"I think I've found a new favorite author! What an exciting read—tense, suspenseful, and masterfully written!"

"In *Tell Her No Lies*, Kelly Irvin has crafted a story of wounded characters overcoming and fighting their way to the truth. In a world where so many present one facade externally and another inside their homes, this novel shines a light on the power of truth to cut through the darkness. Wrap that inside a page-turning mystery and some sweet romance and it's a story perfect for readers who love multiple threads. This is a keeper of a story."

"With plenty of twists and surprises, this is a story readers will be shocked by."

"Well-established as a writer of Amish romances, Kelly Irvin's romantic suspense novels promote faith after betrayal and encourage readers to learn to love and trust again."

"Irvin . . . creates a complex web with enough twists and turns to keep even the most savvy romantic suspense readers guessing until the end. Known for her Amish novels, this two-time Christy Award finalist shows that her talents span subgenres from tranquil Amish stories to rapidly paced breathless suspense."

CLOSER
THAN
SHE
KNOWS

OTHER BOOKS BY KELLY IRVIN

ROMANTIC SUSPENSE

Tell Her No Lies
Over the Line

AMISH

Amish of Big Sky Country Novels

Mountains of Grace
A Long Bridge Home
Peace in the Valley (available August 2020)

Every Amish Season Novels

Upon a Spring Breeze
Beneath the Summer Sun
Through the Autumn Air
With Winter's First Frost

The Amish of Bee County Novels

The Beekeeper's Son
The Bishop's Son
The Saddle Maker's Son

CLOSER THAN SHE KNOWS

KELLY IRVIN

THOMAS NELSON
Since 1798

Published in Nashville, Tennessee, by Thomas Nelson. Thomas Nelson is a registered trademark of HarperCollins Christian Publishing, Inc.

Scripture quotations are taken from the Holy Bible, New International Version®, NIV®. Copyright © 1973, 1978, 1984, 2011 by Biblica, Inc.® Used by permission of Zondervan. All rights reserved worldwide. www.zondervan.com. The "NIV" and "New International Version" are trademarks registered in the United States Patent and Trademark Office by Biblica, Inc.®

Also quoted is the New King James Version®. © 1982 by Thomas Nelson. Used by permission. All rights reserved.

Thomas Nelson titles may be purchased in bulk for educational, business, fund-raising, or sales promotional use. For information, please email SpecialMarkets@ThomasNelson.com.

Publisher's Note: This novel is a work of fiction. Names, characters, places, and incidents are either products of the author's imagination or used fictitiously. All characters are fictional, and any similarity to people living or dead is purely coincidental.

Library of Congress Cataloging-in-Publication Data

Names: Irvin, Kelly, author.
Title: Closer than she knows / Kelly Irvin.
Description: Nashville, Tennessee : Thomas Nelson, [2020] | Summary: "In this fast-paced romantic suspense, a serial killer with a literary bent pursues a court reporter, leaving a taunting new note with every body he kills. And he's getting closer"-- Provided by publisher.
Identifiers: LCCN 2020002143 (print) | LCCN 2020002144 (ebook) | ISBN 9780785231868 (trade paperback) | ISBN 9780785231875 (epub) | ISBN 9780785231882 (audio download)
Subjects: GSAFD: Romantic suspense fiction. | Christian fiction.
Classification: LCC PS3609.R82 C58 2020 (print) | LCC PS3609.R82 (ebook) | DDC 813/.6--dc23
LC record available at https://lccn.loc.gov/2020002143
LC ebook record available at https://lccn.loc.gov/2020002144

Printed in the United States of America

20 21 22 23 LSC 10 9 8 7 6 5 4 3 2 1

To my grandchildren: Brooklyn, Carson, and Henry.
You are the hope of a new generation. (No pressure!)

1

Six pounds of pot, a .38 Special, and a by-the-book cop.

Teagan O'Rourke rolled the words around in her head. They sounded like the opening lyrics of a classic rock-and-roll anthem instead of evidence in a murder trial. Weary to the soles of her black pumps, she stared out the window of the San Antonio Police Department vehicle and watched small, unassuming homes built along a long, narrow city park whiz by. Park Boulevard failed to deliver on its grand name. Latino kids screamed and laughed on the playground. Seniors stretched on outdoor fitness equipment. Teenagers engaged in a fierce pickup game on the covered basketball court. Only the tennis courts stood empty and forlorn, their nets waffling in the breeze. *Play with me. Please play with me.*

No one looked up at the SAPD unit. Cop cars were as common as mosquitoes during a humid summer in this neighborhood. If her mother were here, she'd say, *"You reap what you sow, Teagan Catherine O'Rourke."* Twenty awkward minutes in a car with a newbie wasn't so bad. Officer Moreno had unbent enough to tell Teagan she had plans to go to a movie with her fiancé that evening. After much debate they'd decided on a superhero action flick. Officer Moreno preferred dramas. Her fiancé liked what she'd termed "stupid" comedies. "A lot of bathroom humor and raunchy—that's his idea of funny."

Like a lot of men in the arrested development stage.

Maybe by the time they returned to Teagan's Prius in the parking garage across from the Paul Elizondo Tower downtown, she'd know the officer's first name. Most trials didn't require such an expeditious disposal of the evidence to SAPD's evidence room, but Judge Ibarra had ordered the immediate return of this evidence due to the nature of the trial and the involvement of opposing gangs likely to retaliate over its outcome.

Teagan didn't mind. It meant less evidence she had to worry about storing in her crowded office vault.

"We're almost there, Ms. O'Rourke." Officer Moreno came to a full stop at the corner of Park and Academic Court, where the glass-covered police department recruitment center and property room facilities glinted in the late-afternoon sun.

A smile brought out dimples on Moreno's cherub-cheeked face. Her assignment to escort a court reporter and the evidence to the property room was almost to the halfway point. Teagan had told Moreno to call her by her first name, but the patrolwoman couldn't seem to manage it. "I'll get us through security, we'll stow the evidence, and I'll have you back to your car in a jiffy."

Did people still say "in a jiffy"? Teagan's grandma might, but this woman was no more than twenty-four. A couple of years younger than Teagan. She studied the officer's face as she turned onto Academic Court and accelerated. The woman was for real. A straight shooter determined to be successful in a man's world.

Teagan smiled, but Moreno had already returned her gaze to the road, hands at the proper ten and two positions on the wheel. "I know there's plenty of other things you'd rather do than babysit evidence—"

The driver's side window exploded.

The force knocked Teagan's head against her window. Sudden pain pricked her face. Fragments of glass pierced her cheeks and forehead.

The car swerved, jumped the curb, and crashed into the wrought-iron fence that protected the academy.

Was this what Mom felt the day she died? The inevitability of it?

Air bags ballooned.

Teagan slammed back against her seat.

I'm sorry, Max.

I'm sorry I never said it.

A second later the bag deflated. The smell of nitrogen gases gagged her. Powder coated her face. The skin on the back of her hands burned.

Time sped up in an odd, off-kilter *tick-tock*.

Teagan struggled to open her eyes. Pain pulsed in her temple. Her stomach heaved. Waves of adrenaline shook her body as if she'd grasped a live electrical wire.

I'm alive. Today's not my day to die.

The evidence. Protect the evidence.

"Officer Moreno?" She tried to sit upright, but her seat belt bit into her sore chest. "Officer?"

Head down, Moreno slumped to her right, held back by her seat belt. Blood coursed down her face. A lot of blood, considering the air bags should have protected her from a hard hit from the wheel or the windshield with its safety glass.

Teagan struggled to lean toward the officer. Her seat belt clenched tighter. Her lungs refused to cooperate. "Officer?" The strangled word barely broke the sudden, ringing silence.

She wiggled toward the woman. She stopped.

Six years of slapping evidence stickers on crime scene photos and listening to medical examiners' testimony forced her to admit what she was seeing. Officer Moreno had a hole in the side of her head near the temple.

A bullet had pierced her skull and scrambled her brain.

Teagan forced her gaze from the dead woman's face. A warm, humid breeze wafted through Moreno's window, sending the smell of blood and human waste to assail Teagan's nose.

She'd written official court records for dozens upon dozens of murders, attempted murders, and aggravated assault cases. She transcribed those court records. She proofread them. She added her official certification to each one.

Now she knew. Death stank. Murder stank.

Vomit rose in her throat.

"No, no, no." Teagan fought with her seat belt. Her hands shook. "Come on, come on."

"Deep breaths." Her father's Dallas drawl filled her rattled brain. *"Just breathe."*

Teagan inhaled and exhaled. She unhooked the belt. Gently, she touched Officer Moreno's wrist. Her pride in that navy-blue uniform had been so obvious.

Warm skin rewarded Teagan's efforts. Wisps of brown hair grew above the woman's wrist. The details flooded Teagan, trying to drown the one salient fact.

Officer Moreno had no pulse.

The baby-faced officer didn't have to worry anymore about potty humor.

She didn't have to worry about anything at all.

2

Officer down. Officer down. In the intersection of Academic Court and Park Boulevard next to Collins Garden Park's tennis courts."

These magic words would bring help. Teagan dropped the mic. The dispatcher's soothing voice continued to talk, but Teagan had no words left.

The door jerked open. Hands reached for her.

"I'm okay." Not okay. So not okay. "It's the officer. She's dead."

"Are you hurt?" The man touched her arm. "Let me help you out, *mi hijita*."

Mi hijita. The words of endearment soothed Teagan's soul. He sounded like the father of her best friend from high school, Jessica Hinojosa. Mr. Hinojosa called all Jessica's girlfriends *"mi hijita." My little daughter.*

"I'm okay. It's the officer. She's . . . dead."

The man, dressed in a green parks department uniform, guided her from the car. "Help is on the way."

Screaming sirens confirmed his words.

Teagan's body swayed. Her legs refused to do their job. They collapsed under her. The man and his companion, a rotund woman in a matching green uniform, settled her on the curb a few yards from the mangled vehicle. "Put your head between your legs," the woman urged in the raspy voice of a chronic smoker. "Don't pass out on us. You'll conk your head."

5

"My evidence." She hung on to the one thing she knew for sure. Her job remained to preserve the chain of evidence. They were here in this spot because of her duty to the court. "I can't leave the evidence."

"You have stuff in the cop car, *mi corazon?*" *Corazon. Heart.* Just like Mr. Hinojosa. He'd died of a heart attack the year after seventh grade. She and Jessica had that in common, only Teagan's mom died in a car accident the summer after fourth grade. "That car isn't going anywhere. Don't you worry. Just rest."

The next few minutes were blurred, like the old family videos her mother had loved to show at family get-togethers. A fire truck hurtled down the street, its Klaxon horn blaring repeatedly as residents scurried to the curbs while trying to capture the scene on their cell phones. Teagan shooed the first responders toward the SUV and Officer Moreno.

An ambulance followed. A dozen police units. Officers swarmed the scene, drawn by word of a fallen comrade. Yellow crime scene tape fluttered in the dank air. Officers pushed the growing crowd of onlookers back until they stood around on the grassy stretch that separated the tennis courts from the street. Officer Moreno's comrades in arms did everything they could to keep the proceedings respectful, but nothing dignified came of a sudden, violent death.

Mothers with babies in strollers chatted. An elderly man yelled the sordid details into the ear of a lady in a flowered housecoat. Tattooed gangbangers dressed in wife-beaters and baggy jeans squatted on the tennis court, smoked cigarettes, and thumbed texts on their cell phones.

A regular circus attraction.

Eventually an EMT focused on Teagan. He took his time plucking tiny glass shards from her cheek and then covering the cuts with small bandages. She closed her eyes and concentrated on the pain pricks that told her this wasn't a nightmare. It was real. A wispy memory hovered. Mom never let her have bandages unless there was blood. She'd put ice in a plastic bag for a boo-boo, as she'd called it.

Once Teagan fell off her bike and cut her knee. Not one but three Rugrats Band-Aids had been applied. Along with kisses. Her mother felt the wound worthy of her badges of honor.

Wounds of the heart took much longer to heal.

Max. She needed Max.

"Let's get you checked out at the hospital." The EMT closed his kit. "I'll help you up."

"I'm fine. I don't need a hospital." She managed a smile. "But thank you. I can't leave my evidence."

"Are you refusing to be transported?"

Fortunately, she understood legalese. "Yes. Thanks."

He wasn't buying the "fine" thing, but the EMT urged her to see her physician if she had any residual pain in the next few days, then moved away. Teagan would have plenty of pain, but none that a primary care physician could fix.

She drew her legs up, crossed her ankles, and rested her head on her knees. Texting Max was out of the question until her hands stopped shaking. A busy line of ants paraded past her scuffed, dusty shoes, headed for unknown parts. She began to count them. Anything to take her mind from the medical examiner's wagon that rolled in just as the fire truck departed.

"Hey, Teagan."

The deep familiar bass that delivered those words made Teagan lose count. *Darn it. One, two, three, four . . .*

"T?"

"Hey, Justin." She brushed her hands together and forced herself to look up at Homicide Detective Justin Chamberlain. Of course it had to be him on this day inhabited by Murphy's Law from the time she spilled a full cup of expensive Starbucks on her fresh white blouse. "Shouldn't you be home with Lilly?" Teasing her brother's best friend since ninth grade about his marital status was force of habit for Teagan. "Are you here in an official capacity, or are you checking up on me?"

Justin removed his Ray-Bans and stuck them on top of his slicked-back curls. Someone should tell him to ease up on the hair product. He squatted in front of her and brushed her tangled hair from her face like the pseudo–big brother he'd always been. "Lilly and I aren't joined at the hip. We have a very healthy relationship. I called your dad and Billy as soon as I caught the call, and they told me you were involved."

Billy she could deal with. Her stepbrother knew better than to treat her like a second-class citizen because she hadn't joined the family business.

"I'm okay. I don't need him to come." The words came automatically. She'd worked hard to stand on her own two feet in a family of cops. "I'm fine."

"I can see that."

"Did you ask for this case?"

"You know it doesn't work that way. Me and Alisha were up next."

His partner, Alisha Martinez, stood talking to the ME investigator. She turned at that moment and waved. Teagan returned the gesture.

Justin swiveled on the toes of his glossy leather loafers and plopped on the curb next to her. He removed a notebook from his suit coat pocket. The official capacity part was about to begin. "I know it's been a rough day, but I need you to run through what happened. Think you can do that?"

"I'm not a hothouse flower." She bristled in spite of herself. Justin knew better. She picked strands of fresh-cut grass from her suit pants. "Where do you want me to start?"

"At the beginning."

So helpful. Teagan outlined the trip to secure evidence at the PD evidence storage facility.

Justin underlined words in his notebook. "What trial?"

"A couple of gangbangers got into it during a drug deal. One of them tried to book with the product and the money. The other one shot him. He tried to claim self-defense, but nobody was buying that."

"So he was convicted?"

"Manslaughter. They were both habitual offenders." Teagan suspected jurors had a hard time caring in cases like this when both perpetrator and victim were criminals with long rap sheets. "It's not likely the guy will appeal, and he's not smart enough to realize the court reporter is in charge of the evidence."

"His attorney is."

"Lenny Soto caught the case."

"There you go."

"He wouldn't risk his career for a lowlife druggie gangbanger." Despite his penchant for long-winded opening and closing arguments, Teagan liked Lenny. He was a no-holds-barred public defender into winning, social justice, and making a name for himself—not necessarily in that order. "For a poor immigrant, maybe, but not for a guy who got greedy and offed a guy for a few pounds of pot."

"What if the gangs involved want payback?"

"Do you see them using a high-power rifle to kill a cop? It's overkill, and they're smart enough to want to avoid the scrutiny of the entire SAPD and the capital murder charge. More likely they'll go after the families involved. They'll keep it in-house."

Justin scratched his nose and frowned. "Then what? A random shooting? A hit on a patrol officer? Have you made anyone mad lately? Any irate boyfriends?"

Teagan snorted. Justin didn't smile. "I'm serious. You're a court reporter. You're involved in murder cases, sexual assaults, aggravated

9

robberies, commitment hearings, capital murder cases. Maybe someone decided to take you out and missed."

"Seriously? People don't even see me in the courtroom. They think I'm a stenographer." A glorified typist. She had an associate's degree in court reporting: computer-aided transcription technology. She wrote 230 words a minute with 97 percent accuracy in real time. During a trial she did this as much as eight to ten hours a day. "It's more likely it has something to do with Officer Moreno."

"She was a second-year patrolwoman. We'll dig into any recent calls she took and arrests, but it'll be small potatoes."

Small potatoes. The woman died for small potatoes. "What was her first name?"

Justin looked up from his notebook. His forehead under thick black curls furrowed. He cleared his throat. "Her name was Kristin Moreno. She went by Kris."

"I want to know who did this and why. I want him caught. I want him put away for life—"

"Whoa, whoa. Kris was a fellow officer. We work every homicide with equal zeal, but you can rest in the fact that we'll throw every resource at finding this maniac."

"I feel so . . . I want to help."

"Your dad, Billy, and Gracie are the police officers. You prepare court records. You don't solve cases." Justin's voice softened. "It's not an uncommon reaction, though."

"I'm a witness. I should be able to help."

"You can help by telling me everything you saw or heard. Anything unusual from the time you left the courthouse until the time of the shooting?"

Teagan closed her eyes. She'd been thrilled that the sun was shining when they walked from the tower and crossed the street to the patrolwoman's SUV. Not a cloud in the early May sky. They couldn't tell what the weather was like inside the justice center. The heat made her remove her jacket and sling it over her shoulder. She kept her wheeled basket with the packages containing the pot and the weapon close. She was anal about her evidence—any court reporter worth her salt was. The rest of the exhibits were on their way to the district attorney's evidence warehouse, where they would be retained until they could be legally destroyed. Only weapons and drugs went back to PD.

The drive took them from downtown to I-10 East, exiting on Nogalitos Street. Nothing. Then they turned onto Park Boulevard by the H.E.B. grocery store and past the Collins Garden Library, and farther along Park Boulevard. Nothing. Quiet. Cars parked on the house side of the street. No perpetrator strolling along the sidewalk with a rifle slung over his shoulder.

As if that wouldn't be obvious. How had the killer got off at least twos shots and walked away without being noticed? Teagan touched the bandage on her cheek. And with such accuracy? "What kind of weapon was used?"

"We won't know until the ME does the autopsy." Justin tugged at the knot in his tie. Fine perspiration dotted his forehead. "Some sort of high-velocity rifle."

"Where did the shots come from?"

"Good question. We're corralling everyone we can in the park and in the neighborhood, trying to locate someone who saw something."

"We stopped at the stop sign at Park and Academic Court," Teagan thought aloud. "She looked at me and said something about getting me through security. She turned left. The window blew out. I have no idea if someone was standing at the corner. I was oblivious to my surroundings. Could the killer have shot from a passing car?"

"It would be a heck of a shot. He'd have to hit a moving target." Justin's gaze roved over the crowd that refused to disperse. "Totally dependent on being in the right place at the right time. That's not much of a plan."

"Unless it truly was a random drive-by shooting. Gangbangers going through initiation or getting back at PD for arrests on their turf."

"Which is up to SAPD's finest to figure out. Not you. Your job is to go home, rest, and recuperate from a traumatic event." Justin's tone was a wisp away from sarcastic. He knew her too well to expect her to rush home and throw herself on the bed. "You might also consider finding someone to talk to about all this. It helps. If you promise to do that, I promise to keep you apprised of what's going on with this case. Even though it's not necessarily protocol."

"I appreciate that." He knew she would pester him until he told her what she wanted to know, just like she did when he knew her siblings' plans to apply to the academy. "And I'm fine."

"From the level of prickliness you're displaying, I'd say you're determined to be fine. That's not the same thing. Take it from a nine-year veteran of this stuff." He shoved off the curb, stood, and held out his hand. "Hang tight. When we're done here, I'll get someone to drive you downtown to make a formal statement. Then your dad wants you to come to the house. Or he said he'll get Gracie to give you a lift if you're not up to it."

"I need to go home and feed Tigger. She'll be starving." Teagan ignored his hand and stood on her own. It took her last ounce of strength to keep from swaying. Tigger would be all the medicine she needed. The pit bull weighed fifty pounds, but at two she was still a puppy who thought she was a lapdog. "I'm not in the mood for a family powwow."

"Get Julie or one of your other *amigas* to take care of Tigger. Let your dad cook for you. It'll make him feel better. We lost one of our own, and that hurts."

Her headache ratcheted up another notch. Julie Davidson, her court coordinator and friend, would be happy to feed Tigger, but she had plans this evening—a granddaughter's dance recital—and

Teagan had no intention of bothering her. She hadn't even thought about her dad. "Sorry. I'm so wrapped up in myself. Did he know Officer Moreno—did he know Kris?"

"He taught a couple of classes at the academy when Kris was there. Yeah, he knew her."

"I'll call him when I get home."

"You'll be here awhile longer, so try to be patient. Get someone to feed Tigger if you can." Justin grabbed her hand and squeezed. "I'm glad you're okay. If you ever need to talk, I'm available. You're always welcome at the house. Lilly loves to feed strays."

Leave it to Justin to be nice in one sentence and insult her in the next. It was his MO. His wife was far too sweet for a guy like him. A whiff of long summer evenings spent splashing around at a neighborhood pool drifted over her. Justin lording it over the younger kids as a lifeguard, buff and bronzed in swimming trunks, a whistle hanging on a lanyard around his neck, dark hairs just beginning to sprout on his chest, the smell of chlorine and sunscreen in the air. She'd been watching the girls fawn over him and wondered what they'd think if they knew how he belched after drinking soda or chewed with his mouth open just to annoy her stepsister, Gracie. "Thanks. I'm . . . that's nice of you, but like I said—"

"You'll never be the same. You shouldn't be—"

"Teagan, Teagan, over here!"

Annoyance flitted across Justin's face, but he backed off and looked over his shoulder. Teagan waved at Brian Lake, a one-man band from the local ABC affiliate. He stood out in a crowd, mostly because he was six feet two, weighed two hundred pounds, and had a big nose even for that football player–sized body.

A hopeful look on his craggy face, Brian waved back. "What are you doing here? I thought you'd be at home with your feet up by now."

"So did I," she called back. "Wrong place, wrong time."

"Don't even think about it." Justin turned to face Brian. He pulled his sunglasses from his head to his nose, hiding his dark-brown eyes. "Chief is on his way. He'll do the usual news conference."

"Brian's a friend. I know better than to share too much." Dealing with members of the media who visited her courtroom had taught Teagan to tread carefully on the high wire of being friendly without revealing more information than her job allowed. "I thought you liked him too."

"I do. I don't have any beef with him or the rest of them. I just don't want the chief chewing me out for stealing his thunder with the media."

"Come on, guys, give me a hint."

Brian was a nice guy who followed all the judge's rules—no shorts in the courtroom, muted cell phones, no showing the jury on the news, and so on. If Teagan dropped him a tidbit on a juicy upcoming trial now and then, she wasn't the only one. It was nice to have a photographer who doubled as a reporter who actually understood how the system worked, who was who, and got the story right. He was older, probably in his forties, with enough experience to use diplomacy to finesse his way into the information he needed.

"I'll fend him off." Justin adjusted the sunglasses. "I can talk to him on deep background. He won't burn me. You stay away from the media."

Teagan couldn't help the eye roll. "Yes, sir."

Justin's lips rolled up in a sardonic smile. "As if you ever showed respect for my authority."

The first notes of "Forever on Your Side" by NeedtoBreathe floated from her pants pocket.

Max.

Wednesday night. Youth group.

Would a true believer forget her church obligations in the aftermath of a shoot-out? Mom would say no, but she'd been on track for sainthood. Max would happily feed Tigger after youth group. He was a good friend.

A sudden hitch in her breathing hurt Teagan's chest. The look in Max's burnished amber eyes when he thought she wasn't watching told her he wanted to be much more. All she had to do was say the word. Make the first move.

The ball was in her court. Max would never pressure her. Not because he lacked guts, but because he saw himself as less than worthy.

He was so wrong. Teagan held that title.

Not now. Keep it light. "Hey."

Max's husky voice filled the space around her. "Hey, where are you? You've never missed youth group in two years."

Justin frowned and walked away.

"I'm having a bad day."

But not nearly as bad as Officer Kristin Moreno's day.

3

Even a fifty-pound pit bull terrier couldn't protect a woman from a sniper's bullet. Not something Max Kennedy expected to worry about in his hometown. He'd had enough of that in Afghanistan. He shoved the thought away.

The gentle rumble of his Indian Scout Bobber soothed him. He let the motorcycle idle in the driveway as he sat contemplating Teagan's small 1940s wood-frame home in Southtown, a stone's throw from San Antonio's downtown. The distant hum of I-10 traffic mingled with crickets chirping and the occasional dog barking.

Security lighting cast its rays on her small cement porch and a series of hanging moss-lined containers, some filled with Bossa Nova Orange begonias, sweet potato vines, and silvery dichondra. Max knew the names of these plants because Teagan liked to sit barefoot on the front steps in the dappled sunlight of early evening, paint her toenails sparkly purple, and tell him about them. They gave her pleasure, and her animated voice as she reeled off their names did the same for him.

Teagan had asked for his help. She didn't do that much with anyone. Even friends. Some would think feeding a dog a minor request. Not Teagan. She counted Max as a member of her small group of close friends. Being a part of that group was a privilege.

He dismounted and headed across the yard to the Little Free Library Teagan had built near the wide sidewalk in her equally small front yard. The scent of basil and rosemary she'd planted on the roof of the three-story mini house anchored on a five-foot cedar post wafted over him. He slipped his goddaughter's copy of *What the Dinosaurs Did Last Night* into the children's section, trying not to think about how she'd outgrown it already. Babies grew so fast. He wanted a few of his own so he'd have an excuse to read silly children's stories every night.

Should a guy with his past have kids? It was an old argument. Faith and Hope Community Church obviously thought so. They trusted him to pastor two dozen rowdy middle and high schoolers. He had them for a few hours a week and on a couple of mission trips a year. Little chance of thoroughly messing them up and plenty of opportunity for shepherding them closer to Jesus and farther from the miry pits that had ensnared him.

Could he trust himself to be a husband and father? He needed to know. Only then could he ask Teagan to venture into territory beyond friendship. To trust him.

A beige folded sheet of stationery floated from the first-floor box of adult classics into the thick St. Augustine grass. Borrowers and lenders often left sweet notes for Teagan, one of the many things she loved about having the library, where she sometimes served lemonade or gave away cherry tomatoes and cucumbers grown in her backyard garden. Some court reporters drank after work or went to the gym to drown out the day's proceedings. Teagan grubbed in the garden or worked in the youth group pumpkin patch and ran a library in her front yard.

Lucky for Max. He stayed out of bars these days.

He scooped up the note and squinted in the motion-detection solar light that allowed evening visitors to see the books.

The words buzzed in his ears. He read it again.

The thin sheet fluttered to the ground a second time. Goose bumps prickling on his neck, he glanced over his shoulder. Swallowing against bitter bile, he bent to retrieve the paper again, this time with his fingertips.

With his free hand, he dug the key Teagan had given him as backup for when she lost her own from his jean pocket and tromped across the yard to the front door.

A half-strangled scream shattered the night.

Key halfway to the door, Max froze.

The scream rose. "Stop. Please stop. Help me, someone help me, God, help me!"

Mrs. Conklin. Max thrust the note in his back pocket, whirled, jumped the two steps, and pounded toward the neighbor's house.

"I'm coming." He jerked open the fence gate that led to the back-yard. "Where are you?"

The screaming stopped.

A horrible silence filled only by his own ragged breathing ensued.

"Mrs. Conklin? It's me. Max Kennedy."

No response.

Mrs. Conklin's spindly back porch light didn't do much to illuminate her backyard. He edged into the yard. His boot thudded against something hard. He dug his phone from his hip pocket and turned on the light. A twenty-pound bag of mulch. He let the light play across the yard.

The dark was preferable.

Mrs. Conklin lay sprawled on her back, arms flung wide, legs bent at a bizarre angle. Her ripped, gaping pink housedress was hitched up above her white knobby knees. Fuzzy pink slippers had been knocked a few feet from her body. Her long white curls wreathed her head, but her blue-rimmed glasses were MIA.

Blood seeped from wounds on her chest, arms, and hands. Her eyes were wide with disbelief.

Max's Army medic training kicked in. He knelt and touched her neck.

Nothing.

His stomach churned. The Whataburger with cheese and tots he'd eaten for supper threatened to make an appearance. Blood pounded in his ears. He sucked in a long breath. "Abba Father, help me."

He punched the button for 911, hit Speaker, dropped the phone in the grass, and made the report as he began CPR.

Counting, counting, counting, then breathing, counting, counting, breathing. Still nothing.

The sound of the dispatcher's voice kept him company. Yes, he was still here. Yes, he was doing CPR. No, she wasn't breathing.

"Help is on the way."

"Thank you. Come on, Evelyn, come on, please!"

He stopped and leaned over to listen. No puff of air on his cheek. No sudden inhale of air.

This wasn't Hollywood, after all.

Counting, counting, counting. His shoulders ached. Sweat ran into his eyes. Yet he shivered with cold.

Nothing.

The metallic taste of dwindling adrenaline in the back of his throat, Max leaned on his haunches and wiped sweat from his face on his T-shirt sleeve. His hands were covered with sticky blood.

He'd seen a lot of dead men and women in his six-year hitch with the Army in Iraq and Afghanistan, but it never ceased to amaze him how quickly the vacancy sign went up. Only a husk remained where once had lived a nice lady who made tasty double-fudge brownies, always smelled like lilacs, and was the first person in the neighborhood to welcome Teagan when she moved in next door. Mrs. Conklin even offered to take care of Tigger when Teagan went out of town. A nice gesture considering the exuberant dog knocked the lady on her keister once in Tigger's excitement to see her. In Tigger's defense, her neighbor often kept doggie treats in her pockets. Her Chihuahua, Princess, had passed away, but she still stocked the treats for neighborhood dogs.

Mrs. Conklin lived alone. She had no family here in town. For now, Max would be her family.

The crickets went back to their chorus. Mosquitoes buzzed him. The sounds became Humvee engines straining on the mountainous terrain of Afghanistan and the *whop-whop* of blades as helicopters hovered over screaming men with broken bodies and blood pouring from deadly wounds.

When his counselor said it was better to face the triggers for his PTSD, surely he didn't have this in mind.

Sirens sounded in the distance. Finally. It really didn't matter. Mrs. Conklin wasn't going anywhere.

A branch snapped. Leaves rustled.

Max unfolded his legs and stood in a single motion. "Who's there?"

Quick, furtive footsteps.

A dark figure flung himself—or herself—at the six-foot wood-plank privacy fence that surrounded the backyard.

Max raced across the grass and scaled the fence. Note to self: steel-toed leather boots didn't work for pursuit of bad guys.

Since when did a part-time youth minister, part-time mechanic chase bad guys?

He dropped into the pitch-black alley. Gravel crunched under his boots. The putrid stench of full garbage bins struck him in the face. Straining to hear, he panted. Left or right?

Right.

He turned. The blow caught him across the forehead and sent him smashing into the bins.

Pain.

Lights out.

4

A trip to SAPD's headquarters downtown had not been on Teagan's itinerary earlier in the day. But a witness to the murder had to give a formal statement in an interview room with the digital recorder running. That ensured a good record for when the case went to trial. When the perpetrator was caught. Teagan hung on to that optimistic thought as she climbed into her car in the courthouse parking garage.

By now Officer Moreno's body had been transported to the medical examiner's office for the final indignity of an autopsy. *An autopsy.* How many times in her career had Teagan written records of testimony by a Bexar County medical examiner investigator? Two, three, four hundred times? How many times had she gone back to check her work, searching the transcript's numbered lines to make sure every word was clean? What would the investigator's testimony sound like in Kristen's case?

```
 7   A. She was in a body bag and her hands were bagged
 8   with paper bags. She was partially dressed. Part of her
 9   clothing had been cut away. And she looked to be an
10   adult female with injury-
11   Q. All right. And in-in-and when you're
12   doing an autopsy and you're-and you're examining a
13   body and you're looking at the clothing, were you able
```

14   to determine basically what did it appear had been the

15   reason for this person dying?

16   A. What was obvious on first examination with-

17   was that she had a gunshot wound of entry in her left

18   temple. And a second one in her left neck.

19   Q. Was there an exit wound to either?

20   A. For the neck wound, yes, but not the head wound.

Teagan might have written a hundred records with medical examiner testimony over the years but never the autopsy of someone she knew. Someone who'd been sitting next to her talking one moment and blown away the next.

The dry heaves hit her hard. *Breathe, in and out, in and out.* Thank God she hadn't eaten lunch.

Gracie had shown up and given Teagan a ride to her car after the interview. Which meant sitting in her stepsister's so-called eco-diesel Dodge Ram Lone Star edition, dissecting the situation in minute detail for another forty-five minutes before Gracie finally released Teagan with the admonition that she must go directly home, lock her door, turn on her security system, and sleep with Tigger at her side.

Which was what she usually did. First she wanted a cool glass of iced peppermint tea and a quiet few minutes on her back porch, enjoying a soft breeze. She needed space and silence.

She turned the corner onto her street. Flashing lights. An ambulance. A crime scene unit SUV. Cop cars.

Crime scene tape.

She slowed, then stopped. A nightmare on repeat? It couldn't be. She'd left the crime scene but here it was, slapping her in the face all over again.

Max. Had she sent him into harm's way when she asked him to feed Tigger? If anything happened to Max, it would be her fault.

The dry heaves returned. She swallowed again and again as purple dots danced in her periphery.

The first responders weren't in front of her house. Instead they swarmed the next house down. Evelyn Conklin?

Her empty stomach tied in double knots. A patrolman she didn't recognize refused to let her get any closer, so she parked the Prius in front of the Nixons' house three down.

She grabbed her wallet and exited the car. Driver's license in hand, she approached the officer. His name tag read DIAZ. "Officer Diaz, I live right there. See?" She pointed to her address on the license. "What's going on? Is Mrs. Conklin okay?"

"Ma'am, I need you to back up. We'll get you into your home as soon as we can."

He cocked his head toward the crowd of neighbors huddled across the street. Most of them were young professionals who were rehabbing old houses just like Teagan. Evelyn was an exception—an original property owner who hadn't given in to the pressure to sell her aging, crumbling home. She did her own yard work, climbed a ladder to clean her gutters, and handed out homemade Rice Krispies treats on Halloween.

"I need to find my friend. He was headed here to feed my dog."

"He may have come and gone before the incident occurred."

"He's not answering his phone." She edged past the officer. Max's motorcycle was parked in her driveway. So where was Max? "Just let me take a quick look in my house."

"Ma'am, back up. Now."

She had no choice. She backed up. And tried Max's phone again. No answer. She texted him.

Where R U?

No answer.

Unease mixed with dread, making nauseating muck in her gut.

Breathe. Just breathe.

Dana Holl, a defense attorney who owned the forties bungalow-style house on the corner, slid in next to Teagan. Her sweat-stained workout clothes suggested the well-muscled blonde had just come from the gym and not the courthouse. "It looks like it must be Evelyn. They've got CSU there and the ME's investigator. Who would murder a sweet old lady?"

Teagan didn't bother to reply to her rhetorical question. Dana knew as well as Teagan that sweet old ladies were targeted by criminals because they so often were defenseless. However, Evelyn wasn't defenseless, and woe to the thug who underestimated her. She had a state-of-the-art security system installed after her husband died. She kept a baseball bat, pepper spray, and a Taser in strategic spots throughout her quaint four-bedroom, two-story house built in the fifties. She stopped short of a gun because she believed the experts when they said an assailant could easily turn it around on her. "How did they get in? Evelyn wouldn't open the door to a stranger."

"I don't think she did. I think the thugs caught her in the backyard. All the activity is back there." Oscar Benavides, Teagan's neighbor to her right, was a professor of Latinx culture and creative writing at UT San Antonio. He shared the Victorian cottage with artist Carlos Chavez, who owned a renovated warehouse that held an art gallery, rental studios for artists, and a coffeehouse.

As usual Oscar was dressed in tight black jeans, a black T-shirt, and high-end sneakers, and his silky black hair was pulled back in a man bun. Also per usual he sounded eager to pounce on any morsel of gossip he could. "No one is saying anything yet, but that's the way it looks."

"Thugs? There was more than one?"

"I think. They've got cops spread out, going door-to-door in the neighborhood. I saw the PD copter overhead a few minutes ago. And they've got your friend the motorcycle man back there."

His heartthrob smile didn't hide the fact that he was dying to drop that tidbit on her and see her reaction. One of the few disadvantages of living in a neighborhood where people actually tried to know each other's names and help each other out when the car battery was dead or the dog got loose or the electricity went out was that they also knew each other's business.

"You saw Max?" Her heart began to beat again. Air flowed through her lungs. "He was okay?"

"I couldn't tell for sure, but from here it looked like he had blood on his shirt. An EMT was looking him over, but he was walking around."

"If he was walking around, he's okay." Dana offered her a sympathetic smile. "I'm sure they're interviewing him as a witness."

"It makes me sick how everyone is just standing around watching or taking videos on their phones so they can post them on social media." Stephanie Nixon parked her jogging stroller containing two-year-old Charlotte who had passed out, pacifier firmly affixed in her mouth. Stephanie owned a cupcake shop on Alamo Street while her husband worked trauma surgery at University Hospital. They were refurbishing a Craftsman three houses down from Teagan. "The media trucks are lining up on the next street over."

The modern age. More and more amateur phone videos showed up on the local and national news every day, but that didn't keep the professionals from converging on crime scenes in hopes of getting their money shot of a pool of blood.

"It's almost like a block party." Oscar rubbed his hands up and down his tawny brown arms. "Only everyone turned out. Do you think the murderer is mingling with this crowd, surveying his handiwork with delight?"

Oscar's love of murder mysteries was showing.

The question made Teagan shiver despite heat that lingered even in the dark. She glanced around. Her neighbors and the media comprised most of the crowd. Lots of strangers, too, but she couldn't know everyone in Southtown.

She wanted her dog and her couch and the afghan her grand-mother made.

She wouldn't mind having Max around either. He was an amateur boxer with a license to open carry. And he put up with her.

Teagan tried his number yet again.

His husky voice urged her to leave a message. *"Be God's,"* he concluded as he did every email and every message. "Where are you, Max? I see your bike but no you. Call me back. Please."

She could hear his response now. His golden-amber eyes would spark and his full lips curl up in a lazy smile. "Are you worried about me, T?"

Yes. She worried about all her friends and family members. A person who'd lost her mother at the tender age of nine did that. With Max it was necessary when he took his bike on long road trips to clear his head of the cobwebs left over from a war that left him emotionally scarred and drug and alcohol addicted. He drove too fast and leaned into the turns far too much for her liking. Almost as if his carelessness might be intentional.

But she never told him that. Instead she said stupid stuff like, *"Why can't you drive a minivan like a normal youth minister?"*

"No such thing as a normal youth minister," he would retort.

And he would be right.

"Officer, I need to get into my house. I need to see if my friend is there. His bike is out front, but he's not answering his phone."

"Sorry. As soon as the detective in charge of the scene gives the all clear, I promise we'll let you in." Officer Diaz had the earnest delivery of a new guy on the beat. "Sorry for the inconvenience."

"Who's the detective? Is it Billy O'Rourke, by any chance?"

"No, ma'am. Detective Siebert."

Siebert was old school. Closer to her dad's age than her brother's.

The gate to Evelyn's backyard opened. Max trudged through it, Detective Siebert at his side. A CSU officer lagged behind a few steps with a wad of paper evidence bags under one arm and a camera hanging from his neck.

Thank You, Jesus.

"Max!" Teagan dodged the officer, ducked under the crime scene tape, and raced across the yard. "Are you okay? What happened?"

A bandage on his forehead didn't begin to cover reddened skin already starting to turn purple. Something dark muddied his white T-shirt. Max shot forward and enveloped her in a hug. His sandy five o'clock shadow rubbed against her cheek, and his strong arms squeezed the breath from her. "I didn't get to feed Tigger. Sorry."

"Seriously?" Teagan pushed back to get a look at his face. Trauma etched lines around his mouth. His eyes were red rimmed. Max didn't need this. He'd had his share—more than his portion—of trauma. She managed a reassuring smile. "Tigger will survive. What happened?"

"Who are you?" Siebert intervened as Diaz took Teagan's arm and tried to tug her free from Max's embrace. "How do you know Mr. Kennedy?"

"Don't touch me." Teagan drilled Diaz with the famous O'Rourke glare inherited from a mother who had all the redheaded Irish temperament of her forefathers and mothers. "This man is my friend. He's the youth minister at Faith and Hope Community Church. He came here at my request to feed my dog."

She turned back to Max. "What happened?"

"As I explained to Detective Siebert, I heard screaming. I ran to Mrs. Conklin's backyard and found her on the ground." Max's voice faltered. He ducked his head and stared at his boots. "I performed CPR, but I couldn't revive her. She had been stabbed several times."

A wave of nausea hit Teagan in tandem with dizziness that had nothing to do with lack of food since breakfast or a long stretch of sleepless nights. "I just talked to her this morning. When I left the house she was watering her roses. She told me people think roses are

27

hard to grow here, but her Belinda's Dream roses bloom nine months out of the year."

She needed to stop babbling. The matching sympathy in the three men's eyes didn't help. They saw a poor woman who needed consoling instead of an experienced court reporter with two capital murder trials under her belt. Teagan gulped air and steadied her voice. "She brought me a bouquet of cut roses last week. They're pink and they have a light but sweet fragrance . . ."

Max slid his arm around her shoulders. "Let's sit down."

Siebert stepped into their path. "So you corroborate Mr. Kennedy's story that he has a key to your house and permission to enter it in your absence?"

"Corroborate? You don't seriously think Max had something to do with this?" Teagan corralled fierce disbelief. The guy was doing his job. "I can corroborate it, yes. Max has a key. I asked him to come. Plus, he's a friend of Evelyn's. He stows boxes in the attic for her. He had his youth group kids paint her house and install energy-saving devices in January after that nasty cold snap."

"We found Mr. Kennedy in the alley outside the victim's backyard. He has blood—presumably hers—on his shirt and hands."

"I gave her CPR." Max's Adam's apple bobbed. He cleared his throat. "I tried to save her, but she was already gone."

"Did you find the weapon?" Teagan shrugged free of Max's arm. "Did he still have it on him?"

"No."

"So how did he dispose of it? He left and came back? You actually think he had time to do that before first responders arrived?"

"We're just covering all our bases here. We have officers canvassing the entire area. If the weapon is still there, we'll find it." Detective Siebert's tone held thinly masked impatience. His gaze bounced to Max. "I need to see the note."

"What note?"

Max gripped her hand. "Let's sit on your steps."

"Max."

No response. He strode ahead, forcing her to trot on unsteady legs in his wake. At the small porch he sat and then pulled a creamy-beige folded piece of paper from his back pocket. He held it out.

Siebert plucked it from his hand with gloved fingers before Teagan could react. With great care he unfolded the single sheet of paper and held it up. "Have you seen this before?"

"No." She inched forward. The words were etched in black calligraphy that looked as if it might come from an old-fashioned fountain pen. An invitation? A poem?

A letter.

Dear T,

    I'm sorry about the officer.

    Not really.

    Serial killers aren't capable of remorse.

    If dear Evelyn was too close to home,

    Just wait.

    Tell the reporters I want a proper name.

    Aren't letters a quaint way to converse?

    I'll be in touch soon.

                Cheers!

                Your friend Francois Bonaparte

The author had signed the name with an ornate flourish.

The world spun like a Tilt-A-Whirl. Teagan had never been a fan of carnival rides. She plopped onto the steps. Gorge rose in her throat. She swallowed against the acrid burn. "You need to get Detective Chamberlain over here."

"He's up to his eyeballs with Kris Moreno's case." With a ginger fingertip touch, Siebert handed the letter to the CSU evidence investigator, who slid it into a paper bag. "Do you know this Francois Bonaparte?"

"Justin's case is connected. The writer wants us to know that." She sucked in a long breath. "Francois Bonaparte is a fictional character in Raymond Fuentes's first Jay Southerland novel, *The Code*. He leaves notes with every woman he kills after assaulting them, outlining the so-called moral code that should be used by all serial killers. Like never kill anyone you know, never change your mind once you start, always dispose of weapons properly, and don't be stupid or careless."

All very good rules for killers who didn't wish to get caught.

Max sat next to her, so close their shoulders touched. His solid presence steadied her. He stared at the dried blood on the hand he rested on his grass- and dirt-stained jeans. "How does it connect to you?" His hoarse voice delivered the question in a carefully neutral tone. "What do a young police officer, an elderly woman, and a court reporter have in common?"

"I have no idea, but we need to figure it out." Teagan gripped her hands in her lap and stared up at Siebert. "Did you know Officer Moreno?"

"Not personally, but she was a police officer. A decent one who'll never have a chance to get really good at it." He stared into space, but his expression left no doubt he was imagining her death. "It stinks."

"It does. I'm so sorry for every officer who has lost a colleague today. This creeper is comparing himself to fictional killers like what he does isn't real."

"But there was no letter in Kris Moreno's killing."

"He's used one letter to connect the two murders. It's like he's introducing himself to me." Despite the heat, Teagan shivered. "As a fictional killer. Is it because of my job as a court reporter, or does he know I read mysteries and suspense?"

"Don't try to apply logic to the thoughts of a psycho." Max rubbed her back and let his hand drop. "It'll only make you crazy."

That seemed to be the idea. Francois Bonaparte aka Serial Killer wanted to frighten her.

Teagan straightened. She refused to play the victim.

A man who hid behind a fake name was a coward.

Bring it on, Franky.

5

Murder turned a home into Grand Central Station. Teagan's tiny house bulged with an onslaught of law enforcement types. She led the way into her home so they could confirm the perpetrator hadn't entered it. She corralled poor Tigger. The dog knew better than to jump on her, but she licked Teagan from forehead to chin, whimpering the entire time. After feeding and watering her, Teagan shut her into the kennel with repeated promises to make it up to her soon.

A CSU investigator told her to wait outside. Curbing a surly response, she obeyed. Another CSU guy took photos of Max, head-to-toe, then asked for his clothes. Max grabbed his saddlebags from his bike and went to the guest bathroom to change.

Seconds later Justin's unmarked Crown Vic skidded to a stop behind the SAPD units. Gracie's Ram and Billy's Tundra rolled in behind him. Gracie's undignified streak across the yard didn't give Teagan much time to brace herself. Her stepsister, almost six feet tall to Teagan's five-five, swooped in for a crushing hug followed by twenty questions.

Billy's more reserved approach involved a glaring review of her person followed by a short, hard hug. By the time Max returned, dressed in gray boxing gym sweats, a T-shirt with ragged cut-off sleeves that showed off his eye-popping muscular biceps, and dirty Nikes, her front yard looked like a cop convention.

A review of the killer's calling card resulted in worried stares and curses—mostly from Gracie, who would defiantly toss dollar bills into Teagan's swear jar later.

"Poor Evelyn is close to home, but it sounds like he's planning to get even closer." Her stepsister's hand went to the Smith & Wesson M&P40 on her hip. In her SAPD uniform, dark-brown hair pulled back in a tight bun, she looked every inch the cop she was. More than one perp who tried to take advantage of a female officer had lived to regret it. Her black belt in karate helped. "The guy plans to torment you specifically. Why?"

"I have no idea. I'd never met Officer Moreno until today. But Evelyn . . ." Teagan choked on the name. Sweet with a pinch of vinegar. That's the way Mom would've described her neighbor. A firecracker. Teagan gritted her teeth. *"Suck it up, kid,"* is what Dad would say. "What kind of psycho kills a defenseless elderly woman to make a point with me?"

"A monster." Billy stripped off the Nitrile gloves he'd used to examine the missive. "He's telling us he's a serial killer. An arrogant son of a gun. And he's made it clear he's not done."

"We need Dad here. I'm calling him." Gracie tugged her phone from her pocket. "I remember him telling stories about a couple of cases he's investigated involving serial killers."

"The department has all kinds of resources for that. It doesn't have to be Dad." Teagan was already neck-deep in concerned family members. Adding her father—Billy and Gracie's stepfather—to the mix would only complicate the matter—and her life—more. "Don't you have a profiler?"

"Dillon will have a personal stake in this. He'll throw everything he's got at it." Max's voice floated from behind her. "And he's retired now, so he has the time to do it."

Supposedly Dad had retired six months earlier. As retired as a guy could be who consulted for law enforcement agencies across the country, taught classes, and wrote true crime books. Some men played golf. His hobby was crime.

"So what exactly did you see, Max?" Justin didn't bother with pleasantries, which suited Teagan fine. They were all tired, and given the history between the two men, it would be hypocritical. "Siebert says you weren't particularly forthcoming."

"I didn't say that—"

"It's okay." Taking his sweet time, Max handed the paper bags containing his shirt, jeans, and boots to the investigator. He nodded at Billy and Gracie, who returned the favor. If they were less than enthusiastic about Max hanging out with their stepsister, they'd had the good sense not to mention their reservations to Teagan. "Any chance I'll get those boots back? They're not cheap."

The investigator shrugged and trotted away. Max shrugged and turned to Justin. "The light from Mrs. Conklin's back porch doesn't reach the rear fence. I bet your buddy will let you tour the scene if you don't believe me. I heard sounds, looked up, and saw someone dart from the bushes that line the fence. I took off after him—"

Billy's hand shot up like an eager student who wanted to be teacher's favorite. "It was a man?"

"I can't be sure. It's just an impression. I know it's a cliché, but it happened so fast and it was so unexpected." Max rubbed bloodshot eyes. "Believe me, I wish I could be more specific. Dark clothes, a hooded sweatshirt maybe. He-She catapulted over the fence like a high jumper, so someone physically fit."

"And you didn't see anything in the alley?"

"It was pitch black. He whacked me before I had a chance."

"We found an old piece of wood—like a table or chair leg—on the ground next to the trash cans," Siebert added. "It may be the weapon used on Max. CSU collected it, but the chances of getting fingerprints are slim to none."

"You're lucky he didn't stab you too." Nausea pummeled Teagan.

She worried every day about losing Gracie or Billy to violence on the street. She never expected to have to worry about a youth minister who'd turned into her closest friend. Someone who occupied her thoughts more than she cared to admit to him or to herself. "It would've been my fault for asking you to come over here."

Justin snorted. He stuck his pen behind his ear. "So why didn't he stab you? Why not kill you? The note makes it sound like he wants to hurt people . . . close to Teagan."

Teagan studied the books in her Little Free Library. Time to add some of the paperbacks she'd picked up at a library fund-raiser. *I can't lose anyone else, God. How much do You expect me to take? She got it. Nothing was guaranteed. Live every day like today was your last day. Live for eternity. So take me. Not Max.*

Intellectually the concepts were easy to grasp. Emotionally they resulted in train wrecks.

"T?"

She met Justin's gaze head-on. "The author of the letter knows things. Personal things. Like the fact that family members call me T. Family, close friends like Max. How could a killer know that? Has he been stalking me? Does he listen in on my conversations?" Her voice rose. She stopped. More teeth gritting was needed.

"We'll get him, Sissy." Gracie edged closer.

"That's a promise." Billy crossed his arms and glowered. "Take it to the bank."

His face ruddy, Justin shifted his feet. "So that means you're both in danger. We can't offer much in the way of protection. T, you can stay at your dad's—"

"That's not necessary. I'm a big girl."

"He's headed over. We'll talk about it when he gets here." Billy used that calm negotiator voice he'd probably learned in a class at the academy. "But try not to be a stubborn horse's behind when he gets here."

Billy did a better job of policing his vocabulary in front of the youth minister than Gracie did. That he tried usually made Teagan smile. Not today.

"You should probably consider taking a leave of absence from your *jobs*, Max." Justin's unsolicited background check when Max came into Teagan's life still rankled. That he had good intentions wasn't lost on her or Max. "Do you have some place you could go until we get this creep off the streets—relatives out of state?"

Max had been the late-life child of a couple who'd been more like grandparents than parents. They had passed away after a few years of living the quiet life of golf-loving retirees in Fort Myers, Florida. He had no relatives, only a tight-knit church family. "I'm good. I'm capable of taking care of myself."

"That's what most people think, until they end up dead."

"I won't endanger people I care about."

"Take a road trip then."

The testosterone overload in her front yard made Teagan's headache ratchet up a notch. The clusters of neighbors and other rubberneckers behind the crime scene tape had begun to disperse with the lateness of the hour and the lack of discernible activity. Still, her neighbors didn't need more fodder for the grapevine. "Can we focus on next steps, guys?"

"It's mind-boggling that he or she stayed around to watch Max find the victim, call for help, and perform CPR." Gracie slipped behind Teagan and kneaded her shoulder and neck muscles. Teagan lowered her head and closed her eyes, but no amount of massage would remove the tight knot of anger, confusion, and heartache stuck in her throat. Gracie's hands slowed. "He took a huge chance of being caught. Why would he do that?"

"He's an adrenaline-rush junkie," Justin offered. "He thinks he's smarter than the police. Most killers do."

"Why leave the note at all?" Billy squinted as if staring into the distance. The setting sun haloed his wiry dark-brown hair. "It's obvious we have an attention seeker. He wants the media to give him a good name."

"If he's calling himself a serial killer, then there may be other victims we don't know about yet." Gracie's hands tightened. Teagan moved and Gracie let go. She slid around so Teagan could see her face. "Or more to come. You really do need to move back to the house, T, until we catch this guy—"

"Just remember, this is my case," Siebert interjected. "You're PD, but you're also family members. I'll keep you in the loop—"

"*We'll* keep you in the loop." Justin tapped his pen on the slim, reporter-style notebook he favored. "I talked to Sarge. He agreed. We'll team up with a combined investigation into both murders. If it's really a serial killer, it'll be all hands on deck, task force, you name it. Let's get the jump on it before they decide to involve the Feds."

"I don't care who does what. Just do it fast"—Max threw the words down like a gauntlet—"for everyone's sake."

"That's the plan." Justin picked it up with a fierce smile. "This is what I do for a living. Just stand back and watch."

No challenge there.

On that note, Dad rolled onto the scene in his retirement gift to himself—a brilliant blue Charger, fully loaded with a hemi, leather seats, and the latest, greatest stereo system. Officer Diaz obviously knew him. Teagan's father traversed the crime scene tape with barely a pause, whereupon he parted the waters of the tight group surrounding Teagan and made directly for her.

His bone-crunching hugs were legendary among the kids. Teagan might be his only child by blood, but he treated the three he inherited when he remarried after her mother's death like his own flesh and blood.

His pale crystal-blue eyes sharp, Dad gazed into her face first. His fingers touched the baby bandages on her cheeks and forehead.

Fierce emotion towered in his normally granite, clean-shaven face. "I'm sorry, T." He kissed her cheek tenderly and wrapped her in a hug that squeezed breath from her body. "I'm sorry you had to go through this."

The choked emotion in his words invited tears. Teagan dug deep to keep them from escaping. "Thanks."

He studied her face and nodded. "You'll come through this like the champ you are." He turned to the others. "So what do we have?"

They took turns reciting the basic facts. He wouldn't want or need embellishment.

"Let me see the letter."

The lines around his eyes and wide mouth tightened as he read. He ran his big hands over his silver military-style crew cut. He cast his gaze up and down the block. "We've got a big problem. I've seen letters like this before. We thought we caught the guy. It seems we may not have."

His gaze settled on Teagan. "Either a serial killer has my daughter in his crosshairs or we have a copycat out there. Either way, she's in danger."

6

Everyone moved at the same time. Max grabbed Teagan's hand and tugged her toward the house. "Why are we standing outside where you're a sitting duck?"

Dad propelled her from behind. Gracie and Billy closed ranks in their wake. Lockstep into the house, where her father directed traffic with the efficiency of a man who'd spent fifteen years in the Army CID before joining local law enforcement. In minutes they were seated at Teagan's pine table strategically placed across from the granite-topped peninsula that separated the breakfast nook from her kitchen. Billy made the coffee and Gracie served it.

"Here's the deal." Dad sipped black Costa Rican blend from Teagan's favorite stoneware mug. "Certain details of the Leo Slocum case were not made public. He wrote a letter to his victim Olivia Jimenez after he killed her. He had a few sheets of fancy stationery in his van, along with a fountain pen and ink. That and a number of other details tie him to numerous other murders across South Texas, mostly in the Valley. He was a pharmaceutical salesman based out of San Antonio. The murders occurred along or near his sales route."

"The guy convicted of kidnapping, assaulting, and murdering the UTSA student?" Billy scratched his head and frowned. "He's in prison, isn't he?"

"Last time I checked he'd been transferred to Corpus. They think they can get him on a murder charge there—maybe two." Dad stared into his cup as if divining something there. "It's possible he's killed women in Corpus Christi, McAllen, Weslaco, Harlingen, and Brownsville over the past thirty years."

"But he's in jail," Billy said a second time.

"Yes. There was a witness to Olivia Jimenez's kidnapping. A guy who stumbled out of the bar at the wrong time looking to take a whiz before he walked home. Slocum had a stolen revolver, a butcher knife, and a garrote in the back of his minivan at the time of his arrest, as well as the writing tools. He got sloppy. He had a shtick he did with women. He told her he was security for the bar and that someone had tried to steal her car. At least one person overheard the conversation. When they got out in the parking lot, he forced her into his van. He didn't realize the guy was there leaning on a truck, doing his duty. The guy was three sheets to the wind, but he came forward when law enforcement made a public appeal for witnesses."

"What does this have to do with today's murders?" Max traced the condensation on his glass of ice water without looking up, but his tone suggested complete and utter concentration.

"The murders linked to Slocum in these other jurisdictions have a number of things in common, but one of the most notable is the fancy calligraphy letters left by the killer." Dad's gaze came up and touched Teagan. "We've only had the one murder here with that MO. Until now."

"Copycat or accomplice?" Distaste apparent on his deeply lined face, Siebert threw out the question as if testing the waters. "But it would have to be someone who knew the inside dope that wasn't released to the public."

"Technically this letter wasn't left with the victim." Gracie rubbed her arms. Red spots deepened on her fair cheeks. She had her mother's dark, almost black hair and pale-gray eyes. Right now she looked tired. "He basically gave T a warning. How common is that for a serial killer?"

"If Slocum is responsible for the murders in the Rio Grande Valley, he varied his weapons and his method of killing. That's one of the things that has made it hard for law enforcement to pin some of the older murders on him." Dad leaned forward in his chair and splayed his big fingers on the table. "The murderer in the earlier cases was articulate and well spoken—at least in the letters left at the scene, which are his signature. He wanted people to know he was smart. The women he killed were dissimilar. Young, old, black, white, Hispanic, blondes, brunettes, redheads. They were shot, stabbed, and/or strangled. He didn't sign the letters with the names of fictional characters. That's a new development."

All eyes in the room turned to Teagan. As if she knew why a killer would target her. She was twenty-six, college long in the rearview mirror and then only the two years at community college needed for her associate's. Her thick, strawberry-blonde hair settled just beyond her shoulder blades. During the day she wore it in a braid wound into a knot for a more professional look. At home the bun came out but the braid stayed. Same green eyes and long nose as her mother. Two hot-blooded children of Irish immigrants made for immense, explosive arguments and passionate making up, according to her mom. Teagan had inherited their temperament.

One item linked her to the killer more than any other—her love of murder mysteries, thrillers, and suspense novels. Especially Raymond Fuentes novels.

"Anybody need more coffee?" She stood. Tigger whined and did the same. She nuzzled Teagan's hand, seeking a pet. Teagan obliged. "I can make sandwiches. I made fresh sourdough bread over the weekend. I have sliced turkey from the deli—"

"Stop." Billy might look just like his younger sister, but his reserved personality must've come from his father. "Redirecting attention won't work. A murderer has you in his crosshairs. Homemade bread isn't going to divert us. Take it seriously."

"I do. Very seriously." The thought of food made Teagan's stomach turn inside out. "I don't see any reason to get hysterical, that's all. Food helps people think. That's what Mom always said."

One beat, two beats, three. Dad cleared his throat. "She did, didn't she?"

Mom specialized in comfort foods. Vegetable-beef stew and cinnamon rolls made from scratch. Pot roast with potatoes, carrots, and brown gravy. Chocolate pudding upside-down cake. Lemon meringue pie. Fried chicken and mashed potatoes swimming in white, peppery gravy.

Teagan eased back into her chair. She stroked Tigger's warm, soft back. The dog hummed deep in her throat. "This perpetrator is different. He's made this more personal. He didn't glance at me in a bar or a restaurant and decide to get his jollies by killing me. He's studied me."

"That's what makes this so bizarre." Dad pounded his fist lightly on the table. "And troubling. A copycat who's not quite a copycat has set his sights on my daughter. Is it something out of Teagan's courtroom? Is it related to Slocum or some other case I handled? We've got a lot of ground to cover, people. And quickly."

"Agreed. Slocum is in jail, awaiting trial on two more of a series of murders in the Valley that the LEOs think are related. Now we have a killer who's connecting the dots between Officer Moreno's death and Evelyn Conklin's. We have a letter written by the killer, which connects the cases here to those unsolved cases in the Valley." Siebert flipped over a page of his chicken scratches on a narrow notebook. The bags under his eyes had taken on a purplish hue of exhaustion. "On the other hand, Teagan has nothing to do with Slocum. It seems to me more likely that it's somebody in the court system you've PO'd who's familiar with the case. It could even be someone you know in this neighborhood. Lots of legal eagles living in this froufrou area."

Froufrou area. Teagan didn't take offense. Plenty of people felt gentrification was an evil dressed in a pretty urban renewal frock. People liked to put down millennials, but the ones like her were putting their hard-earned money back into neighborhoods close to the heart of the city, coming home instead of moving to the coasts. They were rejuvenating a city quickly becoming a destination known for the arts, a downtown music scene, and a farm-to-fork movement.

"I live and breathe criminal behavior five days a week. I know the masks of normalcy people wear and what they hide." She picked her words carefully. She was not naive. Nor did she discount the millions of people who led perfectly normal lives, never even contemplating breaking a law, let alone actually doing it. "Even so, it's hard to imagine any of my neighbors stabbing Evelyn to death. They certainly don't strike me as criminals capable of picking off a police officer in a moving car."

"All the same, no stone unturned." Billy's tight smile offered encouragement tempered with cynicism. Eight years on the force had fine-tuned his laconic style. "Think hard. Anybody you've made angry? Any arguments recently? Any odd behavior?"

The day's surreal quality ballooned. She'd barbecued turkey burgers with these people and made gluten-free chocolate chip cookies for National Night Out. "Y'all know Dana Holl, the defense attorney. She's been in my court. So has her fiancé. He won his last case against the DA."

"What about here at home? Any beefs with them?"

"You mean does it bug me when their bulldog does his business in my yard and they forget to use a doggy bag? Yes. But mostly we just remind each other at neighborhood meetings that it's the dog owner's responsibility to pick up poo. Do I get irritated when Carlos takes my favorite mysteries from the Little Free Library and doesn't donate anything in return? Yes, but I don't stab him over it. I post cute little reminders to give as much as you get."

"You know what I mean." Billy's jaw jutted forward. He over-enunciated the words as if she needed help understanding them. "Real arguments. Between you and your neighbors or between Mrs. Conklin and your neighbors."

"The most heated argument I've ever witnessed was over leaving recycling bins on the curb too long. I'm telling you this has nothing to do with my neighbors."

"All the same, we'll do background checks on everyone." Justin's tone was more conciliatory. "We'll interview everyone individually and check alibis for both the afternoon and this evening."

"I'm available to help." Dad set his cup on the table as if ready to begin immediately. "I have copies of the case file on Slocum. I'm the closest thing you have locally to a serial killer expert."

"I don't know if the department will go for it. You're retired." Justin's expression turned hangdog. He knew a good offer when he saw it. "I wish you weren't. We could use your experience."

"I consult."

"True." Justin fiddled with his pen. "I'll run it by Sarge."

Gracie grabbed the remote from the counter and clicked on the small flat-screen TV that hung on the far wall of the breakfast nook.

"TV right now? Really?" Teagan mostly used Netflix and Amazon Prime to watch her crime shows—a vice that perplexed Max, who tended toward fixer-upper shows, if deigning to watch at all.

"I want to see what the chief said about Kris's murder."

No one spoke while Gracie spun through the local channels offering ten o'clock news. The ABC affiliate led with the cold-blooded murder of a cop on a San Antonio street. Reporter Brian Lake peppered the chief with questions at his laborious presser on the grass at Collins Garden Park, held strategically at the top of the ten o'clock news block.

"Does the department have any leads?"

"Not yet, but be assured we will track down and arrest the perpetrator of this horrendous act of violence." Chief Gregorio Zavala's voice choked. He rearranged papers on the portable podium. "Officer Moreno was a young woman with only two years on the job. She had a tremendous future ahead of her, not only as a police officer, but as an individual who might one day be a wife and mother. I'm sick of cops being cut down by vicious killers with no respect for the uniform. I'm sick of having to tell loved ones that the worst day of their lives has arrived, the horrible scenario they imagined when their loved ones became officers has become reality."

"A follow-up, Chief. Court reporter Teagan O'Rourke was in the officer's vehicle at the time of the shooting." Lake shouted over other reporters vying for the next question. "Is it possible she was the target?"

"We're looking at every scenario, but it seems unlikely." Zavala glanced at an officer who leaned in to whisper in his ear. "That's it for now. Stay in touch with the Information Office. They'll have updates when possible. Thank you."

"Talk about giving the killer what he wants." Gracie hit the power button. The TV screen went black. "You can bet he's loving this."

"Not yet. The media doesn't know there's a connection between our officer's murder and Evelyn Conklin's." Anger tightened Dad's craggy features. "He doesn't have his name yet or his fame."

Justin pushed his chair back and stood. "Do you want to walk the scene with me, Dillon?"

Her father gulped the last of his coffee and nodded. "Happy to do it. This guy claims to be a serial killer, but until we're sure, there's no reason to involve the FBI. Once we nail this down, we'll want all the resources they can bring to bear. Billy, can you touch base with Corpus PD tomorrow? I'd feel better if we knew the status of Slocum's cases there and elsewhere. He bombed out of law school, but he's claimed the right to defend himself. The guy knows just enough law to be dangerous. He's slick."

"Will do."

A chill skipped up Teagan's arms and curled around her neck. "How many women are we talking about?"

"In Corpus? Two." Her father's attempt at a smile didn't mask his concern. "Altogether? As many as twenty, maybe more."

"This doesn't fit his MO. It's too personal."

"He wants you to know he knows about your life." Her dad ran his hand over his crew cut. "He wants you to know he's hunting you. Killing Kristin Moreno and Evelyn Conklin are opening salvos. He's coming after you, but first he wants to make you squirm. He wants to terrorize you and then destroy you."

His gaze shifted to Max. "He also implies he'll go after people closer to Teagan than Evelyn Conklin. The hint wasn't exactly subtle. Justin's suggestion you lay low for a while isn't a bad one."

Max crossed his beefy arms. "I can take care of myself."

"Do you still carry?"

"Rick asked me not to bring my weapon to the church." Max's tone was even. "I don't agree, but I respect his decision. Some of the parents were uncomfortable with the idea of a gun-toting youth minister."

"Even after Sutherland Springs?" Shaking her head, Gracie grimaced. "In this day and age their kids aren't safe at school or church."

Twenty-seven people, including eight children and one unborn baby, had been killed and twenty more injured as they prepared to worship in their small church. It was the worst mass murder in a church in modern history, and it had happened thirty-five miles southeast of San Antonio. "Let's not debate guns and church violence tonight." Teagan heaved a sigh. "It won't change anything. It certainly won't change any minds in this room."

"Agreed." Hands jammed in his stone-washed jeans, Dad leaned against the door frame. "Max, I'd keep your weapon close for the foreseeable future. I'm sure your pastor will understand."

"I will."

A self-proclaimed serial killer was threatening Max in order to get to Teagan. "Go visit your Army buddy in Arizona." She sought to keep her voice cool. "You've been talking about a bike road trip forever. You have the time coming. Pastor Rick won't mind."

"You're crazy if you think I'm leaving you when a killer has declared he's coming after you." Max snorted. "I'm not going anywhere."

"I don't want any of you shooting or killing anyone on my account. Let's just be clear about that." Teagan let her gaze sweep the room. Two stepsiblings, her father, a family friend, and a friend, all who embraced their Second Amendment rights. She didn't begrudge them their opinions. As a pacifist tree hugger, she clung to her minority status with all the strength of her convictions. "We'll catch the guy, and then we'll let the system work. We all know it does."

"It's been a long, awful day." Max stood. "Let's get out of here so Teagan can rest."

He could read her face like the *Express-News* digital edition, but she didn't need his help on this. "I'm fine."

"We're done for tonight." Dad made a wrap-it-up motion with his index finger. "Good night's sleep, fresh brains in the morning."

"You don't want to go to Dad's?" Gracie stood but didn't move toward the door. "Or I could stay with you tonight. I can call Frank—"

"No, I'm good." Frank and Gracie were newlyweds. Everyone had been shocked when she married the quiet, almost painfully reserved accountant she'd only known for six months. Somehow it seemed a match made in heaven. "Go home to your husband. Max is right. I need to regroup. I need some space to do that."

Billy collected coffee cups. It was so like him. His language of love involved doing things for people. Teagan touched his arm. "Leave them, Bro."

His awkward shrug said it all. She smiled. "Love you too."

"Call me night or day."

"Will do."

The four of them walked to the front door. Her siblings lingered. "You headed out, Max?" Gracie waded in. "I got the impression you're released."

"Yeah, in a few minutes."

He didn't elaborate. Billy's disgruntled look almost made Teagan smile. Almost. Billy pulled the door open. "I'll request patrol-bys. It's the most we can offer with the department's resources stretched so thin."

"I'll be fine. I've got Tigger."

"And me," Max asserted.

"I can take care of myself." She couldn't let him stake more territory than she was willing to give him, even under these circumstances. "But thanks, all of you, for caring. You can all go. It's late and I'm tired. I need to sleep."

Max edged closer, his back to the others. "Can we talk for a minute?"

His soft tone for her ears only made saying no impossible. "Sure."

Five seconds later the others were out the door. She closed it, turned, and faced him. "You could have been killed."

"You could've been killed." His hand came up as if to touch her, then dropped. A muscle pulsed in his clenched jaw. Emotion raged in his burnished-gold eyes. "I couldn't have lived with that."

"I asked you to feed Tigger." Ghosts from the colorless world she'd lived in after her mother's death brushed past her. "It would've been my fault."

"That's so like you. Taking responsibility for something you had no control over. The act of a psycho."

"You ended up knocked out in a dark alley."

"I'm fine."

"I just want to make sure—"

"I'm not going to drink because of this, T. I promise." Hurt seeped into his words even as his expression tried to hide it. "Have faith."

"I didn't mean to imply—"

"But you did." This time he didn't stop. He raised both hands and caressed her cheeks with warm fingers. "Someday you'll realize you can't keep the world safe. You'll realize you have to take a chance on getting hurt. I plan to be around when that happens."

She closed her eyes against the onslaught of emotions. They were perilously close to walking off the cliff. She couldn't do it. It wouldn't be fair to him. She opened her eyes. "You should go. I hate thinking about you driving your motorcycle on Highway 16 at night. It's so dark and curvy."

His hands dropped, but she could still feel the warmth of his fingers. He sighed. "You could come with me. My place in the country is six acres of safe haven."

"I can't, Max."

"What are you so afraid of?"

"Let's not do this now."

His golden-amber eyes filled with heat. "Soon, then." He backed away and opened the door.

Teagan dug her heels into the floor to keep from following him. "Text me when you get home."

He gripped the doorknob so tightly his knuckles turned white. "Turn on the alarm."

"I always do."

He strode away. Teagan closed the door, locked the dead bolt, put on the chain, and turned on the alarm. To keep the bad guy out or to keep herself from racing after Max and dragging him back into her house?

He wouldn't want her when he realized that she couldn't in good conscience give him the one thing he wanted. Children.

7

One step forward, two steps back. Her skin was so soft. The longing in her face, real. Max hadn't imagined it, had he? So why did she always back away at the last second? Why? Because he was a drunk and an addict?

Max donned his helmet, wheeled the Indian around in the driveway, and got on. *God, I don't know how much longer I can take this.* Rick's oft-repeated words droned in Max's head. *"Do you believe that God is good?"* Max did. That didn't mean he always agreed with the great I Am. *A little less tough love would be appreciated, Abba.*

The driver of the cruiser parked at the bottom of the driveway turned on its lights. Nice. Max started his bike and coasted closer. The cruiser didn't budge. He revved the bike's engine. The rumble of the Indian Scout Bobber 69-cubic-inch 100-hp V-Twin engine soothed his irritation. He could wait as long as Justin did. It had to be Justin in the cruiser. The man liked to play the power card, which was probably why he became a cop in the first place. He wore his insecurity like a gold badge.

The lights flipped off. The engine died. A soft breeze rippled through the live oaks and mountain laurels in T's front yard. Mourning doves cooed. Max cut his own engine and waited.

Sure enough. Justin emerged from the car and ambled up the driveway.

"I was beginning to think you'd fallen asleep in there." Max removed his helmet and laid it on the bike. "You're not much of a guard dog if you can't stay awake. I thought Billy said y'all didn't have the manpower to provide overnight security."

"We don't. I'm not." Justin adjusted his belt as if to bring attention to the S&W on his hip. "We just finished up at the scene. Dillon and I were going over the details one more time before he took off."

Yes, I know you're a cop. I know you're tight with T's father. "So you're out of here?"

"Yep. You?"

"Appears that way."

Justin spread his legs and crossed his arms. "Look, I know we got off to a bad start—"

"We're fine. I don't hold a grudge." Max had forgiven. Forgetting proved to be harder. As he had told Teagan, he was a work in progress. "Let's move on."

"I'd like to."

"What's stopping you?"

"I shouldn't have done the background check without T's permission. I agree. But you never addressed my findings." The guy apologized out one side of his mouth and proceeded to bang away at Max out the other. "How can you set yourself up as a role model for a bunch of impressionable kids when you've done what you've done?"

"Defended my country, you mean? Survived hellholes in Afghanistan? Is that what you're referring to?"

"Thank you for your service. Believe me, I respect it."

"I appreciate that."

"It's what you did when you came back that concerns me."

"Putting myself through the Dallas School of Theology, you mean?"

"You know what I mean."

"The Pastor-Parish Relations Committee at the church did the same background check you did. They hired me. I've given my testimony before the entire congregation at three consecutive services." Max had puked in the church's bathroom twice that day, but Justin didn't need to know that. "They operate under the assumption that when God pardons sin, they should do the same. When He doesn't stay angry forever but delights to show mercy, they should do the same. When He has compassion on us, they should do the same."

"I get it. They're good Christians. I spend my share of time in church, but I'm also a cop. I see human nature as it is in this messed-up world." For the first time Justin dropped his gaze to the driveway. "I don't have brothers and sisters of my own. The O'Rourkes have been family to me since I was a kid. I don't want to see any of them hurt."

"Yet you egged Billy and Gracie on when they decided to apply to the academy even though you knew how much Teagan was against it. You became a cop yourself." *Easy, easy. Speak softly. He cares about T. That makes him a good guy.* Max reached for a more conciliatory tone. "T comes on like she's all tough, but she's really a marshmallow inside. She lived with her dad being a cop all those years after her mom died. She didn't want more of the same for the rest of her family."

"These guys can take care of themselves. Trust me on that."

"I imagine Officer Moreno told her family the same thing. Now her parents are planning her funeral. Teagan still worries and prays every day that something awful doesn't happen to the people she loves. Unlike most people in this world, she knows that bad things happen to good people. She sees and hears it every day at work." Max longed to give her the gift of innocence once again, but it wasn't possible. "The blinders were torn away when her mom died. Teagan can't ever get that blind, blissful existence—that ignorance—back."

"So much for having faith in a good God."

"Faith is believing God is good even when bad things happen. Not just when life is good."

"Tell her that."

"I do."

Even so, the fear that lived inside her—the fear of losing another loved one—kept her hamstrung. She edged out on the high wire of love and commitment, only to turn back whenever the fear overcame her. He'd spent two years getting to know her since she joined his church. Group volunteer projects such as Magdalena House, Haven for Hope, and Habitat for Humanity. Church social activities such as Mission games, Spurs games, barbecues, potlucks, and chili cook-offs. The more time he spent around her, the more she burrowed under his skin. The few times he'd ventured into deeper territory, she shut him down.

"For the record, there's nothing going on between Teagan and me. You don't have to worry." Not on her end, anyway. "She's made it clear friendship is all she's looking for."

"But you've made it clear you're looking for more."

"I respect her feelings." Even if he didn't agree.

"This psychopath wants to play with her feelings. Make her hurt. What if something happens to you? What do you think that will do to her faith?"

The killer would be another reason for her to build walls and hunker down behind them. They needed to grab the guy and put him away. "The killer couldn't have known I would be around this evening. This was total spur of the moment on my part. Now I know to be on guard." For himself, but even more so for Teagan. "You want to make me leaving her alone an argument for her spiritual well-being? Do your job and it won't come to that."

"Did you tell her you tried to kill yourself?"

The question hit Max with the force of an IED. The metallic taste of adrenaline burned his throat. Fight or flight?

He stood his ground. No one should know about such a private, painful, agonizing time in his life. Getting into a veteran's records couldn't be easy. Not impossible for a cop with connections, though. "My medical records are confidential. No one has a right to know about that. Least of all a jerk like you."

Justin took a step closer to the bike. He flicked a clinging moth from the headlight with one finger. "Is that what this is—the latest method to your madness? Take a curve a little too fast someday and all your problems disappear?"

For Max, picking his poison had been easy. Pain pills for his back. His dad's favorite smooth whiskey. A cocktail on an unending brilliantly sunny summer day. Unfortunately—no, fortunately—his housemate, another vet with better control over his demons, came home from work and found Max in time.

The suicide attempt was his hit-bottom point, and from there it had been a long, arduous, but steady clawing ascent from the dark, miry pit to the light. Ninety-nine percent of the time, he chose not to look back. That other one percent sent him back to AA, his sponsor, his pastor, and close friends. He had backup.

"Just the opposite. The motorcycle was a graduation gift to myself when I hit five years clean and sober. Not that it's any of your business."

"You make it my business when you mess with the O'Rourkes. T is the little sister I never had." Justin jiggled his keys. The noise, like everything about the man, was irritating. "Everybody deserves a second chance. I get that. I believe it. But when it comes to her, I see trouble written all over you."

"Lucky for me, it's not up to you. It's up to Teagan." *Thank You, God.* "She knows everything she needs to know about me, and for some reason she still hangs around me. Get over it or get lost." Max started his bike and revved the engine.

Childish maybe, but it felt good.

Instead of fencing with Justin, Max should be working with him to keep Teagan safe. "Just do your job. Find this killer before someone else gets hurt."

"That's the plan."

"If there's anything I can do to help—"

"Stay out of the way."

Reconciliation took two. "How about I pray?"

"That is something you're good at." Justin touched the gun on his hip. "Leave the rest to me."

Prayer was far more powerful than any gun, but the two together upped the odds of success.

Would they be enough?

8

Rest in peace, Evelyn. You didn't deserve this.

The cataclysmic events of the previous day on repeat in her head, Teagan lay in bed for a few minutes, staring at the ceiling.

Rest in peace, Kristin Moreno, you did not deserve this.

Evelyn should be eating her oatmeal in preparation for her early-morning gardening. Kristin Moreno should be gearing up for another day on patrol. Instead they were in the medical examiner's suite. Were their gurneys side by side? Who would go first? Teagan's throat ached as she fended off the images.

```
20   A. We then open the body and take a look at
21   the organs inside the body. We take each organ
22   individually and weigh it and examine it. Again, we're
23   looking for any evidence of natural disease or any
24   evidence of trauma.
25   We also take any fluids from the body:
26   urine, blood, vitreous, which is the fluid behind the
27   eye, and we test those fluids for any materials, say
28   drugs, that may be present. We take all of this
29   information and we use it to determine a cause and
30   manner of death.
```

This morning a medical examiner would remove each one of Evelyn's organs and weigh it. Nausea rocked Teagan. She bolted upright and threw her legs over the side of the bed, ready to dash to the bathroom sink. She gripped the sheets and kneaded the silky material with both hands. *Breathe, breathe, breathe.*

Tigger whimpered and slid from the bed with a thump. Her nose nudged Teagan's hand. Teagan managed to loosen her grip on the sheets so she could slide her hands along the dog's muscular frame. *Easy, easy.*

Normally her next step would be to run. She needed to blow off steam and she would. The monster behind two murders wanted to take this everyday routine away from her by placing a target on her back. He wanted her to cower in the corner, afraid to leave her own home.

She simply refused.

Standing on shaky legs, she donned her athletic shorts and tank top. As soon as she had her jog, she would head to the courthouse and review her files to see if anyone popped out as a potential perpetrator seeking revenge. The names should jog her memory. Then she could use the date and case number to find the real-time transcript of the case stored on the cloud, if necessary. Mostly, Justin and Siebert needed a name they could run through the databases and pull his arrest records.

The hundreds of cases that came through Teagan's courtroom tended to meld together. It was better that way. They might haunt other reporters, but when she tucked the manila folder containing the basic essentials of a case into the metal filing cabinet in her office, she made a concerted effort to move on. She always had another case to take its place.

The ability to compartmentalize kept her sane. So did running. Teagan laced up her Reeboks and took Tigger's leash from its hook by the front door. The dog's cute butt wiggled in ecstasy. Her beautiful snout turned up in a gleeful smile.

"Yes, we're going out, sweet pea. I won't tell the cop squad, if you don't. We both need a good run after yesterday. Evelyn wouldn't want us to wallow in our grief, would she?" What would Kristin Moreno have wanted? Did she go to the gym? Did she work out or run?

Evelyn scorned exercise of any kind. She said vacuuming, mopping, and gardening were more productive and just as healthy. Unless a wild animal was chasing her, she found running undignified and a waste of time. Teagan closed her eyes and let her mind run.

```
14  Q. All right. And-and did she also present with
15  any items of clothing with her?
16  A. Yes.
17  Q. And how would you describe those items of
18  clothing?
19  A. She was clothed in a pink gingham housecoat,
20  a white nightgown, and fuzzy pull-on slippers.
21  There were some things in the pockets of her housecoat.
22  Dog treats, butterscotch candies, clothespins, and a cell
23  phone.
24  Like I said, the housecoat and nightgown had rips from
25  stab marks and being cut open.
```

Despite her own admonition, tears choked Teagan. Evelyn always had doggie treats for Tigger. The elderly woman loved butterscotch candies. All sweets, in fact. Every room in her neat little house had a candy dish, just in case she had visitors who shared her not-so-secret vice. Teagan grabbed a tissue and wiped her nose. "Allergies are bad today, aren't they?"

Her expression anxious, Tigger cocked her head. "Woof."

"You're so right about that."

Teagan armed the security system and let Tigger lead the way. The dog's excited bark alerted her to a guest at the Little Free Library. Guests. Keeping Tigger close to her side, she went to greet Cole

Reynolds and his gorgeous chocolate Lab, Huck, whose tail did the cha-cha upon seeing Tigger.

Cole, dressed in basketball shorts and a gray T-shirt, pushed back a black-and-silver Spurs ball cap and smiled. "Still no classics. The Russian novelists are good. Have you ever read *Anna Karenina* or *The Brothers Karamazov*?"

The borrowers from her library weren't interested in the classics. Romances went well, of course, and mysteries. "Can't say that I have." This wasn't their first discussion of tastes in literature. Teagan enjoyed sparring with Cole even if she found him to be a bit of a literary snob. "I have, however, read *The Outsiders* and *The Bell Jar*." In high school. Two years of junior college had not included a literature course.

"If you ever want to broaden your horizons, let me know. I have all of Charles Dickens's books and everything Mark Twain ever wrote."

"I'll keep that in mind." Filed in File #13. Cole always looked like someone's fitness trainer, but he was a speech and communications instructor at San Antonio College. He had cerulean eyes, curly honey-brown hair, a toothy smile, and a nice physique. Hoping he couldn't read her mind, she smiled. "How's the renovation coming?"

Cole owned a two-story Victorian partially renovated by flippers who ran out of money. He'd lived in the neighborhood about a year. "The downstairs is done. I haven't had time to work on the bedrooms, though. Too many papers to grade."

His Lab's soft *woof* was met with delight by Tigger who immediately tugged at her leash, begging to be allowed to play. "Tigger still wants a playdate."

They always talked about getting the dogs together, but they never did. The story of busy professionals whose lives touched but never really connected.

"I know. Huck too. But my schedule has been crazy." He stuck the book back on the shelf. "It's wishful thinking to suggest I'll have time to read a book for pleasure. What with all the amazing projects my students must turn in between now and the end of the semester." Sarcasm dusted the words.

Did he know about Evelyn's murder? If he did, he didn't show it. The muscles in Teagan's shoulders knotted. What if the killer was watching them right now? What if he picked off Cole Reynolds the way he did Kristin Moreno?

She tugged at Tigger's leash and edged away. "I'd better get moving. I'll be late for work. Good luck with grading papers. I hope you'll be able to read to your heart's content soon."

"Thanks. It just isn't meant to be. I'm teaching a couple of summer sessions. I complain, but I really enjoy teaching. Taking nervous freshmen and turning them into public speakers is a challenge." Ignoring her obvious desire to move on, he stepped forward and stroked Tigger's head. Huck nuzzled his other hand. Double-dog duty. "I like coming home to this neighborhood too. I'm glad I decided to buy here. It was love at first sight."

A reader and dog lover with a yen for an old house. At first blush the perfect neighbor. Maybe even a perfect man. If he were older, she would introduce Julie to him. His eyebrows lifted. He probably expected a response. Teagan studied his house across the street over his shoulder. "Mine was love at first sight too. But it wasn't a flip. My family and friends were my construction team. I paid them in pizza and blueberry cobbler." Sweat equity turned a crumbling two-bedroom two-bathroom semi-shack into a cozy home with just the right touch of rustic. It was still a work in progress, but it was home. "They couldn't see what I saw, but they hung in there with me, and now I can't get rid of them!"

Not that she wanted to get rid of any of them. The Saturday night barbecues were epic.

"It's a beauty. I really like the blue color you chose. It's very sunny."

He cocked his head. "All the flowers help too. If I ever get around to landscaping, I know who to ask for tips. I'm not much of a gardener."

The guy liked her house, her dog, and her flowers. Good friend material. Not on Max's level but decent. "We really should take the dogs for that run we're always talking about."

"It's a date." He grinned and hunched his shoulders in mock embarrassment. "Sorry. Slip of the lip. A playdate for the hounds. Not us."

With a determined smile, Teagan took off running. The smile lasted until she glanced toward Evelyn's tidy gray home with white trim and a mass of pink roses in front.

Who would water and prune them now?

Teagan's normal easy lope evaporated into a frenzied pace that had Tigger straining to keep up. Six or seven miles usually satisfied Teagan's urge to punish herself. Today she hit her max at eight after a longer-than-usual foray through the King William District and back. Usually imagining the founders of that historic neighborhood and what their lives were like in early San Antonio filled her thoughts as she ran. Not today. She slowed to a stagger a block from her house. Tigger raised her head and barked for more.

"Sorry, girl, I'm done." She slid her hand down the dog's warm, muscled body. "Save it for tomorrow."

Her phone dinged as she dragged herself up the steps to the house. Max.

How r u?

Good. U?

At church.

Max always tried to arrive at the sprawling church campus early for devotions and prayer before the other staff members showed up. He and Rick seemed to have an unspoken competition going on to see who could unlock the doors first.

Good. That's good.

Are u really okay?

Really.

Be safe.

U too.

Praying.

Me too.

Be God's.

Always.

She did her best with her prayers, but Max knew that. He did a much better job of keeping in touch with God. Her prayer life was more a series of discussions between an Abba Father and his recalcitrant daughter.

Their text language reminded Teagan of the one she used on her writer. People who bothered to ask found it hard to understand how she typed hours of dialogue using fourteen blank keys. Court reporters who made it through the training—only three from her class of twenty graduated—learned to type phonetically, combining numerous sounds.

Be safe. Just seeing Max's name come up on her phone made her feel safer.

Cheered by the thought, she picked up speed and headed to the shower. She chose her favorite blue suit and low heels. Normally when she didn't have a trial on the docket, she walked the mile and a half to work or grabbed one of the ubiquitous electric scooters now available on every corner downtown. Today she would heed the cop squad's warnings and play it safe by driving. Ninety minutes later she strode into her office behind the 177th District Court at the Bexar County Justice Center.

Julie Davidson didn't bother with a greeting. She simply folded Teagan into a hug and patted her back. Her signature gold bangle bracelets jangled. Julie was at least forty-five but looked thirty. She never had a brown hair out of place or a wrinkle in her simple but elegant Anne Klein ensembles. Under her able administration, the

177th's team was a well-oiled machine. "You should've taken the day off. The judge would understand."

"I'm better off working." Teagan hugged back and broke free from her willowy friend's grasp. She was late, no time for their usual give-and-take about their evenings. "What's on the docket today?"

Hearings on a variety of topics usually filled Thursday's docket if they weren't in trial. Julie perused the document that served as her bible as they headed down the hallway behind the courtroom that led to their offices. "A PSI on a sex assault of a child, several motions to revoke, and several trials that will probably plead out or could get settings." She glanced at the smartwatch on her wrist. "Judge will be ready to take the bench in about fifteen minutes."

That gave Teagan enough time to grab a cup of coffee and check her email. On trial days she often didn't communicate with the outside world for eight or ten hours. Nothing urgent for now. She slipped into the courtroom where the assistant district attorneys had taken over two tables inside the gates that separated the bench from the gallery. The 177th was one of the smaller courtrooms in the Paul Elizondo Tower. The walls were a soft coral and the carpet sturdy gold. U.S. and Texas flags adorned the space behind the bench. Her home away from home.

She made the rounds. Everyone had a theory on the events of the previous day. Everyone wanted her take on it. She kept her responses short. She knew little more than they did and she'd been there.

Bailiff Pete Sanchez waved and turned back to the prisoners who shuffled into the jury box, where they would wait for consults with their attorneys already gathering to hash out plea deals and contested Motions to Revoke with the assistant DAs.

As usual Thursday meant organized chaos in the 177th.

She slid into her chair just below the judge's bench and smoothed her fingers over her writer. Plain, simple, and her touchstone. It brought order to chaos. She'd been doing this so long, she could type lengthy voir dire of potential jurors and plan her grocery list in her head at the same time. Attorneys might argue on top of each other, the judge might mumble, the defendant might stare, but she let nothing get in the way of the words.

"I heard you had a bad day." Hand on his service weapon, Pete paused by her tiny work space with just enough room for her machine, her computer, and a few technology odds and ends. "Sorry about that."

"Thanks." Teagan scooted closer to her desk. Some days the defendants in the jury box behind her were too close for comfort. "I just feel bad for Officer Moreno's family. She was so young."

"Quiet in the box." Pete turned and shot a fierce frown at an orange jumpsuit–clad man with the state of Texas tattooed on one cheek and a nasty cold sore on his upper lip. "You just can't shut up, can you? Stop talking." Pete turned back to Teagan. His smile returned. "Moreno knew what she signed up for. It doesn't make it any easier for the family, but Moreno was a police officer. She died with her boots on."

Small comfort for Teagan too. What if it had been Gracie or Billy? Families of law enforcement officers knew they had to suck it up and swallow their fears.

She busied herself making sure her computer was up and running, ready to do real-time transcription so the judge could see the record. She'd transcribed two capital murder trials in her career. She never wanted to do another one involving a police officer. Her mind tapped out the record she prayed would never be needed for Gracie even while her brain demanded she stop her fingers.

```
2   A. The actor, the driver, he's now unable to
3     get over the fence, and he turns around and confronts the
4     officer. A large guy, a big guy, much bigger than
5     Officer Gracie Evans Gomez. And the officer tells him to get
```

6   down, to surrender. She's wearing her full police

7   uniform. It's broad daylight. She's telling him to give

8   up, he's caught. He waves a gun around.

9   Officer Gomez is backpedaling,

10   starts to-starts to backpedal. Pulls

11   her gun. Tells him to drop his gun. He does not. Comes at

12   the officer. The driver shoots at Officer Gomez one time

13   in the chest and Gomez falls to the ground in the middle

14   of the yard. The officer tries to call for help.

15   and-and shooting. The officer takes two more blows. She

16   takes one to her-her left thigh and then she takes one

17   to-through her boot into her ankle. She's hurt bad, but she

18   returns fire. The neighbor retreats back into his house.

19   He gets on the phone.

20   He's calling 911. He goes to get his own gun. It's

21   upstairs. To load it up, but you'll find by that time

22   Officer Gomez is deceased.

Deceased.

Teagan's stomach twisted. Sudden tremors shook her. Maybe *fine* had been the wrong word. *Shake it off. Sitting at home would be worse.* She didn't need more time to think. She needed to work.

"Teagan. Teagan? Teagan!"

Startled, Teagan jolted from her chair. "Is the judge ready?"

"He's still on the phone in his chambers." Julie grinned and cocked her perfectly coiffed brown-haired head toward the door. "You got a delivery. Run take a look before he comes in."

"Are you sure?"

"After the day you had yesterday, this will cheer you up." Julie opened the door with a flourish. "Somebody loves you, and I think I know who it is."

With a glance at her watch, Teagan dashed down the hallway to her office. Amid the mess on her desk sat a cut-glass vase containing at least two dozen pink roses. Their sweet aroma overcame the usual scent of old paper, stale coffee, and dust. Spring had sprung in her dingy courthouse office.

"They're gorgeous." Teagan breathed in the deliciousness. They reminded her of Mrs. Conklin. She raised her head and stepped away from the bouquet. Someone knew they would. Max, probably. He knew she loved flowers, and he managed to make them into a friend gesture—just behind the line she'd drawn between them. "That's so thoughtful."

"Who sent them? Was it Max?" Julie clasped her manicured fingers in front of her like an ecstatic child waiting for a gift to be opened. Her bangles clapped with her. "I bet it was Max."

Her coworker labored under the illusion that one day Teagan would open her eyes and see that Max was a perfect match for her. She was one of the few people whom Teagan had enlightened as to why they were not, in fact, a perfect match. That didn't stop Julie from hoping.

Teagan tugged a small cream-colored envelope from amid the greenery. Instead of the usual typed message that resulted from a telephone call or an online order, she found a note penned in thick black ink. A familiar script that read:

Dear T,

    These are no match for Evelyn's lovely Belinda's Dream roses, but I hope they lift your spirits. Blue is your color. I wonder how red will look on you. Tell your father I said hello.

                Your friend,

                Phillip Meek

Teagan eased into her chair and laid the card facedown on her desk. She examined the envelope without touching it again. No florist name or address adorned it. That should've been her first clue.

"Who's it from?" Julie's smile died. Her hazel eyes grew somber behind stylish red frames. "What is it, girlfriend?"

"I need to call Justin."

"Why would he send you flowers? He's married—"

"They're not from him either."

"Who then?"

"They're from the killer—Evelyn's and Officer Moreno's killer."

Julie's court coordinator mask slid into place. "I'm on it. I'll let the judge know and get Pete in here."

Roses would never smell sweet again.

9

Same book second chapter. Teagan rubbed her pounding forehead with both hands and tried not to get in the CSU investigator's way.

"Who's Phillip Meek?" Alisha stood in the doorway doing the same thing. "Another literary friend?"

"No friend of mine, but yes. Phillip Meek is a fictional serial killer in *Death So Sweet*. More accurately, a hit man who gets paid to kill but also enjoys it." Suddenly cold in the tepid air generated by the courthouse's overworked AC, Teagan shivered. "He kills his victims in various violent ways and then butchers them to freeze the meat. His version of taking trophies. He's a gourmet chef, by the way."

"Lovely. How does Fuentes sleep at night?"

"He was a reporter before he wrote fiction. He knows bad stuff happens to good people and bad people are everywhere."

If it sounded like an oversimplification, too bad it wasn't.

The CSU investigator didn't bother to take the roses with her. They came from a shop on South St. Mary's, delivered by their employee who brought them through security and carried them directly to their offices. She dusted the card and the envelope and then placed them in evidence bags. The once lovely scent of roses now gagged Teagan. She grabbed the offending flowers and stuffed them into the wastebasket. She had to smash down the stems in order to close the trash bag and tie it off.

"Good job." Alisha leaned against the wall, arms crossed, watching Teagan's semi temper tantrum. Justin's partner was a solidly built woman slightly taller than Teagan with deep cocoa-brown hair and eyes shaped with a hint of her Mayan ancestors. "You showed them."

"They stink."

"I can see why you'd say that." Alisha pulled away from the wall and tried to pace in the space between the desk and the door that led to Teagan's evidence vault. Her long ponytail swayed with each step. "I know you can't tell me anything about the flowers, so let's just concentrate on what you did this morning."

The killer had been watching her. He knew she wore a blue suit. Her favorite Calvin Klein notch-collar jacket with silver buttons and matching pants would no longer be her go-to outfit. Its price tag made it too expensive to burn, but it would make a nice donation to Dress for Success San Antonio, a charity that helped women experiencing homelessness get jobs.

Shuddering, Teagan sipped the water Julie had brought her and studied the mosquito bite on her wrist just below her Fitbit. "I went for a run." It sounded so self-absorbed said aloud. "I needed to clear my head. Tigger needed to stretch her legs. I owed her one."

"You don't have to justify your actions to me." Alisha went back to leaning on the wall. Her fingers tapped a brisk beat on the painted drywall behind her. "I worked out at the gym for an hour and a half last night. I couldn't get enough of the punching bag."

She did understand. A punching bag was far better than the twelve-pack some officers chose. Teagan grabbed her tension ball from her desk and squeezed it. "That was it. I did eight miles, dragged my butt into the shower, and came to work."

"Nothing unusual? You didn't see any strange cars in the neighborhood? You didn't pass anyone on your run who seemed out of place?"

"No one. No one out of place." Teagan rubbed her forehead. She dropped the ball, grabbed her leather satchel, and dug through the contents until she found a travel pack of Tylenol. She extracted two. "I chatted with my neighbor from across the street. He's one of the least strange people on my block." She took the pills and swallowed them with a gulp of water. "Unless you think bibliophiles are strange. He likes to browse through the books in my Little Free Library, mostly so he can critique the collection. He thinks I should have more classics."

"Name?" Alisha tugged her pen from behind her ear and produced a small notebook from her jacket pocket. "Anything different about him?"

"He's into Victorian decorating, but that doesn't make him weird. He bought the house over a year ago from flippers who ran out of money. He's finished the downstairs and started on the bedrooms upstairs." Teagan blabbered when she was nervous. "Cole Reynolds, San Antonio College instructor of speech and communications."

"I'll check him out."

"You should. He's cute, physically fit, and has a dog named Huck." Alisha was single and ready to commit. She hadn't been able to find the right guy or one who didn't mind her job. Teagan tried to help her out. As if she had this guy thing figured out. "He's into DIY projects and he likes to cook. He's nearly perfect."

"No beef with Evelyn Conklin? We don't have a lot to work with here."

"What about the flowers? Isn't that a stupid thing to do?" Teagan went back to squeezing her tension ball. Maybe she could pretend she was squeezing the killer's neck. Probably not very Christian. *Turn the other cheek. Kill 'em with kindness. Heap burning coals of kindness on their heads.* "He calls a flower shop and buys flowers or, better yet, orders online?"

"Except he didn't." Justin swaggered into the room. The guy thought he was all that and a bag of chips. His scent of Polo and hair product arrived slightly before him. "The flower shop clerk says a

CLOSER THAN SHE KNOWS

woman came in and ordered them. She brought the card with her. She claimed her boyfriend asked her to order them for him. It was a surprise for his mother on her birthday. She paid cash."

The news poured cold water on Teagan's tiny flame of hope. "What woman would do that?"

"It's not unusual for psychopaths to have girlfriends."

"Could the clerk describe her?"

"Average height, white, long brown hair, brown eyes, cute, thin. Mid- to late-twenties."

Like thousands of women in one of the fastest-growing cities in the country. San Antonio boasted a rapidly expanding population of 1.3 million. Many were millennials drawn by its reasonably priced housing market, a thriving, culturally diverse downtown, and job opportunities. "Her fingerprints have to be on the envelope."

"We'll see—"

Max burst through the door, a sudden impression made up of shaggy sandy-brown hair, a TobyMac T-shirt, faded, holey jeans, and boat shoes. Pete the bailiff—Teagan always thought of him that way. Did his wife?—followed with one hand on his gun and the other on his ASP baton. Pete didn't look happy, but Max looked even more agitated. "Are you okay? Confirm for this guy that you told me to come."

"I told you it wasn't necessary for you to come." Teagan rose and slipped around her desk. The office barely held the space for her desk, two chairs, and some filing cabinets. Now it had to play host to a law enforcement convention and one larger-than-life youth minister. "But I knew there would be no stopping you. There's a subtle difference."

Max muscled his way between Justin and Alisha. Teagan barely had time to brace herself before he delivered the hug. "You're okay?"

"He sent me flowers. He didn't come himself." Teagan edged from his space even though every muscle urged her to lean into his broad chest. "I'm fine."

"How did the flowers get up here?" Max looked around as if to browbeat someone into answering his question. "I thought this was a secure building. Where was Pete the bailiff?"

That he used her name for Pete reflected the number of stories he'd listened to Teagan tell about the hard-nosed bailiff's antics in the courtroom.

"The flowers went through security." Justin had asked the same question. He didn't need to consult his notebook for the answer. "This is a public building. That's how all the jurors get in, the defendants, the attorneys. What were you expecting? Alcatraz?"

"Looks like they don't need any stinkin' security in Corpus, either." Billy stuck his head through the doorway. "Hi, Sissy, how you holding up?"

Another LEO heard from. Soon her office would be like the Volkswagen Beetle vying for a Guinness World Record for the greatest number of law enforcement officers who could be stuffed into one ten-by-twelve office. Teagan returned to her side of the desk, Max in tow, a fact that didn't bother her no matter how much she'd love to be the macho woman in this scenario. "Come on in, Bro, the more the merrier."

Billy wedged himself between Justin and Alisha. He didn't look happy. "I thought you should be the first to know. Our serial killer is in the wind."

10

Suspected serial killer Leo Slocum had escaped from Corpus PD custody. Billy's monotone delivery of the news didn't fool Teagan. Her brother was livid. Personally, she didn't know whether to sob, throw up, or faint.

Of course she would do none of the above. Grown-up women—especially O'Rourkes—didn't engage in histrionics. From an early age Mom had bombarded her with role models like astronaut Sally Ride, Supreme Court associate justice Ruth Bader Ginsburg, Madam Curie, Eleanor Roosevelt, and of course, Wonder Woman. At the moment Teagan wanted Wonder Woman's superhuman strength to open the window behind her, her ability to fly away from San Antonio, and her superhuman speed to go far, far away.

Justin and Alisha cursed at the same time. Good thing Corpus PD couldn't hear what SAPD homicide detectives wanted to do with their peers up I-37.

Max's hands slid onto her shoulders. His fingers tightened. Maybe he could be Superman to her Wonder Woman and they could fly away together. "How is that possible?" She managed to pose the question without a quiver in her voice. "What kind of security do they have at their jail?"

"He insisted on mounting his own defense, so their guys took him back and forth from the jail to a law library at the courthouse—"

"And he escaped." Justin rolled his eyes. "Do these guys not recognize the Ted Bundy scenario?"

"The prosecutor said the guy actually fancies himself as smarter than Bundy. He doesn't admit to killing anybody, but he says if he'd defended himself in San Antonio, he would've been found not guilty. He's claiming his attorney was incompetent."

"Escaping is no way to show innocence." Alisha peeked over Billy's shoulder at his notebook. "How long has he been gone?"

"Two days. A guy went into a convenience store Monday to buy cigarettes and lottery tickets. He got to talking to the clerk, and pretty soon he looks up to see his Infiniti driving away from the gas pump. He'd just filled it with gas."

"And the idiot left his keys in the car?" Teagan groaned. "Why do people do that?"

"Nope. Not quite. Apparently, the thief hot-wired it. But the money he used for toll roads and such was in the console. Cameras clearly show it's our guy Slocum."

"He's not my guy." Teagan squeezed into her chair. Max slid behind it as if to stand guard. "It's a five-hour drive, depending on traffic, from Corpus to San Antonio."

"The Infiniti was found abandoned in Victoria." Billy's gloomy expression squashed any hope that his report would get cheerier. "No sign of Slocum."

"Let's assume he boosted another car and has made it into San Antonio." Justin slapped a folder on Teagan's desk. "Have you ever seen this guy before?"

The man staring up at her looked familiar, only because his photo had been published in the *San Antonio Express-News* during his trial. Slocum had thick black hair that had gone silver at the temples. He favored a stylish salt-and-pepper five o'clock shadow. His cheekbones were high, his cheeks hollow, and his lips thin. But it was his eyes that captured a person's attention. Deep-blue eyes framed by long dark lashes. Bedroom eyes. Not a face a person would forget. Especially a woman. "I've never seen him before."

"Think. Where have you gone in the past three days?" Justin pressed. "Grocery store. Gas station. Starbucks."

"She said she hasn't seen him." Max bristled like a bulldog who had discovered an alley cat in his territory. "Don't treat her like some street thug you just arrested."

"Easy, Max. I was in trial until yesterday afternoon." Teagan touched his hand with her fingers for a second, then withdrew. She didn't need him or anyone else to defend her, certainly not from Justin. She'd gone head-to-head with him plenty of times. "Earlier in the week, I worked all day and went home to scope the transcript and clean it up, like I always do during a trial. You know where I was last night."

She handed the photo to Gracie, who whistled. "No wonder he has a girlfriend."

"The clerk said the woman looked to be in her midtwenties, maybe even younger," Justin pointed out. "Seems way young for this dude."

"Daddy issues?" Alisha suggested. "Sugar daddy? It doesn't really matter. If Slocum is in town and he's hooked up with an old girlfriend, finding her could lead us to him."

"I'll get a sketch artist to sit with the clerk, see if we can get a decent sketch," Billy said. "And I'll go through the prosecutor's files on the kidnapping case with a fine-tooth comb—"

"How are we doing in here?" Stately in his black robe, Judge Simon Ibarra squeezed his portly body into the office. They really were going for the Guinness record. "Teagan, it appears you're in good hands. I'm so sorry for what you're going through."

Ibarra was Teagan's second judge in her six-year career. Her first judge got booted out by voters in a clean sweep of Republicans in the last election. As a judge's fate went, so, too, went his or her support staff. Ibarra was kind, he didn't talk too fast, and he kept reasonable hours. His decision to keep Teagan had been a blessing.

"Thank you, Judge. I'm so sorry we're holding up court. I'm ready to go if you are."

"No worries. I asked Julie to call temp services and get us a court reporter who can sub for you as long as needed."

"That's not necessary." Teagan would not let this creep keep her from doing her job. Where would she be safer than in the Bexar County Courthouse? She stood. "You all go do what you do. Find Slocum and figure out if he killed Officer Moreno and Evelyn. I have work to do."

A hubbub of protest rose around her. Teagan bulldozed her way through the crowd. Billy was the most vociferous. She shook her finger at him. "Go on, get out of here. Don't make me sic Pete the bailiff on you."

Billy put both hands in the air. "Going!"

"Forget it." Max stuck to her like Tigger's fur on her linen suits. "I'm staying."

Teagan had invited Max to observe her in action during a trial. He'd never been able to find the time.

This wasn't quite what she had in mind.

*   *   *

Despite his best efforts, anxiety slithered along Max's spine, crawled into his gut, and made itself at home next to the Pop-Tarts and coffee he'd eaten for breakfast. Rick claimed one of the reasons Max made such a good youth pastor was that he still ate like a kid.

Sometimes. For fun. Sugar and caffeine were his drugs of choice now that no others were available, but he didn't make a habit of eating like a middle-school kid. He joined the parade led by Judge Ibarra down the hallway to the courtroom. Pete the bailiff held the door while the judge entered, followed by Teagan and Julie, who hovered close to her colleague like a bodyguard dressed in the latest fashionable business suit. Before Max could get through the door, Billy tapped his shoulder. "Hey, got a sec?"

Not another "*What are you doing with T?*" discussion. "Now?"

Billy scowled and jerked his head. "Now would be good."

"Are you coming?" Justin hollered. He and his partner were headed out the exit at the end of the hallway rather than going through the courtroom. "We need to powwow."

He definitely wasn't talking to Max. "Go on. I'm good here."

"I'm right behind you," Billy assured his cohorts. He pushed the courtroom door shut. "Did you come down on your bike?"

"No. In my truck."

The '74 Ford wasn't slick and pretty like Billy's flashy Tundra, but it got the job done. The time Max had spent tinkering with it and restoring the engine ensured that. "It was sprinkling. Plus I wanted to bring my Smith & Wesson M&P. I figured I couldn't bring it into the courthouse, so I drove the truck."

"Smart thinking. Where'd you park?"

"Ground lot next to Tommy's Restaurant. The garage was full."

"You'll walk her to her car?" Billy wasn't trying to separate Max from Teagan. He wanted to keep her safe. Points for her brother. "Or better yet, get her to let you drive her home?"

They were on the same page. "Look, I can handle this. Go do cop things."

After a long, level stare, Billy turned and hiked down the hallway. At the door he glanced back. "Don't let her push you around."

No one knew Teagan's dedication to her independence better than her siblings. Max nodded. Billy took his leave. Max tapped on the courtroom door. Julie let him in with a quick smile and an index finger to her lips. He followed her to the swinging gates that led to the gallery, where a motley crowd of people watched the proceedings.

Max's heartbeat did a *cha-cha-cha*. At least half a dozen times T had offered to give him a tour of "her" courtroom and introduce him to her colleagues. He always found an excuse not to accept the invitation. No matter how many years passed, he still turned into a sixteen-year-old misfit whenever he thought of courtrooms. His brushes with the law had been minor—vandalism, underage drinking, possession of a doobie, being out after curfew.

After his parents got done with him, he never wanted to step into a courtroom—or a jail—again. Which was why he'd confined himself to legal drugs during his checkered past. Zoloft, Xanax, and Ambien liberally mixed with alcohol had done the trick for a time.

"Turn it off." His therapist reminded him at every session to be on guard against dwelling on old memories. Flip the channel. Choose a good memory. Rewind it and watch it again. A version of *"Find your happy place."*

No happy place here. He studied the spectators. Unless Leo Slocum was a master at disguises, no way he sat among the unhappy spectators who observed the proceedings. Was he a chameleon? The unknowns took turns pounding on Max's temples. The coffee sloshed in his stomach. His throat burned. *Focus on others.*

Today's show was reality TV better than *Judge Judy* any day, watching Judge Ibarra wade through a mind-bogglingly quick series of hearings. The fine art of negotiation resulted in a plea deal that gave a woman the chance to do inpatient drug treatment rather than going to jail after an on-the-spot urine analysis revealed she'd come to court high on coke. Another woman pleaded no contest to trafficking a person for purposes of sex. She was young, attractive, and apparently worked in a restaurant. How did she end up a pimp?

A plea deal ended with a victim-impact statement in which the father of a middle-school student chewed out a twenty-one-year-old guy who'd been "dating" his daughter. In Texas that was sexual assault of a child. A fourteen-year-old couldn't consent to sex. The tearful father tried hard to be fair as he insisted the defendant look at him. Pete the bailiff had to ask the distraught father to back up twice. The young man received deferred adjudication, which meant if he stayed out of trouble, his record would be expunged. His attorney assured the judge that after ten days in jail, they need not worry about the kid bothering the victim again. He was led away in handcuffs to begin inpatient treatment as a sex offender.

Max leaned back in the hard wooden seat and breathed. The intensity of that five-minute encounter made his chest hurt. Teagan rarely talked about her work. She said she'd learned the hard way that most of her dates didn't want to hear about murder, sexual assault, home invasions, and family violence. It made dating, particularly if the relationship lasted very long, difficult. Why people didn't want to hear about it was apparent, but how could they claim to care about her and not be concerned for her emotional well-being when she had to hold all this in?

She needed a regular prescription for TLC, and Max could fill that one.

He didn't have much time to contemplate human frailties. After another hour of motions to revoke and presentence investigations, Teagan came through the swinging gates with her purse and her leather satchel. "That's it for today. The judge ordered me to go home early. I agreed, only because there's no need to go through my files if Slocum is the guy doing this."

"It sounds ridiculous, but I hope it is him. At least then we know who we're up against. Your judge seems like a nice guy." Max held the door for her, and they took a left into the flow of people headed back to the elevators. "Was this a typical day for you?"

She shifted the satchel from one hand to the other and shrugged. "Getting flowers from a serial killer, you mean?"

"You know what I mean. That victim impact was brutal."

"That was nothing." Teagan scooted closer to the elevator door and punched the down button a second time. "Try being there when family members rip into a defendant who murdered a loved one.

They cry and scream. Sometimes they faint. Occasionally they try to take a run at the killer."

"It must be hard to get all that down."

"Actually, we don't have to transcribe the victim-impact statements." The elevator doors opened. She lowered her voice as they squeezed into the tiny box with a dozen other harried individuals, most of whom either seemed like they were having very bad days or were courthouse employees. "I try to do something else while they're talking."

"So it doesn't affect you so much?"

"Yes."

They were shoulder to shoulder in the back of the elevator. Max squeezed an arm around her and took stock of their companions. A Bexar County sheriff's deputy, a gray-haired, hump-shouldered woman using a walker, a couple who appeared to be in the middle of a furious whispered argument over how to pay for their son's bond, and an amiable-looking, middle-aged, completely bald man in a suit and tie. Probably an attorney.

Nobody looked like a serial killer. Of course, that begged the question: What did a serial killer look like? Women claimed Ted Bundy was handsome. The BTK Killer was a husband and father who taught Sunday school and helped with a Boy Scout troop. Max loosened his grip on Teagan. "No wonder you garden and bake and read so much. You fill your house with beautiful photos of the flowers you grow. You make the world you come home to each day beautiful."

"Self-preservation."

Out on the street, the piercing sunlight made Max squint. "I left my sunglasses in the truck. Why don't we just take it to your house? You can leave your car overnight in the garage, right?"

"I'd rather not. You don't need to be my bodyguard."

"He was watching you. He sent you flowers."

"I'm well aware."

The light turned green and the little neon person appeared. "Walk now. Walk now. Walk now." Max scanned the open real estate between them and the six-story parking garage ahead of them. Open surface lots bordered them on either side, the courthouse behind them. They were vulnerable to attack, the way soldiers were in Afghanistan when they marched across the valleys, mountains surrounding them. With a cluster of other pedestrians, mostly civilian court employees, jurors, and attorneys, they started across Nueva Street catty-corner to the garage. The light counted down the seconds available to make the crossing. Sixteen, fifteen, fourteen, thirteen . . .

Pop-pop-pop-pop.

Gunfire.

11

Max hurled himself at Teagan.

They hit the curb with a bone-rattling thud. Teagan screeched in protest, but Max covered her writhing body with his. All air whooshed from his lungs. Adrenaline flowed. His heart pounded.

Gun. His hand went to his hip. *In the truck.* It had no value if he couldn't carry it on him.

"Max, Max!" Teagan struggled beneath him. "Get off me. What are you doing?"

"Stay down! Stay down!" He raised his head. One of the attorneys stood over him, a hefty man in a gray suit and matching fedora. Max edged away from him. "Shots fired. Get down, man!"

"There were no shots." The man had a soft Mexican accent that gave the words a musical lilt. "A truck backfired, *señor*. That is all."

Darkness threatened to take Max's vision. He gagged on the bitter lump in this throat. "I heard gunshots."

"Only a truck." The man held out his hand. "I help you up."

Ignoring the hand, Max drew a shaky breath and scoured the scenery behind the man. The light had turned red. Cars were stopped in the intersection. A horn blared. A man leaned through the open window of his black BMW, a phone to his ear.

Probably calling 911.

An SAPD officer trotted across the intersection. "What's the problem here? Do we need an ambulance?"

"Get off me, Max. Get off." Teagan shoved at his chest with both hands. "Just a misunderstanding, Officer. My friend thought he heard shots."

Max rolled off her and dragged himself to a sitting position on the curb. Teagan did the same. She brushed at dirt on her no longer pristine suit. Road rash decorated the back of her hand. Angry red welts rose on her bare legs. A Bexar County sheriff's deputy loomed over them both. "Are you okay? What's going on here?"

"We're fine, Joe." Teagan waved the guy off. "Thanks. He's a friend. He just overreacted."

"A little." The deputy's grin was sympathetic. "Ease up on the caffeine, buddy."

"Right." Max closed his eyes and shame washed over him. He hadn't done this in years. "Sorry."

"Don't be sorry." Teagan's hand sought his and squeezed. "It's not your fault. All this tension isn't good for you."

"For me? Look at you." He turned her hand over and stared at the damage he'd inflicted. "I'm a nut case."

"You're a veteran with PTSD. You don't need the added stress. I'm the one who's sorry."

"Don't pity me."

"I wouldn't dream of it." She patted his knee. "Go home. Or go to the gym. Punch the bag for a few rounds. Take a nice, cool shower. Take a nap in your hammock."

What he should do was take a meeting. "That all sounds nice. It would be nice to have you for company."

The concern on her face faded, replaced by uncertainty. "I need to go home. You're better off not hanging around me."

"Not in a million years."

A steady stream of pedestrians flowing around them, they sat on the curb on a busy downtown intersection, staring at each other.

She broke the deadlock first. "I don't need you to babysit me."

A woman wearing a hijab pushed a stroller past them. Two small girls trailed after her. He schooled his voice. "I told Billy I'd get you home."

"Billy doesn't tell me or you what to do."

"In this case he's right. You need backup."

Teagan stood and picked up her satchel. "I'm tired. I'm headed home to make some fresh iced peppermint tea. I'll sit on my back porch and watch the cardinals play hide-and-seek in the trees. The goldfinches will complain because the squirrels keep emptying the feeder. The hummingbirds will buzz the honeysuckle and the snapdragons. I won't think about anything else."

But she would. And so would he. "I'll follow you."

"Don't." The stubborn jut of her jaw said the conversation was over.

Surely his face told her it wasn't. "I'm walking you to your car."

She whirled and started toward the garage. With a limp.

Lord, couldn't we be allowed to curse once in a while? I'd love a free pass now and then.

Not allowed. Max silently counted to ten and hurried to catch up. His left arm ached. A patch of skin burned on his hand. The muscles on the left side of his body hurt.

None of that mattered. He'd hurt Teagan. He slid his arm into hers. "Let me help you, please."

"If it makes you feel better."

They were silent for the rest of the trek to her blue Prius with its nondescript body and modest frame. She opened the door and looked back at him. "Text me later?"

"Are you sure you don't want company?" *Not even my company?*

"I have Tigger. I have a state-of-the-art security system." She opened her door.

Come on, come on. Let me in. Please let me in.

She turned. The satchel dropped to the ground. Her arms came up, and he stepped into the hug. Her scent reminded him of rain on a spring day—fig, grass, and green musk. "I don't like what this is doing to you," she whispered. "I don't want my friends hurt. Consider staying away for a while, please."

"A friend has your back. He doesn't run away. There's nothing in the world that would keep me away from you." He leaned back so he could see her face. "Get that through your beautiful head right now. I stick like Velcro to my friends. I don't bail when things get tough. You've been there for me, remember."

He didn't like it, but Teagan had insisted he put her on his list of people to call when he found himself hanging from the ledge by his fingertips. One drink. One shot of tequila with a beer chaser. Anything to dull that persistent thirst that made it hard to swallow against the pain of simply existing from one day to the next.

He'd only had to call her once. And then it had made his stress worse, not better. He didn't want her to see the cracks in his facade. She should see him as fixed, the outer finish completely smooth after years of sobriety.

Every drunk knew the cracks were still there. Waiting to burst under the pressure of the floodwaters. He could blame bloody, grotesque memories of what he'd seen in Afghanistan—young men and women blown to pieces by roadside bombs and IEDs—or he could admit that the seed was already there waiting to be watered. No excuses needed.

"You just experienced your first PTSD flashback in years." She drilled him with the O'Rourke stare, knowing full well it had no effect on him. His mother was Italian. "You need to call your therapist and your sponsor."

"You don't need to mother me."

"You're my best friend, Max. I'm entitled to meddle in your life. You certainly meddle in mine. If I feel like taking care of you, I will."

The knot in his throat ballooned. He swallowed hard. Who was comforting whom here? Or was it *who*? "You're my best friend too. If you would just let me in—"

"Don't. Please don't." Teagan broke free and slid into the car.

Max didn't wait for her to drive away. He didn't wait for the elevator, either. He darted to the stairwell, raced down four flights of stairs, and jaywalked across Nueva to the lot where he'd parked his pickup.

Three minutes later he wheeled into traffic and turned onto Flores and headed toward South St. Mary's. A creature of habit, Teagan would take South St. Mary's to Alamo Street and be at her house on Simon Street in a matter of minutes. Still early, traffic was light. He picked up her trail before she made it to Alamo Street.

It only took him a minute or two to realize that he wasn't the only one following her. Justin's unmarked Crown Vic edged into the turn lane ahead of him.

Max beat a rhythm on the wheel to Zach Williams's "Chain Breaker." Justin didn't trust Max. Why should he? Once he heard about the fiasco in the middle of a busy San Antonio intersection, he would never let Max hear the end of it. A familiar dry ache burned his throat.

He grabbed his water bottle from the seat and removed the lid. The lukewarm water did nothing to slake his thirst. He picked bits of gravel from the raw patch on the palm of his hand, focusing on the pain instead of the rising thirst.

Ignoring the whisper in his ear that sounded like one of his high school buddies who worked with him at a fast-food joint on Bandera Road and who provided Max with his first six-pack and a dime bag, he glanced in his rearview mirror. Billy's unmarked unit tailed him.

A regular caravan. Teagan would be so irritated.

She called them the cop squad.

He pulled onto Simon Street. Dillon's blue Charger sat under the carport next to her Prius.

Really irritated.

A serial killer was stalking her.

Enough said.

12

They meant well.

Teagan repeated these three words like a mantra as she stood on her small cement porch, arms crossed, body aching from Max's bruising tackle. They meant well, but a line existed between a simple, caring hug and actual suffocation. Dad sat in his Charger, a phone to his ear. Justin and Billy sandwiched Max's blue-and-white Ford between their PD vehicles. The three of them converged on the yard at the same time. Nobody looked happy. The abrasive stench of testosterone overpowered the light mingled scent of honeysuckle and snapdragons. A ruby-throated hummingbird whirred away, no doubt frightened by the stomp of men feet across the stamp-sized green St. Augustine lawn. It was so small, she cut it with a Weed Eater instead of a mower.

"Seriously? Did all y'all have to come?" She turned her back on them, intent on unlocking her door. Tigger's ecstatic bark greeted her before she could open it. "I'm planning to take a nap. You can stay out here and talk about me behind my back."

Dad's hand stilled hers. She glanced up. Her father's expression warned her. "What?"

"Let us have a look around first, why don't you?"

"The alarm is on. And even if it wasn't, do you think Tigger would let a stranger in my house?"

"Call me overly cautious."

Leaving the key in the lock, she backed away. The men paraded in front of her. Her very own cadre of bodyguards. If it weren't so ridiculous, she'd laugh.

"Come on in."

Billy gave her the go-ahead after the thirty seconds it took to clear her 1,510 square-foot abode. Tigger's happy squeals broadcast her delight at visits from so many of her favorite men friends in one fell swoop. *Traitor.*

Teagan tugged off her pumps and padded into the house. Tigger dragged herself away from Billy's noogies and romped toward Teagan, fifty pounds of pure muscle and puppy love. "I'm surprised you even saw me here." Teagan hugged and petted her and submitted to Tigger's thorough face licking. "You are a fickle girl, aren't you?"

Tigger at her side, Teagan moved to the breakfast nook and deposited her satchel on the table that also served as her desk. "I have iced tea and water. Someone start talking while I serve. You're supposed to be out there finding Leo Slocum."

"Either." Dad's phone dinged. He thumbed the screen and studied it for a few seconds. "Anyway, here's the plan. Billy, can you get back to Corpus PD? Find out if he had any visitors since he was transferred down there? Justin, can you do the same here? Who visited him before or during the trial? I'm touching base with my old partner and the legal team that prosecuted Slocum. Let's find out if he had any admirers who might be upset with how the trial turned out."

"Why does this guy want to pick on T . . . ?" Billy's voice trailed off.

"I'm guessing it has to do with me." Dad placed his phone facedown on the table, leaned back, and crossed his beefy arms. "She's my daughter. What faster way to cut a father to the quick?"

The unspoken words knocked into each other as they filled the small nook and overflowed into the cozy kitchen. Everyone in the room knew Teagan and her dad had a contentious relationship. He was the center of her world for the first nine years of her life. Then

Mom died. Their world shrank to just the two of them. Making PB and Js and chocolate milk with Hershey's syrup for supper. Sleeping on the couch in front of a fire in the fireplace. Watching Mom's favorite romcoms until dawn.

Then twelve months later, he'd done the unforgivable. He'd married again. Instead of pining away for Mom, he'd married a divorced personal trainer and health fanatic with three kids.

"Maybe this *doesn't* have anything to do with you, Dad." Teagan ventured into the sudden silence. "Maybe some defendant in my courtroom spent too much time staring at me during his trial. He's fixated on me. He followed the Slocum case and is using the details to send us down a rabbit trail."

"You were the one who said no one pays attention to the court reporter," Justin pointed out. "How does he know about the letters?"

"All the same, in the interest of thoroughness, go through your records, see if anyone pops." Dad's gaze glossed over all the underlying tension. "Billy and Justin can run down the ones who aren't in prison or who just got out of prison and decided to get a little payback. You can bring your laptop with you to the house."

"You don't understand how this works. I need to go back to the courthouse and go through my hard files. That will jog my memory regarding any cases where a defendant might have some bizarre behavior or whatever that might circle back to this scenario. That will give me a name, case number, and date. Then I can pull the archived materials if we need the entire court record."

"We're better off pursuing the copycat angle." Max's statement fell into the silence after her explanation. No one wanted her to go back to the courthouse.

Dad grunted his agreement in that he-man way that always amused Mom. "Tomorrow. Right now you're headed to the house as soon as you pack a bag."

"No, I am not."

"Guys, why don't you give us the room."

Max shifted. "T—"

"It's okay." Dad was right. Better to have this discussion without an audience. "Give us a minute."

"I'll take Tigger for a walk around the block, but I'll be right back."

Max's tone made it a promise. Ignoring her dad, Teagan smiled at Max. "She'll love you forever for that."

Max squeezed her arm and moved past her chair. Billy and Justin meandered down the hall, likely headed for the front porch and less emotionally charged air.

Teagan slid into a chair across from her father. "You know I haven't spent a night in *your* house since I turned eighteen and graduated from high school."

He would get her emphasis on the word *your*. It had once been Mom's house. A rambling three-bedroom fixer-upper on San Antonio's northwest side. Dad had added two bedrooms when he married Jazz. The wooden fort and swing set they built as a family still stood in the enormous backyard beneath the shade of a dozen live oaks, mountain laurels, mulberry trees, and burr oaks. Mom's roses covered a trellis along the deck where they'd barbecued steaks for him and turkey burgers for Teagan.

In the summer the yellow finches, cardinals, blue jays, and mourning doves flocked to the feeders. Hummingbirds buzzed each other in territory fights. A cadre of squirrels took turns swinging from the feeder that held black sunflower seeds, determined to get their share of the manna from heaven. Tent sleepovers with her friends under his watchful gaze had occurred in that backyard. He'd taught her to catch a baseball and hit in that backyard.

Now he lived there with a woman who went by Jazz even though her driver's license indicated her name was Deborah. She still taught Pilates, spinning, and Jazzercise at the gym where she and Dad had met.

"I talked to Jazz. She thinks it's a good idea."

"I don't care—"

"Careful what you say, sweetheart. You're too nice a person. You know you'll only regret it later." He splayed his fingers across the table and fixed her with an earnest stare. "She's decided to do a girl's weekend in Vegas with her sisters and their friends. They're leaving for the airport in a few minutes. They won't be back until Sunday."

Read between the lines. He expected to end this nightmare in the next three days. "And what did your wife say about me bringing my dirty dog into her clean house?"

Jazz was a germophobe. Not that she cleaned house, but she did use Dad's hard-earned dollars to employ a cleaning lady. When Dolly, their sweet Lab, died of old age the year after the wedding, there had been no talk of adopting a new puppy.

"The cleaning lady comes on Mondays to clean house."

"Good timing."

"This isn't about the house. It's about you and your safety."

"I have my own house. I have security. I have a pit bull."

"Who loves everyone who walks through the door." He smoothed back his ruffled hair. His wedding band was silver instead of the gold he'd worn representing his love for his first wife. "Tigger wouldn't hurt a flea."

"She would if someone was hurting me."

"We're not having this argument. Get your bag packed."

"You're not the boss of me." Only her dad could make her feel ten again. "Don't you have enough to worry about with your stepkids— the ones who followed in your footsteps?"

The words dropped like stones.

A deep-red flush burned across his face. His fingers tightened into fists, then slowly straightened again. His deep sigh filled the silence. "Just because Billy and Gracie chose to become police officers doesn't mean I love them more. I would've been okay if they'd decided to do something else, something safe, but I want them to be happy. Being police officers makes them happy, so it makes me happy."

Because he chose to ignore the risk involved, just as he'd done in his own career, never acknowledging the toll it took on those who loved him. "Does Jazz make you happy?"

"You never gave her a chance."

"You sprang her on me. You came home one day and introduced me to a stranger and told me she was moving her family into our house. She changed everything. Even the yellow gingham kitchen curtains Mom made with the rickrack on the bottom." Tears choked Teagan. She swallowed them. "Did you really think making me share a room with a stranger would make the transition easier?"

She closed her mouth. Why was all this coming out now? Now that she was the one in danger. All these years of walking on thin ice to keep the peace. As an only child, she'd lived in her own world. She spent long summer afternoons in the hammock in the backyard, reading book after book. She loved her quiet, small, close-knit family of three.

"Jazz tried. She thought freshening up the place would remind me less of your mother." His voice turned hoarse. "It was a dark time for me, too, but Jazz and her kids brought light back into the house. Noise and laughter and craziness. And she loves me, which never ceases to amaze me. She's not your mother, but no one could be. I didn't replace your mom. It couldn't be done."

Shame tightened like a noose around Teagan's neck. Dad deserved to be happy. Mom would've wanted that. Teagan knew that. She'd always known it. What she couldn't understand was the choice of a woman the polar opposite of his first wife. A woman who preferred Thai takeout or sushi to cooking. A woman who wore skinny jeans and tank tops and pierced her nose on a whim. "I still miss Mom," she whispered.

"Me too. I never forgot your mother. I never stopped loving her." Dad managed a wan smile. "But I had room in my heart for another love. Maybe someday you'll understand that."

"I do understand it. I do. I want you to be happy."

"Thank you. Leyla's home from law school. She'd love to see you."

The youngest Evans-O'Rourke had chosen law instead of the academy. As long as she became a prosecutor and not a defense attorney, her siblings might eventually stop giving her guff about it.

A headache that started behind her ears and thudded in her temples made it hard to think. Teagan rubbed her neck with both hands. "It might be better if she went back to Austin until this is over."

"The lease on the apartment she shared with her friends is up. They're looking for something better—cheaper, in other words—but it's a quick visit. She's got an internship at a law firm for the summer."

Too many people to keep safe. "My being at the house puts her in danger."

"I'm at the house." Dad's hand went to the Glock on his hip. When he retired, he returned to his favorite weapon, eschewing the new Smith & Wesson SAPD officers now carried. "Billy and Gracie will be around. She's safe. You're safe.

"One other thing." He swiped the air with his index finger as if to give his words weight. "I have all my personal case files on Slocum at the house. You could go through them. Maybe you'll see something I don't."

Dangling a sweet carrot in front of her. He knew she'd never be able to resist a chance to be involved in this investigation. "I'll pack my bag, but I'm only staying until they catch Slocum."

"Good choice."

She stood. Dad grabbed her hand. "Spare a hug for your old man?"

"You're not old." She swooped down and hugged him hard. "Sorry for being a pain in your rear."

"You're your mother's daughter, sweetie." He planted a hard peck on her cheek. "And that's a compliment."

The best compliment possible. Teagan fled.

13

Hello, my dear friends. How I've missed you.

The aroma of spilled beer and fresh cigarette smoke tickled Max's nose. Like a peculiar brand of air freshener manufactured just for people like him. He slid onto a stool at the bar and eyed the bottles of booze that lined the wall behind it. Wild Turkey had always been his favorite. Johnnie Walker Black next. Then Crown Royal. A shot of Patrón Silver tequila chased with Corona. He liked variety. Not on the same night, of course. That only worsened the hangover. He chose his poison and stuck to it. He was a drunk, but he was a smart drunk.

Four o'clock and the Biker Blues Bar on Loop 1604 West across from the UTSA campus verged on comatose. Two guys in black leather vests and baggy jeans, sporting long leather key chains and bandannas turned into headbands played pool. The dozen longneck Corona bottles lined up on the table suggested they'd been at it for a while.

A woman in jean shorts and a sagging tank top bent over a vintage jukebox, her hands thrumming to the beat of an ancient Creedence Clearwater Revival tune. She had the leathery skin of a sun worshiper. A couple sucked face in a booth by the door, oblivious to the people around them grossed out by their ecstatic PDA.

The tune took Max back to the days in high school when he'd worked on his first car in the garage while his dad, who loved classic rock, sat in a beach chair giving him life pointers.

"Never kiss a girl on the first date. She'll think you're after one thing and one thing only."

"Dad! Things aren't like they were forty years ago when you started dating Mom."

"Being a gentleman never goes out of fashion."

Two years in and Max still hadn't kissed Teagan. Friends didn't kiss. Dad wouldn't understand his son's relationship with Teagan. Max didn't understand it himself.

However, he had thrown her to the asphalt on a busy downtown street for no reason other than a car backfiring.

"What'll it be?" The bartender, a heavyset man in a Metallica T-shirt pulled tight over broad shoulders and a flat belly, wiped his hands on a dish towel and dropped it on the bar. "It's happy hour. Two for one."

Happy hour had once been Max's favorite time of day. "A large Sprite with lots of cherries and lime. Extra ice."

The guy's black unibrow did a dance, but he smiled and nodded. "Coming right up, buddy."

Max dug his seven-year chip from his jean pocket and laid it on the scarred pine bar. He picked it up and spun it. At first he'd gone to meetings every day, sometimes twice a day. He hated them, right up there with the twice-weekly sessions with his therapist after the suicide attempt. They were like pouring rubbing alcohol in an open wound. Every meeting reminded him he couldn't control himself. He couldn't fix himself. Gradually the routine became a comfort. He had a place to go. A place to be. With other broken human beings willing to say it out loud. *We can't control ourselves, but God can.*

"My wife has one of those chips." The bartender slapped a napkin in front of Max and placed the soda on it. "Takes a lot of willpower to get one. Are you sure you're in the right place?"

"Just visiting old friends."

"If you need anything else, let me know." He shrugged. "I hope you don't, but it *is* a bar. My lady has started over twice."

"How far is she now?"

"Two months and two days. Her longest stretch was four years, three months."

"But she keeps trying." Max squeezed the juice from the lime slice and inhaled the clean citrus scent. "That's what counts."

"She knows we can't be together if she drinks. I won't leave the kids with her."

"She doesn't mind you working in a bar?"

"I'm not an alcoholic. A couple of beers during the big game and I'm done. This is what I do. I own the dump. It's how I met her."

It made about as much sense as anything else in this screwed-up world. "I'll pray for y'all."

"I appreciate that." The bartender moved on to an old fart with a ZZ Top beard at the end of the bar who had been trying to wave him over for most of the conversation.

Max bit into a maraschino cherry and savored the sweetness. He dropped the stem on the napkin and took a swig of soda. The fizz burned his throat and his nose. The heady sweet drink did nothing to slake his thirst.

He closed his eyes and breathed, concentrating on the sounds. The smack of cue stick against ball, ball against ball, the classic rock 'n' roll that pounded with a quivering bass through massive speakers, and the baseball game on the flat-screen TV over the bar. The click of ice poured into glasses. The hiss of the AC. The sounds pulsed louder and louder. His head pounded.

When he first got sober, he'd missed the bars almost as much as the alcohol. The camaraderie, the loose, easy feeling after a scotch on the rocks or two that he and his friends could talk all night about everything and nothing. Politics, religion, life, death, love, family, and everything that kept a guy up at night. The cacophony drowned out the screams of a dying twenty-year-old whose legs had been blown from his torso.

Drowned out the feeling that nothing really mattered.

The slide toward oblivion had been easy. Even enjoyable.

He took another sip of soda. His stomach protested. He hadn't eaten since breakfast.

To have a drink now would be the most abject kind of selfishness. Teagan needed him, even if she wouldn't admit it. The kids at church needed him. Rick had taken a chance on him.

One shot of Jose Cuervo. One Heineken. Just enough to take the edge off.

The lie every alcoholic told himself.

His parched throat ached. His hands shook. Just the imagined scent of the old man's gin and tonic made Max light-headed.

He fumbled for his phone. Jabbed the number in his Favorites. Damon answered in that deep, mellow, jazz-DJ voice on the first ring. "Hey, Bro, what's up?"

"It's been a day."

"That kind of day?"

"Yeah."

"Where are you, man?" His AA sponsor's tone didn't change. Damon was a 240-pound former NFL tackle who lost his dream job because of drinking. He now raised goats, hogs, and horses and grew vegetables on a hundred-acre spread in the Hill Country. "I hear music."

Max named the bar.

"Did you drink?" The question held no judgment. Damon was in information-gathering mode.

"No, but this looks like the day. Any excuse looks good."

"What happened today?"

Max offered the salient details of his meltdown.

"It's been a long time since you had a flashback that severe. Do you know what brought it on?"

He didn't want to get into it on the phone. "It doesn't really matter.

I knocked the woman I love to the ground in the middle of the street like we were in the mountains of Afghanistan. I hurt her."

Damon knew about Teagan. He was an expert at excavating information. "Do me a favor and walk outside. Get some fresh air. I'll be there in ten."

"No. You don't have to come."

"I want to come. It's my job as your sponsor."

"I just needed someone to give me a verbal slap upside the head."

"I'm not doing that. You don't deserve verbal abuse for being human." Damon's voice remained as smooth as vanilla pudding. "Let's take a meeting together."

"I'll meet you there."

"Are you sure? It's no problem for me to swing by and pick you up."

"Then you'll have to bring me back here to my truck." Which would be conveniently parked at a bar. "Meet me there."

"You got it, friend. If you don't show up on time, I'm coming for you and it won't be pretty."

"I'm leaving now." Max hung up first. Phone still gripped in one hand, he slid from the stool and inhaled the aroma of oblivion one more time.

He swallowed the last of the soda and slapped a ten on the bar. His chip lay next to the damp napkin. Max picked it up and wrapped his fingers around it.

It felt light yet solid.

One day at a time. One hour at a time. One minute at a time. That's how he'd gotten through those seven years.

That's how he would get through the next seven years. One minute at a time.

14

Do not pass go. Do not collect two hundred dollars. The old Monopoly game admonition sang in Max's head as he trudged up the steps to the portable building on the edge of Faith and Hope Community Church's parking lot. Damon's lemon-yellow Mustang hadn't appeared yet. This group met in the portable because it allowed participants a place to smoke under the overhang. It used to be they could smoke in the ten-by-twenty room where the meetings were held. Even that became an issue. The church elders didn't want to put any more obstacles in the way of these people's sobriety, but they couldn't have smoking inside their facilities. Even in this dank room that smelled musty and like the old clothes they used to sort here for the church's homeless outreach.

Today the aroma of coffee mingled with the less desirable odors. Max needed caffeine. Maybe it would assuage the desire for a drink. Not likely. Only death could do that. He filled a Styrofoam cup, bypassed the obligatory donuts, and settled into a folding chair in the circle. The facilitator liked the circle. Nobody could hide in the back row. At least that meant they didn't have to stand and walk to the front of the room to do their sharing.

A woman in faded blue jeans, a retro hippies-style peasant blouse short enough to reveal a belly button ring, and pink Converse sneakers hesitated in front of him. "Is this seat taken?"

"Nope. Help yourself."

She smelled like patchouli, orange, and cardamom. A nice clean scent not easily overpowered by the mustiness of the room. Max leaned back and tried to relax. Maybe there was something to the aromatherapy craze the girls in youth group talked about.

"I'm Charity." She held out her hand. Max shook it. Her firm grip didn't match her thin, almost frail, frame. She had light-brown eyes and long brown hair. "I just made my thirty days."

"Congratulations. I'm Max." He didn't share that he had seven years in the rearview mirror. One more minute at the Biker Blues Bar and tomorrow he'd be thirty days behind Charity. "I haven't seen you here before."

"My first time at this one." She tugged the strap of a leather bag that could've served as luggage for a long trip from her skinny shoulder and plopped the purse on her lap. "I moved to this area last week. It's closer to UTSA. I'm a graduate student. I'm doing my thesis on alcoholism and the dysfunction of the creative mind."

"So you figured you needed to gather data?"

She fingered a dainty gold hummingbird hanging from a gold necklace and giggled. "No, there's a ton of famous writers and artists who were drunks. I just like to drink."

"Welcome to the club."

Damon plopped his Humvee-sized body into the chair on the other side. Whoever arranged them never allowed for a man big enough to lead the league in quarterback sacks four years running. His oversized presence and clean scent of aftershave provided the same odd sense of security it always did. "What's shaking, dude?"

Max fisted his hands so the tremors wouldn't show. "Life in the fast lane."

He jerked his head toward Charity and made the introduction. The two shared nods and relaxed into their seats without further ado.

The group facilitator, a wheezy man who always had coffee stains on the one-size-too-small polo shirts he favored, called the meeting to order. He asked who wanted to start.

Max did not. He never wanted to share. Sharing was a lesson in humility. So he did. "I will. Hi, I'm Max, I'm an alcoholic."

"Hi, Max."

Without naming names or revealing the gory details, he sketched an outline of the last two days. "It kills me that my first reaction is to want a drink. I'm not stupid. I know that will never go away. I know how it would disappoint my friends. I know I would likely lose my job. I need to get over it. Suck it up."

He shut his mouth and studied his hands. His knuckles were white.

Charity nudged him with her elbow. "Good job."

"Thanks."

Damon's gaze held empathy. "One day at a time, bud."

The hour passed in a litany of similar admissions. Not that anyone else dealt with life-threatening situations involving murder, but every participant had a cross to bear that his buddy Beelzebub said would be easier to bear if he simply gave in and had a drink.

They stood, held hands, and ended the session as they always did with the Serenity Prayer.

According to Bill W., cofounder of Alcoholics Anonymous, the key to sobriety was giving up control. Max agreed. He didn't like it, but he agreed. Which made his predilection for pills and booze so hard to understand. His parents, both gone for a few years now, had assured him that no history of alcoholism existed in his family. Nope, it was on him.

He stretched. Every bone in his body ached. Damon wandered off toward the coffeepot. Charity stood closer than she should. "That was good."

"You didn't share."

"Just getting the lay of the land. Maybe next time. I'm sorry about your friend. That sucks. If you ever want to talk, I'm available. We could grab a cup of coffee. Lunch. I'm a good listener." She leaned in.

Her collarbones stuck out. "I know a lot of meditation and massage techniques that can help you relax."

Max stumbled back. His sneaker smacked against a chair. He flailed to keep from landing on his rump. "I'll keep that in mind. I'm more into boxing at the gym and running. I work on my truck. Sweat a lot. You might talk to the facilitator, though. He can help you find a sponsor, if you want."

"I have a sponsor. I don't want to give him up."

Max's Spidey senses tingled. "Your sponsor is a he? I'm surprised. They don't recommend that. It's really frowned upon."

An ugly brick red crept across her porcelain cheeks. "I know, I mean, don't say anything. He's been great and there's nothing going on there."

Nothing didn't usually result in a flush of embarrassment. And something else. Something that looked distinctly like fear. "Hey, it's none of my business." It wasn't, but the youth minister in him wouldn't shut up. "Just be careful, okay? There's a reason for that rule. There are three or four women in this group who would make great sponsors."

"Naw, not necessary. My sponsor's a saint, I promise." She grabbed the suitcase-slash-purse and brushed past him. "See you around."

Her tone suggested not-if-I-see-you-first. A 360-degree turn. From heat to ice in fifteen seconds flat.

"See you."

"She seems nice." Damon sipped his coffee and checked his smartwatch. "Let's grab a taco at Tink-A Tako. We haven't talked in a while. You can fill me in on what's really bothering you. I'll drive."

"Murder and mayhem isn't enough?" Knowing Damon as he did, Max didn't bother to put up a fight. They hit their favorite hole-in-the-wall taco place, gorged on one too many tacos *de carne guisada con queso* on corn tortillas with fresh salsa. By the time he finished venting about his feelings for Teagan, Max felt somewhat better.

Damon listened, didn't offer clichés, and whistled at the appropriate times.

"It's enough to drive a guy to drink." He chortled and threw his long, beaded dreadlocks over his shoulder. "If we can't laugh, we have to cry, right?"

"And I want her to be happy." Inhaling the aromatic scent of grilled jalapeños and onions, Max shredded his napkin over a plate empty except for a few sprigs of cilantro. "And safe. I want her to be safe. She's right not to trust me. If I confront the issue, I could end our friendship. If I don't, I may never know for sure why she won't take things to the next level."

"That's between you and her. I don't give advice to the lovelorn." Damon had five kids he rarely saw because of two divorces. Five reasons he'd spent five years swimming in whiskey sours. "Instead of going to a bar, head to that church of yours. Pray about it, if that helps. That's all I'm saying."

AA might be faith based, but Damon had so far rebuffed any attempt Max made to talk to him about Jesus. "You're right. I had a weak moment."

"The way I see it, you had a strong moment. You didn't drink. Congratulations."

Perspective ruled. "Thank you."

"Now get your behind home and get some sleep. The sunrise is guaranteed to knock your socks off. Another thing that God of yours did right. No matter what happens, you have a good friend in Miss Teagan. With all the people in this entire universe, you met her. What are the chances?"

Before Max could respond, Damon swept up the bill and lumbered to the counter to pay. They said their good-byes in the church parking lot with Damon demanding a promise that Max would call him next time, before he stepped into the bar rather than after.

Max dug his keys from his pocket and trudged to the truck. From the church it was a simple hop-skip-jump to Loop 1604. From there he could hit Bandera Road, aka Highway 16, and head north. At this time of night traffic would have dissipated from the gridlock that persisted throughout the day on the thoroughfare through San Antonio's fastest-growing neighborhoods.

He cranked up The Message Sirius XM when Mandisa began belting out "Unfinished." That was him. A work in progress. He would always be a work in progress. Which meant Teagan could never trust him. Trust was the foundation of any relationship. Could he subject her to more scenes like the one downtown earlier in the day? Could she trust him to stay sober year after year? How could she trust a drunk with her heart?

Yeah, he wanted control. How could he not?

One of the best things about driving Highway 16 was the speed limit. Sixty-five miles an hour felt good after the day he'd had. No slow-moving traffic held him up on the one-lane stretches. The poor truck shook with the effort to maintain speed on the dark, winding road. People who lived out here complained about frequent accidents, but that could be chalked up to slowed reflexes of the elderly and poor eyesight, others argued.

An occasional vehicle headed into town cast light on the dark asphalt. The lack of company didn't bother him. He sang along with Mandisa, then Chris Tomlin, and Zach Williams.

"Fear, he is a liar." That was the truth.

The bright eyes of a critter—possibly a possum—stared at him in the middle of the road.

He hit the brakes.

Nothing happened.

He swerved, missed the furry creature, and hit the brakes again. Nothing. Not good.

The speedometer needle inched up instead of down.

God have mercy.

He stomped on the brake. Nothing. Nothing.

Jesus, please don't do this to Teagan. Spare her this.

The wheel spun. He fought for control. The truck careened to the right. He hit the grassy ditch doing seventy-five. The jolt knocked him against the window. His head banged.

The truck bucked, skidded, and hurtled through a wood post and barbed-wire fence. Still, they didn't slow. Max spun the wheel to the left in time to avoid a massive live oak.

The truck slammed into a cluster of juniper trees. Pollen rained down on the windshield.

All movement stopped.

Yet the world spun off its axis.

15

If only walking through a door could turn back the clock. To be six again, dressed in a swimming suit, running full tilt toward the Slip 'N Slide. Teagan studied the framed photos in the hallway that led to the O'Rourke living room. Baptisms, birthday parties, prom pictures, graduation pictures, Christmas family photos—a multitude of landmark moments in the O'Rourke family from her baptism to Dad's marriage to Jazz.

Amazingly, the photo of her dad and mom on their wedding day remained at the far end of the long hallway. She wore a full-length white dress with an empire waist and an endless train. A tiara of tiny yellow roses sat atop red hair pulled up in poufy curls. Dad looked young and dashing in his electric blue tux and ruffled shirt. They were the perfect couple. They should've been together forever.

"She did make a beautiful bride."

Teagan faced her dad, who stood behind her, a longneck bottle of beer in one hand. She summoned a smile. "I'm glad it's still here. I thought maybe after I moved out Jazz would take it down."

"She gave me a gift when she agreed to live in this house that belonged to the woman I loved before her. I didn't want to uproot you. She agreed. It was very gracious of her." He popped the lid from the bottle, held it up as if to say, *Cheers*, and took a long swallow. "I'd offer you a glass of wine, but I assume you're still abstaining."

Teagan had signed a covenant that included abstaining from

alcohol when she agreed to be a youth group lay leader. No more Friday night margaritas at Rosario's. "You're right. To be honest, I don't think I could've done that."

"She has a good heart. She did a good job raising three kids on her own for five years."

Jazz's first husband was a plastic surgeon who ditched his marriage for one of his medical assistants. Despite a successful practice, he regularly fell behind on child support payments and consistently missed the special occasions in his children's lives.

No wonder they liked their stepdad better.

Teagan studied the photo taken the day her dad married Jazz.

His new bride wore a sleeveless, beaded coral dress with a plunging neckline that had caused Grandma O'Rourke to wonder if the bride had it on backward. Jazz's black hair cascaded down her back to her waist. She weighed no more than one hundred pounds sopping wet, and every ounce was muscle. Dad wore a Western-style sport coat, bolo tie, jeans, and his best cowboy boots. In this photo he looked older and wearier but still happy. That man deserved to be happy. They gazed at each other with the kind of megawatt smiles that made photographers' jobs easy. "She was a beautiful bride too."

"Thank you for saying that. Billy and Justin told me about what happened downtown today."

Of course they did. Billy was a major league tattletale. "Max's PTSD isn't a secret."

"I was in the military. I have more than a passing understanding of post-traumatic stress disorder."

"So don't judge him."

"You know I'm not."

Teagan traced her fingers over a photo of her with Justin and her two older stepsiblings. They wore swimming suits and held huge chunks of watermelon. "Sorry. Max is jumpy because he's worried about me. That should endear him to the family."

"Max is a good guy. He has problems. We all do, but right now I want people around you who can be counted on in a crisis."

"He has the most important skill down. That's praying."

"Knowing how to take down a psychopath is the most important skill right now." Dad turned and headed for the hallway that led to his office, his bare feet padding noiselessly on the hardwood floor. "I could use some fresh eyes on the Slocum cases."

Teagan followed. The cramped office that held her dad's extensive collection of crime-related textbooks, law books, biographies, writing craft books, fictional thrillers, suspense, and modern mysteries had been turned into a war room. A large dry-erase board on rollers sat behind the scarred oak desk that had graced the room for as long as she could remember.

Ignoring the rush of memories was impossible. She'd learned to read in an overstuffed chair that threatened to swallow her while her dad sat at the desk paying bills or studying case files, looking up every now and then to correct her pronunciation or applaud a particularly difficult sentence. She'd been four and insisted he teach her. *Thank you, Daddy, for those days.* They'd been less and less as she grew older and his job took more of his time.

Then Mom died. Then he remarried and three more kids shared the crowded spotlight. Resentment crept in. Her teen years had been full of shouting matches and long stretches of silence.

Teagan strode straight to the board. Faces of women—twenty in all—with their names, locations, and dates of death written under each one. Taking her time, Teagan examined each face. These women had plans. They had hopes and dreams. They had loved ones. Had that last day been a good one or a bad one before that horrific realization that she had made a terrible mistake? At what point did she see the monster behind the stranger who'd made a simple plea for help? The monster had counted on these women's kindness, their inability to say no when someone asked them for help.

They'd all seen those terrible news stories where a person lay dying in the street, crying out for help, and no one stopped because they didn't want to get involved. These women didn't want to be that person who walked on by.

He used their innate humanity to ensnare them. A simple ruse. It worked every time. Because no matter how much the media focused on death and destruction, the all-consuming pool of blood at the crime scene, and the vitriolic hate in this world, good remained. It was the chink in their armor.

A hard knot caught in her throat when Teagan touched the first photo. Tiffany Conrad, Corpus Christi. She was twenty-four. Maricela Gonzalez, Brownsville, age thirty-four, single mom of two. Jessica Miller, Harlingen, thirty-nine, twice divorced. She and Tiffany could be sisters. All three women smiled as if they didn't have a care in the world.

One by one, Teagan studied each photo until it was engraved on her heart, along with their names. These women were more than victims. They had families and lives.

Without speaking, Dad took a seat at the table and waited.

Finally she joined him. The table to the left of the board was covered in copies of police reports, witness statements, court documents, newspaper articles, and photographs of crime scenes.

"So many documents." She picked up the photo of student Olivia Jimenez. Bruises and dried blood darkened her face. Her open eyes stared unseeing at a future gone black. A second photo showed ugly bruises and scratches on her arm and wrist where the perpetrator had handcuffed her. The woman had fought for her life. Even in death Olivia's beauty shone through. The killer had picked her out for a reason.

Teagan laid the photos down and took another set from her dad. The crime scene from Tiffany Conrad's murder in Corpus Christi. An ugly, gory death. The killer wasn't content to simply take life. He enjoyed making a mess. Teagan picked up the report and read several paragraphs. Gorge rose in her throat and she swallowed hard. When she was sure she could speak without a quiver, she turned to her father. "Do you think Slocum came back to San Antonio to get revenge on you and your team? It's a stupid thing to do. Better to disappear into the woodwork some place up north or south to Mexico."

"You have to understand the psychology of some serial killers. They often think they're smarter than law enforcement. It can be a game to them, one they're sure they can play two moves ahead."

"The letters have Slocum written all over them—no pun intended." Teagan picked up a photocopy of a letter left with one of the victims allegedly killed by Slocum. Similar script.

Dear Joanie,

Thank you for a lovely date. I hope you enjoyed it as much as I did. Short and sweet—for you. The pink posies are a nice touch, don't you think?

Don't worry. I'll visit you if I can. If not, it was nice while it lasted.

Me

"*Me.*"

"Yeah, a deliberate change by Slocum, or is it a copycat who doesn't know how the other letters were signed?" Her dad removed his glasses, then placed them back on his nose as he squinted at the letter. "The LEOs in the Valley did the VICAP report and submitted it to the FBI's BSS folks. The profile is nearly a perfect fit for Slocum."

"Speak English, Dad."

His goofy grin was reminiscent of the times he went crazy describing scenes from his favorite Bruce Willis movies. Mom and Teagan always rolled their eyes and sighed. "The cops filled out the Violent Criminal Apprehension Program—VICAP—report. The profiling section of the Behavioral Science Services, otherwise known as Investigative Support Unit, came up with the report."

"They don't actually run the investigations?"

"Not typically. They might send out a profiler to assist on-scene, but mostly they work in an advisory capacity."

"Did this killer actually go back and 'visit' his victims?"

"We don't know. It's hard to tell with the level of violence and, in some cases, the amount of decay."

"What does he mean by posies?"

"He dropped rose petals on her mangled body."

Teagan picked up a *San Antonio Express-News* article from Slocum's trial in San Antonio. "What about his family? What happened to them after he was arrested?"

"His wife, Diana, stuck with him for most of the trial. After he was convicted, she bailed. His daughter is a dentist on the East Coast with a husband, two kids. She didn't come back for the trial. His son, Chase, visited him at the Bexar County Jail during his incarceration before the trial."

The image of a cold-blooded killer barbecuing hot dogs and playing in a blow-up wading pool with his little boy danced on the movie screen in Teagan's brain. "What does he say about his dad? Did you talk to the wife?"

"Whoa." Dad held up both hands, palms out. "It was a homicide. We had no reason to interview any of them at the time. It wasn't until LEOs from the other jurisdictions got in touch that we realized who we might have in our jail."

"Why didn't the DA's office pursue for the death penalty?"

In Texas a homicide during the commission of a felony such as kidnapping, armed robbery, or sexual assault fell under the umbrella of capital punishment. The law was designed to discourage perpetrators from killing their victims to avoid being identified by them.

"Slocum had no criminal record. Upstanding citizen of the community. Family man. He had an excellent attorney, and the only witness was a guy who admitted to drinking a six-pack of beer and half a dozen shots that night. The DA took heat for it from the family, but he felt lucky to get the murder charge to stick."

"We have to talk to the son."

"Agreed. His wife has made it clear to the folks in the Valley that she wants nothing to do with any of this. She gave them the name of her attorney and hung up. The daughter is the same way."

"I'm trying to imagine having this man as a father." An involuntary shudder ran through Teagan. "Being told your father is a monster."

"The BTK serial killer volunteered in his church and with Boy Scouts. He had a son and a daughter. He and his wife stayed married until he was arrested and confessed to ten murders." Dad leaned back in his chair, tossed his reading glasses on the table, and rubbed red eyes. "Gary Ridgway, the Green River Killer, had a wife, a son, a house, a steady job, and he killed forty-eight prostitutes. There are dozens more examples of Joe Blows leading secret lives as serial killers."

"Are these killers insane? Wouldn't they have to be insane to kill in such grotesque and horrific ways?"

"Not usually. Not legally. All the research confirms that these men—they're almost always men—know the difference between right and wrong. They don't care. They're psychopaths, sometimes used interchangeably with the term *sociopath*." He took a breath, obviously just getting warmed up. "Psychopaths don't experience fear the way we do, so they don't have the same conscience normal people do. They can be charismatic and manipulative, and they pretend to have normal emotions when they don't. They have no remorse and can rationalize everything they do. The victim deserved to die for x, y, or z reason. Serial killers are the same way. They're often charming, grandiose, lying, shallow, callous, living off others, impulsive, promiscuous, a juvenile delinquent, et cetera."

"How is that not insane?"

"Look at Slocum. He had to have a plan. He had his tools in his van. He had a vehicle that served his purpose. He killed away from home, while on trips. He had to catch these women off guard and con them into helping him or make them believe he was a security guard."

"It was premeditated."

"Not a term we use in the state of Texas, but yes. He can't claim heat of the moment to try to get it down to manslaughter."

"Does your head ever hurt from having all that gross crime stuff in your brain?" Teagan studied his chiseled face. It was as familiar to her as the one she saw in the mirror every day, yet he'd aged and somehow she'd missed it. "Don't you want to balance it out with sweet stuff so it doesn't explode?"

"Hey, I'm waiting for them to offer a *Jeopardy* show for crime experts." He threw both hands up in victory signs. "I figure after winning a few dozen times, I'd be set for life."

"Hey, Sis!" Leyla pranced into the room. No other word described her dancer's gait. She'd studied ballet, tap, modern dance, and flamenco for most of her twenty-three years. The spitting image of Jazz, Leyla was the most like her mother, with cocoa-colored eyes and waist-length, shimmering black hair. "Long time no see. You look mar-va-lous."

"You lie like a dog." Teagan rolled from her chair and enveloped the elegantly thin woman in a hug. She smelled like grapefruit and cherries. "But you are so kind. Now go back to Austin."

Instead of obeying like a good little stepsister, Leyla traipsed over to the murder board and studied the photos in much the same way Teagan had earlier. "You need to get this monster." Her perfectly manicured fingernails touched the border of Maricela Gonzalez's photo. "Anything I can do to help?"

"Go back to Austin." Teagan tugged on her arm as if that might propel her toward I-35 North and Texas's capital city, home of UT, the legislature, liberalism, and the Texas music scene. "Go now. Stay there."

"You're not the boss of me." Leyla's use of the family mantra made Teagan smile despite herself. Leyla's gaze skipped to Dad. Like her siblings, she looked to him for approval. "I might see something you don't."

She didn't mean to be snooty. Her law degree would trump Teagan's associate's degree in court reporting. But Leyla would never catch up when it came to experience. "And this guy might see you. Run, don't walk."

"Okay, girls, enough bickering." Dad rolled his eyes at Tigger. "Some things never change. We can use a fresh set of eyes and a sharp mind. It's good experience for a future prosecutor."

"Or public defender." Leyla liked to push her stepdad's buttons. She snatched the first folder off the stack. "How far back do these killings go?"

"Thirty years."

"Pizza, anyone? Meat lover's special!" Justin tromped through the door with two large Papa John's pizza boxes in his arms, as well as a six-pack of Angry Orchard. "Get it while it's hot."

Teagan's stomach clenched and her throat closed. It was the thought that counted. "Thanks."

"I'll get paper plates and napkins." Dad pushed back his chair and stood. "You want me to keep the alcohol cold?"

"That stuff will kill you." Leyla turned up her nose. Her omnivorous siblings enjoyed ribbing her about her long-standing status as a vegan. She never failed to return fire. "Do you know how long it takes your body to digest animal? How can you eat something that has eyes and gives birth?"

Ignoring her, Justin handed over his stash. Her father took a bottle from the cardboard carrier and set it on the table. "For later." He strode from the room.

Justin turned to Leyla. "Hey, kiddo, how's college treating you?"

"Not a kid and it's law school." Leyla didn't care for Justin's brother-slash-uncle routine any more than Teagan did.

"You should tuck yourself in bed and stay safe until we catch this guy."

"I have plans." Leyla grabbed the Angry Orchard from the table and headed for the doors. "My evening will be far more enjoyable than yours."

"Watching old Chris Pratt movies and mooning over him?"

"I have a date." She pranced from the room. "An old married guy like you probably can't remember what dating is like."

"I'm blessed. The woman I married made me forget about dating. Dating stinks. I feel sorry for people who are still dating."

"Don't. I'm still young enough to enjoy it, unlike some people I know." Leyla sashayed from the room with the same pizzazz she'd employed to enter it. "Ta-ta. *Au revoir, buenas noches.*" Her voice floated after her.

Justin plopped into a chair. The smell of cigarette smoke mingled with the more enticing aroma of pizza. When had he started smoking? The Justin she knew in high school would never have despoiled his athlete's body with nicotine. He and Billy had been all-American kids who played basketball, ran track, dated cheerleaders, and made the honor roll.

To have that innocence back. A person couldn't put the genie or the memories back in the bottle. "How is Lilly?"

"Pregnant."

His deadpan delivery made Teagan rerun his response to make sure she'd heard him correctly. "You're going to be a daddy?"

With all his practice playing brother, he would be a stellar father. Teagan's elation fizzled. Another child in the world who would grow up worrying about whether daddy would come home at night. On the flipside, he had a gun and he knew how to use it. Having children in this world took blinders to the horrific mess humans had made of it.

Her fears were her own. She stood and held out her arms. "Congratulations."

He rose and accepted her offering. "Thanks. Lilly will be a good mom. We'll see how I do."

"You're a shoo-in for Father of the Year. Don't be so modest."

"Thanks for that, pip-squeak. You're not so bad yourself. You should try it—you might like it."

No way would she discuss her issues regarding motherhood with Justin. How did Lilly get through the day, knowing she might end up a widow at any given moment? "Where have you been, besides picking up pizza?"

"It's my mother's birthday."

She'd totally forgotten. Justin's mom had been a single mother who worked many night shifts as an ER nurse while raising her son. "How is she?"

"After a day that included a massage, manicure, pedicure, and haircut paid for by yours truly, I believe she's having dinner with a gentleman friend from her church."

"Good for her. I suppose you ran a background check on him too."

"You bet your behind I did."

"I'm glad you take care of your mom. She took good care of you."

"She did and she does. She deserves to be spoiled." He spun a pen around and around on the table. "So are we talking about what happened downtown?"

"It was absolutely not necessary for you to tell my father about that."

"Billy and I agree you shouldn't be relying on Max for anything. The man's got obvious problems."

"Max knocked me to the ground and covered my body with his. What more do you want from him?"

"To be able to distinguish between an imagined threat and a real one."

"Not fair."

"Not fair is getting taken out by a murderer because your boyfriend is in la-la land."

"Why do you have to be such a jerk?"

"I'm just trying to protect a friend's—"

The first notes of a Lady Gaga song floated from his shirt pocket. Still looking as if he might spit nails at her, Justin dug his phone from the pocket, tapped it, and stuck it to his ear. "Chamberlain."

Teagan only caught his side of the conversation, but Justin's morose expression spoke volumes. He hung up and took a swig of his beer. "That was Siebert. He's trying to find other killers in Bexar County who might fit the pattern better than Slocum. We really need for you to go through your files."

Much safer ground. "First thing in the morning."

Dad stalked back into the office. "While I pay Chase Slocum a visit."

"I want in on that." Teagan took the paper plate he offered and set it on the table. The thought of food made her jaw clench. "Don't go without me."

"We'll go to the courthouse first, then pay Slocum a visit."

"Neither of you is a principal on this investigation." Justin paused in his effort to slide a slice of meat lover's pizza from the box without losing the melted cheese. "Dillon, you don't have any authority to interview potential witnesses or suspects. Teagan, you're a potential victim."

Fierce anger whirled in a tight, black funnel in her like her own personal tornado. "Do not call me that. I am not and have never been a victim."

"You know what I mean—"

"I'm not planning to interview him in any official capacity,"

Dad intervened. He opened the other pizza box, plopped a piece of Canadian bacon and pineapple pizza on a plate, and set it next to his beer. "I'm writing a book on serial killers."

"His father technically isn't a serial killer—not in terms of the legal system."

"And he won't be if they catch him and nail his behind to the jail cell wall," Teagan added. "The more information we collect, the more pieces we can put together."

"Don't you think the guys in the Valley have already spoken to him?"

"They have their own agenda." Dad laid a piece of vegetarian supreme on a plate and handed it to Teagan. She averted her eyes and fought the urge to pinch her nose against the smell of food. "Besides, I'd like to have Teagan's impressions. She's an astute observer, and a woman might help Chase Slocum feel more comfortable."

"Thank you."

"You're welcome. Eat your pizza."

"I can't."

Understanding followed by empathy warmed Dad's blue eyes. "It's been a long day. Do you want to turn in?"

"I may never sleep again."

"I'm sorry about your neighbor."

"Thank you. She was a sweet lady and a good neighbor. I'll miss her."

A look of satisfaction on his face, Justin belched and patted his chest. Some things never changed. "Fine, the two of you can interview Chase Slocum, but it's not official police business."

Never in her wildest imagination had Teagan considered working with her dad on a murder case. But then she'd never imagined a scenario where a serial killer stalked her friends and family.

She would need every bit of Dillon O'Rourke's expertise. And then some.

16

The darkness seeped away. The pain refused to go with it.

Eyes closed, Max heaved a breath, then another. He opened his eyes. The truck lights illuminated a crazy, tilted view of thick juniper branches dripping with green pollen. The cracked windshield made the entire view seem like a piece of abstract art.

Gradually, night noises resumed. Crickets chirped. Mourning doves cooed. Strangely idyllic sounds that didn't jive with the pain in his head, chest, and arms.

Adrenaline shook his body. Was this why some people chose speed as their drug of choice? Talk about loss of control.

He eased forward and tried to turn off the truck's engine. His hand shook so hard he couldn't get a grip. "Come on."

With two hands, he managed. "Okay. Okay. Easy."

Talking to himself aloud seemed to help. He was still alive. His voice shook, but no one could hear his semi-panic except himself. And God.

"Thanks, God."

Warm liquid dripped from his lip. It tasted salty. He touched his fingers to his nose. It might be broken. More blood slid into his left eye. He felt his forehead. A cut over his eye. The disadvantage of an old truck was the lack of air bags. But the truck had a solid metal frame. There was that. Ribs, maybe broken, or just bruised. He worked his way down. Nothing else major.

The shaking subsided enough for him to unbuckle his seat belt.

"Moo-o-o. Moo-o-o."

Come again?

Pain sliced from temple to temple. He eased around to look out his window. A sooty brown cow stared back. Behind him, his cohorts gathered. A crowd of staring, bewildered cows confronted him.

Did that make them a herd? He might be from Texas, but Max was a city boy. "Sorry, guys, I didn't mean to crash your party."

"Moo-oo-oo."

"I get it. I really do." *Please God, tell me I didn't hit one of them. I didn't kill a cow, did I?* "I'll be out of here as soon I can."

With deference toward the pain that swept through his muscles, already aching from the contact sports of the past two days, he gingerly reached up and turned on the overhead light.

Bluetooth and OnStar had not been invented when this truck slid off the production line. His phone no longer lay on the vinyl seat. He listed to one side until he could reach the glove compartment and grab his flashlight.

The dark recesses under the seat yielded his phone. And something else.

A thin, folded sheet of paper lay on the floor mat. The creamy beige stood out against the black rubber.

Just leave it there. Don't touch it. It's evidence.

Read it.

He could do without the competing lawyers in his head.

With his fingertips he raised the letter to the seat and let it drop. Then he rummaged through the glove compartment until he came up with a pen. With a delicate touch, he opened the sheet enough to see the now familiar script:

Dear T,

     Max was a good Christian boy. He'll go to heaven. That's what you believe, isn't it? Why are you sad then? Truth is, he didn't have the guts to kill himself, so I did it for him. Killed two birds with one stone. Your friend gone before you had the guts to admit you have the hots for each other. I bet you wonder who's next. I'll let that be my secret. Just know that it will hurt just as much, maybe more, if I'm lucky. That's right. You don't believe in luck. Don't say I didn't warn you, T. I expected more coverage from our media friends by now. Perhaps you should let your reporter friend in on what's going on.

Your friend William Quinones

Another fictional character, obviously. Teagan would know. The urge to wad up the paper and toss it out the window blew through Max. He jolted back and focused on his phone instead. GPS indicated he was on a Bexar County ranch. Just barely. A few more yards and he'd be talking to Medina County sheriff's deputies. He called 911. After requesting an ambulance and a sheriff's deputy, he asked them to get a message to SAPD Detective Justin Chamberlain. *Call your buddy, Max.* Regarding what? Regarding a killer who'd murdered two people and almost made it a third in twenty-four hours?

To call Teagan was a luxury Max couldn't afford. Her sweet voice would be a balm that soothed his pain, but it would be selfish. She had to be protected at all costs.

The minutes dripped by slower than ketchup from an old-fashioned glass bottle. Finally, his phone warbled a tune that told him the caller wasn't in his contacts.

"What do you want?" Justin didn't sound any friendlier than he had the previous evening. "Isn't it past your bedtime?"

"Somebody cut my brake lines. And there's something in my truck you should see."

"Where are you?"

He gave Justin the information and hung up.

Less than ten minutes later a Bexar County sheriff's deputy

showed up right behind an ambulance. The deputy insisted on nosing around the crash before returning to question Max under the lights of the ambulance.

"Did you fall asleep?"

"No. My brakes failed."

"What is that—a seventy, seventy-one?" The deputy shoved his hat back and scratched his forehead. "How many miles on it?"

"Seventy-four. Ford F-100. The odometer turned over before I bought it from a guy in Grandview. It has sixty-five thousand miles on it now."

"So when did you last have it serviced?"

"I did the work myself after I bought it." Another form of therapy. Keeping his hands busy proved helpful. Sitting in the house in front of a TV did not. "Shocks, hoses, tires, sparkplugs, brakes, everything."

"Could you have messed up something?"

"I think I would've noticed before tonight."

The EMTs insisted on loading him onto a gurney to transport him to a hospital for X-rays and a CT scan. The deputy ordered a blood draw for alcohol when it became apparent Max would not be able to perform simple field sobriety tests. Max's explanation that he'd been driving home from AA didn't faze the man.

"I'm not leaving until Detective Chamberlain gets here."

"That's up to the EMT." The deputy nodded at the EMT, whom he apparently knew. "I can get a tow truck out here after it gets light. We'll want to take some photos. I reckon the property owner will want that too. We'll get him out here first thing in the morning."

"Don't touch anything. Detective Chamberlain will let you know what he wants done with it." Like towing it to the PD impound lot as evidence. "It's super important—"

"I get it. This detective is a big shot, but this accident scene is in the county, which makes it our scene."

At that moment Justin pulled into the makeshift parking lot where Max had destroyed the rancher's fence. The cars blocked the exit of the cattle, most of whom had heeded the shooing of another deputy afraid they would make a break for it and end up hamburger on the highway.

Justin wasn't alone. Teagan raced across the lumpy, weed-covered terrain and shoved between the deputy and the EMT. "Max?" She grabbed his hand and squeezed so hard her grip hurt.

"Easy."

"Your face looks like you got the knockout punch in the tenth round." She picked up steam with each word. "I told you an old truck with no air bags was a bad idea."

She chose anger to keep her fear of loss at bay. Teagan worried about air bags, food poisoning, snake bites, drowning. She didn't let reality keep her from living life, but she made no secret of the fact that she'd like to wrap everyone else in a cotton cocoon for the duration.

"You know I have a superhard head."

"We're taking him to University Hospital." The EMT tugged at the gurney. "You're welcome to meet us there."

"Hold your horses." One hand on the gurney, Justin interceded. He flashed his badge. "I'd like to interview this man first." He did like to throw his weight around.

The EMT didn't seem inclined to listen. He and his partner kept moving. The deputy held up his big, dark-brown hand. The EMT muttered under his breath, but the stretcher remained stationary.

"I left the letter on the truck seat." Woozy, Max leaned his head back and closed his eyes. "I barely touched it."

"You shouldn't have touched it at all." Justin snapped his pen open and shut. "Details."

Max ran through his evening. When he arrived at the part about the AA meeting, he hesitated. Anonymity was the heart and soul of those meetings.

"There was someone new at the meeting." He danced around the details. Lives were at stake. His and, more importantly, Teagan's. "That person said something that seemed odd at the time."

Justin frowned. "So who was this person? What did this person say?"

"I can't tell you much. It's called AA for a reason. The thing is, this person claimed to have a sponsor of the opposite sex. That's frowned upon. But no way this person tampered with my brakes."

"It's got to be a woman." Annoyance in her voice, Teagan's nose wrinkled. She hadn't let go of his hand, which was good. "That's really sexist. You don't think a woman could tamper with brakes?"

"This person was inside during the entire meeting. Before and after it, a whole swarm of people congregated in the parking lot smoking. She'd have been seen."

"Either way, we have no last name. I think Teagan's right. Your mystery guest is a woman." Justin clicked his pen again. An annoying habit. The guy was full of them. "What did she look like? This woman may be a killer. She may know our killer. AA or not, Max, you have to help us out here. For Teagan's sake."

Max couldn't contain a groan. The EMT grabbed the gurney. "Wait, wait. Okay. Charity. Thin. Shorter than me. Fair complexion. Kind of cute. Long brown hair and brown eyes. She said she was a student at UTSA, the main campus, getting her master's in some strange psychology thing."

Teagan and Justin exchanged glances.

"What?"

"Sounds like the woman who ordered the flowers for her 'boyfriend.'"

Not being able to take people at face value sucked the life from a person. "Being a fake would explain why she didn't know that AA doesn't allow members to have opposite-sex sponsors."

"Which gets you off the hook on the anonymity thing. She's

probably not an alcoholic at all. CSU is on its way. I'll take a look at the letter." Justin cocked his head toward the ambulance. "Y'all can go ahead and take him."

"Whoa." Max struggled to sit up. Head spins knocked him back against the pillow. "I don't need to go to the hospital. I'll walk home if I have to."

"We'll be the ones with whiplash," the EMT groused. "You're strapped in, buddy. You're going."

Teagan clung to his hand. Her soft, smooth skin felt good against his. She kept up with the moving gurney. "Can I ride with him?"

"No room, ma'am. Meet us there, okay?"

Teagan squeezed his hand again and let go. "I'm sorry about all this."

"Not your fault."

"He came after you because of me."

"Whoever he is, he's a psychopath. Something in his brain sprang a leak."

"I'm right behind you."

If he could just hang on to her hand, everything would be all right. "All I could think about was you," he whispered. "I refused to die. I refused to put you through the loss of another person you care about. I won't give him that power over you. We have to talk, T. Life is short—"

"Just rest." Her effort to smile seemed painful. "We will talk. Later."

No. Sooner, not later.

*　　*　　*

The crumpled blue-and-white carcass of Max's truck told a story Teagan didn't want to hear.

"He's lucky he survived." Justin shone his LED mag flashlight through the shattered driver's side window. "If he'd hit one of those bigger burr oaks, he'd be flatter than a pancake."

"Nice. First, we don't believe in luck." Teagan kept her phone light on the ground. Meeting a rattlesnake in the dark wasn't on her bucket list. Nor was twisting her ankle in a hole. "Second, I'd appreciate it if you didn't egg on my imagination. I already know all the ways he could've died."

The possibilities left her with pain in the vicinity of her heart so sharp, she couldn't heave a breath. He could've died. Again. What would her life be like without Max? Empty.

"*Life is short,*" the take-the-leap angel on her right shoulder whispered in her ear. "*It's selfish and you know it,*" the look-before-you-leap angel on her left shoulder cautioned, leaning in closer.

Both were right. She stifled a groan.

The CSU crew hustled to set up spotlights. The team's lead investigator didn't seem pleased with the situation, but she acquiesced when Justin asked her to retrieve the letter. She laid it out flat on the truck's bed. Justin added his light to hers.

"It's addressed to you, T."

Of course it was. The cocoa sloshed in Teagan's belly. Despite the humid night air, a chill raced through her. She rubbed her bare arms. "He didn't expect Max to survive."

Together they bent over the letter and studied its contents. "*Truth is, he didn't have the guts to kill himself, so I did it for him.*"

Teagan jerked her hand back from the bed's smooth rubber surface. "What does that mean?" Justin didn't respond. His gaze studiously avoided hers. "What didn't y'all tell me?"

"Max originally entered rehab from a hospital where he was taken after trying to kill himself with booze and pills. Billy figured you knew. Max said he told you everything you needed to know about that period of his life."

Max didn't think she needed to know this. A cold-blooded killer knew all his secrets. All hers, too, apparently. He had no right to bare Max's secrets to Teagan. He'd stripped away Max's dignity with one line of fancy script. "It doesn't matter."

"The guy's yanking Max's chain. And yours too." Justin motioned for the investigator to bag the letter. "So lay it on me—who's our latest character?"

"A film professor who shoots digital recordings of his victims and makes snuff films out of them. It's called *Caught on Film*."

"This guy is seriously irritating me." Justin smacked the truck with his gloved hand. "He's toying with you, terrorizing you."

And doing a good job of it. "The big question is, who will he go after next?"

"We can't put a detail on every person in your family indefinitely, and he knows it."

"I can't lose anyone else."

"You won't." He couldn't promise that.

His phone dinged. He glanced at the screen. "I'm gonna take this."

Teagan studied the sad heap of a truck. Max loved this truck, and the killer knew that. It would've been easier and more deadly to drive him off the highway when he was riding his motorcycle.

The CSU investigator hooted and yelled for one of her compadres. The two peered into the Ford's engine compartment.

Teagan squeezed in next to them. "What is it?"

They both looked up and went back to their commiseration.

"Come on, guys. I'm with Detective Chamberlain. I'm . . . consulting on the case."

"The brake line was cut. Not completely. There was probably enough brake fluid in the lines to get him going, but eventually the line busted and the brakes no longer functioned." The investigator had the gall to look happy. "We're talking attempted homicide."

The letter already proved that. They had motive and means. If

Justin's theory held water, opportunity occurred while Max recited his Serenity Prayer at AA.

"We have to go."

She turned just as Justin bolted past her. "Yeah, I know. I need to go to the hospital."

"It looks like we just found Max's friend Charity."

She slogged through the weeds after him to the car parked haphazardly behind the Bexar County Sheriff's Department vehicle. "We don't even have her last name."

"We do now." He jerked his door open and paused for a nanosecond. "According to the driver's license they found in her purse, it's Charity Waters."

"Her purse? Where is she?"

"In a Dumpster behind your church. And he left us—you—another letter."

17

Dear T,

Let that be a lesson to you. This is what happens when you make a mistake. Mistakes are not permitted. I am a hard task-master. Charity served her purpose. Your lover boy is true blue; he didn't take the bait she offered. However, this was necessary to teach sweet Charity a lesson. I will miss her. When the time comes, you'll want to give me that which I require. Complete and perfect submission. Until then, *adieu*.

Your friend River Flows

Teagan didn't wait for the detectives to ask. "In *Death Comes Quickly*, the killer is known as River Flows. He uses a ceremonial knife to slash their throats and then performs a Native American ritual before burying them in an old, abandoned cemetery."

"As if we don't have enough grotesque evil in the world without making it up." The CSU investigator, a lanky redhead, shook her head and walked away.

Teagan waited for Seibert and Justin to do the same before she sank against the bumper of Justin's Crown Vic. Thank goodness she hadn't eaten the pizza. Charity Waters's battered body still lay draped over trash bags in one of the Faith and Hope Community Church's Dumpsters at the back of the parking lot. Only one pink Converse tennis shoe showed on a leg slung over the side. Another CSU investigator had hopped into the bin with the victim. Teagan had not been allowed to cross the crime scene tape. Nor did she wish to do so.

"Fancy meeting you here."

She jumped and screeched.

Brian Lake shifted his digital video camera to his other shoulder and grinned. "Made you jump."

"Seriously, you're like a little boy sometimes. How did you get past the unis?"

"I'm in stealth mode." He made a motion like an airplane flying in front of him. Despite the hour, the journalist wore neatly pressed Dockers and a short-sleeve button-down, collared shirt. The only signs he'd had a long day were the white-and-gray five o'clock shadow that covered his narrow chin and his mussed sandy blond hair. "The question is, what are you doing here? Isn't this the third crime scene you've visited in less than forty-eight hours? What gives?"

"How did you even know? You're not nightside."

"The freelancer photog who does our overnight coverage called me. It just so happens we had a beer together last night, and I was telling him about how your life had been strangely touched by two tragedies in one day. We commiserated on your behalf."

Over a beer. At least he recognized that these were tragedies. "So you hopped out of bed and zipped down here to get a shot of the pool of blood?"

"I'm sorry this is happening to you." Brian's East Texas drawl became more elongated when emotion peeked through his crusty exterior. "I truly am. I didn't mean to make light of your suffering. I know this isn't just a story to you. I'm only trying to do my job."

Which he tried not to take home with him at night. Reporters suffered from some of the same nightmares as court reporters and police officers. At least the good ones did. "Thank you. I appreciate that, but I still can't talk to you."

"Off the record. Steer me in the right direction." He gave her that puppy-dog look he employed when she had chocolates on her desk.

"Talk to Detective Chamberlain or Detective Siebert."

"How is this related to Officer Moreno's death? Or the murder of your neighbor?"

"What makes you think it is?"

"Number one, you're here. Number two, the two detectives you named, along with their partners, are working the cases together. That's unusual. Three, the scuttlebutt around the courthouse is that San Antonio may have its very own serial killer."

The magic words. *Serial killer.* They would light up the media's world. Which was exactly what the killer wanted. His time in the spotlight. His fifteen minutes of garish fame.

Teagan clamped her mouth shut tight. She had no intention of furnishing this letter-writing creep with the joy juice he wanted. He would only keep killing in order to get more and more of the high he craved.

"Come on. A high-powered rifle killed Officer Moreno on the near west side. You were in the car. Evelyn Conklin was stabbed to death in her yard in a quiet millennial-infested near-south side neighborhood, coincidentally next to the very house where you live. Now we have the body of a woman in the Dumpster where you attend church. It doesn't take a genius to figure out you are the common denominator. Was this victim shot or stabbed? Did you know her? Is she a member of your church?"

Brian was far too observant and had too many PD contacts.

Charity Waters had bled to death after someone slashed her neck from ear to ear. One clean, fell swoop. She let the killer get close. Justin said there were no defensive wounds. She'd been laid out on the trash bags with her hands crossed over her chest, her purse nestled by her side, the letter inside of it. So far, no weapon had been found. Not even Charity's fingerprints appeared on the purse. Nor did the letter have prints. The guy was not an idiot.

They knew from Max's statement that Charity had attended the AA meeting from seven to eight o'clock.

One of the homeless men who used the church's prayer garden as a place to drink and sleep after dark had found the body when he foraged for the staff's lunch scraps in the Dumpster. That meant the murder occurred between eight and eleven at night.

Officers were canvassing the area for potential witnesses. So far nothing. They would interview everyone who attended the AA meeting earlier in the evening—all the church staff, and anyone who had been at church meetings scheduled in the education building that evening. Did the killer know his plan to murder Max had failed, or did Charity simply die for a slip of the lip over her sponsor? If he knew Max hadn't died, how did he know?

How could a guy stalk her and Max at the same time? Accomplices plural? If he killed them off for such minor offenses, he wouldn't have them for long.

Surely someone had seen something.

The violent, ugly evil now permeated every part of her life. Her job. Her sweet, peaceful, neighborhood. Her friend's classic pickup truck. Now her church.

Too much.

Teagan clenched her fists and breathed. This guy had nerve. So did she. This would not end well for him. She had resources. She had guts.

He'd picked a senseless fight with the wrong woman.

"I have to go." She brushed past Brian and ducked under the crime scene tape.

"Hey, Teagan, come on, give a guy a crumb."

"PD's PIO is on his way. He'll give you more than I can."

She marched across the asphalt in the harsh parking lot lights augmented by the CSU's floodlights. The stench of garbage and excrement billowed in the dank humidity of a South Texas night. Her stomach lurched. *Stop it.*

"You don't belong in here." Justin stepped in her path the second she entered his line of sight. "Wait for me by the car. I'll get you home as soon as I can."

Still treating her like the little sister he never had. He hadn't wanted her to come to the crime scene. She'd insisted. Now she had what she needed. "I'm leaving. I'll get an Uber to take me to the hospital. I need to be there for Max."

"You're not going anywhere by yourself." Justin took her arm and propelled her away from the others. Alisha rolled her eyes and grinned. Siebert simply looked confused. Justin didn't seem to notice or care. "If I have to arrest you, I will."

Teagan tugged her arm free. "As I have said numerous times—"

"I'm not the boss of you. I know." Justin's bass deepened, a hoarse shadow of itself. "I'm only trying to keep you safe. For Billy, for Gracie, for your dad. If something happened to you, think about what it would do to them. You're your own worst enemy, you know that, right?"

"You have three related homicides to solve. Why not focus on them and let me take care of myself? I'm not a kid anymore."

"Then don't act like one. Do you know what your dad will do to me if something happens to you?"

The stare down lasted several long seconds. Teagan backed up a step. "Could you have someone give me a ride to the hospital? I'll ask Billy or Gracie to give me a ride home from there. They're armed and dangerous. Is that good enough?"

He actually had to take time to consider the proposal. "Fine. Alisha will drive you. She can take Max's statement when the doctors are done with him. Then she'll drive you home. Got it?"

"Got it, Uncle Justin."

"Sarcasm will win you no points."

"But it makes me feel better." Actually it didn't. Justin acted the way he did because he cared. "Justin?"

He looked back. "What?"

"You be careful too."

The sardonic expression that so often adorned his face these days disappeared. "I will, Sissy."

"Love you too, Bro."

18

Seventeen years and the smells of a hospital still had the power to send Teagan hurtling through space to when she'd been a scared little girl who wanted her mom back. The antiseptic smells, the squeak of the meal cart's wheels, the telephone ringing at the nurses' station. Worried faces. So many worried faces. People telling her it would be okay. They lied. Grandma and Grandpa arguing with Daddy down the hall. Grandma won. She took Teagan's hand and led her into Mom's room. Teagan was a smart kid. She understood this was good-bye. They were taking her mom off life support. She understood. But she still expected it to be okay. Mom would open her eyes and ask Teagan how school had been that day.

Only she didn't.

Teagan picked up her pace.

"You okay?" Alisha had been tense on the walk from the parking garage. Now she seemed to relax a little. "You look green."

"I'm fine." Teagan checked on the room number.

Alisha identified herself as a police detective on official business. The nurse shrugged and noted that the patient was likely sleeping. Together they found the room. Teagan pushed open the door to find Pastor Ricardo "Rick" Chavez sitting next to Max's bed. His posture, body forward, head bent, elbows on knees, and hands clasped, suggested prayer or deep meditation. She closed the door with a gentle push. He didn't look up. Max's eyes were closed. Deepening purple-and-black bruises ran rampant across his left cheek, eye, and forehead. His nose was swollen to twice its normal size.

A white bandage on his right cheek stood out in stark relief to the ugly bruises. His upper lip was swollen and split. She moved toward the railing. Rick glanced up. "Hey." His gaze traveled to Alisha. "What's up?"

"How is he?"

"Cranky." Rick straightened and stretched. The burly pastor of a three-hundred-plus-member church wore faded blue jeans sporting grass stains on the knees and a wrinkled white CHRIST IS RISEN T-shirt. "He called me because he thought he needed a ride home, but the doctor decided to admit him overnight for observation. If all goes well and all the tests come back clear, they'll spring him in the morning."

"I bet he loved that."

"Yep. He uttered a few words that made this innocent pastor blush."

Rick had grown up poor as the son of a Mexican-born migrant farmer. He hadn't been innocent for many of his thirty-plus years. Still, Teagan managed a smile to reward his effort at a joke. "How long has he been asleep?"

"Twenty minutes or so. They gave him something for the pain. They had to convince him it was nothing that would send him spiraling into addiction. You know how he is. Absolutely petrified of narcotics." Looking distinctly uncomfortable, Rick nodded toward the door. "Let's go in the hallway."

They traipsed from the room.

"You're not going to wake him, are you?" Fixing Alisha with a stern stare, Rick shoved his hands in his pockets and did his father-knows-best imitation. "Can't you wait until morning?"

Rick didn't like police officers. Teagan filed that fact away with other biographical information about her pastor. He'd participated in

Dreamer protests numerous times and traveled to Washington, DC, to testify. He was legal. His parents weren't.

Alisha made a show of looking at her phone. She thumbed a text and then turned to Teagan. "I have something I have to check on. Billy will pick you up when you're ready to leave. Don't go anywhere on your own. Text me in the morning. We'll arrange to interview Max at PD when he's up to it." She nodded at Rick. "Nice to meet you."

"Same here." Rick's response remained lukewarm.

Together they watched her walk away, phone to her ear.

"Wow, could you be more obvious?"

"Sorry." Rick didn't look sorry. "Force of habit. I need coffee."

Teagan followed him down the hallway to a waiting room/break room with three snack machines, a soda machine, and a coffee machine. "Convenient."

Rick tugged his wallet from his hip pocket. "What's your poison?"

She shook her head and watched while he selected coffee with cream and sugar. The resulting swill was gray. Rick had something to say, and he would eventually get around to it. Another person with an opinion about her situation, no doubt. At least he knew Max as well as she did, maybe better.

Stirring with a plastic swizzle stick, he studied the snack machine. "Caffeine and sugar. It reminds me of my college days."

"What did Max tell you about the accident?"

"Not much. He was more concerned about a letter he found and the author's obsession with you." He set his coffee on a nearby table and bought a package of mini chocolate-covered donuts. "Don't tell Noelle."

Rick's wife, a vegetarian, grew her own vegetables, canned said vegetables, made her own bread and pasta, homeschooled their four children, and taught third-grade Sunday school without missing a beat.

"I'm no tattletale." Teagan ambled back into the hallway, Rick following behind. "Now I have to tell Max a woman he met at AA tonight is dead because he caught her in a lie."

"How could you possibly know that?"

How much did Rick need to know? Was it necessary to sully his world with this incomprehensible, needless string of crimes? "We just do."

"Max is more than a colleague to me."

"I realize that."

"He puts on this big show of being a funny biker dude veteran who likes to sing and play the guitar, but on the inside he's a romantic who just wants to be loved."

"I also know that."

Rick paused at the door to Max's room. "So put up or shut up."

"Pardon me?" She put one hand on the door and held it. They faced off. "Seriously?"

"Max and I've worked together for four years. We've known each other for five. I consider him closer than my own brothers." Rick peeked into the room. "He's still sleeping. Let's not take this inside."

She let the door close.

Rick set his coffee on the counter at the nurses' station and tugged a donut from the package. How could he eat at a time like this? The brown skin around his ochre eyes crinkled as he enjoyed the donut. He swallowed. "What are your intentions with Max?"

"My intentions?"

"Max cares for you deeply."

"This is a conversation that needs to occur between him and me."

"He's afraid to cross the line. He thinks you don't trust him because of his disease."

"Because of the alcoholism? That's ridiculous." She trusted Max more than any man she'd ever known. "It has nothing to do with him. It's me."

"You know that's what people always say when they want out of a relationship."

"We don't have a relationship. We can't. I can't let him yoke himself to a woman who can't give him what he truly wants."

"What exactly is that?"

It was one thing to tell her dad or Julie, who understood the line women walked between motherhood and careers, who understood the risks involved in caring that much for another human being. Still, Rick was her pastor and a counselor. His discretion could be counted on.

"I care deeply for Max, it's true. But there's a bigger obstacle involved." She explained her predicament in as few words as possible. "I know you don't understand a good Christian woman not wanting children. Few people do."

"That's not true. I see a lot of millennials today choosing not to start families. Having children doesn't fit with their lifestyles or careers. They have staggering student debt. Child care costs are exorbitant. Housing is expensive." Rick's effort to keep his tone neutral was patently obvious. "Ultimately—and I know many of my pastor colleagues will disagree with me on this—having children is not a requirement of a godly marriage. People who truly don't want children shouldn't have them. Children deserve parents who are all-in, nothing less."

"Yet I can see you judging me. Why isn't it okay for me to make that choice?"

"I'm not judging you. I'm offering an observation based on love and caring. Your choice is based on fear. You don't trust God with your life and the people you love."

"For obvious reasons." She couldn't contain the fierce anger that boiled up in her. She put her hand over her mouth and closed her eyes for a two count followed by a long breath. "I'm sorry. I know you mean well. I know you care about Max—"

"I care about you, Teagan. We are both members of the body of Christ at Faith and Hope Community Church. We build each other up. We hold each other accountable. As children of God, that's our job, to be family to each other."

"I can't see bringing children into a world full of people like the man who is currently obsessed with me. Does that seem unreasonable?"

"What about bringing children into a world also filled with people like Max? A man after God's heart who loves you and loves children?"

"This world is falling apart. Glaciers are melting. The ocean is filled with plastic. Entire species of animals disappear every day. It's filled with politicians so bloated with ego and self-interest it's a wonder they don't implode. This is not negativity. I love my small piece of the world. I love hummingbirds and homemade bread and tamales and luminarias at Christmas. That's not what my hypothetical grandchildren will inherit. They get the sewer that's left. Why do that to them?"

"Because we trust in God's plan. Maybe those grandchildren will be the ones to save this world. Maybe they'll be statesmen and scientists who'll change everything. Did you ever think of that?"

An argument she had with herself in the dark night when she slept alone and longed to feel Max's solid body in the bed next to her. Just when she thought she'd swung to the God-side, she wrote another court record in a trial in which a monster broke into a house and violated the occupants in ways no human should have to endure. She brushed past him. "This is between Max and me."

"No. It's between you and God."

That was Rick. He always had to have the last word. "Can I have some time alone with him?"

"Of course. I need to call Noelle and update her." He tugged his phone from his pocket and walked away.

Still shaking her head, Teagan shoved open the door and went in. Max smiled up at her.

"You're awake."

"Where's Rick?"

"Outside eating chocolate donuts and drinking caffeine sludge. Feel free to tell Noelle about it."

He laughed and then winced. "Ouch. Broken ribs." The humor faded from his mangled face. "Rick said you had to go to another crime scene. Who was it?"

She picked up a plastic pitcher and poured him a glass of water. Then she told him the story of Charity Waters's demise.

His face white with pain and anguish, he leaned back on his pillow and closed his eyes.

"It's not your fault."

"She was a kid."

"She was my age."

"I rest my case." He coughed, winced, and reached for the glass of water. Teagan helped him take a sip. "If she hadn't talked to me, she wouldn't have let it slip about the sponsor."

"He wanted her to talk to you. That was the whole point of her being there. He thought he could tempt you with another woman. Just another way to hurt me."

"So he doesn't know as much as he thinks he does."

Max rarely dealt in sarcasm. He tended toward humor instead. There was no humor in his face now. Marshaling her defenses, Teagan took a minute to set the glass aside. "You don't think it would hurt me to see you with another woman?"

"I don't know."

"You're hurt. We're both exhausted." She couldn't help herself. She brushed his hair from his face. "Let's not do this now."

"Teagan, about the letter, what it said I did—"

"Don't worry about it. That also is a discussion for later."

They would have it, but not when he was in pain and lying in a hospital bed.

"You're right." He closed his eyes, breathed, and winced again. "I wonder if she saw it coming."

"Take it from an expert. Don't think about it."

"Can I pray for you?"

"Yes." She laid her forehead on his arm and closed her eyes.

How easily Max talked to God amazed and astonished her every time. As if they were friends sitting on the porch, drinking lemonade and shooting the breeze. When she prayed it always felt like an argument, like making her case to a skeptical father. Max's words flowed over her. The tension in her neck dissipated. Her angst seemed at least more manageable.

"In Christ's holy name, I pray."

The words ceased. She raised her head and Max smiled at her. "Go home. Get some sleep. God is on your side. Our side. Evil will not prevail."

"Can I sit with you awhile?"

His grip tightened. "I'd like that."

She laid her head down again. When his grip on her hand slackened, she raised it. The snoring through his swollen nose sounded painful. She kissed his forehead and his cheek. "I love you, Max Kennedy," she whispered. "We will talk. I promise."

He murmured something unintelligible. She backed away and tiptoed from the room to find Rick and say good night.

Evil would not prevail. She had Max Kennedy and God on her side.

19

Sweet silence. Teagan made herself a cup of ginger tea to settle her stomach in the kitchen of her childhood. She sat on a stool at the butcher block–topped island, Tigger at her feet, and let her mind go blank. Billy had taken her admonition seriously that there would be no talking on the ride home from the hospital. He walked her to the door, unlocked it, and trudged away with his own orders: *"Get some sleep."*

If only she could. The thought of lying down in her old bedroom had its charm, but closing her eyes would only invite the images to invade her brain—Officer Moreno's bloodied head, the way her head lolled to one side, Charity Waters's pink Converse sneaker hanging over the side of the Dumpster, Evelyn's blood on Max's T-shirt. Max's bruised face and mangled truck.

Teagan stirred more honey into the tea and added a squeeze of fresh lemon. The scent soothed her. She picked up the transcript from Slocum's trial in the murder of Olivia Jimenez. The 145th District Court reporter had done the transcript. She was fast and meticulous about detail.

The image of Max's battered face danced in her head, keeping her from seeing the pages in front of her. Red-hot anger coursed through her. "What's the deal, God? Mom died, wasn't that enough?"

Apparently not.

Teagan smacked her fist on the walnut and cherry wood strips that comprised the butcher block island topper. "Give me a break!"

No response.

Tigger barked and scrambled to her feet.

"Sorry, shhh, don't wake Dad."

"Too late."

Her father stood in the doorway squinting against the bank of lights illuminated over the island. He was clad in basketball shorts and a white oversized T-shirt.

"Nice jammies, Dad."

"You're lucky I didn't come out here in my boxers."

"A visual I didn't need." She cupped her hands around her tea and sighed. "You couldn't sleep either?"

He extracted a half gallon of skim milk from the refrigerator and a box of Cinnamon Swirl cereal from the cupboard. "I'm not used to sleeping alone."

"Another visual I didn't need." She nodded at the oversized box of cereal. "Jazz approve of that?"

"I might have made a run to the store after her flight took off." His abashed grin made him look twelve. "Hey, her idea of a midnight snack is fat-free yogurt with dried fruit."

"Why bother?"

"Exactly."

Did all men hide their food choices from their wives? Max wouldn't. He ate oatmeal with fruit and almond milk in the winter and granola with fruit and almond milk in the summer. He'd abused his body too much to take it for granted now.

"How's Max?"

Her dad had always been good at reading her mind. "If all goes well, he'll be out in the morning. Rick was with him when I left."

"He's a good friend."

"He's also a good pastor. You should check him out some Sunday morning."

Dad slurped down several serving spoon–sized bites of his cereal before he responded. "The women in my life are the religious ones in the family. You know that."

Grandma O'Rourke had picked up where Mom left off when it came to church attendance. Teagan spent at least one weekend a month with Grandma O, who taught her to garden, bake bread, hate war, and love Jesus. Jazz made sure she went to church the rest of the time. "I'd like to see you in heaven. I don't think it's possible to be sad in heaven, but no one wants to think of their loved ones languishing in hell for an eternity."

"That's a heavy topic for the middle of the night." He wiped his mouth with his sleeve—some men never grew up—and laid the spoon on a paper napkin. "What brought it on?"

"If Max had died this evening, I would've been devastated. Heartbroken. Probably as decimated as when Mom died." Her throat tightened. She sipped her tea and inhaled the lemony scent. "But I would've been happy for him. He knows where he's going. He's ready to go at the drop of a hat. I'm not so sure about you. We've never had that conversation. We should."

"It's your job, right?"

"It's my job to spread the good news. I do the grunt work, but God does the heavy lifting." Heat curled around her neck. She longed for her comfort zone. "That's what we are called to do."

"How 'bout them Cowboys?" Dad burped quietly. "You think they'll make it to the Super Bowl this year?"

"Dad, it's baseball season."

"I know. I was never sold on God to start with. I went with y'all to church because my wives asked me to do it. Now that you're older, Jazz is less insistent." The bravado disappeared, replaced by sadness rarely displayed on his craggy face. "After your mom died, I felt like my doubts were well justified."

"And then He led you to a new love."

"We can debate this from here to eternity—"

"Not if we're not heading to the same place in eternity."

He went to the sink, rinsed his bowl, and stuck it in the dishwasher. "Let's let this sleeping dog lie, shall we?"

Tigger's head popped up. She whined.

"It's okay, sugar, we're just talking." Dad patted her head on his way back around the island. "If you want a middle-of-the-night heart-to-heart, explain to me why you became a court reporter if you hate law enforcement so much."

"I don't hate law enforcement." Teagan corralled sudden anger. "It made sense to me. I wanted to understand it without being a part of it. I simply record it. I hear the arguments for both sides, I'm responsible for the evidence, I record the closing arguments and the jury's decision. I'm not asked to pass judgment myself, although I admit I often do. I want to understand what makes you do it. What makes Billy and Gracie do it? Why risk it? Why put everyone you love through this?" She ran out of breath.

"So you chose it because you're scared and you want to stop being scared." He slid from his chair and came to her. His big hand stroked her hair. "What does your God say about that?"

"He says 365 times, 'Do not fear.'" She leaned her head on his broad chest. "I just haven't figured out how to do that."

"When you do, let me know."

She raised her head to look into his clear blue eyes. "You're afraid?"

"I'd be an idiot not to be. You're my girl and I don't want anything happening to you."

"I'll pray."

"You do that." He enveloped her in a hug. "And I'll carry my gun."

His bear hugs had the same ability to comfort and heal as they had for a small, bewildered little girl who missed her mommy. She breathed in his smell of milk, sugary cereal, and Dial soap. "You do that."

"You should do the same. You weren't a bad shot in your day."

Years ago he'd insisted she learned to shoot. Grandma O'Rourke had tried to talk him out of it, arguing that Mom wouldn't have approved. No dice. Not only did she have to shoot but she had to know how to load and unload the gun he'd chosen for her. She'd loathed every minute of it. The feel of the gun in her hand, the kick when she fired, the smell, the ear-splitting sound—all of it only solidified her sense that she would never own or use a gun. Guns were not her weapon of choice. Faith, love, and humanity were. Violence perpetrated violence. Barbaric acts of man against man.

"I'm not carrying a gun. Now or ever."

"Fine. So this guy breaks into your house in the middle of the night. What do you do?"

"Tigger will get him."

"What if he shoots Tigger?"

"Dad!"

"The FBI has done extensive studies on the question of how to live through an encounter with a serial killer. The number one recommendation from the experts is flee. Escape. If you can't do that, the next is to resist verbally. Giving in and going along made almost no difference in the final outcome. It depends greatly on what kind of killer he is and what motivates him, but this guy likes to talk. So verbally resist."

Talk about heavy middle-of-the-night conversations. This one would only add to the nightmares. "I took a self-defense course for women. What about fighting my way out?"

His cop face said it all. "He will overpower you."

"I know some moves."

"Honey, kick him in the family jewels if you're that close to him, but I'd rather you not be that close. Keys to the eyes. Bite his nose off. But that means you're too close."

"This is never going to happen. You guys are protecting me every second now."

"I was a Boy Scout. Be prepared. Be prepared to run."

Dad's childhood had included working in his parents' barbecue joint and earning money by delivering newspapers. "You never were a Boy Scout. Run, even if he has a gun?"

"A pistol or revolver, yes. Any cop will agree if you're more than five yards away, your chances of getting hit are slim to none. If it's a rifle, your odds become grimmer."

This was a stupid conversation. It would never come to that.

"I hear through the Evans-O'Rourke grapevine that there's something else you're afraid of."

Great. "As if they don't have enough going on in their lives, they have to mind mine?"

"I hear you don't want children because you're afraid of what might happen to them in this world."

"That's an oversimplification."

"I'm so sorry, baby." Shadows hid his face, but his voice went hoarse. "I never meant to do this to you."

"This is my choice I'm making of my own free will. It has nothing to do with you."

"No. You're afraid of losing the people you love. You're scared of something happening to your brother and sister. You've lived in fear since your mom died. So no kids. It makes me sad to think you'll miss out on the joy of being a mother and a parent and sharing that with your husband because of fear."

"It's not fear. I've made a rational decision based on the condition of this world."

"So how is that trusting in the God you mentioned earlier?"

"God surely understands my position. He can see the state of this world He made and the human race's efforts to destroy it."

With a gusty sigh Dad patted her back. "Get some sleep. Are you going to the hospital in the morning to pick up Max?"

"Alisha and Justin decided that was a bad idea. They don't want us out in the open together. So Alisha gets that lovely duty. Max will not be happy."

"There's nothing to stop him from getting an Uber and escaping. She'll bring him here?"

"That's the plan. No sense in putting anyone else in danger, and they can keep an eye on him so our psycho doesn't take another shot at him."

"Agreed." He leaned against the door frame and rubbed red eyes. "So we're on then for the interview of Chase Slocum?"

"Yes."

"It's outside your comfort zone."

"So many things are these days." She followed him down the hall and up the stairs. "At least I have you to navigate it with."

"That's the nicest thing you've said to me in a long time." At the top of the stairs he planted a kiss on her forehead. "Sweet dreams, baby girl."

Inexplicable tears threatened. "Night, Daddy."

She fled to her room.

20

Two hours and two years of files and nothing popped. Teagan stood at the filing cabinet in her office, going through manila envelopes, staring at defendant names, and trying not to feel violated that another court reporter sat in her chair in the courtroom, writing records for her judge. Dad, who was far too chipper considering their middle-of-the-night meeting in the kitchen, sat at her desk typing notes on his laptop for the true crime book sure to come from this roller-coaster ride.

"How's it going in here?" Julie stuck her head in the doorway. Another far too chipper person. "Can I bring you some more coffee? We have donuts in the jury room."

Teagan held up her oversized mug. "I'm good. How's it going out there?"

Dad's phone rang. He took the call and sauntered from the office with an apologetic nod at Julie.

"We're on a break. I think the judge drank too much tea." The court coordinator took Dad's place in Teagan's desk chair. As usual she looked perfectly put together in her sleek salmon Donna Karan skirt and jacket paired with a silky white blouse, pearls, and gold bangle bracelets. "I know not being in there is eating you alive. Don't worry about it. No one can take your place. Sandy is a fine substitute, but that's all she'll ever be. A sub."

"You're sweet to say that. I didn't realize how much work anchors me." Teagan studied the names on her paper list that included the defendant's name, case number, and dates of the trial. "Troy Sullivan. Troy Sullivan. Does that name mean anything to you?"

Julie tilted her head and wrinkled her nose. "I've been doing this for ten years. With the exception of the capital murder cases, they're pretty much one big blur."

"Same here, and I've only done six years." Teagan peeked inside the envelope. A voir dire list and a witness list. When she first started court reporting, she'd stored her real-time on disks. Now she preferred the cloud because of the large audio files. "Troy Sullivan killed his father in a dispute over his curfew."

"I do remember that one. His mother sat in the courtroom and cried every single day of the trial."

"She lost her only son and her husband over a stupid argument." Teagan moved on to the next name on her list. Rebecca Chavez. She was convicted of killing her two-year-old daughter with a vacuum cleaner hose because she wet herself. Anyone who still claimed to be a human being would remember that name. "Tell me something good. Right now."

"I had another date with Nathan the Nose."

Nathan the Nose had made it to date number two after the initial introduction through a dating app. Not many made it that far with Julie. "And it went well?"

"We had lunch. I met him at Aurelio's. He chews with his mouth shut. He doesn't smell. And he doesn't talk about his ex-wife. He tells a joke well and uses good grammar."

Julie had learned not to set the bar too high in her latest foray into dating.

"Are you seeing him again?"

"Ball's in his court. He said he'll call. We'll see if he does."

Julie did single beautifully, but now that she wanted a partner in life, Teagan wanted one for her. "I'll say my prayers."

Julie grinned. "I'm saying mine for you."

"Don't start—"

Dad strode into the office. "Have you found anything?"

"Not so far. I've gone back two years. Why would someone wait more than two years to start exacting revenge for something that happened in my courtroom?"

"Maybe he or she was incarcerated." Julie tapped her long, pale-pink nails on the desk. "That would inflame the desire."

"So why not go after the prosecutor and the judge?"

"I'm with Teagan on this one." Dad closed his laptop and picked it up. "The letters tie these murders to Slocum and therefore to me. His son, Chase, has agreed to talk with me."

"I'm coming." Teagan shoved the filing cabinet closed, scooped up her laptop, and grabbed her purse. "This is a waste of time."

Time they didn't have.

Dad didn't bother to argue. "Get a move on then."

Julie slipped into Teagan's path, bringing with her the lovely scent of Chanel Coco. "Be careful, please. Good court reporters are hard to find."

"Very funny."

Court reporters could easily be replaced. Friends could not. She accepted Julie's hug. Her friend stepped back and straightened Teagan's collar. "Seriously, I want you back here in one piece ASAP."

"My family is all over it. So is Max."

Julie's worried expression relaxed. "It would be nice if one good thing could come of this horrible situation."

Julie had been rooting for Max since the first time she met him at the church's pumpkin patch two years earlier. "We'll see."

"Text me when you get a chance."

Twenty minutes later, Teagan strode up the sidewalk ahead of her father through the Slocums's spacious front yard. The sparse grass needed water and the live oak trees could use a trim. She concentrated on the broken, jagged sidewalk that led to Leo Slocum's old house. Had Slocum played tag with his kids in this yard? Had he planted the yellow bells that lined the front porch? The roof sagged. The gutters needed cleaning. The fake daisies on the WEL-COME TO OUR HOME wreath were wilted. The entire two-story wood-frame house needed painting.

An older model gray Jeep Cherokee sat in the driveway. Had Slocum returned here and found the place wanting after his escape from the Corpus jail? It seemed unlikely that his son would tell them if he had. He'd agreed to the interview only when Dad had made it clear he was a retired police officer, not on official business.

Chase opened the door after the first tinkling chime of the doorbell. A tall, muscled man, he bore a definite resemblance to his father. Straight dark hair, blue eyes. Only his long face and overly narrow nose kept him from being model material. "I can give you thirty minutes. My kids will be home from school then, and I'm not talking about their grandfather in front of them."

"Of course."

A suspected serial killer had grandchildren. Sweat dampening her hands and armpits, Teagan followed the man into a living room with furnishings best described as shabby chic. A chintz-covered sofa and love seat sat catty-corner from a fireplace that hadn't been cleaned after the last fire of the winter. Barbie dolls and all the detritus that goes with them vied for space on the chunky coffee table with a plethora of Matchbox cars, at least half a dozen Transformers, Llama Llama books, coloring books, and a basket filled with crayons. A flat-screen TV on the opposite wall was tuned to an afternoon talk show, but the sound had been muted. "Is your wife here?"

"No. No wife."

If his failure to elaborate on this statement was an indication of how the interview would go, they might as well call it a day now. Teagan glanced at her dad. His eyebrows did a little dance. He shrugged. They sat.

"I don't know what you expect me to say." Chase settled into a wingback chair with a lap quilt slung over the back. A slinky gray cat immediately joined him. He didn't seem to notice, even when the cat's purr filled the air. "The police have already been here. I haven't seen my dad. I haven't talked to him."

"Then you know he's suspected of killing more women than just Olivia Jimenez here in San Antonio. The two women he's accused of murdering in Corpus Christi are just the tip of the iceberg," Dad dove in. Seeing him don the role of a law enforcement officer—however retired—and interview this innocent man—whose life had been recently shattered—only made the moment more surreal. "You know they're watching the house, waiting for him to show up here? I imagine they're getting a warrant to tap your phones in case he tries to contact you."

Teagan kept her face neutral. Her education regarding tactics to get witnesses to spill included this one. Her siblings often grumbled over the inability to get judges to approve phone tap warrants unless all other means of getting information had been exhausted. Of course Leyla, the future attorney, argued for the right to privacy and against fishing expeditions.

Never a dull dinner table conversation at the O'Rourke house.

"He won't." Chase snatched a tissue from a box perched on top of a stack of books on the end table next to his chair. He liked legal thrillers. John Grisham. James Scott Bell. Cara Putnam. *Good choice.* "He wouldn't put the kids in danger."

A strange dichotomy. He killed women and couldn't see how his actions affected his loved ones. Teagan wiggled. Her instructions had been to keep quiet and observe. *Tough beans.* "You don't think he did any of it, do you?"

"My father was—is—a hardworking family man who has always tried to better himself so he could provide for us better." Chase's voice cracked. Instead of using the tissue, he twisted it into a knot and began to shred it. The cat on his lap batted at the pieces, knocking them to the tan carpet as if her friend had invented a new game. "That's why he was taking law courses. He traveled a lot, but when he was in town, he went to my sister's dance recitals and to my basketball games.

"He and my mom had date nights, for crying out loud. They used to come home after dinner and a movie and dance to the old Frank Sinatra records they collected—the moldy oldies, me and Skyler called them. They drank champagne from crystal flutes my aunt gave them as a wedding present. I used to sit at the top of the stairs and listen to them giggle and smooch until my dad would tell me to go to bed. 'Nothing to see here,' he would yell, and she would giggle even harder. He said he had X-ray vision and she had eyes in the back of her head. They could always see me."

"It's obvious you love him—"

"And he loves me and Sky and my mom." His earlier calm a distant memory, Chase's Adam's apple bobbed. His eyes turned red. It was hard to know if he was trying to convince them or himself. Either way, he was begging them to see Leo Slocum through the eyes of a son. "Once a dog wandered into our yard. She was limping. It looked as if she had a broken leg. Dad wrapped her in a blanket and took her to the vet. He paid the bill for a dog that wasn't even ours. He made sure the vet found a home for her. He took us camping at Garner State Park. We did father-son projects together—he taught me how to change the oil in a car, stuff like that."

His words churned in Teagan's mind, already forming a transcript that one day would paint a picture of Leo Slocum for jurors.

13 A. I asked what his plans were with it and he

14 mentioned that the Jeep could be a father-son project.

15 Q. So you worked on the car together with your dad?

16 A. I did. All that summer after my freshman year.

17 Q. Did he give you the Jeep when you learned to drive?

18 A. He did, but it wasn't about that. I mean, it wasn't

19 something I asked for. We rebuilt the engine together.

20 We spent time together.

21 Q. Were you and your dad close then?

22 A. Yes.

23 Q. Would you say he was a good dad?

24 A. Yes, very good.

The picture Chase painted made it hard to see Leo Slocum as a sadistic misogynist who murdered women and dumped their bodies in places where he hoped to be able to visit them again. On the ride over Dad had given her a detailed lecture on how murderers were frequently able to compartmentalize their actions and their lives. Kill a guy with a hammer and then stop for milk on the way home to supper with the wife and then listen to the kids' prayers before tucking them into their beds.

His narrow eyebrows arched, Dad frowned at Teagan and then directed the question at Chase. "Is that why you visited him while he was in jail here? You think he's innocent."

"He's only been convicted in the one incident, and he's appealing his conviction. He says it's a simple case of mistaken identity."

"And the DNA they found under his victim's nails?"

"He says it was planted." His voice faltered. Even he could hear how ludicrous that sounded. "He also says he has migraine headaches and blackouts. That he may not have been in his right mind when it happened. He's also appealing on the grounds of ineffective counsel and not being allowed to represent himself."

Throwing everything at the wall to see what would stick.

"Do you remember him having headaches or acting erratic?"

"He sometimes stayed in bed all day. Mom would tell us to be quiet because he needed his rest."

"What did you talk about when you visited him?"

"At first I was mad, I didn't want to go, but he kept calling me and writing me, telling me he wanted a chance to explain, that he deserved a chance to explain." Chase swiped at his face with the back of his hand. "My mom packed up and left, leaving me with no one to watch the kids while I work. My sister wouldn't even come back for the trial. I'm all he has left."

"At first you were mad, but now you're not?"

"Yes, I am, at a system that crucifies an innocent man. If you spent a few minutes talking to my dad, you'd see. He's no killer. He reminded me of what he used to say when Mom would try to pick a fight with him. 'I'm a lover, babe, not a fighter.'"

Not a statement Teagan could imagine her father making to one of his children. No one wanted to think of her parent as a lover in the physical sense. "What else did you talk about?"

"The kids. I showed him their school photos." He pointed to a row of photos in cheap gold frames on the fireplace mantel. His kids were cute, with his dark hair and blue eyes. But they had big smiles. The girl had missing front teeth and wore a shirt with a pink unicorn with a shiny gold horn on it. "I told him about Serenity winning the spelling bee and Cullen's home run in T-ball and Todd's obsession with Captain America."

"Nothing about the crimes?"

"He told me he wasn't even in those towns when the women disappeared. He said when he goes to trial, they'll see they have the wrong man. That right now, the real killer is out there, running free, probably still killing, while he's sitting in a cell, wrongly accused."

"Did he have a room in the house that was off-limits or a shed he kept padlocked?"

"Of course he did. Didn't your parents?" Chase rolled his eyes. "We weren't allowed in his office because he kept important work papers in there and stuff from his job."

"Was your mom allowed in there?"

"Yeah, she was." Chase sounded less sure of himself. "I know I saw her in there . . . once or twice."

"What about a shed?"

"Everyone kept their sheds padlocked. Otherwise the mowers and tools got stolen. They still do. It proves nothing."

"You use his office for something else now?"

"If you're asking me if any of his stuff is still here, the answer is no. The cops took his laptop and boxes of papers."

"What about the shed?"

"The cops went through everything. I don't know what they took."

Dad did. He'd read the reports. Sometimes family members didn't share all the nooks and crannies with law enforcement. If Chase had withheld information, he wasn't forthcoming about it now. The police hadn't found the hoped-for trophies in Leo's shed. Nor had there been human blood or DNA other than his own on his tools. He had another hiding place.

The front door swung open. Five kids in varying sizes raced through the door, darted through the living room, and slowed when they saw the company. They were step laddered in heights. Beautiful. Innocent. Four of the five ran straight on through. Probably to the kitchen. That was Teagan's first stop after school. A slim, leggy woman followed at a more sedate pace. She closed the door and strode into the living room behind them.

"Daddy, I got all my spelling words right." The oldest one ran to Chase and threw her arms around him. The cat meowed her distaste, jumped from his lap, and trotted away. "You said we could have ice cream if I did."

Chase kissed her golden-brown hair. "Good job, Serenity. We'll get pizza and have ice cream for dessert."

"I want ice cream now."

"Have a snack."

"Who are these people?"

"They're people from my work."

Serenity looked Teagan over. She must've passed inspection, because the girl approached and picked up a Barbie dressed in an elaborate ball gown. "Do you like Barbie's dress?"

"I do. It's beautiful. Is she going to a dance?"

"She is. Ken's taking her."

Such sweetness. "I always liked G.I. Joe for Barbie. He's not as pretty as Ken."

Serenity grinned. "I like soldiers, but G.I. Joe doesn't have a tux."

"We need to fix that."

"Serenity, go to the kitchen." His voice strained, Chase pointed toward the door. "Have your snack and start on your homework. I'll be out in a little bit to check it."

"Are you staying for supper?" Serenity removed her pink-and-purple backpack. She unzipped it and placed Barbie and Ken at the top, arms out, so they could ride along without being lost in the backpack's contents. "We're having pizza and ice cream."

"Serenity, go!"

"We can't." Teagan let her regret at not being able to spend more time with this enchanting little girl show on her face. "Congrats on the spelling test."

"Thank you." She started for the kitchen. At the door she looked back. "You're pretty. Like my mom."

She disappeared through the door, but the words echoed in Teagan's head, making it hard to think. Little girls should have mommies who played dollhouse with them and washed their hair for them and taught them about boys. Serenity's mother hadn't died. She abandoned her child.

Who did that? All little girls needed mommies. Playing Barbies and eating ice cream after a spelling test should be considered an honor and a privilege.

The woman who'd shepherded the children into the house shifted until she stood next to Chase's chair. She cleared her throat. Chase made the introductions. The woman was his housemate Joanna Dean, who had moved in when his mom moved out.

"The house is paid for, but it's tough raising my kids and paying all the bills on what I make. Mom was watching the kids for me when I worked, which saved me a bunch of money."

"Yeah and I have a deadbeat husband, so it helps to share costs. Two of those screaming meanies that raced through here were mine." Joanna tossed her long braids of silky brown hair over her shoulders. She wore skinny jeans and a tank top that matched her charcoal eyes. "Chase watches my kids when he can. We met at a park play day and hit it off. So did our kids."

The woman had volunteered more information than needed. But then, talking to cops made most people nervous. They either babbled or they clammed up. Joanna was a talker.

Teagan picked up another Barbie doll. This one had long black hair and dark eyes. She wore an evening gown with sparkly silver sequins and spiked silver shoes. "Your daughter is beautiful. And smart."

"She loves to play with dolls." Chase's faint smile came and went. "Cullen just likes to throw them around like missiles and hide them from her. Anything to be a thorn in her behind. I spend all my time picking this stuff up."

Parenthood was hard. Doing it alone was even harder. How did Chase manage under the crushing load of suspicion and uncertainty? He was blessed to have found Joanna. Or had she been the real reason his wife left? If she was more than a friend, she'd taken over the wife spot quickly. Like Jazz had for Dad. Shame whipped through Teagan. An exercise in what-ifs. *Is that what this is, God? I get it.*

She grew up with a law-and-order man who loved his family and loved his job as a cop, mostly in that order. She'd resented his choice of profession, the time it took away from her after her mother died.

Lying in bed at night, listening to the sirens, she pulled the blankets over her head. She prayed that it wasn't her dad out there getting blown away by a meth-crazed punk or a felon wanted on a warrant who refused to give up without a fight.

Chase Slocum had a dad with a safe job. He traveled a great deal, but when he was home, he gave them his undivided, loving attention. "I'm sorry for your pain, for what you've lost. I truly am. I can't even begin to imagine what this is like for you."

"No, you can't." His jaw worked. Then he took a long breath. "Thank you, but I don't need your pity. He'll appeal. He'll be exonerated. Y'all really need to go. The kids will want their snacks, and they have homework to do."

And they didn't need to know Grandpa might be a serial killer.

Dad stood and held out a business card. "If you think of anything else—"

"I know, give you a call. I've heard the spiel." Chase took the card and stuck it in his jeans pocket. "You think my father is a killer. It's up to you to prove it. Don't expect me to do it for you."

"Those women were loved by mothers and fathers, boyfriends, brothers and sisters. They were sadistically tortured, killed, and dumped like trash in places where the killer thought they might never be found." Teagan remained planted on the sofa. "Doesn't that bother you?"

"Sure, it bothers me. I have a daughter." Chase stuck his thumb over his shoulder in the general direction of the kitchen. "But I know that the man who taught me to tie my shoes, my division tables, how to improve my jump shot and perfect my bunt, didn't kill those women. He's kind and decent and a good grandpa to those kids. He wouldn't do that to me. Or to them."

"He's a good man." Joanna edged closer to Chase's chair. She put a hand on its back. "He raised Chase. He can't be bad."

"Did you know him personally?"

"No, no, but like I said, he's a good father and provider. That's more than I can say for my ex."

Chase scowled at her. "You don't have to defend him or me to them. They don't know us. They can't know. They'll believe what they want to believe. They decided Dad did it and they never looked for anyone else."

"The evidence was overwhelming and certainly not circumstantial." Dad's tone was gentle. "But I can understand why you feel as you do. Believe me, I never lose sight of the fact that there are always more victims than the one who died. But my duty as a police officer—before I retired—was to the one who ended up in the morgue. To that person's family."

"Save the speech. I've told myself all that a thousand times." Chase stood. "You need to go."

Joanna stepped forward. They stood side by side, a united front.

Dad didn't move. "Mr. Slocum, where's your wife?"

"Not that it's any of your business, but she left after Dad was convicted. She didn't walk, she ran for the hills."

"And left her kids?"

"I figure she looked at me and wondered if the apple didn't fall far from the tree." He stuffed his hands in his pockets and stared at Teagan's dad. "She probably is afraid her kids are demon seed. She talks to them on the phone and she writes to them, but she hasn't been back since the jury delivered a guilty verdict."

"My daughter and I'll get out of your way." He drilled Teagan with the O'Rourke stare more commonly associated with his first wife. "Thank you for your time. I know it's not an easy thing to contemplate, but for your sake and the sake of those kids, I hope you'll be careful if he does decide to come here."

"Just get out." Chase marched across the grubby beige carpet to the door, Joanna right behind him. "If you come around here again, I'll sic my lawyer on you."

At the car Teagan paused to look back. A forlorn basketball hoop with no netting graced the top of the driveway. A shabby white Plymouth van had joined the Jeep. Had Slocum played twenty-one with his kids on long summer nights?

"What?"

She turned. Her dad leaned both arms on the Charger's roof. She shook her head. "Did you get a weird vibe between those two?"

"I wondered if you'd picked up on it." Dad's forehead and nose wrinkled. He stared at the house behind him. "Very connected."

"Not like a housemate?"

"Like comrades in arms. Joanna did act like she knew Leo, but it could just be from osmosis. I imagine Chase has hashed and rehashed the situation a million times since meeting Joanna. She came into his life and filled a hole. Such perfect timing."

"It's something to chew on." Truth be told, the intensity of the relationship didn't bother Teagan as much as the other thoughts niggling at her. "What if Slocum is telling the truth? What if we're focused on his father when the real killer is murdering women right beneath our noses?"

"Or maybe that's what he wants us to think." Her dad patted the Charger as if it were his pet. "It's just as realistic to think he has someone killing for him to muddy the waters. An accomplice who makes it appear as if Slocum was never the killer. That gets him off the hook."

"Do serial killers have accomplices?"

"They do, or sometimes they kill in pairs as equals." The cadence of his voice changed as he slipped into criminal justice professor mode. "For example, the Hillside Strangler was actually two people. Cousins Angelo Buono Jr. and Kenneth Bianchi, who moved out to California, and over a four-month period, they killed ten women and dumped their bodies in the Hollywood Hills.

"And we won't even talk about the Charles Manson effect. Groupies. Lots of them. Male and female, who do anything to make this man, their new christ, their new father, happy. They were family and disciples all rolled into one."

"I'll take double jeopardy for two thousand, Alex. The answer is an accomplice who went through my courtroom."

"And the question still remains, who's trying to get to Dillon O'Rourke through his daughter?" Dad's jaw worked as he smoothed an imaginary spot on the car. "I worked Slocum's case here. Because of me, he's going to prison. Maybe he's living vicariously through his accomplice."

Would a serial killer turn his own son into an accomplice? A loving father and grandfather? Which was he?

Dad hit the remote and turned off the alarm. "Get in."

She did as she was told. He plugged his phone into the charger lying on the console, pushed the button, started the car, then used Bluetooth to call Billy.

"Hey, Dad, I just picked up the phone to call you."

"How deep a dive did the detectives do on Chase Slocum?"

"Deep. I have news—"

"We need to—"

"Dad, listen. Slocum is back in custody."

Teagan slumped back in her seat. *Good news. Thank You, Jesus. Thank You.*

"So he was never in San Antonio."

"Nope. He was headed this direction, but he didn't make it. He's not talking about the whys and wherefores."

"Why not head south to Mexico?"

"Because he had unfinished business in San Antonio?"

Slocum had not killed Officer Moreno, Evelyn, or Charity Waters. Someone close to him or someone who aspired to be like him had killed three people and tried to kill Max.

Teagan closed her eyes and listened to the hum of the AC and vintage Hank Williams Jr. on the radio. Back to the theory that they had a copycat or accomplices determined to move suspicion away from Slocum. "What are the chances of someone outside law enforcement circles knowing about the letters?"

"Small. It's possible. A leak. But not probable."

"So we're back to the accomplice."

Dad raced through the high points of their visit with Chase Slocum, while Billy contributed an occasional "*uh-huh.*"

"Revisit the background on Chase Slocum. Take a closer look at this housemate."

"On it."

Dad hung up and peeled away from the curb.

She waited a few seconds. Nothing but Hank Junior crooning about a country state of mind.

"Well?"

He growled.

"You'll have to be more specific."

"One down, one or two to go."

She leaned against her seat and rested her eyes. "I like your perspective. Let's get them and get on with our lives."

21

The powwow took place in Dad's war room. Teagan had just enough time to hit the bathroom before Detective Siebert and Justin arrived. Alisha had the task of serving as Max's chauffeur. Teagan's offer to accompany her had been nixed by Dad. Gracie and her partner had been involved in a high-speed chase of a suspected shooter in a drive-by that ended with the suspect's car ramming into a house on the west side. She wouldn't be joining them.

Billy rolled in next and he wasn't alone. A stocky Hispanic man in a deep-blue guayabera and neatly pressed gray slacks followed. He carried a bulging leather satchel in one hand and rolled-up maps in the other.

"This is Detective Hector Solis from Brownsville." Billy waved the man into the closest chair. "He's here to compare notes on behalf of his colleagues in the Valley."

"Welcome." Dad made the introductions and motioned toward the carafe of coffee he'd placed on the long table that sat perpendicular to his desk. "Help yourself."

"My eyeballs are sloshing in coffee." Solis had that soft lilt that said English had been the second language learned in his childhood home. "Four hours in the car by myself, I was afraid I would drift off."

"The suspect broke out of jail and went south. So much for your theory, Dad."

"Which brings us back to square one." Siebert sipped from the ubiquitous Starbucks cup that was never far from his person. "We have a psychopath who's watching Teagan, he's writing her letters, and he's killing people around her and threatening to do more than that."

"Thanks for the recap." Dad didn't bother to muzzle his sarcasm. "It's not Slocum, true, but it's someone who knows more about the case being built against him than the average person. That narrows the parameters considerably. It has to be someone who knows him, spent time with Slocum, admires him, and wants to be like him. Or someone he's influencing to make it look like law enforcement is going after the wrong guy. So let's start with the cases Hector and our colleagues in the Valley have amassed and work from there."

"We made it. Finally." Max pushed through the door ahead of Alisha. "What did we miss?"

"We're just getting started." Teagan wrangled her feelings into their box. All those years of calling herself a pacifist, and all she wanted to do was pummel the person responsible for Max's battered face. The psychopath behind this mental torture knew exactly which buttons to push. How was that possible? "We have autopsy reports for Officer Moreno and Evelyn. Hector is going to give us an overview of the cases in the Valley that they plan to charge Slocum with."

"This guy needs to be hunted down and put in jail regardless of the reason he's doing it." Max squeezed a chair in between Billy and Teagan and sat. "He will kill again. It's only a matter of time. I'd like to get my hands on him for what he did to Charity Waters. And it's a small, small thing, but I loved that truck."

"Easy, big guy. Nobody's going off the reservation." Dad slid a bottle of water covered with condensation across the table to Max. "Cool off. Believe me, I understand the desire. This is my daughter in his crosshairs, but good police work will catch him, I promise you."

Hector stood and handed out thick documents. "The Behavioral

Analysis Unit profile matched Slocum in a number of ways. White male, thirty to forty-five—Slocum's older, of course—married, holds down a job, may have killed in the past but has no criminal record. Until Slocum was arrested for the murder here in SA, he had no record. He's fifty-eight. Old for a serial killer.

"Like our murders in the Valley, Slocum is organized. He is methodical and above average in intelligence. He's socially competent. This is not a spur-of-the-moment killer. Our crime scenes were deliberate, cold, and the victim was a targeted stranger. In every case restraints were used. The body was hidden. No weapon was found and very little evidence."

With Billy's help Hector stuck a map of South Texas on the bulletin board catty-corner to the dry erase board. The detective had used blue and yellow highlighters to delineate a route through a half dozen cities from San Antonio to the Valley and back. "The blue stars are cities on Slocum's sales route. The green stars are locations where the unsolved murders of women have occurred over the years. The stickies are the dates. It's been almost impossible to pin them to one killer because he's so smart. He varies the ages and races of his victims, but they're all adult women. He varies his MO, rotating between shooting, stabbing, and strangling."

Parallel lives. Slocum routinely traveled the 143 miles from San Antonio to Corpus Christi via I-37. From there he took US-77 to Harlingen, another 136 miles. His route then took him a quick half-hour drive to Brownsville deep in the Valley on the Texas–Mexico border. Then his route headed back north to Edinberg and from Edinburg to Falfurrias on US-281 North. His final stop before returning to San Antonio was Alice. Lots of small towns along the way.

"What a perfect job for a serial killer." A chill curled around Teagan's neck. She sipped her coffee, but it did little to warm her. "Going from city to city, anonymous, in and out of hotels, restaurants, and bars. No family member who'll notice you didn't come home until midnight or that you have a bloody knife, gun, and garrote in the trunk of your car."

"As you can see we have unsolved female homicides in Corpus Christi, Harlingen, Brownsville, Edinberg, and Alice. Possibly another one in Weslaco." Hector stabbed at the small town of Weslaco between Brownsville and McAllen with his pen. "The remains were just found in an illegal dumping ground last week. Because of the state of decomp, identifying the victim will be difficult. We know it's a woman. It's possible she is from one of the bigger cities and the killer simply dumped her body in Weslaco."

Teagan forced her gaze to the documents in front of her. Copies of police reports, crime scene photos, toxicology reports, autopsy reports, and witness statements. The sheer amount of information made drawing conclusions difficult. "Aside from being women, what ties them together?"

"Lifestyle. Mostly single, divorced, widowed, never married. They were last seen coming out of bars or restaurants where they were hanging out with friends." He pointed to a photo of a Hispanic woman with dark curly hair that hung below her shoulders. "Mariel Santos was a marine biology major at Texas A&M–Corpus Christi. She finished her shift at La Tropicana restaurant about eleven at night and walked to the bus stop a block away. When she failed to show up for work the next day, her boss called her housemates, who said she never came home. Her decomposed body was found in the dunes of a Corpus nature preserve a month later. Cause of death was blunt force trauma and strangulation."

"So how do you tie these deaths to Slocum?"

"In three cases, we have women who were approached by a man fitting Slocum's description around the time of the murders. For whatever reason, the women spooked and he wasn't able to convince them to go with him. Another woman saw one of the murder victims with a man with a similar build but didn't see his face.

"We subpoenaed his credit card records and financials. We have cell phone records. We have records from his employer showing where he made sales over the years. The number one thing that ties the murders to each other, however, are the letters."

"Which brings us to our three murders in San Antonio post-arrest and conviction of Slocum for Olivia Jimenez's murder." Dad passed around copies of police, CSU, and autopsy reports. "We have letters for two of those murders. Officer Moreno's murder was a shot across the bow, apparently, to get Teagan's attention. To get my attention."

Teagan let her hand rest on the thick folder. Opening it meant subjecting herself to images and words that would be indelibly etched on her brain. She gritted her teeth and flipped to the first page.

Billy went to the board and taped Officer Moreno's photo on it. She looked so young and sweet in her academy graduation photo. "The ME's report indicates Kris was shot with a long-range, high-velocity sniper rifle. Two bullets were recovered during the autopsy, but both were mangled. They appeared to be full metal jacket. They penetrated the vehicle's glass. One hit her in the forehead, the other in the neck. The shot to the head was the kill shot. The bullets are too degraded to tell us much else about the weapon used. They've been sent to the forensic firearms examiner, but I wouldn't hold my breath.

"The examiner is working with CSU on a crime scene recon-struction based on the ME's report on angle of entry. They hope to get a bead—no pun intended—on where the shots came from." Billy tacked photos of the vehicle and a map of the area where the shoot-ing occurred to the board. "Obviously, the shooter had to have been on the park side—the driver's side—of the vehicle. The PD facility has surveillance cameras. They captured nothing."

"A canvass of the area produced not a single witness who saw our perp hanging out with a sniper rifle over one shoulder?" Siebert flipped the top off his Starbucks cup, looked mournfully inside it, and tossed lid and cup into the wastebasket at his feet. "How is that possible?"

"Not one. The accuracy of sniper rifles is unparalleled these days." Billy tapped the map with his index finger. "My best guess, he knew where Teagan and Kris were going. He moved in ahead, parked on Academic Court a few minutes ahead of time, long enough to get set up in the backyard of one of the corner houses at South Park Boulevard and Academic Court. A decent shooter could hit his target anywhere from three hundred to a thousand yards."

"Not a skill the average person has." His jaw tight, Dad twirled his reading glasses with one hand. "Military background?"

"Maybe, or an avid hunter of big game."

"So basically we've got nothing to go on in terms of physical evidence." Dad laid the glasses on the table, leaned back, and scratched his head. "We can't even canvass sporting goods stores if we can't narrow down the type of sniper rifle used. Our only option is to go to everyone in town and ask if they've sold a sniper rifle recently. He might not have bought it here."

"And hunters who use them covers a lot of people in Texas," Hector pointed out.

"If we come up with a weapon at some point, the examiner may be able to match the lands and grooves in these bullets." Billy's offer sounded weak, and from his expression he knew it. "It may be in one of the federal databases."

"The killer's too smart to hang on to the weapon." Teagan ignored Billy's attempt to interrupt. "He never uses the same weapon twice. That and varying the victim types makes it nearly impossible to tie him to the murders. He knows that. And he wants people to know just how smart he is. Thus the desire for publicity."

"That's a lot of money to throw away after only one kill," Billy objected. "One of those sniper rifles can go for as much as four thousand dollars or more." Teagan agreed, but this killer valued his freedom more than money. "I'm just saying."

Billy plopped into a chair next to Teagan. "Siebert, you're up."

The detective stood. His knees cracked. "I'm getting too old for this stuff." He trudged to the board where he hung an autopsy photo of Evelyn under Kris Moreno's photo. "But this guy really gets under my skin."

Up-close photos of Evelyn's stab wounds followed. Five of them. Teagan ducked her head and closed her eyes.

"Are you okay, T?" Max's hand covered hers.

"I'm fine. Just tired."

"You don't have to sit through this."

"Yes, I do."

"The ME's report indicates five stab wounds to the abdomen and chest. All were deep and inflicted with the blade's sharp edge facing upward and through an underhanded thrust. The borders were clean. The knife was sharp." Siebert pointed to the middle photo. "The wound between the rib cage and the navel was the deepest and most likely the fatal one. The victim—"

"Evelyn Conklin." Teagan couldn't help herself. "She has a name. Evelyn."

"*Mrs. Conklin* died of exsanguination." Siebert's tone bordered on exasperated. He sank into his chair with an exaggerated sigh. "She did have some defensive wounds to the hands. She put up a fight. But no blood or DNA was found other than her own."

"Nothing? How can this guy be so lucky?" Billy grabbed his water bottle and knocked back a long swallow. He burped and slapped the bottle on the table. "There's got to be something."

"He's not lucky. He's smart." Teagan reiterated for the twentieth time, it seemed. "He has practice. He's experienced. He's not Slocum's copycat. He's a serial killer in his own right."

"So why the letters?" Hector returned to the board and pointed to copies of letters he'd posted earlier. "Let's stop for a moment and consider the letters. Slocum allegedly wrote the letters to his victims. The letters here are written to Teagan. Why? If it's to torture you, Dillon, why not write them to you?"

"Are you a parent?"

Hector nodded. "Two boys, seven and nine; two girls, twelve and fourteen."

"Don't you agree that stalking and harassing your daughters would more effectively torture you than if a psycho went after you directly?" Dad's face hardened. His eyes turned cold. "Like Max, I'd like to rip this guy's face off and bury him so deep his body would never be found. That's what he wants. He's tapped into a father's love. Believe me, he knows what he's doing."

A father's love. A parent's love. Nothing compared to it.

Teagan would never know. Did that make her a coward? Or someone with eyes wide open knowing her limits, understanding more than most what came of loving someone so much she would be willing to die for them? Or kill for them?

Teagan squirmed in her seat. Eyebrows lifted, Max caught her gaze. He mouthed the words, *Are you okay?* She nodded and willed herself to sit still.

"The basics are the same. The paper used, the black ink, the ornate cursive script." Hector tapped the letter found in Teagan's Little Free Library. "I had a long sit-down with the department's handwriting analysis expert. The challenge we're up against is the passage of time."

"Come again? I thought a person's handwriting was unique. The department has handwriting experts work on check forgeries and handwritten notes all the time." Siebert stood and walked up to the board. He peered at the letters. "I'm no expert and even I can see huge similarities."

"Let the guy talk." Billy might need an afternoon nap. He was getting cranky. "You're a homicide dick. What do you know about handwriting?"

"My girlfriend is in white-collar crime."

Recently divorced, Siebert had jumped back into the dating pool with no looking back, according to Gracie. Not that Teagan needed to know about the man's personal life. "Can we get back on track?"

"As we age, our handwriting changes." Hector patted his shiny forehead with a paper napkin. "Our health, a stroke, vision changes, hand injuries, drugs, alcohol—they can all affect our handwriting as we get older.

"Our forensic document consultant said these letters are probably a match, but she can't be sure." He pointed to the words *your friend*, repeated in the letters to Teagan. "Look at the slant of the lowercase *f* and the size of the *e*, look at how the letters are connected, the spacing between the words, the capital *T*'s and the lower-case *d*'s. The new letters have a high probability of being written by the same person. "The older letters are similar but still different."

"What about errors or word choice? Do those tell us anything about the killer?" Teagan threw the question out there, unafraid. She knew nothing about handwriting analysis. "Do the letters tell us anything about his personality?"

"He doesn't make errors in grammar or punctuation, so we can assume he's educated." Hector swiped at his face again. His lovely brown skin had a sheen of perspiration. Teagan rose and turned on the ceiling fan. He smiled his thanks. "As far as personality, that's not in the bailiwick of a handwriting expert. That's called graphology and it's not a science. Not one that we want to rely on, for sure."

"So we get a handwriting sample from Slocum."

"We know he didn't write the new letters," Teagan pointed out. "And Hector just said the writing will be different as the man ages. He's in his fifties now."

"It can't hurt to do a comparison." Dad's forehead wrinkled as he considered the possibility. "*U.S. v. Mara* says he can be ordered to provide it."

"If we can get an existing sample, that's one thing." Hector settled back into his chair. "The problem with having him give a new sample is he can simply disguise his writing. He'll know why we want it."

Teagan nodded. "He has no reason to cooperate with law enforcement. Plus he knows enough about the law to be dangerous."

"Let's stick a pin in that for now." Hands steepled, Dad studied the board. "Let's go at it from another direction. What about alibis for Teagan's neighbors?"

"Everyone was offended that we asked." Bill shuffled through pages of notes. "We're double-checking their responses against witnesses. Dana Holl was in a conference with a client and then at the gym. Stephanie Nixon took her daughter to a well-baby checkup and then home to make supper for her husband. Carlos Cavazos and Oscar Benavides alibied each other as setting up an exhibit at Carlos's gallery in the afternoon. Which is suspect."

"Why?" Teagan interrupted when Billy took a breath. "Carlos is an artist. Oscar is part owner of the gallery. It's natural they'd work together. And I saw Oscar that evening when Evelyn was murdered."

"Maybe they're also partners in crime. One of them killed Kristen while the other came back to the neighborhood to stab Mrs. Conklin."

"Why? For what earthly reason—"

"Motive. The one thing we don't have to prove." Billy laid on the sarcasm. "You of all people know a rational reason doesn't have to exist—"

"Keep checking." Dad broke in. "No stone unturned. Let's not get tunnel vision on this case, okay? In the meantime, I want dibs on interviewing Slocum's boss and coworkers. He was still working when he was arrested here. Maybe they have some insight into his behavior in years prior."

"You're not PD," Siebert objected.

"I may get more out of them for that very reason. I'm just a consultant, a guy writing a book."

Shrugging, Siebert subsided.

Dad looked at his watch. "It's getting late. We've covered a lot of material. Let's let it marinate until morning. We'll divvy up chores and get back at it."

"Tomorrow's Sunday," Teagan and Max spoke in unison.

"Right." Dad stood and stretched. "Anybody who needs a break for church take it. We'll reconvene after lunch."

"Y'all are invited to Faith and Hope Community Church." Max's gaze swept the room. "We have services at 8:15, 9:45, and 11:15 a.m. And we always have cookies—lots of cookies."

No one spoke. Billy and Siebert edged toward the door. The others followed.

Teagan grabbed her dad's hand as he walked out. "I want in on those interviews."

"We'll talk later." He kept walking.

"We certainly will," she called after him. "After church."

No response.

"No worries. It's an open invitation." Max's aw-shucks grin made Teagan smile. He shrugged. "At least I know you'll be there."

"You certainly know how to clear a room."

His grin faded, replaced by uncertainty, an emotion Teagan rarely saw on his face. "I need to take a meeting, but I can't see myself going back to that portable right now."

"Call Damon. He'll be able to point you to another one. One that's closer. They'll probably want an officer to go with you." She fought the urge to touch his face, his bruised lips, kiss his forehead. To offer comfort. For him to admit to her his weakness represented another step forward in a relationship deepening despite her best efforts. "The fact that you always choose a meeting over a bar shows how far you've come."

He studied his hands. "I have to be honest with you. I did go to a bar." He raised his head and met her gaze. "I didn't drink, but I came close. I called Damon. That's why I was at the meeting last night."

And the killer was following him. A chill ran through Teagan. She wrapped her arms around her middle and tried for a smile. "A good choice. I'm sorry for all this. It wouldn't be happening if you weren't my friend."

"Oh, Teagan." He closed his eyes and opened them. "Bad stuff happens to people. You know that. A faith not tested is a weak faith. I have to be able to live life in all its messiness without resorting to a crutch."

"So call Damon."

His hand stole across the table. His fingers entwined with hers. "Eat something. You look haggard. Take a nap. You're safe here." He raised her hand to his lips and kissed her fingers. She didn't resist. She simply couldn't. His touch, so long denied, sent a host of tremors through her.

He smiled as if reading her thoughts. "Don't back away, please."

"Max."

"I'll see you later. Tell your dad I appreciate him letting me stay here."

"I will."

He gave the back of her hand one last kiss and left.

Teagan didn't move. Her legs were too weak to hold her. Her heartbeat refused to slow. The movie playing in her head featured her sitting on her back porch with Max at her side. They were drinking fresh-squeezed lemonade. He had his arm around her. They were counting the hummingbirds at the feeders.

It came to a screeching halt when a little girl with carrot hair toddled across the yard pushing a play mower.

22

The crush of worshipers at Faith and Community Church's early service Sunday morning felt like home. Teagan sank onto the pew after Rick's benediction and listened to the Faith Band's final playful notes of "How Great Is Our God" before she rose to join the flow of friends who'd become family in the two years she attended church here. No matter how dire the circumstances, a person went to church on Sunday morning.

Even after all these years, her mother's voice echoed in her ears. *"Teagan Catherine O'Rourke, I don't care how late you sneaked around reading your book under the covers with a flashlight, get your buns out of that bed."*

Her scent of Dove soap and Charlie cologne wafted on the air, like a hug from the past.

Max had already left for church when she dragged herself down the stairs to the kitchen at six thirty. He and the other staff members gathered early for prayer before the first service. How had he slept in Billy's old room down the hall from hers? Probably as well as she had. Fitful dozing and dark, broody nightmares between long bouts of staring at the ceiling.

"Hi, Teagan, how are you doing?" The elderly lady's syrupy tone matched the curious look on her shar-pei face. "We heard about your trouble."

Her trouble? This woman meant well. Teagan sent her irritation packing. "I'm fine. This too shall pass."

"If we can do anything—"

"Pray. That's what I need most. Prayers."

The woman didn't even try to hide her disappointment. "Of course. Our prayer group has you on the email prayer list for marriage and children. We know that biological clock is ticking. *Tick-tock-tick-tock.*"

"I'm not in any hurry. I have a great job and a wonderful family." Normally she wouldn't engage. She knew better. But exhaustion and shredded nerves opened her mouth before her brain could scream *no-o-o-o*. "Not every woman is destined to be a stay-at-home mom with her own children."

The woman's eyes widened until her penciled eyebrows touched the artfully arranged, silver-dyed curls on her forehead. "Oh, honey, I know it's hard not to be sour when the years are passing you by and you hear that *tick-tock-tick-tock* grow louder and louder in your ears. Pray earnestly and God will give you the desires of your heart. Scripture says so."

"According to His plan and in His time." Taking Scripture out of context was one of Teagan's pet peeves. Right now the desire of her heart was to flee. "Thank you. I have to see Pastor Rick. You understand."

"Of course, of course. He is a good counselor."

A good friend who wouldn't push his agenda on her.

When she made it to the front of the line, she shook his hand, but Rick drew her into a quick, fierce hug. "How are you doing?"

"Hanging in there."

"I was hoping the events of the past few days might encourage your family to attend church this morning." Rick never ceased to hope or to pray for Teagan's wayward love ones. "Did you offer an invitation?"

"As usual. The response was something about lightning and God smiting someone."

Rick chuckled. "They didn't get the memo about no one being perfect?"

Aware of the folks behind her waiting for a quick word with the pastor so they could race to their cars and head to Bill Miller's to be first in line for barbecue and sweet tea, she squeezed his hand again and let go. "I'm headed to Sunday school to help Max with the youth."

"He's in a state this morning."

"I imagine he is."

"You'll calm him down?"

"Or stir him up."

"Godspeed."

Teagan threaded her way through the crowded narthex that mixed the contemporary service folks with the mostly older members who would attend the traditional service, dodging and swerving like cars on the busy I-10/410 highway interchange. By the time she ran up the stairs to the second floor of the education building, she was winded and tired.

Not a good state in which to run into Noelle. Three-year-old Ricky Junior, a mini-me of his father, toddled along behind his mom who carried a box filled with crayons, construction paper, toddler scissors, and other alien-looking crafty stuff. "I'm glad you're here. With all that ugliness threatening you, you need to keep your faith tank full."

"Just seeing your face makes me feel better."

Even with a box on her hip, Noelle managed to drop a curtsy in a denim dress with a hem that hung to her shins. "Thank you. Even churches have their little crises. All heck has broken out here now."

Noelle launched into her spiel. The four-year-old class needed a sub. Their teacher was out because her child was projectile vomiting. A vacuum was needed posthaste in the five-year-old class because they'd decided to dump out all the popcorn that was supposed to be used for a craft project. Little Joel had wet his pants, removed his shorts and underpants, and run buck naked down the hallway to the bathroom—apparently an afterthought.

"Where is Kathy?" Kathy being the children's pastor. "Shouldn't she be riding herd on this?"

Pastors' wives often picked up the slack, especially in smaller churches like Hope and Faith, but this seemed a bit extreme.

"She has some sort of stomach bug."

"Aha. Where shall I start?"

"No, no, your mission, should you accept it, is to ride herd on Max. He's looking pretty beat up this morning, and the teens are hopped up on doughnuts, Nutella on white bread, and Big Red. Or Dr Pepper. They picked their poison."

"That's just gross." Teagan wrinkled her nose.

"Or nectar of the gods, depending on who you ask."

Ricky Junior took that moment to wail. Noelle handed the box to Teagan and picked up her youngest. The move gave Teagan a better view of the normally svelte woman's protruding belly. "Are you expecting again?"

The words popped out. Probably not PC to ask before the information was volunteered. Maybe she'd eaten too much of her own scrumptious cooking.

Noelle grinned as she snuggled Ricky Junior. "I am. We're gluttons for punishment. I love my boys, but I really want another girl. Don't tell them I said so." Her grin faded. "Rick told me about your conversation the other night in the hospital. I'm sorry. He can be such a horse's patootie. I'm sorry about Mrs. Conklin and the police officer. If you ever want to talk, I'm here."

"I'm fine, hanging in there, all that stuff." Teagan stifled the urge to pinch Ricky's chunky cheeks as Noelle nuzzled his dark curls with her chin. What would it be like to hold your own baby? Read *Fancy Nancy* books over and over? Play ring-around-the-rosy? Run through the sprinkler screaming? Sing the "Alphabet Song" forty times and then sing it again? "Do you think I'm wrong?"

"About having children?" She hitched Ricky onto one hip and held out her hand for the box, which she balanced on her other hip. "I think you would be a fabulous mom. It makes me sad to think of what you'll miss. But I respect your decision, and I know it's one only you can make. You and the man you love. I know one who would be perfect for the job. He's right down the hall."

"We're only friends. Good friends. That's all we can ever be. Max deserves to have his greatest wish."

"God is good and He is mighty. Sometimes we simply have to stand back and let Him do His thing. He surprises me every single day."

"Are you sure you shouldn't be the one doing the preaching?" Teagan smiled despite the pang her friend's words caused.

"My plate is full." Grinning, Noelle hustled past Teagan, then paused to look back from the top of the stairs. "Neil and Jana just adopted their second little girl—the one they've been fostering. There are so many unwanted children who desperately need homes. They're already here, brought into this messed-up world by messed-up parents. They need forever homes and loving parents who take seriously the state of this world they'll inherit. Just a thought." She disappeared down the stairs.

So much for not trying to influence her decision. Teagan shook her head and laughed. They said it took a village to raise a child. Faith and Hope Community Church certainly had that one figured out.

The humor in the situation didn't obscure the sad accuracy of Noelle's words. The Texas foster care system desperately needed parents willing to do a hard, heart-wrenching job loving children who'd been failed by their own families.

Not now. Not today. Teagan batted the thoughts away. Her brain couldn't take another angst-filled issue today—nor could her heart.

She ducked into the double classroom that served as home base for the sixth grade through high school Sunday school classes. They would start here, then divide up into their grades for small-group lessons. Tables and chairs crowded the room. Someone had written JESUS REIGNS in big pink letters with a heart over the I on the dry erase board.

Max sat on a wooden stool, acoustic guitar in hand, his gaze fixed on sheet music on a stand in front of him. Bruises in an array of colors decorated his face. He plucked several notes and winced. No doubt every muscle in his battered body hurt. Two of his high schoolers stood nearby, their guitars at the ready.

"You guys have been practicing."

"Are you sure you're okay?" Odie Needham asked. "We can lead the song if you want to rest. I can get you a soda and Pop-Tarts."

"If I rest any more, I'll roll over and die." Max grinned to show he was kidding. "Thanks for the offer, but I drank two Dr Peppers for breakfast. Any more and I'll have the shakes."

"We heard what happened and we weren't sure you'd be here today," Jess Wampler added. "We could lead the open, you know."

"I have absolute faith in you two. In fact, I'll take you up on it. Odie, you lead the prayer. The two of you can handle the two songs, and then I'll chip in with the announcements and breaking up into groups. Sound like a plan?"

Their expressions reflecting their desire to please, the boys nodded.

Max had such an easy way with kids. It didn't matter their age. Whether it was nurturing sixth graders still shell-shocked from starting middle school or navigating the scary landscape of eighth graders caught exploring their sexuality in the prayer garden. Not to mention the constant battering from a world where society now normalized behaviors far beyond what Scripture called godly. How did kids navigate in a world of social media bullying, sexting, more than fifty gender choices, and myriad drugs available for numbing the pain? Max covered it all, with relieved appreciation from most parents who were kept in the loop every step of the way.

Here more than anywhere else, Teagan stood in awe of this man. His weaknesses, his experiences, and his innate talents combined in a way that God could use him right here and now.

His gaze traveled beyond the boys for the first time. When it reached her, he smiled. She smiled back. He stood, weaved slightly, and laid the guitar on his stool. "Take five, guys."

Odie glanced around. He saw Teagan and gave her a knowing grin. "Sure, Preach."

The kids insisted on calling Max that even though he insisted he was no preacher. Just a guy with a guitar.

The boys clomped out with the obligatory salutations of, "Hey, Miss T."

"Hi, guys." Teagan waited until they were gone to turn back to Max. "Hey."

"Hey."

The silence stretched.

Who started it wasn't entirely clear, but a few seconds later Teagan found herself locked in a crushing embrace.

"How did you sleep?" His breath tickled her cheek. "You looked tired."

"I didn't."

"Me neither." Did he lay in his bed aching to feel her body next to his? Teagan swallowed the question. "I'm terrified and angry and disgusted and I feel helpless. I don't like feeling this way. I hate it."

"I'm here and I'm not going anywhere." Fierce emotion blazed a path across Max's face. "You can count on me."

His hands rubbed her bare arms. Goose bumps rippled in their wake. The heat in his eyes singed her skin. Her gaze found his lips. She fought to look away but couldn't.

He leaned in.

She swallowed against the sudden rush of desire that pulsed through her body. "We can't."

"We can work this out," he whispered. "What are you so afraid of? Is it my past? I can understand that—"

"This is not the time for this discussion." Teagan tore her gaze from his lips. "We're in the middle of a crisis. Our emotions are all over the place."

"The way I feel about you isn't going to change. Tell me you don't feel the same way about me and I'll back off. I'll stay away from you."

"That's exactly what I don't want to happen. I don't want to lose your friendship. I can't."

"Here's the deal. I love you and I'm worried about you and I want to keep you safe." His hands cupped her face, then worked their way down her shoulders and her arms. "So there it is. I know you can take care of yourself, but I want the job. Maybe you can see your way to letting me do that."

"I don't want kids."

Finally. The truth revealed. Relief danced with fear.

Max's hands fell away. Disbelief washed over his chiseled face. "What?"

"I decided a long time ago not to have kids." The desire to take the words back warred with relief at having this boulder of an obstacle out in the open. "I should've told you before, but I couldn't bear to see that look on your face, the one I'm seeing right now."

"How is that possible? If any woman in the world would be a good, nurturing mother, it's you." His voice cracked. His body stiff, he took one step back. "You play mother to your brother and sisters. You always have. You mother the kids in youth group. You babysit Rick's kids."

"It's not the same. I won't bring babies into this world."

"How can you not?" Disbelief turned to desolation followed closely by despair. "All kinds of women have babies who shouldn't. You, on the other hand, have motherhood written all over you."

"The world is a cesspool. It's imploding on itself. It's a grotesque caricature of what God intended it to be."

"You think God doesn't know that?" Max's voice rose. He stopped, the struggle to gain control obvious. "You think he's not in charge right now, in this moment?"

"We're destroying the planet. What will be left for our grandchildren and their children?"

"Have a little faith, woman."

"I do have faith. I also have the brains God gave me. I understand what's at stake." She managed to bring her own voice down a few decibels. "I care about you, Max, very much, but I also know I'm right about this."

"We'll have to agree to disagree on that." The muscle in his jaw pulsed. His voice turned raspy. "God will never give up on His creation. He'll never give up on the human race. I'm not giving up on us."

"I won't let you give up on your dream of having children."

"Do you trust me just as I am: a drunk, an addict?"

"I trust you more than anyone in the world. I want this to work out. I've always wanted it to work out. I just can't see how it can."

Max licked his cracked, bruised lips. He heaved a fractured breath. "It's a back burner issue until we stop this murdering psychopath. Agreed?"

Nothing would be different then. "Agreed, but I won't change my mind."

"Back burner."

"Okay."

His gaze never leaving hers, Max picked up his guitar and plucked a single note. "We're in this together."

"Together."

Setting aside her fears for the future to focus on today. One day at a time. The way Max lived his life as an alcoholic. Having faith. "I'd like for you to stay at my house for the duration of this crazy nightmare. If you want to, that is."

The sudden decision sent a shock wave through Teagan. She'd made it despite herself. "If you don't want to, I totally understand, but I'm going home to my house. My stepmother will be back from Vegas tomorrow and I don't want to be in her way. You shouldn't be alone in your house. What do you think?"

"I can do that."

"Are you sure?"

"Back burner." As much as he kept saying that, Max's expression spoke of something different.

His dreams for the future were crushed and she was responsible.

23

Two funerals in two days had turned the world into a dreary place despite South Texas's May sunshine. Teagan threaded her way through a crowd of familiar faces in Evelyn's modest home. If the pomp and circumstance of Kristen Moreno's funeral had reflected a short life filled with service to her country and her city, Evelyn's funeral one day later reflected the elder woman's life. Planned, frugal, and simple.

The reception at her home was much the same. Teagan accepted the tall glass of iced sweet tea Max offered her, raised it to him in a silent *cheers*, and sipped in the dead woman's honor. The cold liquid did little to dislodge the knot in her throat. It had been there since she woke up at four o'clock to contemplate a day in which they would say good-bye to a woman who epitomized the word *neighbor*.

With everything planned and paid for in advance, it hadn't taken Evelyn's children long to schedule the memorial service at the Baptist church Evelyn had attended for the past forty years, followed by a reception at her house. It seemed strange to be in her house without her. Her grandchildren ate cake under the watchful eyes of her daughter and daughter-in-law.

Her son-in-law walked around openly staring at pieces of furniture. Teagan could almost see the dollar signs clicking in his head as he added up the sale of her antique curio cabinet and the contents, including a complete mix-and-match set of vintage Fiesta dinnerware from the late 1930s, a walnut dining room table and eight chairs made by his father-in-law, a grandfather clock inherited from Evelyn's parents, and an antique rolltop desk of unknown origins.

"Is he for real?" Teagan muttered as she reached for a brownie, one of a dozen desserts displayed on a table in the living room. Evelyn's favorites—key lime pie, chocolate pudding cake, and strawberry-rhubarb pie—were nearly depleted by now. Teagan could get behind a funeral reception featuring nothing but desserts. "She hasn't been in the ground for a full hour."

Before Max could respond, Oscar Benavides leaned between them and picked up a flowered paper plate. "Aren't those the detectives investigating Evelyn's murder?" He nodded toward Justin and Alisha, who had been among the early arrivals at both the funeral and the reception. "Isn't it a dime store detective novel cliché to think the killer will show up at the funeral? Or do they still think it's one of us?"

Justin, Alisha, Siebert, and his partner were making the rounds, with studiously casual looks on their faces. They weren't fooling anyone.

"They're just being thorough. We all want that for Evelyn, don't we?" Revealing the details of the investigation to Oscar or any of her neighbors would be a no-no. Her neighbors, who were in danger because of a killer's fixation with Teagan, were not murderers. Justin didn't know them the way she did. He hadn't eaten their tamales on Christmas Eve and walked the block admiring the luminarias that lined the sidewalks in each yard. If they didn't have unshakable alibis, it was because it never occurred to them they would need them. "I'm sorry if they were overzealous with you."

"Don't apologize." Oscar toasted Teagan with his dessert plate. "Jousting with your buddies was the most fun I've had in a while."

No doubt. Oscar liked to think of himself as a keen intellectual.

Teagan cocked her head toward the less crowded dining room.

Max nodded. They edged away. Oscar dropped a brownie and two lemon bars on his plate and scurried after them. Carlos Chavez did the same. They were dressed like twins in black jeans, black T-shirts, and black suit coats. Sneakers had been replaced by slick patent leather loafers. There the housemates' similarities ended. While Oscar was young and pretty, Carlos had a grizzled salt-and-pepper beard and flowing silver hair. He was at least twenty years older than his friend. And chunky to Oscar's svelte.

"What happened to you, *mi amigo*? I know you like to box, but you look like you made a mistake and got in the ring with a heavy-weight." Oscar *tut-tutted* in a way so like Mom's, Teagan's heart winced. "You were in Evelyn's backyard with the killer. Did he do that to you?"

Shaking his head, Max glanced at Teagan. Everyone on the team agreed that the incident with Max's truck and its connection to the murders would not be disclosed. It was a double-edged sword. Giving the killer the notoriety he wanted could stoke his desire for more. Not giving it to him could push him to kill again and again until his trail of carnage could no longer be denied as that of a serial killer.

A no-win situation.

"I had an accident, but I'm okay."

"*Gracias a Dios*. I heard they think our neighborhood is being targeted." Carlos let his pie-filled fork hover halfway between his plate and mouth. "The police interviewed everybody—even Araceli Cavazos, and she never leaves her house."

Araceli Cavazos, San Antonio's current poet laureate and some-times novelist, played the part of introvert–hermit–creative genius well. She had her groceries delivered and only ventured out of her hot-pink cottage long enough to collect her mail or stand on the porch and call her two matching tabby cats home for supper.

"She weighs ninety pounds sopping wet, and the heaviest thing she lifts is a large glass of vino." Stephanie Nixon shook her head at the apparent idiocy of San Antonio's finest. "Evelyn would have made mincemeat of her."

"Do we really think the murderer was one of us?" *One of us* being the neighbors in this close-knit community. Oscar had the same bloodthirsty expression on his face that he did when he selected a James Lee Burke murder mystery from her curbside library. "We're all so civilized, at least on the surface."

His face brightening, he stabbed his plastic fork in the air as if it were a weapon. "How about Cole? He is kind of quiet, but *muy hermoso*. Still waters run deep. And he doesn't mix much. He didn't even attend the Fourth of July *pachanga*."

Carlos elbowed his friend. "That's how rumors get started, *hombre*. The guy was out of town over the Fourth last year. He's an instructor. He has a chocolate Lab named Huck, and he has a cute girlfriend. I've seen her leaving the house several times. Model thin, nice hair, big brown eyes."

"What reason would a community college instructor have for bludgeoning Mrs. Conklin? She fed Huck doggie treats all the time. The dog doted on her." Stephanie frowned at them through blue-and-purple-patterned glass frames. She wore a simple black sheath in a shimmering material that didn't try to hide the fact that she was pregnant again. "My money's on Jamison Fargo."

They were such innocents. They still thought murderers had rational motives for murder. Sometimes—often—murders were simply senseless. What if the killer decided to make one of them his next target?

Acid burned Teagan's stomach. She shouldn't be here. Even with three detectives in the house, her simple presence put her neighbors in danger.

Teagan cocked her head toward the door. Max shook his head. They should listen. Her neighbors might know something without even knowing it. That's what he was thinking. She took another long draught of her tea and worked to keep her expression bland.

"Why Jamison?" Max gently nudged the conversation along. "He seems like a decent guy."

Jamison Fargo had a craft beer brewery with an adjacent beer garden beloved among the SoFlo Market vendors and customers who liked to binge on vintage goods, handcrafts, and local art. Sitting outside on a spring night listening to live jazz and drinking craft beer after shopping at the market was the epitome of the Southtown experience.

"He and Evelyn had a throwdown. Didn't you hear?" Oscar's dark eyes lit up with the excitement of knowing something Max and Teagan didn't. "They were feuding over him coming home late at night and letting his muscle car motor rip. He kept waking her up. And then his boxers, who often spent long days in his backyard, would bark when he pulled into his driveway."

Teagan shrugged. "I guess I'm too tired at night to hear either one."

"Old people are light sleepers," Carlos offered. "I should know."

"You're not old, amigo." Oscar elbowed him. "Just aging like fine wine."

"Hopefully that's true for all of us." Max tossed his empty plate into a wastebasket near the small upright piano that stood in one corner of the dining room. Evelyn's husband had played. She didn't, but she never sold his piano. "A noise dispute can get ugly. People have been killed for less."

"Do you really think Mr. Cool stabbed Evelyn in a fit of anger because she threatened to make a noise complaint to the city?" Carlos snorted and rolled his eyes. "The guy is a glacier."

"He blew a gasket when the guys repainting his house didn't allow for the wind that caused the spray to reach his car." Oscar's words dripped with disdain. "He was the opposite of cool. Cool dudes don't have meltdowns in public. He was screaming at them and pitching a fit like *un niño*."

"I don't blame him. That Impala is a classic." Carlos feigned sadness while he contemplated a large slice of pecan pie on his plate. "Having it repainted would have been a nightmare."

"Okay, so he's got a temper." Max brought the conversation back to the topic at hand. "That doesn't make him a murderer."

Their voices drifted far away. They sounded hollow and distant like they stood inside a huge tin can. Evelyn was no longer aging like fine wine. She was dead, but not over a loud engine and dogs barking. She was dead because of something Teagan had done. Or so a brutal murderer with a warped sense of humor wanted her to believe. Here they stood in Evelyn's house cavalierly discussing who her killer might be when all of this was Teagan's fault. If only she knew what she'd done, then she'd know who did it. She tossed her plate on top of Max's and turned away.

"Where are you going?" Max made as if to follow her. "Are you all right?"

"I just need some air. I'll be back."

"Are you sure?" His words and his gaze wrapped her in soft, warm shawl. "You look green around the gills."

"Something I ate."

Or something she did.

But what?

Unanswered questions pestered her like a cloud of ornery, biting gnats as she dodged her way around the clusters of people who stood talking and drinking Evelyn's favorite mint juleps served on the Fourth of July or the sangria she offered on New Year's Eve.

Teagan's throat ached with unshed tears. *"O'Rourke women do not cry in public. If we have to bawl, we do it in the privacy of our bathrooms."* Her mom's voice, sharp yet kind, echoed in her ears. *If only you were here, Mom. I could use your help.*

Facing the family photos that hung on the walls of the hallway, she edged toward the door. An old ten-by-twelve of Evelyn with her husband, Dr. Kenny Conklin, caught her eye. Evelyn wore a fifties-style dress with a belt around the waist and full skirt. She was tall, slim, with long chestnut brown hair. They were in their early twenties when he would've been finishing medical school and she had just finished her degree in education.

"You're Teagan. Mom's neighbor, right?" Robin approached. She was the spitting image of the woman in the photo, except her brown hair was cut in a short bob and her eyes were bloodshot, but her voice held steady. "She talked about you a lot. She said you were a good neighbor."

"I'm glad she thought so."

Her eyebrows high, forehead wrinkled, Robin stared at the photos. "I'm not sure how she'd feel if she knew her murder had something to do with you."

The verbal knife came out of nowhere. Teagan's hand went to her chest as if the hilt might be sticking out. "I'm sorry. So sorry. The police are doing everything they can to find the killer. I promise."

"So they tell me." Now her voice quivered. "From what the neighbors say, you're related to half of them."

"It only seems that way."

"I know it's not your fault. I'm trying to understand. I can't understand." She wiped her red nose with a sodden tissue. "Who would stab a sweet old lady? Who would do that? How would killing my mother prove a point with you?"

"It wouldn't. We don't truly understand how the minds of psychopaths work. As rational, decent human beings, as Christians, we can't begin to understand not having a moral compass."

"I'm not sure I qualify anymore as a decent Christian human being. I'm not sure I can believe in a God who lets that happen." Her half sob broke Teagan's heart. "I'm surer that I would gladly take the knife that killed my mom and plunge into the heart of the worthless bag of garbage who did this to her."

Evil could not win again. *Please God, don't let evil take Evelyn from this life and destroy her daughter's faith.* She would need it desperately in the days to come. "Give yourself time to grieve. Please. Then talk to your pastor. Don't let the man who killed your mother take your faith too. Don't let him win."

Robin's face crumpled. She began to sob. Teagan folded her into her arms. "I'm so, so sorry."

"She's gone. I can't believe she's really gone."

"Me either." Teagan rubbed her back and whispered words of comfort meant for both of them. "It might not seem like it, but eventually you'll breathe again. You'll be able to think of her and recall wonderful memories. With time."

"Mommy? Mommy?"

A little girl with chubby cheeks and her mother's hair color tugged on Robin's dress. She had chocolate smeared on her face. "I want milk. Can I have milk?"

Robin scooped her up. "She keeps asking me were Nana is. Mom won't get to see her learn to ride a bike or go to her first dance. My baby probably won't even remember her."

A hard truth. "She's beautiful."

"And she deserves to have a grandmother to spoil her."

"No one would argue with that."

Robin's husband finally materialized, their son in tow. He also had chocolate all over his face. "Your children have been stealing from the dessert table." He apparently spoke before taking a good look at his wife's face. After a second, he put his arm around her and nodded at Teagan. "Excuse us, will you? It's been a rough day."

Teagan's day had been rough, but not nearly as bad as this family's. Evelyn's son-in-law gently led Robin into the interior of the house. She grabbed the mantel to keep from swaying. Grief, even that which was once removed, took its toll. She edged toward the door.

"Headed out?"

The voice was deep and musical like a southern preacher's. She jumped and turned.

"Sorry, I didn't mean to startle you." A pipe-cleaner-thin man in a baggy gray suit touched her arm before Teagan could get the front door open. "I wanted to catch you before you go."

"I'm getting some air," she offered. "I'll be back in a minute."

"I'm Robert Sandoval, Mrs. Conklin's attorney." He tugged a business card from an inside pocket and handed it to her. "I wanted to let you know that you're invited to the will reading. Both you and Mr. Kennedy."

"Are you serious?"

"As serious as fireworks on the Fourth of July, Ms. O'Rourke." He smiled, but genuine sadness filled his words. "Mrs. Conklin left small bequests to both of you. The timing of the reading has yet to be established. A couple of family members weren't able to be here for the funeral but were remembered in her will. Her children are staying in town to go through her things, set up an estate sale, and put the house on the market, once it's been read. I'll call you when the date and time are confirmed, if you'll share that information with Mr. Kennedy."

"I will. I'm surprised. I don't know what to say."

"I drew up the will for her. She liked you and Mr. Kennedy. She said you were good people. That is high praise from her."

Indeed it was. "Thank you for letting me know."

"We'll be in touch."

What a sweet woman. The tears ganged up on Teagan and pushed against the barricades. She pushed through the screen door and let it close behind her. The dank midafternoon air felt cooler on her skin than the sticky, people-warmed air inside the house. She raised her face to the afternoon sun. South Texas spring was fleet of foot. Soon summer's steamy days with one-hundred-plus-degree weather would drive people indoors most afternoons.

People liked to complain about San Antonio weather. Not Teagan. She wanted it to seep into her bones and force the coldness that invaded them during Evelyn's funeral to leave and never come back.

"You look like you could use a stiff drink."

Teagan forced her gaze from the baby-blue sky to the man standing at the end of the sidewalk. Cole Reynolds held up a foil-covered casserole dish. "Dana Holl told me Mrs. Conklin's children and grandchildren are staying here for a few days, so I threw together a lasagna and brought it over."

"You threw together lasagna?" Teagan trudged down the steps to join him on the sidewalk. "That's a neat trick most people can't master."

"I'm pretty handy around the kitchen." He wiggled his bent arm, from which hung a H.E.B. reusable grocery bag. "Breadsticks and a salad to go with it."

His girlfriend was a lucky woman. "Nice. I'm sure they'll appreciate it."

"You look done in."

"It's been a long few days."

"If there's anything I can do to help, let me know." His empathetic smile made the skin around his eyes crinkle. Warm eyes. "I've been told I'm a good listener."

"Thank you. I appreciate that, but I'm sure the last thing you expected when you moved into this neighborhood was to find yourself touched by the murder of an elderly woman."

He ducked his head. "It's so sad, isn't it? This stuff happens everywhere. It's unbelievable. One of my students was murdered by her boyfriend last year. There's no escaping it."

"It seems that way." Teagan returned his smile. "It's kind of you to think of Evelyn's children. It's been rough on them."

"Could you do me a favor?" He held out the dish again. "I don't want to intrude. I didn't know Mrs. Conklin well, although she always had a treat for Huck. It seems presumptuous for me to barge in in the middle of the wake. Deliver this with my condolences?"

"Are you sure?"

"Please. I was just going to leave it on the bench there by the door, and then you came out."

"I'm happy to do it."

He handed over the lasagna, hot pads still in place, and the bag of sides with a small flourish. "I hope you feel better. Like I said, I'm always available to listen."

"Thanks. I'll let them know to return your dishes and hot pads to you."

"No rush." He did an about-face and headed toward his house. He had a leisurely stride that said he didn't care who watched his progress.

Teagan stood there for a few minutes enjoying the quiet. He looked back once and waved. Her hands were full but she nodded. What a nice man. *Nice* was such an innocuous word. But in the midst of this horrifying season, nice felt good. So would average and ordinary. The more trauma she faced, the more she valued ordinary, everyday life.

"What are you doing?"

She jumped, nearly dropped the dish, and whirled toward the house.

Justin stood at the door. "You shouldn't be standing outside by yourself. Come inside."

"You scared me."

"You should be scared. A psychopath is toying with you. Get in here."

"I wish he'd just get it over with." She stormed up the steps. "I'm ready for him."

Justin's frown grew into a scowl. "Be careful what you wish for."

"I wish for peace—"

Justin's cell phone buzzed like an angry cricket. He held up his finger and answered.

"Uh-huh. On our way."

"What is it?"

Justin grabbed her arm and propelled her down the steps. "When was the last time you drove your car?"

"It's been days. You guys won't let me go anywhere on my own. Why?"

"Billy found a letter under your windshield wiper."

The killer was relentless. And brazen. "How is that possible? He simply sashayed up to my car and left me a note?"

"You've been gone a lot. It's not like we watch your house when no one's there."

Teagan skipped like a little kid to keep up with Justin. "I hate this."

"You and me both, Sis."

Billy stood in Teagan's driveway, cussing a steady stream. Gracie pulled out her cell phone and thumbed a message.

The letter lay on the hood of the car. Hands behind her back, Teagan leaned closer for a better look.

Dear T,

> You just don't get it.
> This will not stop.
> I will not stop.
> Not until I have you.
> The two of us shall dance.
> I'll have my due.

Your family will suffer as mine has.

Then it will be done.

My way.

See you soon.

> Your friend,
> Amos Redding

She straightened, did an about-face, and concentrated on breathing in and out.

"CSU is on the way." Gracie slid her arm around Teagan. "We need to know. What's the reference this time?"

Teagan pulled away. "This one's different. In *Dead or Not* Amos Redding plays a cat-and-mouse game with Jay Southerland. Redding is a psychiatrist. He's smart and violent. He kidnaps a patient and her family. It's brutal."

"Not technically a serial killer."

"No, a kidnapper who's into psychological torture. Which is what this guy is doing to me, isn't it?" She gritted her teeth and gripped her hands together so hard her fingers hurt. *Keep it together. Come on, don't give in to him.*

"He wants you to be scared." Her expression fierce, Gracie put her hands on her hips. "He wants to control you. Don't give him what he wants."

"I have no intention of giving him control."

How long could she hold out?

24

After the emotional firestorm of the funerals, it felt good to know this day would be dedicated to finding the culprit responsible for them. Teagan, fully dressed and made up, whipped into the kitchen to fill her travel mug with coffee. Dad would stop by to pick her up in five or ten minutes, and she didn't plan to keep him waiting. He would need very little excuse to interview Slocum's co-workers without her. The kitchen was empty. No Max. His beloved SAC music station was silent. "Max?"

No answer. Teagan shook a mental finger at her disappointment. No getting used to his presence in the morning to greet her with the coffeepot full and bagels in the toaster. Max was one of those people who arose in the morning determined to make the best and most of every day, no matter the circumstances. The pot was half full this morning, and a bagel laden with strawberry cream cheese sat on a saucer next to it. A yellow sticky note featured a smiley face and Max's crazy signature. He made it hard not to imagine many more such days like this one.

Teagan went to the kitchen sink to wipe down her travel mug, then glanced out the window. Max, wearing a sleeveless T-shirt and basketball shorts, had the hood up on her car under the carport. He'd switched his youth minister hat for his mechanic hat. She hugged Tigger, told herself to behave, grabbed her purse and mug, and bolted out the door.

Max didn't hear her approach. She allowed herself a minute to ogle him like a teenage girl. Yes, she loved him for his mind, but she also enjoyed the biceps and burly shoulders. If only she could give him his heart's desire. Waving her fingers in an attempt to cool her face, she cleared her throat. "What are you doing?"

Max straightened and wiped his hands on an already greasy rag. "Just making sure everything is in tip-top condition."

"I thought you didn't work on hybrids."

"I don't." He shut the hood with a sure touch. "But I know enough to make sure your brakes are in good working order and nothing looks out of a whack."

"Thank you." Teagan forced herself to glance toward the street. Dad would be here any minute. Max's dedication to her safety covered everything from prayer to the practical. And he looked so hot doing it. "You'll be late to work."

"I texted Rick. He knows what I'm up to and gave his approval, 100 percent." Max moved from the driveway to where she stood on the porch. "He told me to take all the time I need."

"What did he say about you staying here?"

"To behave myself."

Exactly what she kept telling herself. Heat once again toasted Teagan's cheeks. "Dad's on his way."

"How about if I make us some supper tonight?"

So far they'd done takeout, delivery, and PB and J sandwiches. They were playing house together. It felt good. How would it feel when the nightmare ended and that issue on the back burner suddenly moved front and center? "You don't have to. I can pick up Thai on the way back."

"Don't do that." Max stepped into her space. He smelled of grease and man sweat. What would it be like to fall into those simmering amber eyes? To run her hands through his sandy-brown hair? He smiled. "Let us have these moments. Let us see how we fit together beyond ball games and mission projects. Trust me, okay?"

"Why are you subjecting yourself to this? This torture?"

"Because you asked me to." His lopsided smile turned sardonic. "Because I want you to know what you'll be missing if you take the easy way out."

"The easy way out? There's nothing easy about this."

"I'm asking you to trust God."

"Where was God when my mother died?"

Max raised his hands toward the sky. "He held her hand and escorted her to the throne."

"I was nine."

"And you've been honed by the fire. There's nothing He can't make good come from."

Teagan stared up at the June sky. Who would she have been had her mother lived? How would her life have been different? Gracie, Billy, and Leyla's lives? Justin's?

"Take a shower." She inhaled his scent one more time and scooted back. "Go to work. You have the mission trip with the kids to plan."

"I'm ready. For the mission trip and for anything else that comes my way."

Dad pulled up to the curb and honked.

Saved by the bell. "See you tonight."

"Be careful."

She scampered to the Charger and slid in without looking back.

"Y'all are looking very cozy this morning." Dad sipped from his travel mug and grimaced. "I'm glad he's keeping an eye on you, but I'm thinking about offering him a tent for your backyard."

"We're just friends. That's all we can ever be."

Dad rolled his eyes. "Uh-huh."

"Good friends."

"Whatever you say, sweetie." He had the audacity to wink at her. "Haven't you heard that love overcomes all obstacles?"

"So what do we know about Slocum's coworker?"

Dad chose to accept her attempt at redirection and spent the short drive up 281 North telling her about the pharmaceutical company where Slocum worked until his arrest for the murder of Olivia Jimenez.

Rayburn, Leo Slocum's former coworker, looked like Rupert Grint of *Harry Potter* movie fame who'd morphed into a middle-aged man with a receding hairline and a beer gut. He didn't have the endearing British accent, but he did have the red hair, dimples, and blue eyes. He also seemed to have trouble meeting Teagan's or her father's gaze head-on. He welcomed them into his office on the third floor of a nondescript building on 281 North and Jones-Maltsberger, where he offered them bottled water or coffee—both of them declined.

"Why ask me about Leo now?" He leaned back in a sleek ergonomic office chair that squeaked under his weight. "He's in prison, isn't he?"

"I write true crime stories, and I'm following up on some background information on his life. I'm just trying to get a true picture of what he was like." Dad's blithe ability to spread the truth so thin begged the question of how often he had done that with family, particularly Jazz, who didn't care for his crime "hobbies." "How long did y'all work together?"

"Almost thirty years. We were like eggs and bacon, chips and salsa of ocular-specialty drugs. At least I thought we were. We played on the company's softball team together. Played in darts competitions. If there was something hinky about this guy, I never knew it."

"What was he like at work?"

"Easygoing. Always telling stories. Liked to play practical jokes." Rayburn rose and went to a framed twelve-by-seventeen photo on a wall covered with sales awards and certificates of appreciation for his volunteer efforts. Light from the floor-to-ceiling windows that looked down on one of the most congested highways in town bounced off the glass, making it hard to see the faces.

Teagan stood and followed him. He tilted the photo so she could see. A bunch of laughing people with leis around their necks and umbrella drinks in their hands crowded together at a Hawaiian luau, complete with a pig on a spit. "He was the life of the party. This was a couple of years ago when all the top salespeople across the country won trips to Maui with their bonuses. He always won top salesman. Everybody liked him. You could've knocked me over with a feather when I found out he'd been arrested."

"He never did or said anything that led you to believe he might be hiding odd proclivities?"

"Are you kidding? He brought his daughter's Girl Scout cookie order sheet to work so we could buy Thin Mints and Samoas from her." Rayburn shook his head. "He took off work to do the camping thing with his son. He was in the running for Father of the Year. He made the rest of us look bad."

"How about Husband of the Year? I don't think that's his wife in this photo." Slocum had his arm around a much younger woman who wore a bikini top, shorts, and not much else. They both had that flushed look of sun and alcoholic fun. Alcohol and business trips often resulted in hanky-panky, even for people who steadfastly believed they would never betray their spouses. "How did he rank in that respect?"

"Diana stayed back to take care of the kids. She was a teacher. She didn't come to a lot of functions because of work. At least that's what Leo said." Rayburn's smile faded. "Women liked him—what can I say?"

"You can tell us whether he liked them back." Teagan turned to face him. "He spent a lot of time away from home, night after night, week after week, year after year. I imagine that would take its toll on a marriage."

"For all of us." Rayburn held up his left hand. It bore no ring. "I'm twice divorced myself. My wives liked the commissions. They liked

205

the bonuses. But they still complained ad nauseam about the travel. As if they didn't know what they were signing up for."

"Was it the travel that bothered them or the extracurricular activities?"

Dad's tone held no judgment, but rosy spots bloomed on Rayburn's typical redhead's white cheeks. "Hey, Leo might have been into having a soft place to fall in every city, but I'm not that kind of guy. In fact, I liked the quiet hotel room and not having to listen to my wife gripe about stuff—"

"So Slocum told you he had women on the side?"

"Mostly one-night stands he picked up in clubs, I think." His flush deepened. "He didn't brag about it. Nothing like that. I heard him on the phone a couple of times and I teased him a little. He admitted he played around some, but he said it was only because his wife was an ice queen. He wasn't getting what he needed at home."

A far cry from the picture painted by Chase Slocum of late-night slow dances to Frank Sinatra tunes. "Nice."

"I didn't say I agreed with it. I'm just repeating what he told me." Rayburn returned to his standard gray metal desk, where he picked up a letter opener that ended in a ceramic pink flamingo. He fiddled with it, his chubby face distorted as if thinking so hard hurt. "There was one woman, though, who wasn't a one-night stand. This was years ago, mind you, but I'll never forget it because he had such a cow about me answering his phone. He'd never cared before."

"How do you know she wasn't a one-night stand?"

"I picked up his phone sometimes when he wasn't around. She would ask for him. I took a message."

"Maybe she was family."

"I don't think so, because Leo was too angry about my so-called meddling. He told me I had no business answering his phone. I apologized up one side and down the other. The guy never got mad."

"What exactly did she say?"

"Once it was just to please have him call her. The next time she said to tell him she needed help. Money. That the kid was sick."

"The kid."

"Yep. Freaked me out too. He obviously was PO'd that I knew about this woman and this kid. I asked him what the deal was and he had a meltdown."

"What was her name? Where was she calling from?"

"Oh man. We're talking twenty-five or more years ago."

"It's important."

Ruminating, he stared out the floor-to-ceiling windows that faced 281 and the Quarry Market. "DeeDee, Diane, Debbie, D . . ." He rubbed his face with both hands, then pointed at Teagan. "Deidre. Deidre Patterson. It was a three-six-one area code."

"Corpus Christi," Teagan and Dad spoke in unison.

"Yeah. Corpus. He always said it was his favorite stop on his route. I thought it was because he loved seafood. Shrimp, lobster, a side of fried pickles, and a cold Dos Equis—that was his favorite meal."

He wouldn't be getting that cuisine in prison. They didn't even do last meal requests on death row anymore.

"Did he ever say anything more about her?"

"Not to me. He did apologize to me a couple of days later. He said she was a cousin bugging him for money."

"You didn't believe him."

"That wasn't the tone of a cousin. No way."

"Anything else about her you can tell us?"

"Nothing. I hadn't even thought about her in years until you asked. Women liked him a lot, but she was the only one who ever called here besides his wife, and she was a sweet lady. I always wished, for her sake, this Deidre was a cousin."

They stood and shook hands. Dad handed Rayburn a card. "If you think of anything else, give me a call."

"Aren't you going to ask me about him getting fired?"

"What?"

His skinny eyebrows popped up, giving him the look of a surprised child. "He didn't tell you law enforcement types?"

"Not a word." Dad looked smooth and suave, but Teagan recognized the telltale signs. Smoke might pour from his ears any second. "Or if he did, it's not in the case file."

"Yeah, they tried to keep it quiet. The boss wouldn't have brought it up, I'm betting."

"Why?" Teagan eased back into the chair. "Surely he knows withholding information would look bad in a murder investigation."

"Jethro is more interested in covering his butt and protecting this company."

"So what happened?"

"I don't dare tell you. I need my job. Just ask Jethro if there were any blemishes on the record of his best salesman. He might not volunteer something, but he won't lie either. He's not stupid."

Maybe not, but a lie of omission didn't make him a genius either.

25

Ten minutes later an administrative assistant ushered them into Jethro Sullivan's office two floors and a world away from Rayburn's cramped office. The tanned, fit president and CEO of the Texas subsidiary of U.S. Ocular Products, one of the largest sellers of ophthalmology products in the country, looked more like a golf pro, despite the smartly cut suit and silky red tie. The practice putting green in the corner of his massive office added to the image, as did sundry photos taken with golfers such as Tiger Woods and Rory McIlroy, along with several trophies.

Sullivan came around the enormous mahogany desk to shake their hands, bringing with him the scent of Polo, the cologne Teagan had given to Max once on a whim. He only wore it on special occasions.

Dad launched the first salvo. "As I told your admin, we're interested in Leo Slocum's work record."

"Why now? The man's been convicted."

Dad ran briefly through the whys and wherefores.

"What exactly do you want to know? Personnel records are confidential."

"What we exactly want to know is whether Slocum was fired, and if so, why, and why didn't you tell the police?"

"They didn't ask. I assumed they knew. Surely they asked Slocum if he was employed. Surely he told them he was unemployed, which begs the question—"

"People who murder tend to lie about all sorts of things," Teagan interjected. "Surely you're aware of that."

"I suppose so. Look, he was a terrific salesman, one of the best I've ever had. No one since has matched his volume." Sullivan scratched his forehead with manicured fingernails. "But I had to let him go because he got a little too friendly with the help. Dumb broad complained. In this *Me Too* era a company doesn't dare ignore that kind of complaint."

"Sexual harassment, you mean?" Teagan wrestled to keep her contempt under control. You could dress a guy up and put him in the corner office, and he would still be a greasy snake charmer. "How do you define 'a little too friendly'?"

"She claimed he touched her inappropriately at a company party—more than once, actually."

"What did Slocum have to say for himself?"

"He apologized. He said he got his signals messed up. That it wouldn't happen again."

"But you still fired him."

"Human Resources did their due diligence. They investigated her complaint and found it had merit, even though the alleged behavior occurred out of the view of everyone at the party. Miss Fancy Pants said she wasn't the only one and there was no way he got his signals mixed up. There were no signals. That just because she's single and his subordinate doesn't mean she has to take that kind of behavior, that the law says the company has to do something about it."

"When was this?"

"About two weeks before he was arrested." Sullivan fingered his tie. "I couldn't believe it when I turned on the six o'clock news and there he was doing the perp walk in front of a bunch of TV cameras. I still can't believe it. He was a good guy—"

"Right up until the day you fired him? He was convicted of stabbing a college student to death."

"I'm well aware of that, Ms. O'Rourke." Sullivan's tone made it clear he wasn't used to being interrupted by a mere woman. "I'm thankful he no longer works here. Of course, I would have fired him immediately upon his conviction."

"Sort of a moot point if a guy is in prison."

"All the same."

"We'd like to meet the woman he harassed."

"Allegedly harassed." Sullivan pursed his lips and wrinkled his nose, the picture of a man who smelled rotten meat. "You already did. My admin Harper Nelson."

*   *   *

The woman who had led them to her boss's office had exchanged her earlier anxious look—they had no appointment and Mr. Sullivan never saw people without an appointment—for a terrified look.

"I have so much work to do." She eased into a soft leather chair in Sullivan's private conference room, used at his request. After all, they couldn't have this conversation in full view of the employees out in the cubicle city in the middle of the offices that ringed the outer four walls of the floor. "I really don't understand why this is necessary. I don't have time for it."

"This will only take a few minutes, Ms. Harper." Dad used his gentle *here-kitty-kitty-kitty* tone. "We want to ask you about what happened with Leo Slocum."

"What happened is he groped me at a company quarterly sales celebration." The terrified woman disappeared, replaced by a much more outspoken, disgusted, and vocal person. "He followed me into the hallway. I was on my way to the ladies' room. He took my arm and whirled me around so that I smacked right into him. Full body." Her peaches-and-cream complexion turned scarlet. "I screeched and said, 'What are you doing?' He said I was giving off subtle signals that I wanted him to follow me. I told him in no uncertain terms that he was sadly mistaken. The guy's old, at least twice my age. Seriously.

"He ran his hands down my bare arms and brushed my hair from my face. He said I smelled good. I told him to stop. He'd been drinking and so had I, but not so much that I didn't know it was a terrible idea. I never indulge in extracurricular activities with my superiors. Especially married ones. It never works out and it's always the subordinate who gets the heave-ho. I need this job. I have student loans to pay back."

"When you said stop, did he do it?"

"He touched my cheek again, and when he dropped his hand, it brushed against my . . . my chest." Her face went from scarlet to beet red. "He apologized, but it was obvious he didn't mean it. He smiled and told me to relax and enjoy myself. It was creepy, the way he said it."

The desire to comfort the woman overwhelmed Teagan. Harper Nelson would not appreciate a hug under the circumstances. "It sounds a little scary."

"It was. I turned and raced back into the party. I got my friends and we left. I didn't even go to the bathroom."

"Had you ever experienced anything similar with Slocum before?"

"No, never. I actually thought he was cute for an old guy, especially when he showed off photos of his grandkids. They're adorable." She ran her hands through her long black hair. "What would make a guy like that do such a horrible thing?"

They were no longer talking about her encounter with Slocum, as awful as it must have been. Teagan exchanged glances with her father. He nodded. She chose her words carefully. "We're just glad you were able to walk away from him. He made you uncomfortable, but he didn't hurt you. That's a blessing."

"You think if I'd gone with him, he might have done to me what he did to that poor college girl?"

"We don't know that. Mr. Slocum is a very smart man, too smart, we hope, to attack someone from the company where he works."

"Worked."

"Yes, you did good." Teagan smiled. Harper managed a tremulous smile in return. "We're sorry this happened to you, but we're glad you were able to keep your job and are working though the experience. Did you get some help?"

"I did. I am." She brushed tears from her face and grabbed a tissue from the box on the table. "I'm also looking for another job. I have a second interview tomorrow for a position in a nonprofit run by a woman."

"Good for you." Dad stood and offered his hand. "We wish you the very best."

"Thank you. I hope whatever you're doing will guarantee he'll die in prison."

"That's the plan."

Back in Dad's Charger, Teagan hauled her laptop from the back seat and turned her phone into a hot spot.

"What are you doing?" Dad rolled out onto the street, headed for home.

"Seeing what I can find out about Deidre Patterson."

"Let Billy or Justin do that. They have more resources at their fingertips. It was twenty-five years ago. Talk about a needle in a haystack."

"What if he killed her? What if she was the first victim?"

"That's pure speculation or imagination. She could also be living the good life in a retirement community in Boca Raton."

"I've got a feeling this woman could tell us something about how Leo Slocum became who he is. What he is. And what about the kid? Could Slocum have another child out there? Does that mean anything to him? Maybe it's a bargaining chip to get him to tell us about his accomplice."

Dad was right. Deidre Patterson was a needle in a twenty-five-year-old haystack. She texted Billy with the information and asked him to do a deep dive in hopes of finding something about this blast from Slocum's past.

"It's grotesque to think he had a family here, a mistress, and possibly even a child in Corpus, and he still trolled for victims to kill."

"Getting fired was probably the stressor that made him kill in his own backyard. He had no excuse to leave town anymore and the impulse drove him." Dad tapped the wheel with both hands. "It's an obsession. All Ted Bundy had to do was disappear into a new life. Instead, within a week of escaping from prison, he killed two women and a young girl, and severely injured two more. He couldn't help himself. He ended up frying in the electric chair instead."

Somehow that fate seemed too good for a man like Ted Bundy.

It was certainly too good for Leo Slocum.

26

No retirement community in Boca Raton. Nor had Deidre Patterson died at the hands of her long-ago lover. Maybe not so long ago. Who knew how long the affair lasted? Teagan tucked her phone between her ear and her shoulder and took a small bite of the Whataburger Junior Dad had insisted she order after pointing out how her clothes hung on her. She'd lost at least six pounds since the start of this nightmare. Billy's call caught her and her dad eating in his favorite burger joint parking lot. Good thing Jazz had decided to travel from Las Vegas to San Francisco to visit her parents. She would not be pleased with her husband's attempts to harden his arteries with a Whataburger and onion rings.

"She's not in AFIS. She's never been arrested. But she has a Texas driver's license and she's received several speeding tickets over the years." Billy didn't bother with preliminaries. "Last known address is in Corpus Christi. She's fifty-one, divorced, and works as a restaurant manager."

Fifty-one years old. The right age for Slocum. "Text me the address and any other information you can give us. A copy of her license, too, so we can see her picture."

"You're not thinking of going to Corpus."

"Why not?"

"Put me on speaker."

Teagan did as requested, only because Billy would hang up and call Dad if she didn't.

"You're not seriously considering driving to Corpus to talk to this woman on the basis of something a guy said who used to work with Leo Slocum. This happened more than twenty-five years ago."

Dad swallowed the last bite of his burger. "There's a kid involved who would be an adult now."

"That has nothing to do with the murders we're investigating." When Billy's voice got heated, he sounded different, more macho. Like his biological father, maybe? "It's interesting background information and I'll pass it on to our compadres in Corpus. They can follow up to see if she's had any contact with him recently. Save the gas. Save the wear and tear on the Charger."

"I have to say, Son, I'm with Teagan on this one. It'll make a fascinating case study. It'll give us even more insight into who Slocum was in the early years when he started killing. Why didn't he kill this woman? Does he have another child out there?" Dad settled back in his seat and grinned at Teagan. "If she's still in contact with him, maybe she's the accomplice. This is important. I want it done right. As a consultant on this case, I have standing to do the interview and I know what I'm doing."

"Okay, okay, stop. I know that tone. You're going." His voice went muffled for a few seconds, then he was back. "I'll let Hector break it to our buddies in Corpus that you're horning in on their territory. Do you at least want to call her first to see if she wants to talk?"

"No. That gives her a chance to lawyer up or rabbit or practice her story. I'd rather show up and see what happens." Dad wiped his hands and face with a towelette and tossed it in the empty, grease-stained onion ring container. "Corpus PD is welcome to send someone to sit in on the interview."

"That's big of you." Billy signed off with the obligatory "be careful driving down there and be careful once there" admonition. Her big brother worried. Teagan could relate. "We promise, big brother, we'll behave."

A pause. "Thanks for saying that."

"What, we'll be careful? We always are."

"No, the other part."

The big brother part. She didn't say it often enough. "We'll report in as soon as we have something worth reporting."

"Are you telling Max you're going?"

"After we get there."

"Smart move."

A quick trip inside the fast-food joint to use the facilities, and they were ready to head out. Thankful for her dad's preference for quiet that allowed him to think on long drives, Teagan spent most of the two hours traveling south on I-37 sleeping. Amazing how restful the soft rumble of the Charger's engine, the cooling AC, and her father's presence could be.

The sense that the car had slowed and then stopped brought her upright. Groggy, she rubbed her eyes and tried to adjust to the change in scenery. Corpus had a foreign country feel that went back to her childhood when her dad loaded up the car and drove them to the beach. Memories came in fits and starts. The smell of the Gulf water and sunscreen, the grit of sand and salt on her skin. The feel of her mother's hands as she smeared the sunscreen from one end of Teagan's body to the other. Running like a crazy girl from the iridescent and purple jellyfish that had managed to beach themselves in the sand. Tiptoeing with her dad up to the chunks of seaweed also stranded above the tide, often teeming with strange little creatures.

They bodysurfed, hunted for shells, and built sand castles with water-filled moats. Those were some of the happiest times in Teagan's life.

After Dad remarried he took the entire gang to the beach on a few occasions, but Leyla was allergic to sunscreen and Billy hated the feel of the seaweed on his legs when he swam. Jazz preferred a pool where she could pull up a lounge chair, set her skinny margarita on the side table, and sunbathe drenched in coconut oil. After a few times, Teagan refused to go. She'd pleaded to stay with the Hinojosas where she could help *Abuelita* make homemade corn tortillas and menudo or gorditas. The family gathered around the table into the wee hours, laughing and talking over each other and telling stories, correcting each other's recollections, playing cards and dominoes.

It felt different.

The GPS lady spoke. Dad made a left turn. "Welcome back to the land of the living, sweetheart."

"Did I snore?"

"No, but you have dried spittle on your chin."

"Do not." She wiped at her face with her sleeve. "Are we close?"

"If Miss Redirecting is correct, yes."

"Sorry I didn't help with navigation." Her job as a kid had been to keep an eye on the map to make sure the directions were accurate. A few times they'd ended up on a dead-end street in a run-down neighborhood instead of at a new restaurant her dad wanted to try. "I guess I was tired."

"Crime fighting will do that to you."

"I don't feel like I've been doing much crime fighting."

"Don't let TV fool you. Crimes are not solved in one-hour segments with five breaks for commercials. It's a marathon, not a sprint. That's one of the hardest lessons for new detectives to learn."

"I'm not a detective."

"No, but you have a detective's mind. And all those years of writing records have filled your head with essential facts about how cases are investigated, what autopsies show, what ballistic experts do, and how homicide detectives approach interviewing witnesses. You understand the law and what we can and cannot do in the pursuit of justice. In my book that makes you an excellent stand-in for a detective."

High praise from her dad. Teagan basked in the warm feeling for a few seconds. "Were you disappointed when I decided not to become a police officer?"

"Absolutely not. Relieved." He glanced her way and back at the road. "If you'd decided to go to the academy, I would've supported you. But not having you in the line of fire gave me some sense of peace. I could do my job with one less thing to worry about."

"Sounds like there's a *but* in there."

"It's a ridiculous sense of security, honey. Haven't you figured that out yet?" His voice deepened, became husky. "We have shootings in schools, in churches, in synagogues, in movie theaters. There is no safe place in America."

"Says the guy who loves his Second Amendment rights."

"At least I carry a gun and I know how to use it. I can protect others around me. But I can't be around to protect you all the time. That's why I taught you how to use a gun. That's why I would like for you to own a gun."

"That's never going to happen."

"I've made my peace with that. If you don't want to carry a gun, you shouldn't. If you don't think you could use it to shoot and even kill a person to stop a lethal threat, you shouldn't carry it. A second's hesitation could be fatal. Guns only work for people willing to use them."

"And this country is full of people willing to do exactly that."

"We'll never agree about this."

On that they could agree.

Dad turned right into a neighborhood that had seen better days. The homes were small, some neatly maintained, others teetering on collapse. There didn't seem to be any in-between. Overgrown lots were home to discarded mattresses, sofas missing their pillows, and oversized black garbage bags. He slowed and halted on the curb in front of a house that might once have been blue. The peeling paint had faded in the corrosive sea salt and waterlogged air. Two steps led to a tiny cement porch. No trees, but a few shrubs hugged the front of the one-story wood-frame house. Someone had hung wind chimes on the porch eave.

"According to Billy's text, this is it." Dad leaned back in his seat. "Car in the driveway. That's a good sign."

The car, a mid-2000 Hyundai, appeared in better shape than the house. It looked newly washed and waxed.

"How do you want to do this?" The question hung in the air like bad dialogue from one of her TV shows. "I mean, do we need a story, or are you going with the truth?"

"I know lots of cops lie to suspects. It's allowed. They even lie to potential witnesses or people of interest. I try to leave it as a last resort. The truth is so much easier to remember."

Now that they were at Deidre Patterson's door, the chill on Teagan's arms didn't come from the AC.

"Second thoughts?"

"You do this for a living. Crashing into a person's life, bringing up old hurts, opening healed wounds. It seems cruel in some ways."

"Maybe the wounds haven't healed. Maybe this is an opportunity for a person to tell her story for the first time. To excise old pain."

"Therapy by cop?"

"Maybe."

She smiled. So did he.

Whatever got him through the day.

"I reckon that's the Corpus detective." Dad nodded at the rearview mirror. Teagan glanced back. A white unmarked SUV pulled in behind them. "Billy said they didn't squawk much about letting us in on this interview, although it was emphasized that they were allowing us to sit in, not vice versa."

A short, squat man emerged from the other vehicle and trotted their direction.

Together they met the detective, who introduced himself as Joe

Cruz, all the while mopping his face with a blue bandanna. He wore a lightweight sports jacket, white shirt, and navy Dockers. Against the dark skin above his open collar lay a gold cross on a thick serpentine chain. "Welcome to the sauna we call Corpus Christi. Detective Evans-O'Rourke filled me in." He offered his large hand to Teagan first. "You really think this lady can shed some light on Slocum after all these years?"

"At this point I'll take anything that helps us understand what this man has been up to for the past twenty-five years."

"Killing women."

"We got that part."

Cruz stuck the bandanna in his back pocket and led the way the scant few yards to the door. The tinny bell dinged after a fashion.

Two seconds later, the weather-beaten door opened. Ms. Patterson looked nothing like her DMV photo. Her long brown hair sported several inches of white roots. She wore large red-framed glasses and no makeup. The baggy embroidered Mexican dress couldn't hide the fact that no fat covered her bony body. She was barefoot and her toenails needed a good trim.

"I wondered when the cops would make the connection and show up." She took a long drag on her cigarette and zeroed in on Cruz. "At least one of you was worth waiting for."

Dad grinned and held out his hand. "I think I've just been dissed."

Deidre shook it. "What can I say? I'm a cougar."

"Can we come in?"

"Sure, but you'll never get me to say a bad word about Leo."

"You don't care that he's probably killed several women?"

"The man broke my heart. It would've been kinder to kill me instead." She pushed the door wider. "Come in and convince me a sweet, kind man could possibly have done what you say Leo did."

They had their work cut out for them. If Leo had cast that strong of a spell over Deidre, no wonder he had gotten away with murder.

27

Deidre, aka the Cougar, enjoyed an audience, no doubt about it. Once Teagan asked if she could record the woman's story—for Dad's book—there had been no stopping Deidre. She settled into a stained beige recliner, curled her legs up under her, and lit another cigarette as she prepared to take them along on a trip down memory lane. Teagan barely had a chance to look around as she set the digital recorder on the smeared glass coffee table that separated the couch from the recliner. Dad grabbed a seat next to her while Cruz dragged a kitchen table chair into the living room.

The interior of Ms. Patterson's house matched its occupant. Cheap Mexican pottery purchased in Reynosa or Matamoros served as ashtrays strung from table to table, room to room. Mexican rugs covered scarred vinyl floors. Dime store variety artwork on the walls featured beach scenes of sand dunes, seashells, and high tide under starry skies. A ceiling fan made a *tink-tink* sound as it relocated dank, warm air. The aroma of tuna mingled with cigarette smoke and dirty cat litter. This time the cat turned out to be a chubby tortoiseshell mommy with soulful eyes and two kittens who followed her into the room and immediately fled upon seeing their owner's guests.

Deidre had the leathery skin of a person who'd enjoyed the Corpus beaches too often. White hair crept from her part and mingled with brown hair caught back in a lanky ponytail. Her eyes were a dusky brown.

"Leo Slocum was the love of my life." Deidre sucked on the cigarette and released the smoke in a steady stream through her nose. "I imagine he was the love of several women's lives. I met him at the Surf and Turf over on Ocean Drive. I was a waitress there. Good tips, decent customers. Nobody pinched my behind or tried to look down my shirt when I served their steak. Not so I noticed leastwise.

"Leo liked his seafood. He came in every couple of months at first. He always sat in my section. Clean-shaven, smelled good, clean fingernails, decent teeth, tipped me good." Hacking up a wet, rattling cough, she studied the glowing tip of her cigarette. When the coughing stopped, she drew a ragged breath. "Excuse me while I hack up a lung."

Joe Cruz stood. "Would you like me to get you a glass of water?"

"Aren't you a gentleman?" Deidre unfolded her legs and pushed away from the recliner. She waved him back into his seat. "I've got just the ticket."

She returned a few seconds later with a glass half full of amber liquid. Unless Corpus Christi had a contaminated water system, her drink did not involve water. Nor did she offer any refreshments to her visitors. "Where was I?"

"You met Slocum—Leo—at the Surf and Turf," Dad said. "What year was that?"

"Who knows? I was twenty-four. Do the math." She cocked her head as if thinking hard. "I bombed out of community college after high school. Too much weed, too many hours working, and not enough sleep. I planned to go to cosmetology school, but I never did, not after I met Leo.

"He talked to me like a real person. He'd read interesting tidbits to me from the newspaper while he ate his key lime pie. He had a thing for that pie. Pretty soon he started coming in more often and staying longer. My boss got irritated. He said I was spending too much time on one customer, so Leo suggested he pick me up after my shift and we could talk somewhere else.

"He bought me drinks at a bar on North Shore Drive. We danced. He was a good dancer. One thing led to another." She shrugged. "Then he was gone again. He left me a note on the nightstand saying he had to finish his route, but he would be back in a couple of weeks. He sold stuff to eye doctors all over the Valley. Made good money. I could tell by how nice his clothes were, and he had a nice watch and a bundle of bills in his wallet. Not that I looked, but he took it out to pay for our drinks.

"Sure enough. He showed up at my place—I had an apartment in those days—every six or seven weeks. I started to look forward to those visits. I lived for them. My girlfriends said I was crazy. They were sure he was married. But I never had a guy treat me so nice. It wasn't always dancing and drinks. Sometimes he brought me flowers and he gave me jewelry. Nice stuff, not costume crap.

"Then he stopped showing up for a while. But he called. Until then I didn't have any way to get in touch with him. It was all a one-way street. But he gave me a number and told me to only call it in case of an emergency."

"Did you think he was married?" Daring to break the flow of memories, Teagan had to ask. How could she not? "Did it bother you?"

"I figured as much. I'm not an idiot. I just wanted to believe in the fairy tale a little longer. I thought maybe he would divorce her and marry me." She gulped from her drink and set it with a clink on the metal TV tray next to her chair. "I know how selfish that sounds, but growing up in Corpus is different from hopping in for a visit to the beach on spring break. Or renting a condo for a week on Aransas Pass. Eating shrimp and getting sunburned while you play in the water. Most of us just grub out a living off the tourists. We can't afford to rent a condo with beach access. We serve your food and clean your hotel rooms. If we can get work."

"So what happened?"

"I got pregnant." She stabbed her cigarette into an overflowing ashtray. "And no, it wasn't on purpose. He never made me feel like he doubted that either. But he told me there was nothing he could do, other than pay to get rid of it. But I wouldn't do that. I went to Catholic school as a kid."

"Did he seem like he wanted you to keep it?"

"He came to the apartment one night, late. Said he couldn't stay. He was wearing a gold band on his finger. First time. He sat next to me on the couch and took out his wallet. He showed me a photo of him and his wife and their babies. A boy and a girl."

Deidre's face crumpled as if the crushing of her dreams had happened moments ago and not more than two decades. The pain was real and fresh on her face. Teagan glanced at the two men. His expression uncomfortable, Cruz shifted in his chair. Dad resembled a tree trunk—immovable, implacable. Fine, this was a conversation between two women, years apart in age and experiences, but women. "That's rough. What did you do?"

"I bawled. I told him I'd do anything for him, just don't leave me alone."

"But he did."

"He ended up sticking around for the night, to comfort me. I made him eggs and bacon in the morning. He liked his eggs over easy. He showed up once in a while at first, even after the baby was born. But it was never the same. It was like he wasn't attracted to me anymore." She lifted her drink to dry, chapped lips and drained her glass. "He seemed more taken with my kid, though. He brought clothes and once a baseball mitt. He said the kid had his eyes."

The kid. "What was his name?"

"Who?"

"Your baby."

"Kyle. I named him Kyle. But who knows what his parents call him."

225

"His parents?"

"After a while, Leo stopped showing up altogether. I tried calling him, but he didn't return my call. I couldn't do it. I couldn't. Kyle was a sickly kid. I needed to work. I couldn't afford decent day care. Then I finally met a guy, a guy who wasn't married to someone else. Kyle cried all the time. He had colic, then croup, and allergies, and he never slept through the night, even when he was old enough to know better. Always coming out of his room, always busting into my room. Peter didn't like it. No privacy. He said he needed to sleep good at night, on account of he worked at a loading dock all day. It was hard work."

"So you gave Kyle up for adoption? How old was he?"

"Four when CPS took him. He was in the foster system for a while. Then a couple adopted him after I gave up my rights."

Old enough to remember his mother. Old enough to feel unwanted. He'd been neglected or even abused or Child Protective Services would not have been involved. Teagan's empathy for the mother drained away, replaced by empathy for a child who'd been, by his mother's measure, too much trouble. "You never saw him again?"

"Who? Kyle? Or Leo?"

"Both, I guess. Either."

"I drove up to San Antonio once and tracked down the office where Leo worked. I sat outside and watched people come and go. I saw him get out of his car and walk inside with a woman. A coworker, I guess. They were laughing and talking. Like we used to do." The long ashes from her cigarette fell on her lap. Deidre didn't seem to notice. "At that point, I knew I was over it."

"And Kyle?"

"Never saw him again. He was better off without me. This way I didn't have to tell him how he was conceived."

Who are you to judge? You're too chicken to have your own children.

The startling thought caught Teagan on the chin like a knockout punch from a contender. She wasn't chicken. She'd come to a reasoned decision about what was best. Better than bringing an unwanted child into the world and giving him away like a sack of ill-fitting clothes.

"Did Slocum's behavior ever seem erratic or odd to you? Did he ever do anything that struck you as odd?"

Finally, Dad spoke. Teagan leaned back and relaxed.

"He went in the other room to take calls, but I figured it was his wife." Deidre wrinkled her nose as if she smelled rancid meat. "He used to leave the apartment in the middle of the night. He said he was an insomniac. He would go for walks at midnight, two, three in the morning."

"And you didn't think anything of that?" Cruz fingered the cross around his neck. Sweat had soaked through his shirt around the collar. "What year was that? Do you have dates for when he visited and took these walks?"

"Seriously? I barely remember what I had for supper yesterday." Her laugh sounded more like a bark. "I wasn't about to question him. The man bought groceries. He gave me gifts. He was good in the sack."

TMI. Teagan stared at her hands.

Cruz didn't seem to mind. "Was he ever violent toward you?"

"In the sack—"

"In general."

"Never. Kind, considerate. Sweet. I still have a photo of us."

She pointed to the coffee table. The color had started to fade, but the framed photo distinctly showed a couple in love. Leo Slocum, tall, jet-black hair, blue eyes, smiling. Deidre was right. He had nice teeth. He had his arm around her. The image caught on film held little in common with middle-aged Deidre. The tanned young woman wearing a coral sundress radiated joy. She had curves. She had long chestnut hair that lay on her chest in curls.

Such hope.

Dad stood. Cruz looked reluctant, but he did the same. Teagan settled the photo on the table. "What about the man you met after Leo Slocum aban—stopped seeing you?"

"I married him. He was an abusive drunk. He broke my nose. Eventually he left me for a biker chick."

"No more kids?"

"Two with Peter. One with a one-night stand from Dallas. I have a couple of grandkids. They live in Weslaco."

"That's nice. Close enough to visit." Some people didn't get happily-ever-afters. Leo Slocum had left his mark here, even if it wasn't the one they were looking for. She joined the men as they moved toward the door, but something made her stop. "I'm sorry for your hurt. I hope things get better. A woman deserves better."

"Thank you." Deidre slurred the words. "I'm not holding my breath." She rose and staggered toward Teagan. "There was one thing."

Both men looked back.

"We always had to go places in my car. It was an old beater with a broken AC, and he drove this nice minivan. He said it was a company car with the name on the side so he couldn't use it for pleasure. Someone would see it parked at a bar, you know."

"That makes sense, I suppose."

"One time I walked by his van. It was parked in the slot next to mine in the apartment complex lot. I glanced in, you know, no big deal. There was a butcher knife on the back seat."

"That's a little weird."

"Next to a roll of garbage bags and a shovel. It still had the price tag on it."

Cruz edged away from the door. "Did you ask him about it?"

"I was scared to, but it was too weird to just let it pass."

"What did he say?"

"He said he was doing some landscaping at home and picked up some things he needed because he saw a sale. The butcher knife was for cutting meat. He likes to smoke briskets and turkeys."

Would Deidre tell a different story in the witness box with an attorney bearing down on her? Teagan itched to record the woman's words with her machine.

```
 3   Q. Did you have an affair with the defendant during
 4       the time period in question while he was working as a
 5       salesman in the Valley?
 6   A. Yes, I did.
 7   Q. Can you tell us if he ever exhibited odd behavior?
 8   A. I'm sorry? Like what?
 9   Q. Didn't you tell the Corpus Christi detective
10       the defendant went on long walks late at night?
11   A. He had insomnia.
12   Q. Didn't you also tell Detective Cruz you
13       saw a shovel and garbage bags on the back seat of his
14       car? Along with a butcher knife?
15   A. He liked to garden and he barbecued a lot.
16   Q. So it's your testimony you found nothing odd
17       about his behavior?
18   A. He was—he is a good man.
19   Q. Isn't it true he abandoned you when you got
20       pregnant with your child?
```

Teagan grasped her hands tightly. Someday soon justice would be served. "And you took him at his word?" Incredulity colored Cruz's words. "You didn't tell anyone about it? Don't you the read the papers?"

"I knew about the women who have disappeared or been found dead over the years. But I figured there were plenty of explanations. Boyfriends like Pete. College kids who get so blitzed on spring break they don't know what they're doing. Just plain bad choices. Leo was a nice man. Good manners, good-looking. He charmed the pants off a person. Literally. There's no way he'd ever hurt a woman. I don't believe it."

"Believe it."

Cruz pushed through the door and left Teagan and her father to thank Deidre for her time.

"The Leo I knew wasn't a killer." Deidre lobbed the assertion after them. "He treated me like a queen."

Until he didn't.

Cruz leaned against his car, picking at a thumbnail. "Can we arrest her for stupidity?"

Dad veered that direction. "Kind of hot under the collar, aren't you?"

"One of the victims was my aunt." His morose stare pierced Teagan. "There was a butcher knife involved. Deidre Patterson saw it. So she proceeds to tell us about her love life and what kind of eggs her booty call liked."

"I'm sorry." Teagan searched for adequate words of condolence. There were none.

Dad opened a package of Doublemint gum, held it out. Cruz took a piece. Teagan waved it away. Dad chewed and contemplated. "The timing's right."

"It still blows my mind that a man can carve up, stab, or otherwise kill women and still have these kinds of relationships with other women." Teagan faced the tepid breeze and let it blow her hair from her sweaty face. The ways this interview confounded her were too many to outline. Her memories of Corpus, filled with the cry of seagulls and crashing of waves, would forever be tainted by the images Diedre had imparted. "How could Leo have a marriage in San Antonio and a mistress here who bore his child? Why didn't he kill her?"

"The FBI has been studying serial killers for decades. A lot is known. A lot is conjecture. Interviews were conducted by analysts, not psychiatrists. And there's much we don't understand about the human psyche." Dad wadded up the gum wrapper and stuck it in his pocket. "For some reason, Slocum took a liking to Deidre. We know from the length of his marriage and from the interview with his son that he had the ability to carry on normal relationships. But he had—has—another darker side that he hides from the world."

"Very well, it seems."

"I don't know." Cruz tugged at his cross. "Not that well. What kind of killer leaves the tools of his trade on the back seat of his company van?"

"You think he wanted her to know?"

"Maybe it was titillating for him to think she might be a little afraid of him, that she might start to imagine what he did with those things. It was part of the game."

"It's possible. Then she had a baby and that changed the dynamic. She wasn't a mistress anymore; she was a mother. I imagine that took the edge off. He had a lot invested in the relationship, but he already had a wife and kids. He didn't need more baggage."

"Dad!"

His grim smile did nothing to lighten the mood. "Spend any time in the heads of psychopaths and you learn something about the way they think."

"And then you take a shower." Cruz tugged car keys from his pocket. "Can I interest y'all in dinner before you drive back?"

"Thanks, but we need to get back to the city."

Teagan stared at the ramshackle home of a woman abandoned by the love of her life. "Leo Slocum has another child out there. I wonder if that ever crosses his mind."

Dad remote-started the Charger. "It would mine, but I'm not a psychopath. Think about the killer writing your letters. He's incapable of remorse. He's incapable of truly caring. He's a consummate actor who plays a part to get what he wants." Dad put a hand on her shoulder and walked her to the car. "He and Slocum are likely cut from the same cloth. I doubt he's given that baby a second thought—or Deidre, for that matter."

"Should we try to find Kyle?"

"Why? So we can tell him his mother gave him up for an abusive drunk and his father is a suspected serial killer? Sometimes ignorance really is bliss."

He was right. Maybe Kyle Patterson had a good life somewhere with a pretty wife, kids, and a satisfying job. Maybe he went to church on Sunday and took the family to Montana to hike the Going-to-the-Sun Road in Glacier National Park for a week in June. Maybe he had a dog named Butch and jogged every morning before work. Maybe they had tickets to Disney World this summer.

To be ignorant of butcher knives, murder, and mayhem would be a gift. It would be a sin to take that from a man.

28

Max met Teagan at the door. Her door, but it still felt husbandly. Her father waved and pulled away from the driveway. The relief that he'd decided not to pop in for a chat brought with it guilt. Max had no reason not to chat with Dillon. He wasn't shacking up with her. Simply providing backup. Dillon should be happy about that. Of course, he didn't know Teagan had insisted Max lock his gun in her document safe instead of placing it in the nightstand next to the guest bed. In the event of an intruder it would do no good.

"You look like you could use a hug." Her revelation regarding children had left Max sucker punched, but he'd learned to bob and weave with the best amateur boxers.

She accepted his offering with a sigh. That she allowed him to get this close was the same gift it had always been. How they would navigate the path from here remained a mystery. Of all the reasons for rejecting a relationship with him, this one had never occurred to him. "Long day?"

"You'll regret getting close to me." She had dark circles under her eyes and her sleeveless blouse hung on her. "I'm sticky and sweaty and I stink. Deidre Patterson smoked like a chimney."

"You always smell good to me." Her scent of eucalyptus and citrus parried with the faint stench of cigarette smoke. "How are you?"

Teagan escaped from his arms and sank to her knees to pet Tigger, who'd patiently waited her turn. "My head is about to explode with all the impressions and reactions from these interviews. I don't know where to begin. I feel like we're onto something, but I'm not exactly sure what."

"I made supper. Why don't we eat and you can tell me about it?" Despite the obvious wilt of exhaustion, Teagan looked excited. Involved. Determined. And never more elusive. Max dragged his gaze from her face and cocked his head toward the kitchen table. "Maybe it'll help you to bounce your impressions off me. Unless you'd rather eat in peace and then talk. That might be better for your digestive system."

"Dad made me eat a hamburger for lunch. I'm not sure I can eat again." Her apologetic smile sent his blood pressure spiking. "For you I'll try. What did you make me?"

"Your dad's right. Not eating only makes you feel worse. I made my specialty—spaghetti and meatballs. They're good, if I do say so myself." He didn't cook much, but his mother had taught him a few dishes "to wow the girls." She said women would be impressed by a man who could cook. His dad claimed manhandling a barbecue grill was the quickest way to impress a girl. So Max did both. "There's a salad, breadsticks, and I picked up a half gallon of Rocky Road."

"No pun intended, I'm sure."

"It could be a metaphor for this season in our lives."

"Or our relationship."

"Nope. Not going there." As much as every bone in his body wanted to argue, cajole, and convince. Prayerful discernment told Max that pushing wasn't the answer. Letting her trust grow and her fears subside held more hope of success. "Let's enjoy the moment."

Max served the meal at her table set with her grandmother's china, cloth napkins, and candles he'd found in her linen closet. Teagan's effort to be enthusiastic was obvious. After two bites, she laid her fork down and picked up the small bowl of fresh Parmesan cheese he'd shredded. "This is excellent. Your mom's recipe?"

"How'd you know?"

"Because you once told me she had a limited repertoire, but what she did make was heavenly."

"She made her breadsticks from scratch. Her pineapple upside-down cake was incredible. So were her cinnamon rolls. We also ate a lot of microwave cuisine when she was busy with her nonprofit."

Max's mother had run an organization that provided clothes to help homeless women dress for job interviews. His dad had owned an auto parts franchise until both retired to travel to Florida in an RV.

He'd loved his parents dearly. The only want they hadn't fulfilled was brothers and sisters. They met too late in life. He wanted a big family. He always imagined he could still have one.

God, how could this be? I'm in love with a woman who doesn't want children. Help me to understand. Is this about sacrificing for the one I love? Or is it about her and what she needs to learn about You?

"I wish I could've met them."

"Me too." He kept his gaze on the spaghetti he swirled against his spoon. That his parents no longer lived left a hole the size of Texas in his world. He wanted them to be around for their grandchildren. They would've played Candy Land with them, gone to their baseball games, and showered them with every good children's book they could find. "Mom would've liked you a lot. Dad too. He liked what he called spunky girls."

"So I qualify as spunky?"

"You're out with your dad hunting a serial killer. I think so."

"While you're here cooking. Does that bother you?"

"No way." Instead images of evenings spent doing exactly this for years to come had followed him around the kitchen. Images that still included burp rags and high chairs. "I love cooking for you. I could see myself doing it on a regular basis. In our kitchen."

Her smile faded, replaced by a sadness for which he had no salve. "Even if it was just the two of us and Tigger for company? I won't let you do that to yourself."

He'd done nothing but think and pray about that question since her revelation at church on Sunday. "It's not up to you only. It's my choice as well."

"You'll end up resenting me."

"That would never happen. I don't blame you for feeling the way you do. You've had enough loss and worry in your short life. I just wish you would trust God's plan for you."

"You should do the same."

"I pray about us and for us constantly. Do you take your concerns to Him? Do you listen for His voice?"

"I'm really tired and I need a shower."

He kept telling himself he wouldn't push, and then he did it anyway. He pushed too hard. "Sorry. Sorry." He gulped his fresh-brewed iced tea and went back to the spaghetti. "Tell me about Deidre Patterson."

Teagan tore a piece from her breadstick and dropped it on her plate. "She was sad. She made me sad."

"Why?"

The story poured out until she arrived at the part where Deidre had a child she allowed CPS to place in the foster care system. Her voice faltered. She sipped her tea and cleared her throat.

"This bothers you more than the fact that she had a child out of wedlock with a suspected serial killer?"

"I try not to pass judgment. She made the right choice to have the child." Her gaze downcast, Teagan drew circles on the tablecloth with one finger. "But she waited until he was old enough to know, to remember. Then she gave him away or allowed CPS to take him away. She replaced him with an abusive drunk who eventually left her for another woman."

"It's a hard truth, but it sounds like he was better off. Maybe he was fostered by a family who adopted him. At four, he was young enough. A white male child."

The realities of the foster care system in Texas were frequently fodder for the six o'clock news. Max's attempt to sugarcoat it would not convince a court reporter who'd written records on cases involving children who'd been abused at home, placed in foster care by the court system, and then didn't make it out of their new homes alive.

"Noelle mentioned Sunday that Jana and Neil from church are fostering kids."

Max laid his fork down. Where was she going with this? "I respect that. It's a tough gig. Many of these children have severe problems because of physical and psychological abuse. They end up in the foster care system through no fault of their own. They deserve better. They deserve forever homes."

"Can you imagine fostering a child and not becoming attached to him or her?" Her expression pensive, Teagan shook her head. "Imagine the court deciding to give that child back to his or her parents after you've bonded. How would that feel?"

"Foster parents are special people. They leave a love imprint on those children designed to help them through whatever comes next. They plant seeds." Sudden hope made Max light-headed. Getting Teagan to see the options before her—before them—might be a way forward. She would make a good mother of her own children and foster children. He could see her teaching a child to read, sharing her love of gardening with a child, teaching a child to make bread. Or was he grasping at the proverbial straw? "They let children know they deserve love. They give children love when people who should've don't or can't."

"The ones who do it well. So many don't."

"It's an imperfect system. All the more reason for people like you and me to do it. My best friend at seminary aged out of the system. It blows my mind. They essentially are dumped out on their own. He made it because he stumbled into a church food bank one day and the pastor saw something in him. He gave him odd jobs, fed him, and helped him find a place to live. He became his surrogate father. I always wanted to meet that pastor and thank him.

"Mark 9:37 says, 'Whoever welcomes one of these little children in my name welcomes me; and whoever welcomes me does not welcome me but the one who sent me.' These children are already on the face of what you see as a ruined world, no place for children. They're here. They don't have the one thing they need on earth besides a loving heavenly Father, an earthly father and mother who will train them up in the ways of the Lord and love them unconditionally."

"It's a strong argument. One you've carefully thought out." Her lower lip trembling, she pushed spaghetti around her plate with her fork. "Maybe too much."

"I try to stay open to the possibilities. I don't know what God has planned for me, but I want to be ready." Max slid his hand across the table and touched her thin fingers. "When He says go, I plan to go all-out."

"Are we still talking about fostering children?"

"I'm praying for discernment." Until his throat was dry and no more words came. "For you and for me. For our future, whether it's together or apart."

"You're a much better person than I am."

"No way. I was the one who made alcohol my best friend when the going got rough. I'm the one who tried to bail out." Emotion caught in his throat. *Not now. Not now.* So much for being a tough guy. Teagan spent her days with macho cops and came home to a spongy-hearted youth minister. "I should've told you about that instead of letting you find out in a creepy letter from a psycho."

"It's your past, and you decide when or if you tell people." Teagan grasped his fingers and held on. "You had the guts to fight your way back and keep fighting every day. You're my hero."

"The truth is I love you and I beg God to give me my heart's desire all the time. I know He'll do what's best for us, but I still want what I want. Which is you."

"Max, please."

"I know. Back burner. We'll save this conversation for later. I better clean up. We can sit on the back porch and eat our ice cream. I bought chocolate syrup."

Teagan had a thing for chocolate. She pushed away her still-full plate and stood. "You cooked. I clean. That's the rule at O'Rourke houses."

"Or we do it together. It'll go faster."

He turned on the SAC jazz station and they cleaned up in companionable silence.

Once settled into beach chairs on the porch with bowls of ice cream drowning in chocolate syrup, the silence continued. Not uncomfortable, more measured.

Fireflies flickered as dusk fell.

"You know what it means when they light up?" Max took another small bite of his ice cream. The cool sweetness eased the ache in his throat. "The males are seeking mates."

"You do have a one-track mind, don't you?" She leaned her chair back, using her feet against the porch banister to balance herself. "Romance among the fireflies?"

Let me in. Please let me in. "Do you think you could give foster parenting some consideration?"

"Back burner, remember?" She patted his hand. "Eat your ice cream."

If eating ice cream on the back porch with the woman he loved was as far as it went, Max would live with it. It was better than not having her in his life—far, far better. "Yes, ma'am."

*   *   *

The best-laid plans. Sleeping in her own bed in her own house seemed like such a good idea. Yet Teagan had marked every hour from midnight to five in the morning on the bright-red numerals of the alarm clock she used as a backup to her phone alarm. Max's words ping-ponged inside her head.

"Promise me you'll think about foster parenting."

Every child should be wanted. Kyle Patterson deserved to be wanted.

Surely no one would dispute that.

Think about something else. Anything else.

The trip to Corpus had been worth it. They knew more than just Leo Slocum's favorite kind of eggs, didn't they? Between the interviews with Rayburn, Chase, and Deidre, they'd painted a much more detailed portrait of Leo over the thirty years he'd been living a double life. On the other hand, they knew so much about his "normal" life and so little about his secret life. The guy liked seafood. He liked Frank Sinatra and dancing. He had good teeth and smelled good.

They needed to translate this feigned normalcy and use it as a key to finding the real Leo Slocum's secret life. He'd left clues, dropped hints, made mistakes.

Everyone made mistakes.

Leo Slocum hadn't made many until he got sloppy. According to Dad, studies showed serial killers who didn't get caught when they were younger tended to settle down. Sometimes they would go years without killing or stop altogether. The BTK Killer killed at least ten people between 1974 and 1991 then went dormant for twenty-five years. Then he started taunting police with what he'd done.

Leo Slocum couldn't let it go. He kept killing. Even in his own backyard.

Let this new information lead somewhere, please Lord.

Tigger woofed, yawned, and snuggled closer. Her heavy, muscled body rested against Teagan's thigh. She felt solid and formidable. The rule about sleeping on the bed had been temporarily suspended due to unforeseen circumstances. That being a serial killer on the loose in the neighborhood.

Was that why Teagan couldn't sleep? Or was it knowing Max

slept in the guest bedroom at the other end of the hallway in her cozy fifteen-hundred-square-foot cottage?

"That's not it, God."

Yeah, sure.

His good-night hug had been brief, but the barely banked fire in his eyes left her tossing and turning.

And imagining. And thinking. And debating.

She sat up and rearranged her pillows. A few punches made them decidedly less fluffy.

I'm not a hormonal teenager. I'm not a hormonal teenager. I'm a chaste, godly woman.

If only she could run seven or eight miles. Dad had assured her he would put her under house arrest in his house if she so much as ventured around the block.

Tigger's head came up. An ominous growl deep in her throat, she rolled and jumped from the bed in one graceful bound.

Sudden adrenaline spiraled through Teagan like a waterspout on steroids. "What? What is it, Tigger?"

Still growling, Tigger pawed at the door.

Teagan hopped from bed and grabbed her SAC sweats from her glider rocker and donned them standing up. Her Texas Rangers T-shirt came down to her knees. Suitably modest, she tugged her phone from the charger and rushed after Tigger who'd shot from the room like a dog on a mission.

Maybe Max couldn't sleep. Maybe he was hulking around the house.

Tigger wouldn't growl at her best buddy.

Her heart beating in her ears, Teagan edged along the hallway toward the front of the house and the foyer. Sweat beaded on her forehead and nose.

Tigger slowed as she approached the foyer.

"Max?" Teagan whispered. "Are you there?"

No answer. The front porch light hadn't come on. No motion

detected. She scooped the Taser from the basket where she kept her keys, pepper spray, and courtroom ID by the front door. "Come on, Tigger, come on, girl."

Tigger's stance stiffened. She didn't move.

Teagan grabbed her collar and tugged. "Let's go talk to Max."

The growl would send a bad guy running, no doubt. It even made the hair on Teagan's arm stand up. "Let's find your buddy Max."

Tigger made her disdain for this suggestion apparent, but she did as she was told. Back to the wall, Teagan edged away along the hallway. She breathed in. *One, two, three, four, hold, breathe out, one, two, three, four.*

At the kitchen door she halted a second time. "Stay with me, girl."

Tigger whined.

I feel your pain. Teagan tiptoed forward and peeked around the corner.

Max loomed over her. With a baseball bat held over his head like a flyswatter.

Teagan screeched. Tigger barked.

Max dropped the bat. "What are you doing out here?"

"What are you doing?"

"I heard something."

"So did Tigger. She's totally on edge."

Max scooped up the bat. "I'm getting my gun."

"No. No gun."

"Seriously? Then call 911."

"For what? You heard a noise? Front or backyard?"

"Front."

"All the way from the guest bedroom?"

"I wasn't in the bedroom."

"Not in the bedroom. Why?"

Max's bruised face flushed. "I couldn't sleep."

That makes two of us. "So where were you when you heard the noise?"

He hesitated.

"You know if you lie to me, I'll know. I can read every nuance in your face."

"Standing in front of your bedroom door."

Teagan put her hand over her mouth and tried to stifle her chortle. Not possible. "Max Kennedy."

"I wasn't coming in. I swear. I was debating knocking to see if you were awake. I figured you were as wound up as I was over the case. I made coffee. We could brainstorm . . . or something. When I heard the noise, I ran to get the bat."

"Way too much explanation, my son." Teagan swallowed her momentary hysteria and cleared her throat. "What did you hear?"

"A thump. And then maybe a car door closing."

"Closing? Or opening?"

"Closing."

"Did you hear a car leave?"

"No."

"So let's take a look out front, shall we?"

"If I can get my gun."

"No gun!"

"This is a stand-your-ground state. If someone is in your yard, you have the right to defend yourself."

"This is my yard, my house, my law. No gun." Teagan held up the Taser in one hand and her cell phone in the other. "These are the only weapons we need. Let's go, Robin."

"Why do you get to be Batman?"

"Shut up and follow me."

Teagan jostled Max aside and took the lead. Tigger passed them both. She stopped at the front door. No growl this time. No soft woof. All-out barking.

Taser in hand, Teagan eased toward the window to the right of the door. She reached for the lacy curtain.

Bang, bang, bang.

She stumbled back and nearly dropped the Taser.

The urgent pounding ratcheted up. Someone would have bruised knuckles.

"It's five forty-five in the morning." Max's growl matched Tigger's. "Who pounds on the door at this hour? Now can I get my gun?"

Breathe in, one, two, three, four. Breathe out, one, two, three, four. Repeat.

"Bad guys don't pound on the door to signal they're ready to tango." Teagan peered through the peephole. The fear drained from her body, leaving her muscles weak and her head swimming. "Cole Reynolds."

"What does he want at this hour?"

"I told him we would go running one day." She laid the Taser in the basket. Max picked it up. "He's my neighbor. Chill out."

"A neighbor you hardly know, pounding on your door at the crack of dawn. This is why you can't be here alone. You're too trusting."

"He's a community college instructor who likes to read the classics. He likes *Anna Karenina*, for crying out loud. He likes dogs." She turned her back on Max, took a breath, and opened the door. "I can't go for a run today."

Cole stood in the stark light of the porch dressed in shorts and a baggy white T-shirt. Huck whined and nudged his owner's hand. Cole didn't seem to notice and he didn't answer.

His expression registered. "Cole, what's wrong?" She glanced around. No obvious signs of a problem. "I'm on lockdown so I can't—"

"I figured." His hoarse voice broke. "I decided to run early because I'm giving finals today."

"You're as white as steamed rice. What is it?"

He jerked his head toward the yard or the library or the street. Hard to say which.

"It's a body," he whispered, "in your yard."

29

The roaring in Teagan's ears sounded so familiar. Like the buzz of fluorescent light about to die. "Whose body?" Her feet didn't want to move. Her arms and hands were frozen. "Did you call 911?"

"I called." Cole's Adam's apple bobbed. "I don't know who. I haven't seen her in the neighborhood."

Hand on Tigger's collar, Max pushed forward, forcing the dog to stay on the other side of the door frame. Teagan made room for Max on the tiny porch. "This is my friend Max."

Cole took a step back. "Oh, I didn't know he was here."

Somehow the words didn't ring true. Max's bike was sitting next to Teagan's Prius. But it was dark and before the crack of dawn and the guy just found a dead body at the Little Free Library. It didn't matter.

A body.

Her. A female.

Teagan pushed Tigger back from the door. "Stay, stay." Tigger whimpered. "I know, sweetie, stay." She couldn't be allowed to contaminate the crime scene. Teagan shut the door and turned to Cole. "Did you touch anything?"

"I checked for a pulse. Was that wrong?" Cole shook his head and gulped in air noisily. "I almost threw up, but I didn't. And I used Huck's leash to tie him to the carport post so he wouldn't get too close and mess something up. I was afraid he would start barking and wake the whole neighborhood, so I brought him with me to your door."

He sounded proud of himself. Understandable. English instructors didn't make a habit of finding bodies.

"No, that's fine. You needed to do that."

Teagan crossed her arms around her middle. The three of them trudged toward the library. The cool sprigs of grass tickled the soles of her feet. Twigs dug into the tender skin of her arches. A mourning dove cooed. The scent of honeysuckle floated on the breeze. None of it made any sense. How could this morning still be beautiful?

The woman lay on her back, staring at the sky. She could've been stargazing. She wore a shimmery white party frock with a full skirt. So different from the Anne Klein suit she'd worn the last time Teagan had seen her. Spoken to her.

Her signature gold bangle bracelets were gone. She looked naked without them.

Teagan's throat closed. Her legs gave out. She crumpled to the ground on her hands and knees. "No, no, no."

Max dropped to his knees and wrapped an arm around Teagan. "I'm so sorry, so sorry."

"You know her?" His voice hoarse, Cole's hands went to his throat. He looked as if he might collapse as well. "She's not family, is she?"

"Julie Davidson. Court coordinator. We work together. She was my friend.

"I checked for a pulse." Cole ran his hands up and down his bare arms. "There was none, but she was still warm."

Julie had taken Teagan under her wing when she arrived at the 177th, a wet-behind-the-ears newbie court reporter, six years ago. She was mother-sister-friend-colleague all wrapped up in a stylish, efficient, organized package.

Teagan bent over, hands on her stomach, and prayed she wouldn't hurl. Julie's perfect makeup had run. Her hazel eyes were wide and perplexed in death. She didn't look scared but rather perturbed. Julie didn't like messes.

Tears blurred Teagan's vision. Julie would've been so peeved at the indignity of it all. Left out in the yard like a sack of fertilizer for all the world to see. "I'm sorry, Julie, I'm so sorry."

My fault. My fault. All my fault.

Julie would no longer sip her Starbucks Venti Iced Matcha Green Tea Latte and thumb through *Home and Garden* magazine while discussing her latest DIY project.

No more running her courtroom like a five-star U.S. Army general.

No more passing around photos of a grandchild while asserting she was the cutest girl on the face of the earth, bar none. No more insisting that she was too young to be a grandmother. Which she was. She married young, had kids young, divorced young.

And died young.

Sirens screamed in the distance. They would be here soon. Vomit in the back of her throat, Teagan forced herself to look at Julie's body. The killer had arranged her with her hands crossed over her heart. Her legs were crossed at the ankles, her feet bare. Her fingernails and toenails were painted a lovely pale pink. Blood had congealed over one, two, three, four visible stab wounds to the chest. Three nails were broken and ragged.

```
3   Q. State's Exhibit—Exhibits 90 through 115, what are we
4   basically looking at? What do these images depict?
5   A. The—the photographs are from the front yard of
6   205 Simon St. They show the—the body of the
7   deceased. They show the deceased's bloodstained
8   clothes, the contusions on her face, broken fingernails.
9   They show her proximity to the property owner's little
10  library and also the proximity to the front door.
```

Julie wouldn't have gone easily. She had a gun and she knew how to use it. She had taken the same self-defense class as Teagan.

Divorced nearly ten years, she lived alone in the Monte Vista neighborhood. She had a state-of-the-art security system. Where had she gone dressed in a party frock? Not a bar hopper, Julie recently had declared herself ready to dive into the dating world. Her choice of weapon had been various dating apps. She would come into work after her date and regale them with tales of her latest fiasco. She gave the men names like Demon David and Henry the Hulk. Big Nose Nathan. Most never made it to a second date.

Where had she gone tonight? She always met her dates at a public place for coffee the first time, then lunch. If they made it to a third date, dinner.

No blood beyond that dried on her body and dress. She had been killed elsewhere and deposited on Teagan's front yard, next to her beloved borrowing library, at her doorstep while she slept. While Tigger slept. While Max slept. Or at least tried to sleep.

Fierce, eviscerating anger burned through Teagan. *Seriously, God, when will this stop? When will You step in and do something?*

She stood. The world tilted back and forth like a crazy, out-of-control seesaw. She sucked in air, trying to calm the rocking. His head down, Max went from a squat to kneeling. No doubt praying for Julie's safe passage through the pearly gates. A longtime member of a megachurch on the north side, Julie knew Jesus well.

"Are you okay?" Cole's fingers touched Teagan's arm. They were cold and clammy. "Do you need to sit down?"

Teagan opened her eyes and cleared her throat. "I'm okay."

"I'm not. I need a belt of scotch. Or two." He knelt and rubbed his face in his dog's fur. Finally, he sighed and looked up. "I'm going home. Tell them I'm ready to give a statement whenever they're ready."

"You should stay at the scene." Max spoke before Teagan could. "You found the body."

He might as well have said, *You killed her.*

"In Teagan's yard. You were both up. Both dressed."

Teagan glanced down at her T-shirt and sweats. Sort of. "Nobody is accusing anyone of anything. Your house is across the street. I don't blame you for wanting to go home and regroup while you wait."

It didn't matter what he did. Turn his back and the scene would still be in front of him, no matter how far or fast he ran. Closed his eyes. No matter. The sight of Julie's body would be burned on the insides of his eyelids for an eternity. What harm could it do to step into his home and close the door for a few minutes?

Max frowned at her. She scowled back.

Cole didn't wait for the standoff to end. He started for the sidewalk. "Do you want me to bring you some hot tea? A shot of whiskey?"

"No. You go. Max made coffee. At some point, we'll bring some out."

The thought of coffee in her roiling stomach sent bile burning up her esophagus. She fought for a smile but couldn't manage it. "Give me your number and I'll text you when they're headed your way."

"Thanks."

They exchanged numbers and he trudged away.

"We only have his word that he found her here."

"I know that. But why would the killer arrange Julie's body here and then knock on our door to share the news?"

"To throw us off."

"Or he could've gone to his house and we never would've known he was out here. He tried to do the right thing. I'm not jerking him around. Besides, he didn't have a drop of blood on that white T-shirt or anywhere else. He was clean and neat."

"Maybe he changed clothes before he came over."

"Seriously?"

"Maybe not. Your buddy Justin won't be happy."

"Your buddy Justin will have to deal with it." She tottered to the porch and sat. *This must be what it feels like to be a hundred years old and wondering why you're still on the planet.* "I'm calling Dad."

"That's a first." Max's gaze stayed on Cole's back as he trudged across the street and up the sidewalk to his house. "A silver lining maybe?"

Teagan ignored the observation. Her dad picked up on the first ring. He sounded wide awake. A night owl, he survived on far less sleep than any human being should.

"Daddy, I need you to come."

"Where are you?"

"Home."

"I'm on my way."

"He killed Julie."

An intake of air greeted her tearful words. "I'm on my way."

No doubt he would be here in half the time it normally took to drive from north of downtown to south of downtown.

Siebert was first on the scene from Homicide, followed by Billy, then Justin and Alisha. Billy's eyes filled with something close to defeat, and he scrubbed at his face with one hand. "We just saw her in your office."

"She didn't deserve this. Her family didn't deserve this." Teagan gritted her teeth and concentrated on the feel of Max's hand around hers. His fingers entwined with hers. "He's killing with impunity and we're not any closer to stopping him."

"Easy." Max's arm slid around Teagan's shoulder. "Everything that can be done, within the law, is being done."

Dad pulled up. Good, she could give her statement once, for everyone, as could Max. Of course, they separated them. Alisha and Siebert took Max's statement, while Teagan gave hers to Justin. Billy and Dad looked on. Both kept opening their mouths and Justin kept shaking his head, forcing them to stuff a sock in their comments and questions.

Justin smacked his pen against his notebook. "You let Reynolds go back to his house?"

"We didn't *let* him do anything. I'm not a cop."

"So he could wash up, take a shower, change his clothes, and get rid of evidence."

"He didn't need to wash up." Teagan gave him the same reasoning she'd shared with Max. "He called 911. He came knocking on my door. Why would the killer do that when he could just walk away and we wouldn't have known the difference? So what evidence?"

"He reported a crime. He should've stayed with the body until police arrived."

"You be sure to tell him that when you talk to him. Him, not me."

Billy put his hand on Justin's arm. Dad did the same with Teagan. Before either could speak, the CSU investigator held up the letter she had tugged from Julie's purse, found under the filmy material of her full skirt.

Teagan breathed. They were channeling their anger at their impotence at each other instead of the true culprit. The killer. This amounted to a hate-hate relationship. Yes, the letter would tell them something, maybe give them a clue that would lead them to this monster. At the same time, it was another opportunity for him to gloat, to prod, to humiliate.

Justin requested the letter be laid out flat by the investigator so they could read it before it was bagged and tagged.

Dear T,

It's time to get acquainted with the ballerina. I'll ask the lovely Leyla for the next dance. You'll be next. The daughters of a retired SAPD homicide detective gone. Simply gone. My deeds will be plastered across newspapers. My nom de plume on the lips of news anchors. What is it, by the way? I'm sure you can come up with something creative by now.

Your friend,
Amos

No. No. No.

He was still posing as Amos, brutal psychopath who kidnapped his victims and held on to them so he could terrorize and torture them.

Leyla. "We have to get Leyla. We need to get Leyla." Teagan darted across the yard to her Prius. She needed her keys. Her purse. She changed directions.

Billy caught her with both arms. "Dad's on the phone with Jazz. Justin is requesting uniformed officers to watch the house until we can get over there. Leyla will never be left alone. We can move her to a safe house if we have to. Or send her to stay with our family in San Diego. I'll personally escort her. I'm headed there now."

"Get to her now. Lights and siren. No stopping at red lights."

"I'm on my way." Billy whirled. His walk turned into a jog.

Max strode toward Teagan.

She shook her head.

He kept coming until he was within arm's reach. "Billy's got this."

He reached for her hand. She recoiled. Even he couldn't help.

"I can't stand this. I need to get some air." Fists clenched, Teagan walked away. Her neighbors congregated on the asphalt. They were scared. They were angry. They felt violated. She knew this because she felt the same way. Their quiet, peaceful neighborhood would never be the same.

Would Leyla, once she knew who was after her? Would she ever feel safe again?

Stephanie and Dana stood huddled on the sidewalk in front of Dana's bungalow. Fighting the urge to hang her head, Teagan joined them. "I'm so sorry."

"I just saw her in court last week." Dana shook her head. Tears trickled down her face. A tough-as-titanium litigator brought to tears at dawn a few yards from her own home. "She was talking about getting a dog. A labradoodle. I told her I thought they were silly dogs. She was offended."

"Why does this keep happening here?" Stephanie wiped her face with a sodden tissue. "Paul and I are talking about moving. We're looking at a subdivision on the northwest side. Gated community with cameras and neighborhood security patrol. Good schools. Low crime."

"The police will get this guy, I promise."

"That's what you said when Evelyn died. This woman didn't even live here. Why is she in your yard?" Stephanie shuddered. "I'll never be able to use your library again."

"They'll catch him. He'll be convicted. His life will be over."

"Not soon enough." Stephanie picked Charlotte up from her stroller and hugged her to her chest. "We have kids in this neighborhood. What if one of them had found her?"

"They didn't."

"What if the next victim is one of our kids?"

The guy had a thing for women. Stephanie had enough fodder for nightmares. She didn't need to know this.

Teagan glanced back at Justin and Alisha. They were on their way to Cole's door. Teagan excused herself from her neighbors and texted him.

They're headed yr way.

Thanks. Yu ok?

No.

Me neither.

Hang in there.

Can you come in? It's the only way I'm letting them in.

On my way.

Would some strange friendship grow out of these grim circumstances? It didn't seem likely. Some day they would pass on the street or see each other at a National Night Out, smile, nod, exchange pleasantries, but they would always remind each other of that day when they waited in the dank predawn air for the cops to show up and bag the body of a too-young-to-die full-of-life woman. There would be no doggie dates among friends who found a dead woman in Teagan's front yard.

"Wait, let me go with you." She scurried across the grass to Cole's front yard. Justin had one hand on the wrought-iron railing that led to the long, narrow porch attached to the Victorian-style home. "He knows me. I can help. He wants me in there."

He didn't know her. Death brought people closer together and more quickly.

Justin's expression didn't just say *no*, it said, *"No way, José."*

Alisha shrugged. "She's already given her statement. If they needed to get their stories straight, they did it before we got here."

"I don't think it's a good idea."

"What we need right now is a break." Alisha's hand went to the doorbell. "He's asked for Teagan to be present. If that helps him relax, maybe he'll remember more details."

"What details? You're assuming he saw—"

"Okay, okay." Justin made a cease-and-desist motion. He reached past his partner and rapped on the door. "Let's see what the man has to say."

30

Cole answered so quickly he might have been standing inside the door listening. His face gave no clue. In one hand he held an etched crystal glass filled halfway with an amber liquid. He'd changed into tan Dockers and a dark-blue polo shirt, but his face remained haggard.

Justin identified himself, as well as Alisha. "A little early to hit the sauce isn't it?"

Cole looked beyond the two detectives to Teagan. "Will they let you come in?"

"They say yes."

"Then, by all means, come in." He opened the door wider and everyone trooped inside.

"Can I get you some coffee or tea? I know it's hot out there, but I can't seem to get warm."

Justin shook his head. "Nothing for me."

"I was talking to the ladies." Despite his words, Cole didn't sound distressed. His gaze, directed at Justin, was assessing. "No matter the circumstances, I try to be a gentleman."

"Good for you." Alisha's conciliatory tone warmed the icy air that hung between Cole and Justin. "If we could ask you a few questions, it would be helpful."

"Absolutely." He waved his free hand at the living room. "I'll bring in the coffee."

He disappeared into the interior of the house without waiting for an answer. Teagan sank onto a floral chintz-covered sofa and surveyed her surroundings. Anything not to think about Julie's body now on its way to the morgue.

A carved mahogany fireplace mantel matched the bay windows, which provided natural lighting for the floor-to-ceiling built-in bookshelves. The remaining walls had been covered with soft red roses on creamy beige wallpaper that met the chair railings about halfway down. Elaborate crown molding decorated the ceilings.

"Good grief." Justin shifted on one of the button-back chairs on the other side of the sofa. "Talk about froufrou."

"It takes a certain kind of man to appreciate the Victorian era." Teagan stood and went to the bookshelves. Art history, architecture, DIY manuals, communications textbooks, and scores of American classics. Moldy oldies. If he watched TV, he didn't do it in this room. His taste in art tended toward still life, portraits, flowers, bowls of fruit, and gardens à la hotel room décor. Cole's home—at least this room—also lacked something. At first Teagan couldn't put her finger on it. She ran her gaze over the room again.

He hadn't displayed a single family photo. In fact, nothing felt personal about the room.

"If you want to borrow something, feel free." His voice floated behind her. "I've been so busy renovating room by room, I still have books to unpack. Not that I'll have anything that suits your taste."

That was it. He still had boxes to unpack. Teagan turned. He carried an ornate silver tray with a carafe and coffee service for four. "Thank you and thanks for the coffee."

"We need to know exactly what you saw. From the beginning." Despite his earlier denial, Justin accepted the cup Cole offered him. "Why were you outside at that hour?"

"Do you want cream or sugar?" Cole directed his inquiry to Alisha.

"I'm good."

He saved Teagan for last. His smile was ragged. "How about you?"

"Both. My stomach is ripped."

He prepared it for her with grace from a different era.

Justin cleared his throat. "Mr. Reynolds—"

"Cole."

"We don't have time to mess around. A woman was killed across the street."

"I'm aware. I'm traumatized for life."

"Then get on with it."

"I went for a run—at least I intended to go for a run—about five forty-five this morning and—"

"Do you always run that early?"

Cole's pained expression reflected his thoughts on Justin's manners. "No. I was supposed to give finals today. I'm an instructor at SAC. Speech, beginning communications for freshmen."

"You locked your door, you ran down the steps, and then what happened?"

"I crossed the street. I planned to head south to the Mission Reach trails for a nice, long run."

"And?"

"And Huck started growling. He never growls. He's a very calm, well-mannered hound unless provoked, in which case you don't want to get on his bad side." The dog, who had followed his owner into the room, raised his head from his spot near the fireplace and *woofed*. "Yes, I'm talking about you, my friend. Anyway, I hesitated. I slowed down. I could see something shining in the solar light by the library, so I crossed over and approached."

He stared into his coffee cup.

"Take your time, Cole." Teagan had traveled this painful road with Officer Moreno's death. "Believe me, I understand how hard this is. You don't see murder victims on a regular basis—or at all—like these guys do. I'm in shock, too, and I've seen many crime scene photos."

"Thank you." Cole sipped his coffee. He moved a coaster closer and set the cup on the coffee table. "Her dress shimmered in the light. At first I thought maybe she had fallen down. Maybe she was drunk. But Huck continued to growl. He became more and more distraught. I got closer. I realized she'd been stabbed. Numerous times."

Huck whined. He stood and meandered over to his owner and lowered himself gracefully on the sixteenth- or seventeenth-century Persian rug at his owner's feet. "I knelt and touched her neck. Only her neck. She was still warm, but she had no pulse. I know you're not supposed to touch anything at a crime scene. I've watched enough TV to know that. But I had to—"

"It's okay." Alisha assured him. "Then what?"

"I stood and ran to Teagan's door."

"Where you should've stayed until police arrived."

"I'm sorry. I've never been first on a murder scene before."

"Did you see or hear anything out of the ordinary or out of place before you discovered the body?" Alisha shot Justin a look, as if to say, *Ease up, bud.* "Cars, people, anything?"

Cole rose and went to the bay window, where he stopped, his back to them. After a second, he turned around. "Now that you mention it, I did see a white SUV or maybe it was a minivan. I don't know. I'm not a car person. It drove through just as I was locking my door. I glanced up because the engine sputtered."

"In front of your house?"

"Having just passed this house, going toward Alamo Street. I hadn't seen it around before, and it was so early in the morning. It's not like this is a through street that people who don't live here normally use."

"We'll need your clothes." Justin grimaced at a spot somewhere between Cole and Teagan. "All y'all's clothes. And we'll need you to come downtown to give your formal statements."

"Again." Teagan stopped. It had to be done. She understood that. Another day spent reliving murder and mayhem in her own neighborhood. "Fine, let's go."

"I'll gather up my clothes." Cole hung back. "Do you want them in a bag?"

"That's fine." Alisha's hand went to her hip where her service weapon hung. "I'll wait for them."

With an encouraging nod to Cole, Teagan headed for the door. Outside the media had gathered along with the same neighborhood residents. From the ramped-up look on Brian Lake's face, they had been exchanging information. "Is it true that the victim worked in the 177th?" he hollered from the tight pack of reporters and photographers. "Is it true she was stabbed multiple times and left at your library, Teagan?"

"We are in the process of notifying the victim's family, so please bear with us." Justin spoke up. "I'd hate for them to find out by turning on the TV."

"So that's a confirmation."

A murmur ran through the members of the media. "Is it true it's the same killer who murdered your neighbor Evelyn Conklin?" the skinny little reporter from KSAT 12 yelled. Her name escaped Teagan's discombobulated brain. "And Officer Moreno? She was shot, the other two stabbed. And another woman was strangled. Does San Antonio have a serial killer on its hands?"

"Where's the chief when you need him?" Alisha muttered to Teagan.

"PIO is setting up a press conference outside the Public Safety HQ in one hour," Justin responded. "I suggest y'all get over there and get set up."

The stampede started before he finished the second sentence.

"Did you just make that up?"

"No!" He winced as if hurt by Teagan's suggestion. "I got a text from the civilian PIO. Let's head over there. Hopefully I can take you in the back side and avoid the presser."

"Stop. Wait." Billy raced across the street. A Mazda pickup narrowly avoided smashing into him. The driver offered him a one-finger salute and a few choice words through his open window. Billy didn't slow. "Jazz called. She can't find Leyla."

31

Sweet, independent, stubborn Leyla was missing. She could already be dead.

Nausea rocked Teagan. She halted. Took two steps. Stopped. Max grabbed her arm. "Easy, easy. She probably spent the night at a friend's house."

"Dillon told her to stay put in no uncertain terms." Billy drew a ragged breath. "She's such a little—"

"Don't say it. She's a grown woman who believes she has a right to a life." Teagan broke free from Max's grip. "I'm going to look for her."

"No, you're not." Billy blocked her path. "I'm sure she took her Glock. And we've got people out searching for her right now."

"When we find her, I'm going to kill her." Teagan grappled with tears she refused to let fall. Leyla was a free spirit in a by-the-book family. She lived in never-never land. "Then I'll lock her in her room for life."

"You'll have to wait in line." Billy's hand went to the gun on his hip. "And hope she doesn't have her Glock on her."

Cole whistled. "She carries a gun?"

He and Alisha were a few short steps behind. Alisha had his bag of clothing in one hand.

"My little sister isn't to be trifled with." Teagan breathed through the nausea. "She used to engage in competitive shooting. Unfortunately, at her age that means she thinks she's invincible."

"I have a sister. She's older. But she has always been self-assured."

"I'm going."

"No, you're not." Justin joined Billy in the roadblock. "You're in police custody. You have to go to HQ to give a statement. Remember?"

"You're kidding me!"

"I kid you not."

"We're not suspects, are we?"

"No, but if you give me any more guff, I can call you a person of interest and slap cuffs on you."

"You'd like that, wouldn't you?" Max cut in. "We have rights. Maybe I should call my lawyer."

"Whoa, we're all on the same team." Dad jogged over in time to hear Max's comment. "Let's keep the focus on Leyla."

"That's what I'm trying to do, Dad." Teagan squeezed between Billy and Justin to confront the elder O'Rourke. "I know all of Leyla's old haunts. Her friends' names from high school."

"She's not with them."

"How do you know?"

"They found a letter in her Mini Cooper." Dad proceeded to read the text of the letter from his phone.

The Mini Cooper. Leave it to Leyla to buy the smallest car to zip in and out of traffic on I-35S, which she shared with innumerable monster trucks and semis.

"Did they find anything else?" To her chagrin, a bit of quiver surfaced in Teagan's voice. She demanded that it stop. "In the car, I mean, besides the letter."

"A sign of a struggle, yes. Her paperwork was scattered around on the front seat. Some snacks. Junk." Dad's gaze sought hers. "No blood."

Thank You, Jesus, thank You. "Can we read the letter, please?"

Dear T,

You didn't move fast enough, my dear.

I've grown impatient.

I plan to dance the night away

With your sweet stepsister.

You can still save her.

Do you tango? Or do you prefer the two-step?

Plaster my nom de plume you've created for me all over the media.

Tell my story for me.

I'll be in touch with further instructions.

Your friend,

Lloyd Carmichael

Lloyd Carmichael. One of Raymond Fuentes's standout bad guys. A paid assassin who appeared in more than one novel as an antagonist Jay Southerland couldn't catch. Until it got personal.

"In *Pay to Play* Carmichael becomes Jay Southerland's nemesis. He threatens some of the most important people in Southerland's life, and he has to protect them. I can't say more without spoiling the outcome."

"Even for Leyla."

"If I think it's applicable, believe me, I'll tell anyone who will listen."

"I've got civilian employees reading them," Justin said. "You've read them over time. The details run into each other. This way if there's any clue in the names he's choosing that helps us, we'll know."

Smart guy. Using all those little gray cells Hercule Poirot loved so much. "He has his gross, horrible hands on my sister." Teagan walked away. It gave her time to swipe at her cheeks and get her game face in place. She turned back. "It's killing me to think what that means."

Billy dug his hands into his suit pants pockets. "We're on it, Sissy. Chief has opened the gates to give us more manpower. There's a BOLO out for a white minivan spotted in this neighborhood—"

"Because that narrows it down so much."

"In a way it does. Most people are driving SUVs now. The old mommy van is passé." Alisha cut in. At their raised eyebrows, she shrugged. "I have friends with little kids. The SUVs are way cooler. When you see a minivan, it's older and more road weary, so to speak."

"Okay. That's something." Billy didn't look convinced. "Teagan, your front porch camera doesn't reach to the library. You need to get that fixed. But in the meantime, we've got nobody who saw anything before Cole Reynolds. So we're proceeding with the plan to take him downtown for a formal interview. He's already contacted a wet-behind-the-ears lawyer he knew in school. We'll need you, too, and Max."

"I'm happy to go downtown, but the statement will have to wait." Teagan squeezed between Alisha and Billy, headed for her car. "I have another pot to stir while I'm at HQ."

"What pot . . . ?" Billy grabbed for her and swiped air. "Teagan, no, no, you can't."

"Watch me."

32

This guy wanted publicity. Teagan would give him publicity.

"This is nuts." Billy slapped both hands on his hips and stood, legs spread. Every muscle tight. His gaze, directed at Dad, blazed with a volatile mixture of anger, fear, and surprise. "You're not going along with this, are you?"

"We will be on top of her every second of every minute."

"Julie was a crack shot with a license to carry. She had a Glock semiautomatic 9mm pistol in her bag." Justin sided with Billy, of course. BFFs to the bitter end. "The guy stabbed her to death before she could pull the gun from her purse."

"I won't have to defend myself, because it'll never come to that." Teagan eased toward the windows in the foyer of the SAPD HQ building with all its fancy accoutrements designed to make it pleasing to the eye. Like putting lipstick on a donkey's patootie. "I'm making a statement."

"Max, are you on board with this?" Billy's effort to shore up his side continued. "She's turning herself into bait."

"He's already done that." Discomfort drew lines deep into Max's battered face with its bruises fading from vivid purple to milder greens and yellows. "However, I've been shouted down twice. It's a stupid plan."

"It'll work." Teagan gripped his hand and squeezed, trying to will her assurances into him. "I know it will. Just believe in me."

"I'll never stop believing in you. I'll pray every step of the way for every word. And for a good outcome."

Prayer, their first and last weapon of choice. Max could keep these things in perspective in a way she could not. "Could we pray now?"

"We really don't have time—"

Billy's quick response was cut off by Dad. "Absolutely."

Her father held out his hand. A little miracle in the midst of such devastation. They joined hands and bowed their heads. Max began. "God, please don't let him hurt Leyla. Don't let him scar and destroy her sweet spirit. Inoculate her against his evil. Don't let him touch her heart and soul. Give her body strength to withstand whatever physical punishment he tries to inflict. Put Your bubble of protection around her, we pray. Give her strength and allow her to use that wonderful brain You gave her to find a way out. Help these men and women to find her quickly through Your saving grace, in Jesus's holy and precious name we pray."

"Amen."

"Thank you." The two syllables came out in a squeak.

"Dad, are you sure about this?" Billy raced back up the food chain as if nothing in Max's prayer had calmed his tunnel vision.

"Sure as a father can be when his children are in harm's way and he has to choose a least-worst-case scenario. I'm not crazy about the idea, but Teagan can handle herself, and like Justin said, we'll be on top of it every second." Dad rubbed bloodshot eyes. "Leyla's life is at stake."

"So you're trading Teagan for Leyla."

"We're not trading anyone." Dad tucked an arm around Teagan and drew her into a tight hug. "We're right behind you, girl. Go get 'im."

Teagan shoved through the doors into the plaza in front of PSHQ. She took a deep breath and stepped up to Chief Zavala's right. He'd been briefed by the PIO staff that she was coming. Still, surprise and concern flitted across his face. Teagan shrugged and cocked her eyebrows. *It has to be done. She's my sister.* Her telegraphed message hit home. His face once again his trademark brown stone with deep scars of unknown origin, Zavala nodded and faced the sea of antsy media.

They were openly anxious to get to their units and file their stories. Most had taped their microphones to the plush portable podium complete with a built-in sound system, perfect for outdoor pressers.

A murmur ran through the small crowd as some, like Brian Lake, recognized her. The mass of journalists leaned forward with a metaphorical *Ahhhh, what have we here?*

"I know you're all chomping at the bit to file stories or get back to the station or move on to the next pool of blood, but you'll want to stick around for my guest." Playing it like a true politician/actor, Zavala patted his face with a folded handkerchief, laid it on the podium, and took a sip of bottled spring water. "Some of you will recognize her. If you're busy doing puff pieces, you might not."

Ouch. Let's not antagonize these folks, Chief.

The sudden appearance of one of the PIOs from the city manager's office suggested she agreed as well. She slid her hair behind her ear and raised her eyebrows.

Apparently the chief caught the signal. Looking duly chastised, he launched into the remarks hastily scribbled by the PIO. "Teagan O'Rourke, court reporter for the 177th District Court, has written records for hundreds of cases in the last six years, but she never expected to be in the middle of a murder spree that has repeatedly hit close to home.

"She is the daughter of a retired police officer and homicide detective, and the sister of two SAPD officers, one a homicide detective. For some reason we're not getting into here, she has been singled out as the recipient of some horrifying notes from a serial killer who has demanded that she share his insights with the world. He wants to be famous, so Ms. O'Rourke and her family have decided to give him what he wants.

"Not because we normally give in to capricious demands from wanton murderers, but because he has kidnapped Ms. O'Rourke's stepsister Leyla Evans-O'Rourke, a law student at UT–Austin. I'll let Ms. O'Rourke share the rest of the information with you."

Cameras clicked in a mad rush, a cacophony of sound until one couldn't be distinguished from another. Bodies crowded the thin line that separated the podium from the media. A uniformed officer stepped in between.

"It's all right, Officer." Gathering her wits around her like spilled grains of wheat, Teagan let her gaze drift over the reporters and then glanced down at the podium. Some eager-beaver PR type had left speaking points for her. She turned the sheets of paper facedown. "I struggle with how to stand in front of y'all and give this depraved killer what he wants." She swallowed. Her dry throat hurt with each syllable. Chief Zavala set a fresh bottle of water, already open, in front of her. She took a long swallow.

Please God, don't let me burp or, worse, cry in front of these people. "But he has my sister. Chief Zavala identified her as my stepsister. Biologically she is.

"But in life, in love, in family, she is my sister and has been since she walked into my bedroom, all of six years old, and announced she wanted the top bunk. I was ten and no way was I letting this little snot-nosed intruder give the orders.

"Leyla is twenty-three now, a gifted dancer, an award-winning competitive shooter, as well as a law student. This man got the jump on her somehow, and now he has her. The only way to pacify him, he says, is to publicly announce my choice for his nom de plume as he calls it. You see, he writes me letters and leaves them at the crime scenes."

Hands shot in the air. Brian's waved like a railroad-crossing red light.

"Let me finish, guys, and then you can ask questions."

She managed another sip of water, praying her stomach wouldn't spew it back out. She explained his choice of signatures, each one different and pertaining to a Raymond Fuentes novel.

"I've chosen the Triple S Murderer, in the tradition of the BTK Killer. I'm not sure what he's looking for. Something more literary, perhaps. But he's not getting it. Not from me. What he's doing is real. It's not fiction. He's hurting and killing women. He's just as desperate as the BTK Killer for publicity. He wants to be famous. As famous as a man who hides his identity behind fictitious names of characters in books can be.

"The Triple S stands for Shoot, Stab, and Strangle. This guy likes to mix up his MO. His victims are woman of various ages, vocations, and ethnic backgrounds. He varies his victims and his MO in order to stymie attempts to capture him. We think the recent murders have been to get at my father, retired detective Dillon O'Rourke. He's playing with me to get revenge on my father. For what, we're not sure. But nothing has to make sense in our minds, only in the mind of a psychopath."

"Is this somehow related to the Leo Slocum case?"

Brian broke protocol by shouting out his question before she asked for them.

"SAPD Homicide, my father, my brother Detective William Evans-O'Rourke, and my sister Patrolwoman Grace Evans-O'Rourke Garcia are running down all leads and all possible connections."

"That doesn't answer my question."

"No, it doesn't."

"My sources say you interviewed Slocum's son recently, as well as several ex-coworkers. Is it typical for a court reporter to participate in an investigation like this?"

"That's a question for the chief, I suppose, but I accompanied my father, who is a consultant for SAPD with standing in this case. I'm not sure how that will change now that a family member has been kidnapped. Either way, the department and my family are pursuing all leads and all possible connections."

"Why have a news conference if you're not going to tell us more?" An AP reporter volleyed that question over the shouts of several of his colleagues. "At least tell us why you think there might be a connection with a man who's incarcerated and likely will be prosecuted in other murders in other cities."

"Right now our focus is on getting Leyla back. The chief public information officer's staff members are emailing all of your outlets jpegs of Leyla, along with news releases with her physical stats, where the abduction took place, and the number for viewers or readers to call if they think they've seen Leyla and the man who abducted her." A sleek PR type handed out printed copies of the release as Teagan spoke. "She was last seen wearing a navy-blue ribbed tank top, denim shorts, and red Converse sneakers with black laces. This man should be considered armed and very dangerous. Please include this information in your reports. And TV folks, we're asking you to banner the number to call on your screens during the stories and for everyone to post the story with the number on your websites, your social media outlets, and your reporter blogs. Everywhere."

Sudden hysterical elation buoyed Teagan. With all these media outlets distributing information, surely someone would call with something that helped them find Leyla before it was too late.

She could already be dead.

More questions peppered her. Most she couldn't answer, not without jeopardizing the investigation. She'd done what she came to do. "If you report anything about this story tonight, use this sound bite: Triple S Murderer, you're no friend of mine. If you hurt my sister in any way, my family will hunt you down to the ends of the earth and make you pay. That's a fact. You wanted publicity, you've got it. Let's make a trade. Me for her. You know where to find me."

"You're baiting him?" Even Brian, who'd covered drug cartel trials, gun-smuggling cases, and capital murder trials involving infants looked shocked. "Are you nuts?"

"Fed up. If he wants to play chicken, I'll meet him on the back road of his choice."

Brian wasn't the only journalist shaking his head.

"What do you mean he's no friend of yours?" The CBS affiliate reporter waved her pen in the air. "When can we see copies of the letters he sent you?"

"I'll turn this back over to the chief. He'll answer your questions regarding the investigation. Thank you for listening."

Brian caught her before she could get to Max, who stood several yards from the news conference, likely to avoid appearing in the camera shots when she stood at the podium. "I'd like to get an interview."

"I've already said all I have to say."

"There's more to this than you're telling us. What else was in the letters? Let me mike you, and you can talk about how you're processing this, getting through it, what impact it's having on your family. How has your faith been impacted?"

"Off the record, it sucks. You want me to spill my guts on camera like so many grieving loved ones do when someone is gunned down in the street in a drive-by and a drug deal gone bad? They cry and sob and say they didn't see it coming despite years of gang activity? I don't denigrate them for doing it. I even understand the need to pour out your pain and suffering to be shared by strangers. But it's not me. All I want is to find Leyla before it's too late. Tell your viewers that. Tell them to pray for us."

"I will." Brian lowered his camera from his shoulder and let it hang from one hand. "I don't mean to be intrusive. I'm just doing my job."

"I know."

"I'll pray."

"Thank you."

When a crusty old reporter said he would pray, she'd hit pay dirt.

Teagan made it to Max. He wrapped her in a hug. "Come on, guys, give us a break."

She raised her head from his chest and swiveled. The media had followed her, including Brian. They were getting the B-roll they adored. Talking heads were no fun. Shots of the bereaved family member collapsing into a loved one's arms were much more appealing. But that's not what she wanted the killer to see on TV. He didn't have her back against the wall. He didn't have control.

"It's okay. We're fine." She took Max's hand and locked gazes with him. "Just fine."

He nodded. Together she and Max walked into HQ. She still needed to give her statement. Dad and the others were upstairs waiting for them, watching the news conference from a live stream from a PD camera. They had a room waiting for them to debrief while Max and Teagan gave their statements. By now Cole would be on his way home. If he was lucky.

She didn't believe in luck. Her intuition said Cole didn't either.

"Vultures." Max waited until they were clear of security and in the elevator to turn to her. "They feed on decent people's lives."

"Just doing their jobs."

"How can you be so calm?"

"Inside I'm a seething caldron of pain, fury, fear, and the desire to shoot that man in the head myself." She leaned against him and took both hands so their fingers entwined. "What does that say about me, Miss Pacifist, Anti–Capital Punishment, Anti-Guns? Anti-violence period. Anti-war. Pro-peace. A disciple of Dr. Martin Luther King Jr. Grandma would be so disappointed."

"She would understand that you're human and you've been pushed too far."

"When we get done here, I want you to lend me a gun. I haven't shot one in years. I need to practice."

"I won't."

"Why?"

"Because you fall in that category of people who will hesitate at the last moment. You won't be able to pull the trigger. You think you can, to protect yourself or the people you love, but you can't."

He brushed her cheek with a gentle kiss, over before she could capture it. "Your beautiful heart is one of the things I love about you. I won't be a part of destroying that. And you would hate yourself for it if you did manage to pull the trigger. If you didn't, the guy would take it away from you and use it on you. He'd kill you with your own gun."

"Wow, you've given this some thought."

"My first inclination when this nightmare started was to force a gun into your hand and make you learn to protect yourself. But I never would do that to you." He slid away and leaned against the wall, both hands behind his back. "I respect your beliefs. I even aspire to them, but I'm damaged goods. I can never go back. I never want you to be where I am. You're a piece of beautiful ceramic pottery that, once broken, could not be remade in the same shape."

"You are not damaged goods." Tears stung the backs of her eyes. She willed them to settle down. "You are a man with a beautiful heart."

The elevator door opened. The officer behind the information desk frowned and shook his finger at them. "You know you have to push the button in order to actually move from floor to floor."

"Ah." Max jabbed the button. The door closed. He jabbed again for the correct floor.

Teagan sank against the wall. "Leyla can't be dead."

"Don't think ahead." Max returned to his post on the opposite wall. "Focus on what we do next."

"Next we find her."

"Agreed."

Ding-ding.

Back to reality. Back to a world where Leyla would not be coming home tonight.

Maybe never.

33

The six o'clock news did its job. The ten o'clock followed up with more human-interest angles. They had a field day with Leyla's Facebook page. A montage of photos from her college days; videos of her dancing and teaching dance lessons; shots of her with various boyfriends, none of whom had stuck, showed what a vivacious, beautiful woman she was. The victim.

Leyla would hate that word. Teagan hated it. The stories were excruciating to watch. Yet she kept watching. They'd recorded as many newscasts as they could, and the rest were being captured from websites.

"Turn it off."

Still dressed in her uniform, her cheeks pink with June heat and her forehead beaded with perspiration, Gracie stood in Dad's living room and held out her hand for the remote.

Teagan laid it on the oversized coffee table instead, nestled amid hunting, fishing, and gun magazines.

Everyone had rendezvoused back at Dad's house, thereby closing ranks. Even Max would stay there. For safety purposes, according to Dad. The news stories had included digital footage of their embrace outside HQ. No one had commented. They had more important things on their minds. Like returning calls received on the hotline number and running down leads, bogus or not. Mostly bogus.

As civilians, she and Max were not allowed to engage in these activities. That didn't keep Max from sitting next to Dad in his office, thumbing through call reports and listening to half conversations, trying to get the gist of what might lead to a true location.

Teagan had done the same until she couldn't stand it anymore. The ups and downs. The possibility shot down by the timing or the location or the description. How many young women were wearing a blue ribbed tank top, denim shorts, and red Converse sneakers with black laces? Leyla wasn't the fashion maverick she thought she was.

Gracie plopped onto the sofa next to Teagan and helped herself to Teagan's tumbler of lemonade. "Anything new?"

"We've got bupkis." Teagan tucked a handful of peanut–dried-cherries–oats–carob-chip granola into her mouth and chewed. Max insisted that she needed to eat. She couldn't stomach much more. "The leads are pouring in, but none are panning out. We'll be up all night."

"They will. You need to sleep."

"You think I can sleep knowing Leyla's out there somewhere? Knowing what he might be doing to her?"

"That was a stupid thing you did at the presser."

"It needed to be done."

"He's gunning for you now."

"He was already gunning for me."

Gracie took her own handful of granola, but she gently shook it onto a napkin without taking a bite. "There's something I want to tell you. This is a terrible time, but it's eating at me and I want you to know before it's colored by whatever happens to this family next."

"Good grief. That sounds serious." Teagan's heart, already a punching bag that should by all rights have been retired with its scarred boxer, flinched. "Don't keep me in suspense."

"We're pregnant. Me and Frank." Tears dripped down her cheeks. She seemed unaware. "It's a girl. We waited until we cleared the three-month mark to tell everyone. Then we decided to wait until the eighteen-week sonogram. Now it's hard to keep it a secret. Everybody probably thinks I just put on weight, but I'm showing—"

"Don't keep it a secret. Share your good news. We need good news." Teagan collected her sister into a hug. She leaned close to her and whispered, "I'm so happy for you, so thrilled. You'll be a super mom."

"Thank you. I can't believe I'm blubbering like this." Gracie grabbed another napkin and sopped up the tears. "It's hormones, I'm telling you. I bawl at the drop of a hat."

"You know Lilly's expecting? You two can compare notes and buy baby clothes together." Baby clothes were so cute. A hard knot formed in Teagan's throat. She would be Aunt T, the supercool single aunt to all her nieces and nephews. "You can exchange babysitting for date nights."

"Justin told me, but I haven't said anything yet. I wanted to tell you first."

"Why not tell everyone at once and get it over with?"

"I don't know." Gracie stared at the sodden napkin in her hands. Her classic-cut solitaire diamond displayed on a simple silver band sparkled in the light. "You're about to do something terribly dangerous to save our sister whose life hangs in the balance. All I can think about is this little nugget inside me. I want her to meet you both. Leyla said she would teach all the grandkids to dance. That would be her gift to us. A sort of IOU until she's old enough."

"Does she know about the nugget?"

"No. We have to get her back so I can tell her."

"We'll do our best." Teagan knew better than to make promises she couldn't keep. "When's the due date?"

"October thirtieth." She sighed. "I'm pulling myself off the streets."

"You're giving up patrol?"

"It's time. Nothing's more important than being a parent." She stopped. Her face reddened. "I didn't mean it that way."

"I knew what you meant. Nothing is more important to you. What will you do?"

"I'm hoping to do white-collar crimes or maybe cybersecurity. I have to take the exam. You know how tough it is to move up. It depends on what's open and who else is applying."

"I think parenting is the most important job in the world." Maybe Gracie didn't mean to imply anything. Maybe paranoia gift-wrapped innocent words intended to celebrate a new life, not denigrate an old decision. "Which is why I've chosen not to go that route."

"You would be a great parent."

"Thank you." No other response worked. It was a sterling compliment. "Let's go tell the others."

"Now?"

"Now. They need this. It'll refuel them."

Fill them up with a light that could overcome any dark.

Gracie slid an arm around Teagan. Together they walked into their father's office. Teagan went to the murder board. All these young women were babies once. They were loved by mommies and daddies who cooed over them, played This Little Piggy Went to Market, made raspberries on their chubby bellies, and taught them to blow kisses.

It was too late for them. All the police could give them would be the much vaunted closure. They would not allow this to happen to Leyla.

The Triple S Murderer would never know what hit him.

34

I'm not sure this is going to work." Teagan's jaw hurt from gritting her teeth in impatience. She and Max had been waiting for the reading of Evelyn's will for more than twenty minutes. "We should be out there following up on leads to Leyla's whereabouts."

Not in Robert Sandoval and his partners' office in a nondescript five-story office building tucked among a plethora of hotels that surrounded downtown San Antonio.

"You threw down the gauntlet at the press conference." Max fidgeted with the sleeves of his navy-blue sports jacket—the one he wore to any occasion that required more than his standard T-shirt and jeans. "He's coming for you. He can't get to you at the house. A slew of cops are watching over you, and even more are following up on these leads."

"Do you think Leyla's still alive?" It took supreme willpower to tame the tremor in her voice.

"Yes."

"Are you just saying that to make me feel better?"

"No, I think he's keeping her alive to bait you, just like you baited him. It strategically serves him better than killing her. He's too smart."

"But he gets off on killing. He may not be able to control himself."

"Or he may make her wish she were dead." Max slid closer and took Teagan's hand. "I'm sorry I said that out loud, but I know you're

279

thinking it. Let's try not to use our imaginations too much right now. Leyla's a smart, savvy woman with self-defense skills learned from your dad. Let's give her some credit too."

Max was right. Imagining the worst had kept Teagan awake most of the night. Every time she'd drifted off to sleep, the nightmares began again. "Do you think he's watching us right now?" Teagan nodded toward the streets below. "Waiting for us?"

"I do. He's watching and he's waiting. He wants us to be on edge." Max tapped on the double-paned glass. "But that's what we want. Our guys are watching and waiting too. If he makes a move, they'll be ready to follow."

"Him who? We don't even know who we're looking for."

"It doesn't matter. They'll follow us, and he'll take us to Leyla. Boom."

Teagan had dealt the hand. Max carried his Smith & Wesson in a holster hidden by his jacket. Cops in plain clothes dotted the landscape outside. A homeless man. A guy eating a raspa. A woman sitting on a bus bench reading the newspaper. They'd put a GPS tracker on Teagan's car. She and Max both had their phones tucked in pockets within easy reach. Her father and company sat in the obligatory nondescript van on the other side of Arciniega Street, waiting.

Now they simply needed the killer to make his move.

"He's not going to do it here. He knows they're watching. He's not stupid, anything but."

This could go on forever. Teagan's nerves stretched tighter and tighter until it seemed her head would explode.

A throat cleared. Teagan jumped. So did Max. They both turned. Mr. Sandoval stood in the doorway to the small waiting room. Today he wore an equally somber dark-gray suit, but his tie was a becoming pale pink. "Sorry to keep you waiting. The family had private matters to discuss."

Having no other choice, they traipsed after him.

The days since the funeral had left their mark on Evelyn's daughter, Robin. She managed a vague smile before patting her cheeks with a bedraggled tissue that held most of the pink lipstick that had been on her thin lips. "I saw you on TV last night. You're either brave or foolhardy."

"More the latter than the former."

Sandoval made it as quick and painless as possible given the circumstances. The house and all real estate and proceeds would be split evenly between Evelyn's two children. Most of the contents would be sold at an estate sale, with the exception of a series of bequests. College funds were set aside for her four grandchildren. To everyone's surprise, Evelyn had substantial investment and savings. She bequeathed a staggering sum of money to the local city-run animal shelter "in support of its efforts to become a no-kill shelter."

Robin's husband grumbled a bit at that one but subsided upon a sharp frown from the attorney. "Ms. O'Rourke, to you Mrs. Conklin left her collection of vintage Fiesta dinnerware and the hickory curio cabinet in which they reside."

"Those early pieces are worth thousands to the right collectors—"

Robin slapped her hand on her husband's. "These are Mother's wishes."

"She's responsible for your mother's murder!"

"I'll ask that you keep your comments to yourself." Sandoval peered over his rimless reading glasses with a frown that would've quieted the most recalcitrant teenage boy. "These are Mrs. Conklin's wishes as recorded in her last will and testament, duly witnessed and signed."

In other words, sacrosanct.

Those beautiful art deco ceramic dishes in the original cobalt, red, light green, and ivory were a gift of great value—not because they were produced by the Homer Laughlin China Company in the early 1930s but because they'd belonged to Evelyn's mother. A lovely gift, but Teagan agreed with Robin's husband. "They should go to Robin. They were handed down from her grandmother."

Sandoval removed his glasses and returned them to his nose. He sniffed. "As I said, these are Mrs. Conklin's wishes." He applied himself to the papers in front of him. "To Mr. Maximilian Kennedy, Mrs. Conklin leaves the contents of her garage, to include a 1966 Ford F150 pickup truck—"

This time the gasp came from Doug Conklin, Evelyn's son. "Wait a minute—"

"This will go a lot faster if we get through the reading before we discuss the contents." The skin on Sandoval's smoothly shaven face turned pink to match his tie. "As well as the Craftsman tools, Craftsman workbench, and any lawn and gardening implements Mr. Kennedy might wish to have for use in the church's ministry assisting seniors with yard work and home repairs. The truck is a personal gift to Mr. Kennedy. However, it can be used as needed to transport materials from the church to the seniors' homes."

Who could argue with such lofty aspirations? Doug, apparently. "Mom didn't even attend that church."

"Your mother was very clear in her wishes."

"It's a very generous gift." Max's amber eyes swam with emotion. "The kids will be touched by it and so am I."

"Mom told me about you. She had a soft spot for people in AA." Robin snagged a fresh tissue and sopped up tears. "My dad went to meetings their entire marriage. It was the only way she would agree to marry him."

Even in death, a person could be surprising.

Sandoval ran through the remaining bequests quickly. The glowering men left immediately thereafter while the women discussed arrangements for the estate sale. "Can you remove your items in the next few days?" Robin's tone was apologetic. "I know it's a lot to ask, given your situation, but we both need to get back to work as soon as possible."

"I understand." Leyla's safety trumped everything else, but this grief-stricken woman couldn't be asked to think clearly at a time such as this. "We'll make arrangements. I just need to be able to get into the house with the movers."

"We're staying there." Robin wrote her cell number on one of Sandoval's business cards and handed it to Teagan. "Just let us know you're coming."

Teagan and Max thanked Mr. Sandoval, expressed their condolences yet again, and left. In the hallway they exhaled in unison. Max groaned. "That was brutal."

"I love that she left those dishes to me, but all I can think about right now is Leyla."

"Let's go."

They headed for the elevator. Two custodians dressed in forest-green uniforms pushed oversized trash bins and cleaning paraphernalia on a rolling cart to the doors, which opened just as Teagan approached. The trash and recycling bins on wheels were big and cumbersome, but the workers manhandled them with eased practice into the elevator.

The elevator's twenty-two square feet of real estate suddenly seemed full.

"We'll wait for the next one."

"No need. No need. We have room." The woman, a tall bleached blonde who wore her hair pulled back in a ponytail, smiled and motioned. "You look tired. Come on in."

"We got room." The man pulled the SA Cleaners cap down over curly black hair that matched an overgrown mustache and a scruffy beard. He shoved the recycling bin farther into the corner. "We're all friends here."

"That's okay." Something in the man's voice seemed oddly familiar. Teagan waved with one finger. "We'll take the next one."

"We need to keep moving." Max tugged her into the narrow confines of the elevator. "I have a feeling they're getting close."

Teagan faced front. Her heart did a weird *hup-two-three-four*. She glanced at the numbers. The elevator headed down at the plodding rate that came with an old building. The camera peered down at them. Good, a camera.

A camera with a lens spray-painted a dour shade of black.

She whirled. Bearded Man was on Max, a gun in one hand, a hypodermic needle in the other. "You're right, buddy, we are close."

Max's hand went for the weapon concealed under his suit coat.

His abductor smacked him across the head with his gun. Max went down.

"Max!"

The gun swiveled in her direction. "Easy, my friend."

Not my friend.

The needle plunged into Max's neck.

"Max!"

"Shut up." Bearded Man smacked the Stop button. The elevator ground to a halt. Max slumped against the wall, then slid down to the floor. The man opened the recycling bin. The woman did the same with the trash bin. "Time to take out the trash, smarty pants."

Bleached Blonde shoved Teagan against the door. Teagan elbowed her in the gut. The woman grunted and doubled forward. Her eyes widened. Dark-charcoal eyes. Joanna Dean.

Joanna Dean with her hair dyed. Or a wig. Dean put her shoulder into Teagan's back and rammed her against the elevator door a second time. Teagan's nose banged against metal. Pain burst forth in a brutal symphony as warm blood flowed over her lip and into her mouth. Salty.

The pain mingled with unreality. *God, not Max, please, God, save Max. Lead Dad to us. We need to find Leyla.*

The needle pricked her neck. Thoughts rearranged themselves in a game of ring-around-the-rosy.

The face of Leo Slocum peered down at her. No. No. Too young. Bearded Man. Chase Slocum. Rough hands lifted her from the floor. Her body slid into the recycling bin.

All fall down.

All fall down.

All fall down.

35

What would perpetrators of horrific crimes do without duct tape? A wad of something rough and dry in his mouth kept Max from asking this purely rhetorical question that swam to the surface with him. He struggled to open his eyes. Nothing happened. Darkness prevailed.

Tape covered the wad. His head pounded. His throat ached. Desperate for oxygen, he inhaled through his nose. Regret immediately followed. Pain blossomed in his swollen nostrils.

Teagan, where are you?

The unintelligible sounds in his ears indicated he tried to speak, but no one answered. He took inventory. No moving his hands or feet. More tape. More around his ankles.

Bound, blindfolded, and gagged.

Teagan? Teagan!

He inhaled again. The stench of burnt motor oil and gas penetrated his aching nose.

His body rocked. His head banged on the floor. An engine raced. A vehicle.

Vague memories of janitors with bins appeared. He'd hit the elevator wall and slid to the floor. Teagan shouted his name. No time to go for his weapon. No time to fight.

He'd let her down.

Again.

Fury boiled and spilled over. He yanked at his hands, flailed. Or attempted to flail. He was trussed like a chicken.

I'm not a chicken, Lord. Give me the strength of Samson. Overcome this evil, please, Lord.

The vehicle heaved to the right, then to the left. It slowed, then sped up. A winding road? Hill Country? Or south to the Valley and Slocum's old stomping grounds?

Who were these people? What did they have to do with Slocum?

A cleaning service. How easy it must've been to steal a few uniforms and slip onto the floor. Better to imagine that scenario than the one where two innocent people had been hurt or worse in order to make this plan work.

Janitors were invisible. No one gave them a second thought.

The vehicle rocked so hard it slung Max's body to the right, then left. He smacked into something warm and soft that smelled of spoiled tuna, burnt popcorn, and moldy bread. The odors of trash. Someone's lunch.

An incoherent grunt followed.

Teagan?

The vehicle stopped moving. The engine died. Doors closed. Then opened. Sweet, fresh air that smelled of lake, juniper, and barbecue swept over Max. It smelled like his favorite place to clear his head—the Hill Country.

At least if he died now, it would be in a place close to God.

No dying now, bud! Not with Leyla and Teagan's lives hanging in the balance. Now might be his chance to break free.

Sure, if he were the Hulk. Or Samson.

Hands touched him. They pulled and prodded and pushed.

For a second nothing held him up. Then he hit solid ground. Air whooshed from his body. His head smacked against a rock.

Do not pass out. Do not. He sucked in air through his nose.

Another thud, then one to his right.

Teagan?

The tape ripped from his eyes. "Urgghh!" So much for being the tough guy. A little duct tape and he couldn't help himself. The mouth came next. "Hey, take it easy!"

"Oh, shut up, you big baby." Brandishing a Glock, the woman bent over him. Her Mexican peasant blouse hung loose from her body. Max had a view of everything from her neck to her navel. He should close his eyes, but he needed to see where they were. He needed a plan of attack. The dark-rimmed glasses were gone. Uniforms and disguises. She grinned at him. "Consider it like a free wax job."

"Who are you? Where's Teagan? Where's Leyla?"

"She said shut up." The man's appearance had changed as well. Glasses, mustache, and beard all gone. This guy was clean-cut with dark-blue eyes and brown hair. Very all-American. "Do it."

Fine. Max raised his head and peered around. Teagan lay on the ground to his right. Beyond her, thickets of juniper, live oak, elegant Spanish Dagger yuccas, and more dowdy prickly pear cacti as far as he could see on undulating ground along a dirt road. To his left, a log cabin featuring a front porch swing missing some of its seat slats, a brick chimney, and a carport filled with firewood. Weeds invaded cracks in the wood planks of the porch.

Hill Country covered a lot of territory. But the smell of fish suggested they were close to water. Hill Country and a lake. If only he knew how long he'd been out, he could estimate how far they'd traveled.

No sense in crying over spilled blood.

Teagan raised her head.

God, thank You.

Her expression glassy, she struggled against her bindings. The woman ripped off the tape. "Hey, chickadee, welcome back."

"You. You!" She gasped and coughed. "Why? Why would you do this?"

She was talking to the man who bent over and ripped the tape from her ankles. He grabbed her arm and jerked her upright. "Let's go."

"Your father is a murderer. You know how that feels. Why would you do this to your kids?"

"Who are they, Teagan?" Max struggled against the bindings around his hands. "How do you know them?"

The barrel of Bleached Blonde's gun touched Teagan's forehead. "Do you want the gag back in? Or should I just blow your brains out and get it over with?"

"If you were supposed to kill us, you'd have done it by now." Teagan leaned into the pistol. "How angry do you think he'll be if you shoot me? Angry enough to kill you? Angry enough to do to you what he had you do to Charity Waters?"

"Teagan!" She knew something Max didn't, but that didn't mean she wasn't playing with fire. These two maniacs were known to Teagan. Both she and Max had seen them. The long-range plan didn't involve letting them merrily trot back home after this—whatever this was—was over. "Let's talk about this. What do you want? Money?"

Not that he had any.

"What we want is for you to shut up." No-Longer-Bearded Man slapped Teagan in the mouth so hard her head snapped back. "Charity Waters was stupid. I'm not. My dad knows it."

His dad. Teagan and Dillon had interviewed Leo Slocum's son. What was his name? Max's head pounded to the beat of the pulse in his ears. *Think. Think.* "You're Chase Slocum."

No-Longer-Bearded Man shoved Max toward the cabin. "Ding, ding, ding! Now shut it."

Max dug in his heels and glanced back at Bleached Blonde. "And that makes you Joanna Dean."

She mimed a ragged curtsy. "If you say so. You guys have a death wish."

The whack between the shoulder blades sent him sprawling on the porch. A gush of warm liquid seeped into his mouth. Forcing back the urge to vomit, Max breathed through his mouth and struggled to his knees.

"Get up, get up!"

Two seconds later they were inside the log cabin. A flashback to his childhood. His parents had rented similar cabins at various state parks over the years so they could fish, swim, and boat. Only Mom would've had a field day with this one. *"Maximilian, don't touch anything until I straighten up. This place needs a deep cleaning, fresh linens, and the windows wide open."*

Her cheerful voice, always brimming with laughter, echoed in his head. *Oh, Mom, I could use that sweetness now.*

An avocado-green refrigerator and gas stove flanked a rusty sink on his left. The doors to three empty rooms stood open. To the right the room opened into a living area featuring a dirty stone fireplace and a blue plaid sofa with sagging cushions. The walls were bare. The odors of burnt mesquite, kerosene, and dust mingled in an unpleasant bouquet.

"Keep moving."

Another vicious shove sent him flying through an open door. The bedroom held an elderly wrought-iron bed frame that had been stripped down to the mattress and a single straight-back chair. Blackout curtains banished any natural light from a single large window. A naked overhead bulb offered tepid illumination.

"Sit."

"I'm not a dog." Teagan seemed determined to provoke. "Try asking nicely."

The blow sent her reeling onto the mattress. She rolled over and blew her hair from her face. "You think carrying out these murders will take the spotlight from your dad? Law enforcement will look elsewhere, leaving him to appeal a single conviction. It'll never work.

Even if he didn't commit the murders in San Antonio, he's good for the ones in the Valley that happened long before he was incarcerated."

"You think you know so much." Chase forced Max into the wooden chair and handcuffed him to a rung. He produced the duct tape and secured Max's legs once again. "My dad never hurt anyone. He is a good man. A good father. Your dad had it out for him from the beginning. You can thank him for this. He did this to you."

"A good man would never ask you to do the things your father has made you do." Max sought a conciliatory tone he didn't feel. "Does a good father make his son kill women on his behalf?"

"We didn't—"

"Shut up, Chase." Joanna slapped a handcuff on Teagan's right arm and handcuffed her to the bed frame. "We're not to say a word, remember?"

"I remember," Chase huffed. "They just think they know so much. They don't know anything."

"Let's keep it that way."

"What harm is there in telling Teagan and me what's going on?" Max strove for calm. To create a semblance of a connection between him and this man whose father was a monster. "Where's Leyla? You have us where you want us. Why not let us in on the endgame here?"

"You know what you need to know." Joanna smiled. Her sharp incisors made her look like a happy rat. "We know better than to fall for any mind games."

"I'm not playing games. I'm trying to understand why two decent, hardworking parents would do this. What happens to you when the police catch you? You killed a cop. That's the death penalty."

"Shut up, just shut up." Joanna's smile crumpled into a thin, fierce line. "You don't know what you're talking about."

"What happens to your children?" Teagan struggled to sit up. The handcuffs clanged against the bed frame. "Their grandpa is in prison. Their dad is next. And yours, Joanna, what about them? Do you have a sister or a mother to take care of them for you?"

"Don't talk about my kids—"

"Shut up, Joanna. She's just trying to get to you." Chase edged toward the door. "Y'all take a nap. Don't bother yelling. There's not another soul within miles."

Guns at the ready, they backed out of the room like bad guys from a B-grade black-and-white movie. The door banged shut.

"Are you okay?" Max jerked at the handcuff. No give in the chair's rung. He flexed his legs. No give in the duct tape. "Why were you antagonizing them?"

"I'm good. I thought we were doing a bad-cop, good-cop thing. I thought maybe they'd get irritated enough to mouth off about their plans." Teagan rattled her cuffs in vain. "I sat in their living room and talked to him for an hour. I met her. He was a loving father shocked by his father's murder conviction. She was a good friend thankful to be able to share a home with him. They seemed to be hiding a secret—that they were involved. But nothing like this. I thought he didn't want us to know he had an affair and that was the real reason his wife left."

An obscenity blistered the air. Joanna's voice raised in anger. Chase's fierce bass mingled with the woman's nerve-scraping shrieks. The topic of the argument seemed to be the kids.

"See, I hit a nerve."

"You can't tell me they didn't consider the consequences before this."

The shouting escalated. A door slammed.

"And just so you know." A sneer on her face, Joanna charged into the room. "That's the beauty of this plan. We can leave you here and go back home. No one will be the wiser. No one saw. Your phones are still in the building. Your car is still there. No one witnessed us take you down. They have no idea where you are. And they have no idea we're involved. I'll be home in time to make mac 'n' cheese and chicken nuggets for the kids' supper. No one will be the wiser. Don't worry, we'll be back to take care of you folks—one way or another."

With that, she whirled and sashayed from the room. The door slammed again.

An engine fired up outside the windows. Tires squealed. The noise died away.

They were alone. Good. They wouldn't be killed immediately.

But bad, because they were hog-tied and possibly left to die a horrible, slow death. No one knew where they were.

No one was coming for them.

36

The quiet had its own deadly sound. The sound of minutes ticking by. Max strained to pull away from the chair. To no avail. "We have to be gone when they come back."

"You have a penchant for stating the obvious." Teagan groaned and wiggled closer to the foot of the bed. "At a certain point, keeping us alive will serve no purpose."

Max leaned as far forward as his bindings allowed. Somehow he had to loosen the tape or rid himself of the cuffs. How? With his teeth? Billy and Justin would know how. Gracie would have a toothpick or a tiny pocketknife or a paper clip hidden in her unmentionables. If memory served, all he had was a guitar pick and seven cents. "Can you tell if they left anything useful on you?"

"Nope. Who knows what they did with my purse." She slid over on her side close to the bed frame and pulled her legs up, knees bent. "I can try to reach the tape and work it off, but there's still the handcuffs."

"One thing at a time. You're short enough. That might work."

"Nice. Kick me when I'm down."

"You're not down. You're never down. I'm awed by your bravery." He swallowed against emotions that could not be allowed to interfere. "I want to save you, but I'm positive you'll end up saving me."

"Okay, that makes up for the crack about my height." Her voice lightened a fraction. "Maybe Leyla is somewhere in this house in another room—in the basement, if there is one."

Max heaved a breath. "Leyla? Leyla!"

Their shouts echoed in the empty space. No one answered.

"If they killed her—"

"They didn't. She was a bargaining chip." Max prayed he was right. "We need to focus on getting out of here and finding her."

Was. Past tense. Now that they had Teagan, they didn't need Leyla anymore. What better way to inflict pain and suffering on their dad than to take not one but two daughters? They didn't need Max either. Why was he still alive?

Because Chase and Joanna weren't killers. They were pawns in a psychopath's plan to make Dillon O'Rourke suffer. Leo Slocum faced the death penalty because Dillon had pulled the string that had unraveled Slocum's secret life. He had to pay. Not a quick death, but a slow and painful descent into hell.

They had to get out. They couldn't let this monster win.

"Do you have any idea where here is?" Teagan asked.

"It smells like lake to me. With the terrain and the vegetation, I'm guessing Medina Lake." Max tried to stand. The cuffs bit into his wrists. His body strained. The chair came with him. Groaning, he plopped back down. "Medina Lake is something like eighteen miles long and thirteen miles wide. It's forty miles from San Antonio. It'll be tough for them to find us. They don't know where to start searching."

"I feel sick thinking about it." Teagan's voice took on that scratchy quality it got when she had a cold. "Poor Dad. First Leyla. Now me. It has to be eating him alive."

"More likely he's imagining all the ways he'll kill the guy who did this."

"They don't have an inkling of who did this. If they did, they could do a real estate search. I'm betting this was a family vacation cabin for the Slocums. But they have to know Slocum's behind it. That his son is his accomplice. He has to be the mastermind. Neither of those goobers is smart enough to have hatched this plan."

"Or killed four women in five days without leaving a bit of evidence behind."

"That's not possible."

"What's not possible?"

"To leave no evidence behind." She tugged at the tape with her free hand. A small piece gave way. "Locard's Exchange Principle says that every time you make contact with another person, place, or thing, it results in an exchange of physical materials."

No doubt this principle had been discussed over family dinners at the O'Rourke house. Or expounded upon by a CSU investigator on the stand in one of the many trials Teagan had been responsible for reporting. "That's all fine and dandy, but the physical materials left at these scenes have not resulted in identifying the perp."

He could talk like a cop as well as the next guy.

"We just haven't figured it out yet."

"There was something about these guys." Max licked his dry lips. His throat burned for a sip of water. "They were afraid of whoever is telling them what to do."

"Agreed. They were following a plan, a script, that someone gave them."

He stared at her across the room. The woman he loved trussed to a bed by two people whose lives had been touched by not one but two serial killers.

At least one, if not two, of those killers held sway over them. No one forced them to kidnap Max and Teagan. They had made the choice. Such was the power that throttled their basic sense of decency.

They could not be allowed to continue. Max leaned forward again. This time he balanced on the balls of his feet, stuck together with tape, and let the back legs of the chair hike into the air. It inched forward a few inches. *Hop. Plop flat. Hop. Plop flat.*

Laboriously, he moved closer to the bed, each time measuring how far forward he could lean without losing his balance and flopping flat on his face.

"You're doing it." Teagan's cheers egged him on. "You can do it!"

Hop, plop back, hop, plop back, hop, plop back.

His grunts resounded in his own ears. His shoulders and wrists ached. Blood dripped from his nose. His sweat stank.

Time passed. Shadows lengthened.

Finally, bed frame and nothing more separated him from Teagan. He heaved to the left until he lined up with her feet, then hopped so he faced away. "Stick your legs close so my hands can get at them."

From there, it took only a matter of minutes for him to tear the tape from her legs.

"Now, your turn." More shimmying and shaking ensued until he parked so he could lift his legs into the air and prop his feet on the bed frame so she could reach his feet.

"I hate to rain on your parade, but this is the easy part." Her tone was matter of fact. "We can't undo the cuffs with our fingers."

"One thing at a time."

Lord, she's right. Give me the faith and the strength of David when he faced Goliath, please.

The *tick, tick, tick* of the clock in his head grew louder with each passing second. *Tick, tock, tick, tock,* until it became a *dong, dong, dong.*

"There, there, I got it."

His legs kicked free and he slapped his feet on the floor. "Thank you, ma'am."

"Now what?" Even as she voiced the question, Teagan's gaze studied the handcuffs and the bed frame. "Remember when we assembled my new bed?"

"Yep, but me first. This chair is old. All this banging it around is loosening up its joints." Max proceeded to demonstrate. He heaved his weight against the back. The wooden frame creaked but didn't give. "Come on." He heaved again. His shoulders screamed with pain. He spent so much time muscle building and punching a bag, when what he really needed was greater range of motion.

Two more times. The wood splintered. The chair gave way. Max slammed to the floor. The center dowels separated from the frame. He rolled up on his knees and let the dowels fall away. "Eureka."

"Seriously, eureka? You're still handcuffed."

"But I'm walking around, which means I can try to find something to unlock them."

"Too bad we don't have a phone or a laptop so we could google it."

"What did people do before Google? Trial and error?" His back to Teagan, Max grabbed the bed frame with both hands and shook it. Also ancient, but still sturdy. "First we get you out of this bed."

"You don't know how weird that sounds."

"Hush."

They went to work, first removing the mattress and box springs. Teagan acted as the eyes of the operation while Max provided the brawn—as much as possible given his circumstances. Below the bed set they found plywood slats and moved them aside. That left Teagan stuck, crouched in the center, handcuffed to the foot of the frame. "This isn't helping. Even if you get the bed apart. I can't run down the hillside dragging a footboard with me."

"You're the one with all the cops in the family. Weren't handcuffs ever a topic of conversation around the supper table?"

"Not that I recall. Cops aren't likely to share that information informally or on the stand in court. They'd rather keep the bad guys locked up. I only know what I see on TV. Bobby pins. Paper clips. Any skinny piece of metal that will fit in the keyhole."

"I need a screwdriver to take the bed apart or a bobby pin for the handcuffs. Whichever comes first. I'll be back."

"Don't be exploring without me." Frustration lined Teagan's face. She tugged at the handcuffs. "You don't know what's out there. Be careful."

Vintage Teagan. Always worried for her loved ones.

"'Have I not commanded you? Be strong and courageous. Do not be afraid; do not be discouraged, for the Lord your God will be with you wherever you go.'"

"Joshua 1:9." The worry lines on her beautiful face softened. "Don't throw worry in my face. God understands. His grace covers my fear. He sees me."

"I would never. I'll be right back."

Right back indeed. The tiny cabin couldn't be more than twelve-hundred square feet. An occupant would know Max was free. Noise echoed from one room to the other. Having his hands handcuffed behind him left him almost completely vulnerable to attack. That didn't worry him as much as his mission did. *Please God, don't let me find a body. Anybody's body. But especially Leyla's body.*

No scent of decomp assailed his nostrils. No doors leading to a basement. Aside from the living room and kitchen, the cabin consisted of a small bathroom off the first bedroom with an empty medicine cabinet, and a second, larger bedroom with its own full bathroom. This room had potential. Someone had lived in it recently. The bedding was semifresh. A dresser housed men's clothing. A few shirts hung in the closet. Men's stuff. What was the likelihood of finding a bobby pin here?

A suitcase shoved against the back wall of the closet caught his gaze. An old leather suitcase with the hard metal frame. Much used. It had no name tag. Max knelt with his back to it and felt along the top until his fingers touched the clasp. *Please God.*

It popped. He shoved it open with what little leverage he could muster, then scrambled around to face the contents.

A pair of ballet slippers, gold bangle bracelets, a gold chain with a hummingbird charm. Blue glasses. They were strewn atop a hodge-podge of women's clothes. He touched a woman's jean jacket à la the eighties, a red silky scarf, and a pink sweater.

Understanding dawned, bringing with it dry heaves that couldn't be denied. Evelyn's glasses and Charity's necklace. Julie's bracelets. The slippers might be Leyla's. These were the killer's trophies left in the closet of a cabin long abandoned by his family.

Max coughed and turned away in fear of contaminating what surely would bring DNA evidence to the table. Connections between victims and the occupant of this cabin. He scooted farther back on his knees. What little he knew about evidence included *don't touch*. He'd already sullied the exterior of the suitcase with his fingers. He'd touched the first layer of clothing.

Clothing that belonged to women who died terrible deaths.

He closed his eyes. *Keep it together, bud. This is no time to be a wuss.* He breathed and opened his eyes.

No bobby pins.

God, help me. Please.

He contorted his body until he could get his feet under his body and stand. A pale-pink T-shirt hung next to half a dozen men's short-sleeved cotton shirts. READING BOOKS IS MY SUPERPOWER. He leaned closer and sniffed. Charity Waters's faint scent wafted and faded as quickly as it had come.

She'd been here. And she had long hair. He moved on to the bathroom. A dish next to the sink held two pair of stud earrings, a scrunchie, two ponytail ties, and voilà, half a dozen bobby pins. Next to it lay a small brown box. The lid slid off with relative ease. A book of matches, gold cuff links, a tie clip, and a miniature pocketknife.

A virtual goldmine for two desperate people on the run from cold-blooded killers.

"Sorry, CSI folks." He backed up to the vanity and fumbled for the pins. His fingers were all thumbs. An earring, a tie, a scrunchie fell on the floor. "Come on, come on."

His fingers closed around the pins. "Thank You, Jesus."

Next the book of matches and the tiny pocketknife went into

his back pocket. His shoulder sockets ached, but the golden liquid of hope ran through his veins.

He took thirty seconds to pray for the women whose lives were snuffed out before the mementos were gathered and then made his way back to Teagan. They would save each other. These psychopaths would not have a memento to remember Teagan by.

Not on his watch.

37

Somewhere in virtual space a YouTube guru was laughing. Using a bobby pin to unlock handcuffs was harder than it looked. Or maybe the fact that Teagan's hands were shaking and her palms sweating made the task more challenging. Perspiration dripped in her eyes. They burned. Her jaw hurt from gritting her teeth. The clock ticked in her ears. Any minute Joanna and Chase would return to the cabin to finish what they'd started.

Stop it. Focus. She concentrated on her attempt to free Max of his handcuffs. "One more time. I'll get it this time, I promise."

"Just relax and close your eyes. Listen for a click."

Hysteria burbled up in her throat in the form of a giggle. "Easy for you to say."

"Not really."

The bobby pin slid from her slick fingers and pinged on the dirty faux wood floor. "Oh no. Oh no. I'm so sorry."

"It's okay, it's okay. I have more." Max eased back so his hands touched the bed frame. He opened his fist, palm up. Three more bobby pins. "Take one and I'll keep the others for backup."

She inhaled, exhaled, and took one pin. Another breath. In and out. *"I can do all things through Christ who strengthens me."* Philippians 4:13. Rick's assertion that a verse existed for even the most exigent situation held true. "Here we go."

Still, executing this delicate operation while handcuffed herself seemed beyond the realm of possibility.

Click.

"I got it, I got it." Tears pricked Teagan's burning eyes. Fear, fatigue, and thirst mingled into a thick slime in her stomach. "Hurry, do mine. We've wasted too much time. It's probably getting dark."

No way to know. Neither of them wore watches. They depended on their phones for the time.

Max whirled and went to work. Seconds later he accomplished what had taken her ten minutes to do. She threw her shaking arms around him and held on. "I can't believe we're still alive."

"Me neither. Did it strike you that those two didn't really know what they were doing?"

"They were following someone else's script." She should let go, but she couldn't. "Why not kill us? Or at least you. The person behind this already tried once."

"Mr. Serial Killer has his reasons. I'm sure we'll find out soon enough—if we don't get out of here." Max's arms tightened around her waist. "Let's not think about it. I'm thankful to God we're both still here."

The air crackled with electricity. Teagan leaned into him. The kiss rocked her to her toes. She wanted this. She wanted to taste him and feel him and know him. Before it was too late.

Max opened his eyes. His feelings were laid bare. "Your timing stinks, but I love you for it."

Love you.

"I know it doesn't solve anything, but if we don't make it out of here—"

"We will. We're going. Now."

The thought of leaving the cabin for the unknown on the other side of its ramshackle walls held less appeal than it had only seconds earlier. "You're sure Leyla's not here?"

"I told you, there's no basement. There's no sign she was ever here."

Maybe not, but the killer had been. The trophies in the suitcase, along with evidence of Charity Waters's presence, told the story. He had used this hideaway as his man cave, his killer cave. And his boudoir.

A deepening darkness and a steady drip, drip of light rain greeted them outside. Not enough to wash away the tire tracks. They headed downhill. The driveway faded into a narrow dirt track barely wide enough for one vehicle. The thick humidity pressed against Teagan's skin. The rain did nothing to cool her.

Elation faded with each step. Juniper branches smacked her in the face. The clouds parted in a tiny crack, but the sliver of a moon gave them no light. She stumbled into a fallen tree trunk. The bark bit into her shins. She fell forward onto her face in a pile of rotting leaves and brush.

Something hissed.

The darkness masked their companion as it slithered away.

"Tell me again snakes are more afraid of me than I am of them," she whispered as she scrambled to her feet. "Tell me you weren't making that up."

"We have psychopaths chasing us and you're worried about snakes?"

"They're not psychopaths. They're sycophants. Followers. Leo Slocum is the family father figure who fills their heads up with what they must do to please him." Talking about it helped fill the space in her head where anxiety and fear had parked themselves. *Focus on unraveling the case.* "They want to show him how much they love and support him. Like Squeaky Fromme and Sandra Good and Tex Watson followed Manson. Only Chase really is related to Leo."

Peering into the darkness, Max climbed over an outcropping of limestone covered with scraggly lantana and coreopsis. "I don't care what you call them. They're crazy, nuts, loco, loony."

"Like foxes. They grabbed us in broad daylight, stuck us in trash bins, rolled us into a stolen van, and drove us out into the middle of nowhere right under the noses of a dozen or more law enforcement agents. That we should be so crazy."

"A carefully thought-out plan." Max nodded. "Is it just me or are you thinking no way they were smart enough to plan the nuts and bolts, the disguises, the uniforms, the timing, the van, watching and waiting for us, getting us into the van? Do they seem that smart to you? They left us in a room together."

"No. And they didn't have Leyla."

The passage of time had gone wonky. It was night, so another day had passed. Another day with Leyla in the clutches of a brutal family of murderers. "Whoever has her is the brains, but he's as much a follower as they are. He's doing this for his father figure, but he's also doing it for himself."

"For himself?"

"Whoever he is, he likes it. A lot." Teagan's foot hit loose dirt. Gravel. She peered ahead. "The road is widening. Look, it's paved. We've hit an actual road."

"Hallelujah!" Max managed to dial back the whoop to a whisper. "Sweet Jesus, thank You."

Headlights blinded them. A car coming up the hill at a steady pace, the lights flickering in and out as it rounded curves and straightened.

"Quick, a car, a car." Teagan waved and yelled. Max did the same. It would be suicide to step in front of the car in the dark, but it might be suicide not to do it.

The car slowed. It stopped.

"Oh, thank You, thank You, God." Teagan stumbled into the road. Max kept pace. "Hello, we need help. We need to use your cell phone."

The door opened. Cole Reynolds stepped from the vehicle.

"Cole, you found us." Teagan worked to focus. How was that

possible? Even if he were part of the pack searching for Teagan and Max, how could he have found them? He alone. In all the places in the world he might've looked, right here, right now. "You're him."

"I am, my friend."

38

C ole Reynolds liked dogs and DIY projects, and he made lasagna for a grieving family.

He was also a serial killer.

The realization hit Teagan like a physical blow. Her neighbor, a community college speech instructor had killed Julie, Evelyn, and Kris Moreno.

A nice guy. Helpful. Sweet. Good-looking.

"The Triple S Murderer in the flesh. No pun intended." Cole shoved the SUV's door shut with his hip and moseyed forward as if he had all the time in the world. As if *they* had all the time in the world. His hands remained hidden behind his blue rain slicker. "You could've done better. It sounds more like a rancher's brand. So commercial. A tad lurid."

"Like yourself. Where's my sister?"

"I have a surprise for you, my sweet." He motioned toward the van. "But not just yet."

"Is she in there?" Teagan plunged toward van. "What have you done to her?"

Cole stepped into her path, a mammoth .357 Magnum pointed at her head, a butcher knife in his other hand. "Don't worry. I haven't killed her. Yet. Titillating, isn't it? I bet your father is dying a slow death all his own. Two of his daughters gone. Trying to find them before it's too late. Wondering if they're already dead. Wishing he could die instead. Just like my father, stuck in that hellhole jail because of him."

Teagan kept moving. She couldn't stop herself. Max grabbed her arm. She struggled to free herself. "I want to see her. Now."

"Easy. He wants you to freak out." Max's soft voice held no emotion. "He's getting his jollies from this. Don't give him what he wants."

"Listen to your boyfriend. Max is a smart guy." Cole smiled. How could she have ever thought that smile charming? He waved the gun toward the van. "Follow my instructions and you'll see her soon enough."

Cold fear mixed with hot anger, creating a violent tornado of emotion. She couldn't think. She couldn't pray. "You're a sick, sick man. I'm not sure you're a member of the human race."

"You can't wound me, dear Teagan, and you know you'll only regret the awful things you say. Shouldn't you pray for me instead?"

"I'll pray for the Lord to give you your due punishment immediately, how's that?"

"If He's real, He will. If He's not, you're doomed." Cole chuckled, a low rumble that matched the distant thunder that promised more rain. "I know which one I vote for."

He tossed zip ties at Teagan. She caught them out of sheer reflex. "I'll let you do the honors. Max first since he's the big he-man."

He would not get his way. He would not do this. Not to Leyla. Not to Max.

God, I need You now. We need You now.

Sorry about this, she mouthed to Max as she did as she was told. *Be ready.*

His gaze like hot pokers, Max nodded.

"Behind, not in front. Good and tight. I wouldn't want to have to shoot your beloved just yet." Cole sounded almost jovial, like a man planning a summer vacation. "I've been noodling this scenario for a while, and I've come to see it as filled with possibilities. A three-for-one if you'll allow me to be so crass. It's actually quite exciting. Something different. Normally, killing Max wouldn't be my thing, but knowing how important he is to you, I can make it work. I'm envisioning a tableau that your father will never forget, never overcome."

Chills like a host of spiders crawled up Teagan's arms. Vomit rose in the back of her throat. Despite the heat she shivered. So many macabre possibilities in a brain so filled with grotesque nightmares just waiting to become reality. She grasped at calm rational thought with both shaking hands. What would Dad do?

Learn as much as possible about the perp. Get in his head. Don't let him in your head. Make a connection. Go along to get along until the time is right. No sudden moves. Be stone-cold sober in your assessments. If ever there is a time for calm under duress, this is it.

"What is your connection to Leo Slocum?"

"I'm his son—well, his bastard son."

Teagan's hands stopped moving. She swiveled and stared at him. The blue eyes, the dark wavy hair. The tall, athletic frame. He had Deidre Patterson's mouth, the shape of her chin, even her dimples. He looked much more like his mother than his father. But now that she'd been told, she could see it in his frame and his eyes.

One plus one equaled three.

The children's A-B-C blocks fell into place. They spelled family. The family that murdered together stayed together.

Or, in this case, grew together.

"So that's what this is about? Earning favor with a father who abandoned you at birth or shortly thereafter? Who refused to leave his wife for your mother?" She eased so close to Max the hair on his arm brushed hers. "Why would you want to do that?"

"The biological imperative, I suppose. Or to show him what he missed by not choosing me." He waved the .357 at her. "Hands."

He zip-tied hers in front. She, not being a big he-man, was no threat to him.

"Why after all these years?"

"Preparation. I never do anything without a carefully thought-out plan. I learned that from Pops. I bought a house and lived in your neighborhood for more than a year. You never suspected. Pops will be proud." His grim smile widened. "I like calling him that. My adopted father insisted on Daddy, which got old by middle school."

"Was adoption so bad?"

"It was good, actually. I won the lottery when it came to foster parents. They liked that I was a 'spirited' child. They adopted me after only a year. They paid for my college education. They made excuses for my bad behavior. They got me out of scrapes. I'm a teacher because of them. In a few years I'll get my master's and move up to a tenured position at a four-year college."

He had goals like a normal man. "Yet you need to curry favor from a psychopathic serial killer."

"Have you heard the maxim 'The apple doesn't fall far from the tree'? I abhor cliché as much as you do, but in this case it's true. I find I'm good at the family trade, and I enjoy it so much more than reading the drivel written by self-important, selfie-addicted kids who wouldn't know a classic if it bit them in the backside."

"What is your endgame?" Max's arm rubbed against Teagan's. He edged in front of her. She jockeyed for position. He would not play the knight in shining armor. "What do you expect to gain from the needless, senseless murder of four women?"

"Six by the time I finish with Teagan and the ballerina. Plus one white knight in shining armor." His face contorted in a mirthless grin. "The more you suffer, the more your father suffers."

"Give me just a little leeway and I'll kill you." She barged forward, intent on unleashing the fury of a thousand O'Rourke ancestors on the man who hurt her sweet, dancing Leyla. "You're a coward, a spineless coward."

The butcher knife came up. It pricked her outstretched arm. Blood warmed her skin, but it didn't really hurt. Not as much as one would expect. Cole smiled. "Even you admit you would give in to your baser instincts."

Teagan's anger drained away, leaving her light-headed, but the determination remained. "No, I'm not an animal like you. I'll let justice have its due. I believe life in prison without parole to be a perfect sentence for a man who wants attention. You'll get it there. Plenty of inmates willing to make you their best friends."

"You'd spare my life then?"

"The death penalty is too good for you. You deserve to suffer for fifty years in a ten-by-ten cell."

"It took me years to track down my father, only to find he'd been a naughty boy. He'd grown sloppy and stalked a prey too close to home. Your father caged him like the animal you say we are. My chance at having a relationship with my father was gone. He wouldn't even see me at the jail. He said he didn't know me from Adam. Your father deserves to suffer. If he hadn't arrested my father, we would have a relationship now. So would my brother and sister. He ruined everything."

"Your father didn't want to see you. That's why you're doing this, isn't it? You want to impress him. You're jealous of Chase and his sister, aren't you?"

The knife came up again and touched her tangled hair. Teagan stood stock-still, forcing every bone in her body to remain unmoving. Cole's smile became almost cherubic. "After Father dearest made the idiotic mistake of escaping, he called my brother. He thought Chase was doing all this. That stupid buffoon. He thanked him for trying to create reasonable doubt."

"Did Chase tell him about you?"

"Yes. Pops denied he had another son. He denied it all." The blade slid across her hair to the bare skin of her neck, down the row of buttons on her blood-and dirt-stained blouse. "I love a good tussle with a beautiful woman. Get in the car. I don't have much time, unfortunately, because I have finals to finish grading. Everything has to be turned in tomorrow."

Parallel universes collided. Chase and Joanna had gone home to make mac 'n' cheese and chicken nuggets for their five children. This teacher was worried about maintaining the mask he'd shown the world. The one he'd shown her with his interest in the Little Free Library, his big dog, and his offer to jog with her. All an elaborate ruse to set her at ease with her neighbor.

Such lengths to go to. "You know nothing you do will change my father's resolve. He'll bury you where your body will never be found."

"I look forward to the denouncement." Cole swished a salute with his gun hand. "Dear Maximilian, let's have you in the back."

His expression grim, eyes blazing with an anger that surely came from the depths of his experiences in a foreign war, Max strode toward the passenger door.

"No, no, that space is taken, my friend—"

"So not your friend," Max ground out.

"Be that as it may, to the back. All the way back." He jabbed the butcher knife precariously close to a spot between Max's shoulder blades. "The modern-day version of the way back."

Max hunched down under the hatch and curled up on the floor behind the back seat. Cole closed the hatch.

"Now, my pretty, you shall see my surprise." He slid open the passenger door.

Leyla curled in a fetal position on the seat. Duct tape covered her mouth. Bruises and dried blood decorated her face.

"*Leyla.*" Surely she screamed the name, but only a whisper sounded. "Leyla?"

"She's quite the spitfire. Just like you. She thought she'd escape. I had to subdue her." Cole nudged Leyla with the knife. She whimpered, but her eyes didn't open. "I may have gotten a bit carried away, but she was so determined, I had trouble containing myself."

God? God! "Forget prison." Teagan raised her bound hands. She swung. Laughing a high-pitched, ugly laugh, Cole danced out of her way. Still swinging, she fell to her knees. "I'll kill you!"

"See there. Given the right circumstances, every human being will resort to violence to get his way."

"You're not a human being."

"I thought you Christians believed every man or woman is a child of God, worthy of redemption." He grabbed her arm in a bruising grip and dragged her to her feet. "Doesn't your God want me to repent and be saved?"

"He does." The words burned her mouth. "The only way you can do that is to let her go. Let me go and turn yourself in."

"Now who's delusional? Hop into the front seat next to me. I like to be cozy with my ladies." He poked her with the gun. She wrestled her gaze from Leyla's inert form and hoisted herself into the front seat. Cole slid the passenger door shut. Ever the gentleman, he gently pulled the seat belt across her body and clicked it in place. "Safety first."

While he trotted around the car and slid into the seat next to her, Teagan prayed. For Leyla. For Max. For a way out. And for her father, who'd done nothing to deserve this. *God, don't give Dad another cross to bear. I'm ready to come home whenever You say, but don't make me a lesson he has to learn. Please.*

Fear not.

The words were distinct and shiny in a world gone dark.

Fear not.

By the time Cole punched the ignition key, she had moved on to reviewing the conversation with her dad that first night in her childhood home. His instructions had been clear. An encounter with a serial killer should first be avoided.

"Flee. Escape."

Too late for that. Next, *"Resist verbally."*

Not working here.

"I took a self-defense course for women. What about fighting my way out?"

The look on his face had been priceless.

"Honey, kick him in the family jewels if you're that close to him. I'd rather you not be that close. Keys to the eyes. Bite his nose off. But that means you're too close. Be prepared to run."

"Even if he has a gun?"

"A pistol or revolver, yes. Any cop will agree if you're more than five yards away, your chances of getting hit are slim to none. If it's a rifle, your odds become grimmer."

He had a gun. Max would know what kind and probably how many shots before he had to reload.

Run. Would Cole run her down in the car? Or shoot her in the back before she made it the requisite five yards? She would not leave Leyla and Max behind. Flee was a no-go.

She contemplated the darkness whooshing by the window. The pain sparred with a sense of unreality. This couldn't be happening. The zip ties biting into her wrists in the same spots the handcuffs had bruised earlier said it was.

That left engaging Cole in conversation. Cole liked to talk, that was apparent. Maybe if he talked long enough, she'd have the chance to make a plan. That's what Dad would do. Make and execute a plan.

"How's Huck?"

"Ever the loyal hound." Cole engaged the windshield wipers. They alternately squeaked and thumped. "I do need to take some time for routine maintenance, but I've been rather occupied of late."

Killing women around her.

"What will happen to him when you go to prison?"

"Who?"

He'd already forgotten the loyal hound with big, sweet eyes the color of walnuts. "Did you get a dog because I have one?"

"Poor thing needed a home. The shelter is full of rescue dogs. I support their effort to become a no-kill shelter."

"Big of you."

"I know it's one of Mrs. Conklin's and your favorite causes, right up there with literacy and feeding the homeless."

He'd used his time living across the street to gather so much information on her. Chatting with neighbors. Talking to her friends. Visiting the Little Free Library. Asking her for recipes. Bending her ear about his renovation project.

He wasn't the only one with inside information. "When was the last time you saw your mother?"

"Over the weekend actually." The light teasing in his voice was a dead giveaway.

No pun intended.

"You didn't."

"I did. She dumped me on CPS because of a drunk who didn't like to share attention with a sickly kid." He drummed a one-two beat on the wheel. "What kind of mother does that?"

He had a point. But Deidre hadn't deserved to die at the hands of her own son. "She was your mother. She had grandchildren. Do you think of those things when you kill? That a woman is someone's daughter or mother or sister or grandmother? Doesn't it bother you?"

"I wish it did. I've tried to care. I've even tried to shed a tear." He patted her hand. "I'm more likely to be able to shed that tear over you. I've become quite attached to you this last year as I've studied you and stalked you."

Madness sat beside her, touching her. Teagan drew a steadying breath. *Show no fear.* "Then don't kill me. Let us go. Disappear. Start over."

"And miss the chance to make your father suffer? No way. He has to understand what loss feels like."

"My mother died when I was nine. He understands loss."

"He's forgotten."

All those nights she slipped from bed and wandered in the dark, seeking her mother's scent on towels, touching her jewelry on the bathroom vanity, peeking into the dark living room where her father sat staring into space night after night. "Nobody forgets. Why kill Officer Moreno? Evelyn, Julie? What about Charity Waters? Did you kill them, or did you have your stepbrother and his girlfriend do it?"

"They're too stupid to be trusted with an actual kill." Disdain dripped from the words. "They couldn't even handle keeping you and lover boy stowed away."

"So you killed four women who aren't related to me, and my father didn't even know them. Why?"

"Don't you get it? You're your father's only child. The only memento from his first and only true love. Making you suffer, putting you in danger, makes him suffer the greatest loss."

"You couldn't have killed Officer Moreno. You're a teacher, not a sniper."

"It's amazing what people are willing to teach a guy. The dark web is full of bad guy mercenaries who'll do anything for the right price. My adopted grandfather died a few years ago and left me a nice little inheritance. Perfect for funding my, shall we say, extracurricular activities."

Teagan's stomach bucked. *Keep him talking. He likes to brag. He likes an audience. He's a narcissistic egomaniac.* "Evelyn was an old lady."

"And you loved her. Just like you loved Julie. She was a fighter. I can't remember when I've had so much fun. I suspect I'm about to have even more."

Teagan swallowed again and again. Her throat burned. Her head swam. "Shut up. Just shut up!"

"You asked." He pulled up in front of the cabin and put the SUV in Park.

Teagan dug her heels into the rubber mat below her feet.

If they went into the cabin, they would not come out alive.

"Shall we, my dear?"

"I'm not your dear or your friend or your anything. I'm not going in there."

"Don't be that way. I have to carry little ballerina. Or I could just kill her here and make you watch. What'll it be?"

"You're going to kill us all one way or another. Inside, outside—what difference does it make?"

More opportunity to run outside than inside.

A smile crept across his face in the console light. His chuckle held a note of delighted anticipation. "Oh my. So many possibilities. A good tussle. A romp in the woods. A swim in the lake."

The lake was close. Cabins on private property dotted the shores of Medina Lake for much of its length. People would be in them, enjoying summer vacations. They would have phones. The county park, shared by Medina and Bandera counties, would be closed for the evening. Not knowing where this cabin sat was a seemingly insurmountable challenge. "I'm not going in there. I'm not making this easy for you."

"Have it your way."

Time sped up despite every attempt to stop it.

Cole opened his door. "Sit tight. I'm coming for you."

His steps quickened as he strode around the car and again removed her seat belt with a kind of reverence. She shrank back from his touch. He leaned in and sniffed. "You smell like sweat and fear. I rather enjoy that eau de perfume, love."

"The least you could do is call me by my name. Teagan."

"I know your name."

"But using it makes me a real person. You don't want to do that."

"I shared a body with you. That's the most intimate act short of—Well, we'll get to that."

She dug in her heels and leaned away from him. He pulled her from the car. She plopped to her knees, intentionally limp.

"These delaying tactics only fan my ardor. You know that, right?" He leaned into the car and produced the butcher knife. "Perhaps a little foreplay to fan yours?" The tip of the knife trailed across her cheek and down her neck. "Stand up."

She stood.

"Stay." He opened the passenger door and pulled Leyla from her perch. Her eyelids flickered and then opened. "There you are, my dear. You'll want to be awake for the fun."

Her eyes widened. Her body thrashed. She tried to scream through the duct tape. Muffled animal sounds.

Teagan threw herself forward. "Get your hands off her!"

"No, no, no." The gun came up again. This time it was pointed at Leyla's head. "Back away."

Teagan backed away.

Cole plopped Leyla on the ground and dragged her writhing body by her shirt collar toward the back of the van. "Come along, dear. You don't want to miss a thing, I promise you."

He tapped the button on his remote. The hatch hummed and lifted.

Max rolled out and head butted Cole in the gut.

Cole stumbled back.

Max's 180 pounds of solid boxer muscle landed on top of him. The pistol flew into the air and disappeared into the dark terrain beyond the cabin's security lighting.

Teagan launched herself at Cole. She stomped on his hand. He dropped the butcher knife. She grabbed it and smacked him in the head with the flat side.

With an angry grunt, he hit the ground a second time. "You're dead. You're all dead."

Max rolled around and kicked him in the gut twice. "Get the gun."

The knife slid from Teagan's grip. She dropped to the ground and crawled through the mud and muck. Her hands, tied together, touched slimy grass, twigs, and indefinable sponginess. Seconds ticked by.

God, I need this gun. I need it now.

Surely not the craziest request God had received, but not one to be expected from His pacifist daughter.

Please, God, please.

Her hands closed around the smooth butt of the gun. She grasped it, struggled to her knees, and turned.

Cole had his arm around Max's neck, the knife to his throat. Blood trickled down Cole's forehead. He had one boot-clad foot on Leyla's head. His grim smile sent shudders through Teagan's body. "It's been lovely, really. I like a challenge, I do. But all good things must come to an end. Give me the gun or I'll slit his throat. I'll stomp your sweet sister's head in."

"Not if I shoot you first." The words came out of her mouth with no hesitation.

"Nobody shoots anyone on my behalf." She'd said those words only a week ago to her family. This was different. She would kill to save Max and Leyla. Pure and simple. Billy, Gracie, and Justin had to make decisions like this because it was their job.

To save lives.

"You won't shoot me, dear. You abhor guns, remember? That's why you didn't become a cop. You didn't have the stomach for it."

"Plant your feet. Steady. Raise your arms and look down the sight."

Dad's calm voice filled her mind. She hadn't wanted to go to the range with him. The other kids clamored for the chance to shoot. The repeated *rat-a-tat-tat-tat* of the bullets firing made her jump again and again. The recoil in the pistol he insisted she learn to fire, disassemble, clean, and reassemble made her arms and shoulders hurt.

To shoot at a target was one thing. To shoot a man with a knife to Max's throat another.

"Come on, T, put the gun down."

T? How dare he? She raised her arms, gun clasped between her hands, and sighted his forehead. Dad always said aim for center mass, but center mass was Max.

She didn't believe in guns, but she believed in him. She believed in family.

She pulled the trigger.

The bullet pinged over their heads into the darkness beyond.

"Oops. You missed."

"But I won't." A semiautomatic weapon snug against his shoulder, Justin raced into the clearing. "Drop it. Now!"

Immediately, a dozen other officers did the same. Billy. Gracie. Dad. All with their weapons pointed at Cole.

Cole might rue the day he brought a knife to a gunfight, but he still had the upper hand.

He had Leyla. He had Max.

39

sn't that special. A family affair." Cole tightened his grip around Max's neck. Max struggled. "You really don't want to do that. What if you hit lover boy here?"

"I just renewed my certification at the range." Billy drew even with Justin. "I've been told I'm an excellent candidate for sniper school."

"Drop the knife." A Medina County Sheriff's Department deputy stepped into the fray. "Don't make it worse. From what I hear, your half brother is back in San Antonio baring his soul to a detective right now."

"Go ahead. Make a move." Dad had pistols in both hands. Both aimed at Cole. "I know they want to take you alive, but after what you've put my family through, I'd just as soon drop you like the rabid vermin you are."

"I'm not giving you anything you want." Cole sneered. Ugly red blotches covered his cheeks and neck. "You put my father in jail. You made sure I'd never have a chance to know him. You deserve to suffer."

"Your dad didn't want to know you. He gave you up a long time ago." Dad jerked his head toward Teagan. She widened her stance and steadied her aim. His gaze went back to Cole. "Nothing you did for him will make a difference. He'll get the needle and so will you."

Dad lifted the pistols higher. "Or I can just take you out now and save the taxpayers a bunch of money."

Cole let loose a stream of vile obscenities. Spittle flew. The knife tightened on Max's neck. Max jerked. A trickle of blood seeped from his skin and darkened his collar.

Reynolds hurled the knife to the ground. He stepped back, shoved Max, who stumbled and collapsed to his knees next to Leyla. "Go ahead, shoot me. Shoot me now. I'm not afraid to die."

Dad's weapons remained on Cole. The desire to give Cole what he deserved etched lines of agonizing fury on his face.

"Dad, no, stand down." Teagan lowered her gun. She understood his desire. She even felt it. But she didn't glory in it. "We're not like him. We're not animals."

"He hurt you. He hurt Leyla. He would've killed you."

"Let the justice system work, Dad. He'll be in prison for years, fighting the death penalty." Teagan moved closer. "You know how it works. He'll sit in his cell day after day, night after night, waiting, knowing he'll die in the end. It's perfect."

"She's right, Dillon, you know she is." His voice soft, Justin approached from the other side. "Give me the guns. Leyla needs you."

With a hoarse sob, her father handed over his weapons. He grabbed Teagan and crushed her to his chest. "Are you hurt? Are you all right?" He pushed her back and gave her a once-over. "And Leyla? Is she . . . ?"

"She's alive."

He threw his arm around her. Together they scrambled across the grass to where Max knelt with her sister.

"I would've killed him," she whispered the words for Dad's ears only. "I meant to kill him."

"I know. You did good."

"I missed."

"It's over. You're safe. That's all that matters." He let go and dropped to his knees. "Leyla?"

Max had removed the tape from her mouth while Billy cut away the ties on her ankles and wrists. "She's out of her mind with fear and shock." Max backed away. "She needs you."

Dad gathered her up in his arms and crooned soft nothings in her ear. She ceased to struggle. "Daddy?"

"It's me, baby, you're safe."

Leyla's eyes closed. Teagan clung to them both for a few seconds, then eased away. "Max."

He smiled. He had the most beautiful smile in the world. "You almost shot my head off."

"Did not." She crawled over to him. "I prayed to God I'd find the gun. Do you think He was shocked at such a request?"

"He might have been a little surprised that it came from you, but nothing shocks God. He knew what you needed in that moment." Max pulled her into his arms. He leaned in close and whispered, "Don't think I don't understand what it cost you to pull the trigger. I'm so sorry you had to make that choice."

"I couldn't let him kill Leyla. And I couldn't live without you. I don't want to live without you."

Teagan slid her arms around his neck and planted a kiss on him that went on and on. They might as well have been alone. The two of them healing each other's wounds, tearing down old walls, making new promises. Even Cole's singsong rendition of Teagan and Max sitting in a tree, k-i-s-s-i-n-g couldn't stop them.

He no longer had a hold over them.

40

Even as Billy dragged Cole to the back of an SAPD unit, the man couldn't button his lips. The steady stream of vitriol directed at her dad only died when the door slammed shut.

Teagan ignored him. Keeping her hand entwined with Max's, she glanced up, seeking her father. He held Leyla's hand while EMTs loaded her on a gurney.

A CSU investigator strode between them, carrying the butcher knife by gloved fingertips.

The feel of that blade against her cheek, pressing against her skin, sent chills through her. Max let go of her hand and slid his arm around her. They both smelled of sweat and fear and mud. They smelled alive. His grip tightened. She looked up at her dad. "How did you find her and us?"

"Joanna Dean told us they had turned Leyla over to Cole before they came after you. She said he has other hidey-holes out here." His voice turned ragged. "They weren't sure if Leyla was . . . alive."

"Joanna turned herself in?"

"No. We had a couple of off-duty guys parked at Chase Slocum's house—"

"You didn't tell me that." Teagan shook her head at a Medina County EMT.

He squatted anyway and shone a flashlight across her battered arms and face. His face grim, he turned to Max. "Both of you need to be examined by a physician."

"No."

"Yes." Dad intervened. "We need it for the investigation. Every bit of this will go into the record to be used in court."

The EMT's partner arrived with a gurney. "I can walk." Teagan struggled to stand and found she couldn't. "Give me a minute."

Dad helped her onto one gurney while the EMT did the same for Max. She held his gaze for as long as possible. He gave her a thumbs-up. She wanted to laugh but her throat hurt too much.

She grabbed her dad's hand. "Tell me the rest of the story."

"One of the employees we interviewed in Sandoval's office building mentioned seeing two janitorial types shoving trash bins into a white minivan. She thought it was weird that it didn't have a cleaning service name on it. I remembered the one parked at Slocum's house. It was a long shot, but these guys owed me."

"Not enough to follow Slocum around."

"Not a tail, a stakeout. I wanted to see if someone unexpected showed up at their house."

"Cole Reynolds is too smart for that."

"He had his claws dug deep into those two. I think Cole wanted to prove he was the better son to Leo Slocum, the true son."

"Competition for their father's approval." A fundamental driving force in the lives of many siblings. But Cole had other primitive forces at work. Teagan repeated what Cole had shared about his dad's reaction to finding out Cole was responsible for the new murders. "Cole might have wanted approval, but he also wanted to make you pay for putting his father in prison before he had a chance to know him or get his approval. Leo Slocum refused to see him. He denied to Chase that he had another son."

"Which only added fuel to Cole's fire."

"He killed Deidre."

"I know. Joe Cruz called me after they found her body. He was broken up about it. He had such disdain for her and now she's dead."

"Do you think he killed her because we interviewed her?"

"No. He'd been planning that since the day she let CPS take him."

The words rang true. Some people exemplified the nature-versus-nurture argument. No parent set out to raise a serial killer. What about Chase? He grew up in a loving home, never knowing of his father's dark side. Yet he allowed himself to be dragged there by a half brother he hardly knew. "How did you get onto Chase and Joanna?"

"They disabled the camera in the elevator in Sandoval's office building, but they couldn't do anything about the one in the lobby without drawing attention to themselves. We got a good digital grab of Joanna's face."

"You recognized her? I didn't immediately. It was her voice that tipped me."

"I had my guys look around their house. They found several wigs, glasses, sunglasses, your garden variety disguises. And guns—lots of guns—in the master bedroom closet. After they returned to the house last night, my guy sneaked a look in the back of the van. The blonde wig was still there. Joanna couldn't bring herself to get rid of it. Her favorite, she said."

"Wait until Cole hears that."

"Neither of them ever committed a crime in their lives. They followed his game plan to the best of their ability. Which isn't saying much. It took about forty-five minutes to break Joanna. She's never even had a speeding ticket."

"And she has two kids."

With Chase's three, five children had been caught in a psychopath's snare.

"Her story is that Cole showed up at the house and introduced himself as Chase's half brother right after their dad was convicted. It was fraternal love at first sight."

"He can be so charming."

"She claims she went along because she's in love with Chase, and she had no place else to go. She also insists she never killed anyone."

Her expression in the elevator didn't jive with her claims. The woman who brought them to the cabin had been enjoying herself. "What does Chase say?"

"He claims Cole did the killing. That they were forced to do everything against their will or Cole would kill their kids."

"Cole doesn't kill kids. Not his MO."

"After she told us where you were, we headed this way. We had parked on the road, and the plan was to walk in quietly and surprise Cole. When we heard the shot, I was sure it was too late." His hoarse voice choked. His Adam's apple bobbed. He sniffed. "Seeing you with a gun pointed at him was the most surprising sight of my life."

"It surprised me more."

"Joanna and Chase are already jockeying for deals."

Deals made the justice system work. They kept the antiquated process moving. Court reporters knew that better than anyone. The system couldn't handle a jury by trial every time a murder was committed. So deals were made even when precious lives had been lost.

Kristin Moreno. Evelyn Conklin. Charity Waters. Julie Davidson.

Four women who left behind devastated families and lost opportunities in lives not lived.

And then Deidre Patterson, whose affair with a serial killer produced a psychopath who killed her.

"No deals, Dad."

"I'm sorry. I wish we could throw them into dungeons and leave them in leg chains for life, but it doesn't work that way."

The guillotine would be more satisfying.

Dad settled onto the narrow bench next to her gurney. The EMT closed the ambulance doors. The engine revved. Teagan closed her eyes. "What about those kids? What will happen to them?"

Dad touched her cheek. His fingers brushed twigs from her hair. "I don't know. I'd like to think Chase's sister or his mother will step up for his three. Joanna Dean doesn't have any close next of kin. CPS is involved."

CPS. Where Cole's life had taken an irrevocable turn years ago.

He was blessed with good foster parents who adopted him—unlike so many other children in the system. But his adoptive parents couldn't be blamed for his fatal character flaws. Nor could his biological mother.

Leo couldn't even be blamed for his son's behavior.

The explanation lay hidden somewhere in Cole's shattered psyche. A single trip into that region had been enough—too much—for Teagan. She never wanted to go there again.

41

The sight of Leyla's bruised face against a bleached-white pillow sent a wave of relief through Teagan. Her little sister looked tiny in the oversized hospital gown. She'd curled up on her side with a half dozen wires running to equipment beside her bed. A bag of saline dripped behind her.

Teagan tugged on the curtain that separated Leyla from the patient sleeping in the other bed and pulled up a chair in the minuscule space left. The rooms in the hospital's older wings were small and spartan. Teagan refused to be admitted. The only way she was spending the night at Methodist was sitting by her sister's side. Leyla needed her and Teagan needed assurance she would be all right.

Leyla's efforts to escape after her kidnapping had earned her a pistol whipping. She had broken ribs, a ruptured spleen, broken nose, broken collarbone, and bruises covering much of her body. She would need dental surgery to repair damage to her front teeth. The doctors said her attacker had not hurt her in any other way.

They were wrong.

She would carry scars on her psyche for the rest of her life. Dad and Jazz had gone to get clean clothes for Teagan and pack a bag for Leyla. Max went to get food and coffee from the cafeteria. They would converge on this room eventually. Leyla would not be left alone while recovering from her injuries. Teagan took her sister's hand.

Leyla opened her eyes with a start and a sob. She grabbed the blanket and hiked it up around her neck with shaking hands. "Teagan? Teagan! Where am I?"

"In the hospital. You're safe."

Her face contorted with fear and uncertainty, Leyla tugged at the blanket until it covered her up to her chin. "You're alive."

"I am. Safe and sound."

Sort of.

"He told me you were dead. He said it was my fault for trying to escape." Her swollen lips, swollen tongue, and two missing teeth garbled her words. "I thought you were dead."

Teagan squeezed Leyla's hand. A hug might hurt too much. "I'm not. We're both here. We're both alive."

"Did they get him?"

"Yes. He's in jail. He's never getting out. He'll get the death penalty."

If the system worked.

Tears tracked down her bruised face, and Leyla shifted on the pillow and winced. "I thought I was going to die."

"Me too."

"I thought I would never see you again. I'd never see Dad and Mom, Gracie and Billy."

"I know, honey, believe me, I know. Dad and your mom went to the house. They'll be back any minute. You'll see them again. Billy's still at the lake, but Gracie's on her way too."

Leyla closed her eyes. The tears cascaded down her purple-and-black cheeks. "I'm still scared. I'm so scared. Is it over?"

"It is over. I promise."

"I thought I was so all-that. I had a gun and I knew how to use it. Chase Slocum took it from me like it was nothing." Leyla struggled to sit up. "My gun. What happened to my gun?"

"It hasn't been recovered. Cole wouldn't keep such an incriminating piece of evidence. He probably dumped it. Don't worry about it right now. You and me, we're smart enough to know we'll need help to deal with this." Teagan stood and bent over her sister so she could get closer. She kissed her forehead and brushed away her tears. "Max goes to a really good therapist. We'll go to see him together."

"I don't know if I can talk to a man." Her voice cracked. "I don't want to feel that way, but I do. He said things. I thought he was going to do things to me . . . What if he gets out of jail?"

"He won't. We'll find the therapist who's right for you, I promise."

If in some strange twist of fate Cole managed to escape, the O'Rourkes would take care of him. Of that, Teagan was certain. God would not approve. The ends did not justify the means, but her father would not take God's position into account. He would never let Cole Reynolds hurt his family again.

"I'm so tired. I've never been so tired." Leyla clutched Teagan's hand. "Can you bring me my blue blanket and my piggy?"

The blue blanket and piggy had been Leyla's best friends through her parents' divorce and the move into a stranger's house. They had a place of honor in her room as she grew older. They'd gone with her to UT when she started college. They came home for visits over the summer. "I will." She kissed Leyla's cheek and brushed her hair from her face. "Try to sleep. I'll be right here."

"So will we."

Teagan turned to see Dad standing inside the door, Jazz right behind him.

"I didn't hear you come in."

He held up a duffel bag. "Your clothes, her blanket, and her piggy."

Jazz had been crying again. She tugged the piggy from the bag and handed it to Leyla, who clutched it to her chest. It was far too soon to tell how Teagan's stepmother would deal with the horrific events of the past few days. If she blamed Teagan, she would be right.

Dad settled the bag on the rolling table next to a pitcher of water. He covered Leyla's hand with his. Her eyes closed, Leyla shifted and murmured something about a gun. "I have mine, honey, don't you worry."

"Dillon, please. No talk of guns." Jazz kissed her daughter's cheek. "What my baby needs now is peace. Lots of peace. We're here, baby, rest."

After a few seconds, Leyla relaxed and faded out.

Dad released her hand, stepped away from the bed, and approached Teagan. "How are you?"

"Fine. She's still so scared. He tortured her mentally and physically."

"She's strong. She'll get through it. And she's got all of us to help her." He cleared his throat. "So do you."

"She'll need professional help."

"You can stop worrying now, T." Dad enveloped her in a hug. "We've got this. We've got you."

Teagan relaxed into the feel of his strong arms around her. "Thank you, Daddy."

"Where's Max?"

"Getting us some food."

"Let him take care of you too." Dad leaned back and smoothed Teagan's hair from her face. "Can you do that?"

"Yes, I think I can," she whispered.

"Go on, go find him."

"He's right, Teagan." Jazz's smile was watery. "Life is short. If anybody should know that, it's you. Go be happy."

Good advice. She swung open the door and let it shut softly. Now to figure out a way to spend the rest of her life with the man she loved.

They'd survived a serial killer. Anything was possible.

42

Don't make big decisions while suffering from grief.

That tidbit, overheard as a child, had stuck with Teagan after her mother's death, but she never really knew what it meant. She dug her bare feet into the grass still cool and wet with dew on this July morning and contemplated her future. Should she—could she—stay in this house and daydream on this front porch? In this neighborhood? Could she let what happened run her out of her dream home? Would she always see Julie's broken, bleeding body lying next to the Little Free Library? Would the Victorian home across the street, now for sale, always be a psychopath's way into her life?

Teagan had two dogs to think about now. Her tiny plot of land didn't provide enough roaming room for the spirited play of a pit bull and a Lab still learning to be friends.

Six weeks had passed since she had fought for the lives of the people she loved at Medina Lake. She slept in fits and starts. Her appetite had yet to make a reappearance. She was on short-term disability leave from work. How could she go back to writing records of horrific crimes again in the courtroom she once shared with Julie? Family and friends had spread Julie's ashes over her beloved Pacific Ocean from a Costa Rican beach. Teagan had not been invited.

Their pain and anger were understandable but no less hurtful.

Tigger and Huck followed her from room to room as if they knew something wasn't quite right.

Don't make any decisions while suffering from grief.

Today, a hot, brilliant day, the sunrise brimmed with the possibility of taking a tiny step forward. She sat cross-legged on the front porch, the dogs on either side, and drank a glass of iced latte. The sweet bite of the coffee touched her tongue, and she thanked God for the ability to taste it. She thanked Him for the chance to see another sunrise.

Stephanie waved as she walked by, her sleeping baby tucked in her stroller. Normalcy crept back into the neighborhood. Dana Holl had started jogging again. Plans were complete for a Fourth of July celebration.

But it would never be the same again. Robin and her family had yet to sell Evelyn's house. People shied away from buying a home where an elderly woman had been attacked and killed. Teagan's house would always be the one where the Triple S Murderer's fourth victim had been found. Both houses, along with Cole Reynolds's, would probably end up on a macabre Halloween tour one day.

But not today.

The legal wrangling complete with finger-pointing continued. Cole had changed his story in the interrogation room. He claimed Chase and Joanna killed Julie and dumped her body in Teagan's yard. He said he only wanted to goad Teagan with his story of having enjoyed killing her friend. He also took back his earlier assertion that he'd killed Kristin Moreno, claiming he didn't have the expertise to do it.

A deep dive in his computer records supported his earlier story that he arranged to buy the rifle and take "lessons" from a dark-web mercenary who taught him well. Well enough to shoot a police officer in a moving vehicle at two hundred yards. Chase claimed Cole had bragged about his long days of preparation. The rifle had not been found. Charity had been Cole's "girlfriend" for six months before her death. Only he could've gotten close enough to garrote her with an electrical cord.

Cole faced capital murder charges. His lawyer had asked to be relieved. A hearing on the request was scheduled for this week. Every time his attorney asked for a hearing, the media resurfaced in Teagan's life. In Max and Leyla's lives. Fortunately, a family of cops kept them at bay.

Plea bargains would get Chase and Joanna out of prison in their fifties or sixties.

Joanna hoped to get a deal that would get her out in time to meet her grandchildren, should there be any. Her children were in foster care. Chase's sister had traveled from Connecticut to pick up her niece and nephews so they could live with her on the East Coast. Their grandmother had declined custody.

Leo Slocum had been indicted on capital murder charges for the string of killings in the Valley. Cole's case would not be tried in Teagan's court. She, Max, and Leyla could be called in the trials of the other three perpetrators. Despite that grim prospect, she didn't want plea bargains. Only the full weight of the law collapsing on the Slocums like an Egyptian pyramid crumbling during an earthquake would be enough.

Work might be the only antidote. The belief that the justice system worked. Would work for her and Leyla and Julie and Charity and Evelyn and Kris. And all the other women caught in a killer's crosshairs. Teagan's fingers on those fourteen blank keys might calm the shakes inside her. Those familiar words:

```
13  On the 5th day of June, the following
14  proceedings came to be heard in the above-entitled
15  and-numbered
```

16   cause before the Honorable Simon Ibarra, Judge presiding,
17   held in San Antonio, Bexar County, Texas.

Or would it mean that more horrific crimes would visit her at night, keeping her from sleeping?

Leyla had decided not to return to law school in the fall. She would live at home until she decided what to do next. She and Teagan visited the same counselor, a woman Rick found for them, twice a week. Some weeks, three times.

Leyla spent a lot of time on her parents' front porch, reading or staring into space. Dad and her cop siblings took turns sitting with her. Jazz slept on a cot in her room. The therapist said it would get better. She would get better.

No one knew if that would take months or years.

Something else to be blamed on Cole Reynolds.

Max pulled up in Evelyn's 1966 Ford F150. It looked good on him. A bag marked Herman's Bagels in one hand, he strolled across the yard, stuck a book in the Little Free Library, and plopped down next to her on the porch. He kissed her softly on the lips and leaned back. "Breakfast?"

He'd been tempting her with her favorite foods for weeks. She'd gained three pounds.

"Blueberry or raisin cinnamon?"

"Both."

"A man after my own heart."

He grinned, opened the sack, and made a tiny picnic between them using napkins and plastic silverware. The bagels were still warm and fragrant. He handed her a tub of cream cheese. "There's apply jelly too."

"Naw. I'm a purist when it comes to my bagels." Her mouth watered. "You're still trying to fatten me up, aren't you?"

"Maybe, or maybe I'm trying to bribe you."

"With breakfast? Spit it out, bud."

"CPS is having an informational meeting this evening for couples interested in becoming foster parents."

Teagan took a swallow of coffee. It still tasted good. The sun still shone. It warmed her face just as it had a few seconds earlier. "What are you saying?"

"I'm saying I hope you'll seriously consider marrying me. I'm saying I can live with not bringing children into this world. After what we went through, I'm acutely aware of your reasons for not wanting to do that." He wiped at his mouth with a napkin, laid the bagel aside, and took her hand. "I'm saying what about the children already in this world who don't have the most basic of all requisites for living—parents who love them and care for them? They're already here. Through no fault of their own—"

"Stop, stop."

"Teagan—"

She tugged the brochure from under her phone and held it up. "I'm in."

"You're in?" Max took her offering and stared at the cover picture of a laughing child sitting on a smiling woman's lap. A man stood next to them looking equally happy. "A CPS foster program brochure?"

"I love you. I want to marry you. I've been thinking about foster parenting since Noelle brought it up at church. I've been thinking about Joanna Dean's children and little Kyle Patterson before he became Cole Reynolds and all those other kids dumped into an overwhelmed system. Some are blessed with good foster parents, but many are not. It's a sad fact."

"You've been thinking a lot."

"I've had some time on my hands. It wasn't an easy decision, but not to try when there's such a desperate need would be an act of cowardice. And I'm no coward."

His amber eyes filled with liquid emotion, and Max stared at her. His jaw worked. His Adam's apple bobbed.

"Max, say something."

"I think I'm in shock. I was expecting this big discussion, and instead you said yes. Not only yes, but you've already done research. You're all-in."

"I was willing to kill for you. I *am* willing to kill for you. That fact opened my eyes to many things. I stopped being afraid that day. Life is short and sweet and too lovely to be wasted on an emotion like worry." Too short to live without the love of her life. Too short to waste one more day.

"I don't know what the future will look like as far as my job. I'm still trying to figure that out. It's unlikely I'll be at the door with supper ready when you walk in from a day's work. I've been thinking about how lovely your six acres in the country are. How peaceful it would be. I'm not sure about any of that yet. But I am sure I will love, honor, and kiss the heck out of you every day for as long as we both shall live."

"I'm still back at you said yes."

"I did. That usually means kissing and hugging and celebrating."

Max shot to his feet. He snagged the Houston Astros cap from her head and tossed it in the air. "She said yes!"

His shout scared the blue jays in the mountain laurel. They scolded him in return. A guy passing by on a scooter hooted and lifted a fist in acknowledgment.

Tigger barked. Huck stood and looked confused. He often looked confused these days.

Max clasped Teagan's hand and pulled her to her feet. "Snoopy-dance with me!"

They had no music, but Teagan took his hand and they jitterbugged across grass that tickled her bare feet. Next came a dramatic tango, followed by the twist, and then the boot scootin' boogie. Barking, Tigger and Huck raced around them in widening circles.

Laughing, gasping for air, Teagan collapsed against Max's chest and closed her eyes. His kiss took her breath away all over again. His hands cupped her face. He took his time. She slid her fingers over his and relished the fervor of his grip.

The Cole Reynoldses and Leo Slocums of the world would not take this from them. They would not take the essence of who she and Max were or who they were yet to become as individuals or as people who loved each other and wanted to spend the rest of their lives figuring out how they fit together.

Scripture promised joy in the morning.

It had arrived right on time.

ACKNOWLEDGMENTS

I had more fun than a person should writing *Closer Than She Knows*. Sometimes authors have so much fun they fudge on the facts or just plain don't get them right. I am so blessed to have had two subject-matter experts to rein me in on this project. My deepest thanks to Kay Gittinger for allowing me to pick her brain about the life and work of a court reporter. Before my writing career took off, I proofread court records for Kay and several other court reporters. I learned a great deal about how the court system works and all sorts of nice details about crime investigations that I can use in my books. But I'm still no expert. Kay's insight into her profession was invaluable.

Once again retired Homicide Detective Richard Urbanek shared his expertise regarding police procedure and homicide investigations. His feedback was indispensable. He also saved me from an egregious and possibly mortal error regarding Texas A&M and the University of Texas mascots. Woe to the writer who gets this wrong. I also found Jennifer Dornbush's *Forensic Speak* an excellent resource.

As usual, any mistakes are all mine.

My thanks also go to Eileen Key for her eagle-eye proofreading that caught the ridiculous typos my eyes refused to see. Her attention to detail saved me from myself.

Whipping this book into shape was a long, arduous process. I'm so blessed to have Becky Monds as my editor. She read the first version and saw not only the big picture but the small details that didn't jive. Line editor Julee Schwarzburg waded through the nitty-gritty details to correct discrepancies in every aspect of the whodunit while polishing the writing. Thinking like a serial killer and solving his crimes were truly a team effort. Bless you, ladies!

A tremendous amount of research went into the writing of a book about serial killers. I think it's important to acknowledge the work done by experts in the field that allowed me to enrich these pages with historical details and information. I spent many nights poring over *Whoever Fights Monsters* by Robert K. Ressler and Tom Shachtman; Ann Rule's *The Stranger beside Me*; and *Double Lives* by Eric Brach, among other resources that outline the history and study of serial killers in the United States. I hope *Closer Than She Knows* is a better story for it.

None of this would be possible without the loving support of my husband, Tim. Love always.

To my readers, God bless you and keep you.

DISCUSSION QUESTIONS

1. Teagan has chosen not to have children for several reasons, including the state of the world. What do you think of her reasoning? Do you believe Christian families must or should have children in order to be complete? Why or why not?

2. How do you feel about Max being a youth minister given his history of drug and alcohol addiction, PTSD, and depression? If you were a parent of a child in his youth group, how would you feel about it? Do you think he has something to teach the youth because of his background?

3. Teagan didn't want her siblings to become police officers because she feared for their lives. Does her worry show a lack of faith? How would you react in her situation? How do you balance being realistic with being hopeful in these situations?

4. The Bible says 365 times, "Do not fear." How do you cope with fear when the diagnosis is grim, the marriage is rocky, a child goes off to fight a war, or natural disasters loom?

5. Teagan has a deep-seated belief that violence is never the answer, that capital punishment is wrong. Yet she's willing to kill to save her loved ones. It's easy to have a philosophical discussion about these issues, but what would you do if you were in her shoes? Take the shot? Or let the system work?

6. How do you reconcile the belief that God is good with the fact that He allows (but does not cause) bad things to happen to good people? What does Scripture tell us about His reason for not always stepping in to change the outcome of a particular situation?

ABOUT THE AUTHOR

Photo by Tim Irvin

Bestseller Kelly Irvin is the author of eighteen books, including romantic suspense and Amish romance. The *Library Journal* said her novel *Tell Her No Lies* is "a complex web with enough twists and turns to keep even the most savvy romantic suspense readers guessing until the end." She followed up with *Over the Line*. The two-time ACFW Carol finalist worked as a newspaper reporter for six years writing stories on the Texas–Mexico border. Those experiences fuel her romantic suspense novels set in Texas. A retired public relations professional, Kelly now writes fiction full-time. She lives with her husband, photographer Tim Irvin, in San Antonio. They are the parents of two children, three grandchildren, and two ornery cats.

Visit her online at KellyIrvin.com
Instagram: kelly_irvin
Facebook: Kelly.Irvin.Author
Twitter: @Kelly_S_Irvin